Praise for *Looks to*

"A nice mix of glamour, mommy lit, and mystery. . . . It's a good thing Kaplan has a sequel in the works." —*Library Journal*

"Stylish and playful . . . *The Devil Wears Prada* for the interior-design crowd." —*Booklist*

"Suspense fans looking for frothy, wacky fun will be rewarded." —*Publishers Weekly*

"Breezy." —*Time Out New York*

"With her trademark combination of savvy wit . . . and classic sleuthing, Kaplan delivers a mystery that will keep you guessing long after your own pedicure has dried." —*Asbury Park Press*

**** (four-star review) —*Romantic Times*

"Lacy is an engaging protagonist. . . . Kaplan's got a future writing this series of fun, frothy, fast, funny, solidly crafted mysteries." —Reviewingtheevidence.com

"An appealing heroine, breathtaking pace, and gilded lives suddenly tarnished make Janice Kaplan's *Looks to Die For* a spectacular mystery debut. Intelligent, beautifully crafted, and riveting." —Carolyn Hart, author of *Set Sail for Murder*

"Lacy Fields sleuths with sass and class and the result is pure delight." —Jacquelyn Mitchard, author of *The Deep End of the Ocean* and *Still Summer*

Also by Janice Kaplan (with Lynn Schnurnberger)

The Botox Diaries
The Men I Didn't Marry
Mine Are Spectacular!

Looks
to Die
For

〰️

Janice Kaplan

A Touchstone Book
Published by Simon & Schuster
New York London Toronto Sydney

TOUCHSTONE
Rockefeller Center
1230 Avenue of the Americas
New York, NY 10020

First Touchstone trade paperback edition January 2008

TOUCHSTONE and colophon are registered trademarks
of Simon & Schuster, Inc.

For information regarding special discounts for bulk purchases,
please contact Simon & Schuster Special Sales at 1-800-456-6798
or business@simonandschuster.com.

Designed by Sue Walsh

Manufactured in the United States of America

10 9 8 7 6 5 4 3 2 1

Library of Congress Cataloging-in-Publication Data
  Kaplan, Janice.
    Looks to die for / Janice Kaplan.
      p.   cm.
    "A Touchstone Book"
    1. Interior decorators—Fiction. 2. Los Angeles (Calif.)—Fiction. I. Title.
    PS3561.A5593L66 2007
    813'.54—dc22   2006050556
ISBN-13: 978-1-4165-3211-8
ISBN-10:   1-4165-3211-0
ISBN-13: 978-1-4165-3212-5 (Pbk.)
ISBN-10:   1-4165-3212-9 (Pbk.)

To Ron,
for walks in the woods

Looks
to Die
For

Chapter One

The night the police came to arrest my husband for murder, I was upstairs, killing myself on the treadmill. If I kept up this pace, I'd finish my three miles in twenty-two and a half minutes, a personal best. So when I heard the doorbell ring, I ignored it, and then ignored it again. But whoever was chiming wouldn't go away and the noise was going to wake up the whole house. Annoyed, I hit the STOP button, threw a Juicy Couture sweatshirt on over my pink running bra and matching shorts, kicked off my all-terrain cross-trainers, which were giving me blisters anyway, and headed downstairs. No personal best tonight.

The Chinese cloisonné clock in the front hall foyer registered 11:50 P.M., not a typical time for guests to arrive at our gated community in Pacific Palisades. I tried peering through the peephole in the door, but the artistically cut crystal sphere had been designed for beauty, not usefulness. I could vaguely make out two men who seemed to be cops, and when I tentatively called out "Hello?" they waved their identification cards, not knowing that from my side, those IDs could have been Picasso graphics. I made a mental note to check out more practical security systems.

Cops at my door? My first emotion was curiosity, not panic, since those I loved and worried about full-time were tucked in upstairs. Grant had turned in early to get some rest before a science test tomorrow, Ashley had communed with two girlfriends until just after ten then gone straight to her own bedroom, and little Jimmy had heard monsters rumbling in his closet but managed to get to sleep after I read him three picture books and pretended to fall asleep first. Even my husband, Dan, had spent forty-five minutes reading medical journals and then set his alarm for dawn so he'd be up for early-morning surgery.

I twisted the ring on my right hand so that the big ruby and two small diamonds pointed into my palm, then opened the door, glancing first at the tall Hispanic cop who still gripped his identification awkwardly, then to the other cop, slightly older and shorter, dour and doughy-faced.

"We need Dr. Dan Fields, ma'am," the older cop said, his voice as rough-edged as his body.

"What for?"

"I'd like to explain that directly to the doctor."

I was sweaty and tired and not interested in conversing with cagey cops. But I had an idea what was going on here, since about a month ago, a three-car police escort had come to whisk Dan to the hospital to take care of a major actress who had sliced off her finger cutting a bagel. My husband was the Saint of Hollywood, the plastic surgeon whose skill at molding, reattaching, and reconstructing meant he could save any face or body part that was seriously endangered. This being Hollywood, he had also nipped and tucked some of the most famous faces on the planet, and the wait for a consultation at one point stretched to eight months. If you couldn't get an appointment, you could at least read fawning articles about him in *Vogue* or *Elle*. No doubt written by editors who figured that with enough sweet talk, Dan would move them to the top of the waiting list.

"Has somebody been hurt?" I asked the cop.

"Someone's been hurt real bad." He took a step toward me, edging in front of his buddy, a sneer contorting his features. "Now go get Dr. Fields for us."

His menacing style wouldn't work. "Look, Dan's gone to sleep already," I said, trying not to sound as intimidated as I felt. "Why don't you tell me what this is about?"

The Hispanic cop glanced back over his shoulder at his partner, who was pocketing his identification, then repeated, "Just get the doctor for us."

"If you're looking for a favor from Dan, you could ask a little more politely," I said.

The cops exchanged looks, then the Hispanic one said, "It's not a favor, ma'am. If you don't call him down, we'll go get him. We know he's in the house."

The guy was a genius. I say Dan's gone to bed and he figures out that he's in the house. "If you don't call it a favor to come by here at almost midnight and ask for Dan . . ." I stopped, because they were both looking at me oddly, and the message finally penetrated that I was off base. Way off base. Maybe not even in the right playing field.

I took a deep breath and, looking again at the doughy-faced cop, noticed that his badge said Detective Vincent Shields and that his buddy was Detective José Reese. Shields quietly said, "I assume Dr. Fields is your husband. He's wanted for questioning."

I stood there, unable to move, and Shields added, "We're investigating a murder." He pointed to the intercom by the front door. "Can you call him down?"

I was suddenly so confused that the intercom might as well have been a moon rock that had dropped into my front hall. I cleared my throat. I pulled myself back together. "Uh, the thing is, we just remodeled the top floor and wiring it into the old system has been a problem, you know? The electrician kept saying he could do it, even though he couldn't do it, so we probably need a whole new system or at least a whole new electrician, if you know what I mean. . . ." I paused, wondering if I could make myself stop babbling. Maybe some action would do it. I stepped over to the intercom, touched the TALK button and the "Master Bedroom" light, and then said, "Dan? Honey? Can you hear me?"

For a response, I got static. I ran my fingers through my curly hair, pushing it back from my forehead, which was still sweaty from the treadmill. And getting even sweatier from the fear suddenly coursing through me.

"We need to go upstairs," Reese said. "You want to lead us?"

I didn't want to do anything of the sort. Having the cops in my marble foyer was horrifying enough. But it didn't really occur to me that I could say no to a man with a badge.

"Mommy? Is it monsters?"

I spun around and saw Jimmy standing at the top of the steps, peering down at us through a railing. His ankles stuck out of his too-short Superman pajamas at an odd angle, and he looked so skinny and vulnerable that I wanted to run right up the stairs and give him a hug. But the cops were eyeing me intently and sudden moves didn't seem like a good idea.

"No, honey, everything's fine. No monsters, just these nice policemen." I smiled bravely and tried to keep my lip from quivering. Jimmy had put on his old superhero pajamas tonight so he could fight any monsters who showed up in his room, but who knew that they'd take this form?

"Jimmy, sweetie, can you do Mommy a favor?"

He stepped back from the railing and eyed me carefully—even at five, he wouldn't commit until he knew the dimensions of the request.

"Go to Mommy and Daddy's room and give Daddy a little shake. Tell Daddy that Mommy needs him to put on a robe and come down."

Jimmy ran off so quickly that I wasn't sure if he'd taken it in or was simply fleeing to hide under his covers. Slowly, I turned to the cops again, but they were muttering to each other. Detective

Shields glanced at his watch and said, "I don't like this. In two minutes you go up."

"Lemme go now. No way the guy's coming down."

Shields nodded, and the two of them headed for the staircase, clambering quickly up the steps two at a time, their smooth-soled shoes slipping on the Italian marble. At the top landing they stopped short, peering at the hallways that headed off in three directions. Reese turned to glare at me as I dashed up the stairs behind them.

"Where do we find him?" he growled.

Trying to catch my breath—lost to anxiety, not exertion—I didn't answer.

"Which of these damn hallways?" he bellowed.

"Our bedroom's to your right," I said, gasping. Then, not meaning to scream, I did anyway. "Dan!" I hollered.

From down the hall, my husband appeared at the bedroom door, his blond hair rumpled, his face blank from interrupted sleep. He hadn't bothered with a robe, just a pair of sweatpants, and he took a moment to register that there were two cops approaching him. When he did, his deep blue eyes widened and he blinked hard.

"What's going on?" he asked groggily.

The cops moved closer, surrounding him as effectively as two people can.

"You're Dr. Daniel Fields?" asked Shields.

"Yes, I am. May I help you?" His refined accent grew more refined as the cops leaned in. Even bare-chested, he maintained his dignity. A well-toned, well-tanned chest can do that for you.

"Well, doc, you can come down to the station house with us. Right now. Quietly," said Shields, with a hint of threat in his voice.

"Would you like to explain why?"

Shields took a moment to answer, digging his toe into the fringe of the Persian rug, then looking at Jimmy, who had slipped out of the bedroom and was edging closer to his dad.

"We need you for questioning," Shields said, discreetly not elaborating while one scared Superman stared wide-eyed at him.

"And it can't wait until morning?" Dan asked.

"No. Now."

"Help me out here, gentlemen. I don't have any idea what this is about or why you need to talk to me." Dan sounded composed and reasonable, as if he were sipping Chablis at his Princeton eating club, not confronting two LAPD cops.

Jimmy anxiously rubbed his hand over the big S emblem on his chest. But the shield wouldn't protect him, and neither would Reese.

"You're wanted for questioning in the murder of Theresa Bartowski," he said bluntly.

"I don't even know who that is. Why would you want to talk to me?"

"She's also known as Tasha Barlow."

Not the slightest wave of recognition crossed Dan's face. "Is this a former patient of mine?" he asked.

"We can discuss it all downtown," Reese said.

"No, let's discuss it here. Or better still, why don't you call me at my office in the morning? I'll pull out my patient records and do whatever I can to help you. But right now, if you'll excuse me, I have to get back to bed. I have surgery scheduled for seven A.M. and I'm not eager to stay up all night talking."

Reese and Shields exchanged another look, and with a move too quick to allow either reaction or resistance, Reese whipped handcuffs out of his back pocket and snapped them on Dan's slender wrists. "You're under arrest in the murder of Tasha Barlow," he intoned. "You have the right to remain silent. Anything you say can and will be used against you in—"

"What the hell are you doing?" Dan's voice, suddenly shrill, warbled through the hall.

"—a court of law. You have the right—"

"Get these off me!" Dan staggered back, holding his arms out-stretched like oddities that no longer belonged to his body. Trying to spin around and make his case for release, he accidentally slammed his handcuffed wrists against Reese, who hastily stepped back and reached for his gun. Shields had his weapon drawn the moment his partner was touched, and it was trained on Dan.

Jimmy began wailing, a high-pitched, hysterical sound that perfectly mimicked what I was feeling. I rushed over and swooshed him into my arms, running down the hall with him, past the stair-case, away from the police and guns, and into his room, which, even infested with monsters, seemed safer than where we had been. In a single motion, I slipped him into his bed and tucked in the covers, murmuring, "You're fine, honey. Everything's going to be fine." He stopped crying, more from surprise at suddenly finding himself under the cozy sheets than from any deeper comfort I'd supplied. I yearned to crawl in next to him and hide my head under his pillow. But as I stroked Jimmy's tear-streaked face, I could hear Dan's plaintive voice from down the hall calling, "Lacy? Lacy?"

My heart banged so furiously that I could hear the pounding in my ears. I'd been a G.I. Joe–banning, Second Amendment–doubt-ing citizen long enough that the simple sight of a gun scared me beyond all reason. Having two of them aimed at my husband blasted me into total terror. I sat down on the bed trying to hide my shock. Jimmy lay suddenly still, as if monsters might be a wel-come diversion from the real-life drama. His eyes were closed and his breathing placid, as if he had willed himself to sleep.

I pulled myself together and hurried back down the long hall-way to the group in front of our bedroom. The cops' guns were back in their holsters, and Dan, still bound at the wrists, was try-ing to reason with Shields.

"I have to get dressed," Dan was saying quietly. "If you take off the handcuffs, I can be quick."

Shields looked skeptical for a moment but then nodded. "Okay, I'll give you three minutes to put on some clothes. But we're keeping you within eyesight. The door stays open so we can see you."

He nodded at Reese to unlock the cuffs, and the detective reached for the key reluctantly. "You want me to call for some backup to surround the house?" he asked, still holding the key. "Don't want him escaping while he's pretending to look for his Calvins."

"I think we're under control," Shields said.

But Reese pushed into the bedroom before Dan. "I'll just wait in here."

I stepped closer to Dan and touched his elbow. "What's happening?"

He turned around to look at me, and his face was tightly controlled, giving up nothing. "I have no idea. But apparently I'm going downtown with these fellows."

"Do you know what they want? Do you know who that woman is? Does this make any sense?" I asked, my questions tumbling on top of each other.

"No," said Dan, one firm negative covering it all. Then calmly, "I'll have to straighten it out."

"How do you straighten it out when they've *arrested* you?" I asked, practically screeching.

Dan picked up my panic, and anxiety briefly flickered over his face. "You should call Jack," he said, meaning Jack Rosenfeld, family friend and attorney.

"Good idea."

We filed into the bedrooom together, and feeling awkward under Shields's gaze, I tripped clumsily against the edge of the rug. But I steadied myself, picked up the cordless phone on the night table, and dialed Jack's house. An answering machine beeped, and I left an urgent message for Jack to call me as soon as possible. I started to stutter out more details but then realized I couldn't figure them out myself.

When I hung up, Dan had pulled on crisp khakis and a navy blue polo shirt and was heading into the bathroom.

"Just a minute," Reese said. He pushed into the room ahead of Dan and jerked his head back in surprise, momentarily staggered by the gleaming marble and brass fittings of our high-tech bathroom. I used to cherish each fancy fixture, but now I couldn't care less. If it would only make the cops leave, I'd gladly trade my Kohler commode for an outhouse.

"A lot of windows in here," Reese called back to his partner, staring up at the arched glass ceiling.

"I'm not trying to escape," Dan said mildly. "I need to use the bathroom."

Reese peered out one of the oversized windows, contemplating the two-story drop. Then he sauntered to the other end of the bathroom. "What's through here?"

"The spa."

Reese opened the sliding door, and the wall of mirrors on the other side reflected his astonishment as he took in the huge Jacuzzi whirlpool and natural-wood hot tub. "Nice setup you've got here," he said acidly. "I'll just wait on this side while you do your business."

The bathroom door clicked shut, and I edged toward the bed, reeling from this bizarre alternate reality in which I'd suddenly landed. Shields kept his back to me, not encouraging conversation, and I rubbed my finger back and forth on the duchesse quilt. If I were dreaming, would I be able to feel the silk fabric sliding against my fingers? I blinked hard a few times and then the bathroom door opened again to reveal Dan back in handcuffs, with Reese at his elbow.

"We're ready," Reese said.

Shields nodded. "Let's go."

Dan took a few steps toward me. "Will you come with me?" he asked. His hooded eyes held mine, needing me.

I thought of the kids down the hall, asleep. Jimmy would likely wake up again, which meant that if I left, Grant or Ashley should be warned.

"No, she won't come," Reese said. "It's not a party. No extra room in the squad car."

"I'll follow in my own car," I said with sudden certainty, his hostility solving my quandary. "Where are we going?"

"Downtown," he snarled.

"There's really nothing for you to do down there, Mrs. Fields." Shields spoke flatly but without anger, the senior man getting the job done. "But here's the address if you really want to go." He handed me a card, and as I glanced at it, the partners soundlessly whisked Dan out of the room. From the hall, I heard my husband calling, "Lacy!"

"I'll be there, honey!" I hollered. "I'll follow you and be there."

I raced to Grant's room, then, remembering that he needed a night's sleep before the test, I moved on to his sister's sanctuary. Fourteen-year-old Ashley, curled up under the flowing canopy on her bed, didn't move when I burst in, so I shook her gently, telling her that Daddy and I had to run out and she needed to get up if Jimmy called. Only half awake, she didn't ask any questions, and before she could think of any, I sprinted downstairs, slipping into the Lexus and pushing the button for the garage door to open. I gunned the car down the block and by the second stop sign—where I definitely didn't bother to stop—I had the squad car within sight. I felt a surge of relief that at least the night wouldn't end with my turning back.

The cop car was going fast but not recklessly, no sirens blasting or lights flashing, and I managed to keep the red taillights within easy view. They knew the neighborhood, winding their way through the dark streets without any hesitation. I kept expecting the squad car to stop suddenly and pull a U-turn in the middle of the road. I'd look in the window and see the faux cops laughing uproariously at getting away with a prank like this. Maybe they represented a medical fraternity doing a grown-up form of hazing. Or they had the starring roles on *Cops 911*, that new Fox show shooting on a nearby soundstage. We'd watch the tape tomorrow and laugh, and Dan would sign the waiver so the episode could air.

But the car kept going steadily forward. We turned onto Sunset Boulevard and suddenly, even at midnight, the traffic was thicker. A red Ferrari slipped in front of me, but I could still track the cops, and when we all turned onto the highway, the Ferrari zoomed ahead and I inched closer to the unmarked LAPD car. As I drove, a name kept repeating over and over in my head. *Tasha Barlow. Tasha Barlow. Tasha Barlow.* I waited for some bells to ring, but got resounding silence. I'd been married to Dan since we were kids just out of college, long enough to read his facial expressions pretty accurately, and nothing had registered when he'd heard the name, either. If this wasn't all a joke, it must just be a case of mistaken identity. Dan was right. The whole mess would get cleared up as soon as he got to headquarters.

From my car phone, I dialed Jack Rosenfeld again, got the same message, and this time left my cell phone number, too. If only I knew his. I flicked on the radio to an all-news station, wondering if I might hear something about Tasha Barlow. But no, just more of the usual—mud slides in Malibu, a loss for the Lakers, and a Brinks truck overturning on the 110 freeway and spilling a million nickels on the road. How to get rich in L.A. I turned the radio off, and when we exited the highway, I focused on negotiating the now unfamiliar back streets.

After some fast turns, the cops pulled into a spot marked PO-LICE VEHICLES ONLY, and I realized we had arrived at headquarters. Of course I didn't see any place to park, so I rolled down the window. "Okay if I leave it here?" I shouted to Shields, who was pulling himself out of the passenger seat of the squad car.

"No, ma'am. Police cars only. You'll have to find parking around the other side of the building."

Instead of dumping the car and telling them to tow it if they damn well wanted, I drove off and wasted five minutes cruising around the ugly block, squeezing my car into a too-small space in front of what had once been a deli and was now a boarded-up store-front. Courage is not exactly my middle name, but I hardly thought about the unsavory characters lurking around as I slammed my car door shut and clicked the remote lock. I started running back to the station house, my shoes making an eerie, clinking sound against the broken sidewalk. I looked down and realized that in my haste to grab footwear as I left the house, I'd slipped into a pair of purple snakeskin Manolo Blahnik mules with high, spindly heels. My Wild Berry Chanel–manicured toenails peeked through the open toes. Above the ankles, I was still wearing pale pink Lycra workout gear. Charging down the street in this getup, I was probably pretty safe— anybody would assume that some pissed-off pimp was chasing me.

Inside the station house, everything seemed surprisingly quiet. A sleepy-eyed cop at the front desk munching take-out from Taco Bell stared at me when I walked in, and when I told her I was looking for my husband, Dr. Dan Fields, she waved toward some chairs at a far wall.

"Better siddown," she said, sounding like a transplant from Brooklyn.

"Can I join him, please?"

"Nope. Siddown."

"He is here, correct? I'm in the right place?"

She shrugged. "I guess so."

"I told the policemen who took him that I'd be following in my car," I said, persisting. "I'm sure they're expecting me."

"Yeah, they set an extra place," she said snidely. She swung her beefy jowls around until she was barely a taco's length from my face. "Siddown, lady. Or leave. I don't care which."

I sat. Antsy, I crossed and uncrossed my legs. My shoes stuck to the floor and made an odd sucking noise as I tried to pull them up. There weren't any magazines around, and the only newspaper was four days old. I ran my fingers through my hair and contemplated the gouges in the wooden floor, trying not to think about what could be making it so sticky. I stared at the policewoman, wondering how much tighter her LAPD uniform would be after that taco. She caught my eye and sat back heavily in her chair, chewing thoughtfully on the taco and gazing at my Manolos. I got up and approached the desk.

"Listen, this is all a misunderstanding," I said, trying to sound calm and friendly. "Please, please tell me where my husband is."

She shrugged without putting down the taco. "Don't really know."

"Your detectives have the wrong person. He doesn't know anything about what they're investigating."

"Heard that one before." She laughed through her nose and took another big bite.

"No, really." I took a deep breath, trying to win her over. Maybe if we became friends, the taco lady could send Dan home. "My husband is Dr. Dan Fields. Maybe you've heard of him?"

"Nope."

"He's a plastic surgeon. He's in the newspapers a lot." Impress her, but still sound modest. "Actually, he's pretty well known."

"Right. Everybody in L.A.'s so important. I'll add him to my list. Let me guess—your husband gives second-rate actresses first-rate boobs."

"Not at all," I said, slightly offended. Then, trying to get back on her good side, I added, "Actually, he spends most of his time doing reconstructive surgery on people who've been seriously hurt."

"Yeah? So he's a good guy?" She looked up, vaguely interested.

I nodded eagerly. "A very good guy. He does facial reconstructions and skin grafts on burn victims. Last week he reattached a teenager's finger after a car accident, and the boy's going to be able to play hockey again—or maybe lacrosse. Whichever he did before, I can't remember," I said, talking faster and faster. "Oh, and cleft palates. Did I tell you about cleft palates? Two years ago Dan went to Chile and started a free clinic and taught all the doctors there how to do the surgery. He's so good, really good."

I paused in the midst of my rant—running out of breath and coming to my senses at almost the same time. If the cop wanted Dan's résumé, she could click onto his website. But probably all she wanted was to finish her shift and go home to her own husband—whose fingers were all attached, and who wasn't in jail tonight.

I kicked off my shoes and sunk about four inches. The cold tile floor of the police station stung my bare feet. "Look," I said, "my feet hurt. I have blisters. My husband's back there somewhere when he shouldn't be. My kids are home alone. I want all this to be over. What do you think I should do?"

"Go home, Mrs. Fields."

For a moment, I wondered how the taco lady had managed to say that without moving her lips from her synchronous chewing. Then I realized that the voice was from the other side of the room, and I got into my shoes again and spun around to see Detective Reese standing there. From across the room, he looked a little like Jimmy Smits in his *NYPD Blue* days, but there was a hardness around his eyes that no actor could simulate.

"I'm not going home without my husband," I said firmly.

"I'm afraid you'll have to." The detective gave me a lazy, contemptuous smile. "He's been arrested, ma'am. Not going anywhere until his arraignment."

"Which is when?"

"Within forty-eight hours, usually."

"Forty-eight *hours*? That's two *days*." I was seething, trying not to scream. "You have no right to do that."

"Oh no? Tell it to the judge, as the saying goes. But just to calm you down, a good lawyer can probably get the case heard in the morning."

"Can't we get it heard right now?" I asked, picturing the dank cell where Dan was probably cowering right this minute.

"I don't think we could find a judge who'd consider this an emergency worth getting up for."

"So why did you arrest him at midnight? He told you he'd try to help you out in the morning. He doesn't know anything about this case. This woman. Whoever she is."

Again, the contemptuous smile. "We knew where we could find him at night. Now as I said, Mrs. Fields, you'd better leave. Your husband is being photographed and fingerprinted and we're running a check on his criminal record."

"He doesn't have a criminal record," I said. "You can't count the parking ticket from last Sunday because it was my fault. Dan always puts in plenty of quarters. He's the most honest man you've ever met."

Reese cleared his throat. "Then he'll have a clean rap sheet." He turned and began strolling away, but his studied casualness was interrupted by a door flying open and a commotion erupting in his face as two cops dragged in a grotesquely bloodied creature, barely recognizable as human. Howling like an animal, he flailed his emaciated arms and legs, then collapsed in a heap, quite literally at Reese's feet. Reese tried to step back, but two blood-caked hands grabbed at his ankles.

"Let go!" Reese hollered, but the man's own wailing drowned out the words, and suddenly the other two cops descended on him with nightsticks, beating him away from Reese. Blood spurted onto the floor and Reese leaped away as the other cops pinned their prey. The howls changed in intensity from plaintive to pained, and the dissipated mess on the floor writhed like a half-dissected frog pinned to the table for a seventh-grade biology class.

"Get him to the back," Reese yelled, and with stunning viciousness, the cops yanked their victim out the opposite door, in the very direction I'd been staring since I arrived.

"No!" I shrieked, running after them. "My husband's back there!"

The door slammed with a convincing thud, locking in the bloodied, the victimized, and the criminal. I crashed against the handle with wild fury, but a lock had snapped into place, and nothing budged. I kicked at the door with the piercing high heel of my left mule, pounding until something seemed to give, but it was the heel, which I felt break away from the sole, dangling like a half-amputated limb.

Reese. Maybe he had a human side. Tears streaming down my cheeks, I twisted around to face him. I would have thrown myself at his feet if I thought it would help—but I'd just seen how much good that did. "Officer, I need you to help me. Whatever you can do, just get my husband out of there. Please, I beg you." My terrified plea ricocheted around the squad room with such high-pitched anguish that Reese actually stopped in his tracks and turned slowly to look at me. He blinked a few times, as if trying to figure out who I could be.

"I can't release your husband," he said finally. "He's in jail. A very serious crime, okay?"

"No, it's not okay! Please don't lock him up all night!" Maybe the room turned humans into wild animals, because my bellows suddenly sounded identical to the cries of the creature who had just been dragged away. Reese didn't bother answering me this time; he just disappeared out the door where he had first come. Despite my broken shoe, I charged after him, but the taco cop stood up with more speed than I would have thought possible and planted herself in front of me.

"Sorry, lady. Nobody leaves this area."

"I've got to help my husband," I said, my voice suddenly shaking.

"Ya not gonna help him here." An edge of sympathy had crept in under her Brooklyn accent. "Look, just get home. Come back first thing in the morning."

"Do you think Dan's in a cell with . . ." I gestured vaguely, indicating the wild man who had just come in.

"Nah. That was probably a drug charge. Your husband's in on murder. Much bigger deal. Probably in seclusion."

My shoe chose that moment to give up completely, the torn heel collapsing and my ankle twisting as I sunk to the floor. My husband was more dangerous than a bloody, drug-crazed maniac. I got up and without another word half crawled, half stumbled to my car.

Driving home, I wanted to think out the situation properly, preparing for constructive action, but instead I kept hearing a mocking voice scream in my head, *Dan's in jail! Dan's in jail! Dan's in jail!* like some endlessly repeated child's tape from the Brothers Grimm. My only images of jail came from TV shows and bad DVDs: I pictured a hostile cell mate, a smelly toilet, and a shaky, lice-infested cot. I tried not to think about the worst—Dan the doctor being beaten up by some nothing-left-to-lose killer, who'd turn his face into a bloody pulp and force needles into his arm.

The highway was empty and I revved the motor, driving eighty most of the way home. Forget the treadmill—my personal best tonight was going to be set in the car. I half hoped I'd get stopped so I could tell my story to some other cop, but nobody came near me. Maybe all the cops in L.A. were busy arresting innocent people tonight.

Back inside the house, I peeked in on Jimmy, but his bed was empty. I dashed down the hall to Ashley's room—where my daughter was sound asleep, with Jimmy curled at the foot of her bed like some loyal golden retriever. I carried him gently back, grateful that he didn't wake up. Making a final stop in Grant's room, I found my oldest son also asleep, his long hair flung across the pillow, a small silver earring glinting in the moonlight that crept in from the edges of the shade. He looked like a Hollywood surfer boy, but under the golden tan was a smart student who had a physics midterm tomorrow. I somehow had to get him off to school in the morning without prattling on hysterically about the police. No use upsetting him before his test. With college applications coming, he needed good grades, and nothing mattered more. I took a deep breath. Nothing mattered more? If only. Whether Grant ended up at Stanford or Swarthmore suddenly didn't seem as serious as Dan's ending up at Sing Sing.

Heading back to my own bedroom, I decided I'd try Jack again at 6:30 A.M. or so. He should be answering by then—Los Angeles is an early-morning town. I lay down on the bed, trying to muster the energy to undress and wash my face, but instead I just closed my eyes.

And then opened them again.

Who cared about the time? With my husband stuck in a cell, I couldn't worry about waking his lawyer. I fumbled in my closet for a pair of no-blister Hogans to replace the broken-heeled mules, then crept quietly down the stairs and back to my Lexus.

Jack lived in Beverly Hills, just north of Sunset on elegant Roxbury Drive, and at this hour, zipping along at a conservative seventy miles per hour, I was there in ten minutes. A thick hedge of trees blocked the neo-Colonial mansion from the quiet street, but Jack, less pretentious than his neighbors, had no gate. I pulled into the driveway, marched up to the front door, and rang the bell.

Nothing. Could they be away? No, his son attended the same private school as Grant, and no self-respecting family with Ivy League aspirations would leave town in March, during midterms of junior year. I rang again. And again. From where I stood on the front porch, I saw the faint glow of a light going on in a distant window, and then a woman's voice over the intercom—at least theirs worked—saying uncertainly, "Who's there?"

"It's Lacy Fields. I need Jack. There's an emergency."

"Lacy?" The voice—Jack's wife, Gina—seemed to perk up. "Hang on, I'll wake him up." The intercom went dead long enough for me to wonder if he was a sound sleeper or in a different bed, but then the front door was opening and Jack was there, tying on a thick terry robe.

"Geez, Lacy, what's going on? Are you all right?"

Jack put his sturdy arm around me, and I felt myself trembling, ready to cry. But I held it together, sensing that if I collapsed now, I'd never get up again.

"I'm okay," I said. "But Dan's in jail."

"What?" His voice ripped through the quiet night, and I envisioned neighbors bounding up from their beds, thinking they'd heard a shot. Jack recovered quickly enough to grab my arm and pull me over the threshold, closing the heavy door behind us with a thud. In the dim light of the foyer, he looked at me uncertainly.

"I want to hear this. Come on in. Do you need a drink? Should I have Gina put on some coffee?"

"Just water," I said. Jack looked dazed, and since he was now dealing with a woman who had shown up unannounced at his doorstep at three in the morning, I couldn't really blame him. We walked down a hall, past the sleekly modern dining room, and then Jack flipped on an overhead light in the kitchen. Gina had been calling me for months to get my professional opinion as a decorator on her room renovation. She had a good eye herself, and now that the kitchen was finished, I could practically picture Martha Stewart coming in to whip up some cream puffs. Good manners demanded I rave about the stainless steel stove and free-form granite counters, but in my current state, I simply wasn't capable of making kind comments about custom cabinetry.

Jack opened the refrigerator and pulled out a bottle of lemon Poland Spring. "What do you mean Dan's in jail?" he asked, saving me from any small talk.

I took a deep breath. "Short version or long?"

"Short."

"Two cops showed up at midnight, crashed through the house to find Dan, and then put handcuffs on him. One of them drew a gun and pointed it right at him." I started shaking, my voice quavering at the memory. I sniffled a couple of times and put my fingers over my lips to stop the trembling. "They took him down to a squad car and to the precinct house downtown, where they locked him up. They won't let me see him."

Jack, still holding on to the Poland Spring, wandered over to the other side of the kitchen and slid onto a bar stool. I followed him like a puppy.

"What's the charge?"

I tried to form the word, but my lips wouldn't do it. Instead, a shudder went through my whole body. "Some woman named Tasha Barlow," I whispered.

Jack furrowed his brow. "She's bringing charges against Dan? What are we talking about here, Lacy? Harassment? Sexual harassment?"

I felt my cheeks getting warm, but I just shook my head. Jack thought he was helping, offering the most dramatic charge he could imagine so I could just nod and not have to say the words. "Worse," I said, my voice barely a croak. "She's dead."

Now Jack glowered at me as if I'd started spouting obscenities. "Murder?" he asked.

Again his voice was loud, and it was all I could do not to cover my ears so I didn't have to hear him. I offered a barely perceptible nod and felt my eyes fill up with tears. "There's an arraignment within forty-eight hours. But the cop said maybe we could get it in the morning."

"Jesus Christ. You know I'm not the one to handle this, Lacy."

"So tell me who is."

"Dave Liggett comes to mind. He's defended a couple of big sex suits lately."

"And you're thinking what?"

"I don't know. False accusations by a woman. This Tasha Barlow . . ." He paused and shook his head. "Forgive me, I'm not completely awake. I guess if she's dead she's not making any false accusations against Dan. Those had to come from somewhere else."

"Of course. False accusations. That's what's going on. Or mistaken identity. I've thought of that one, too." That Dan could be anything less than one hundred percent innocent hadn't yet crossed my mind.

"Chauncey Howell," Jack said suddenly, snapping his fingers "Best criminal lawyer I know. The best."

I liked the name. He sounded like he was from an old New England family, the kind that sailed over on the *Mayflower*. "Can I call him now?"

Jack didn't bother to look at a clock, he just picked up the cordless phone on the counter and punched in a number. We both waited.

"Chauncey? Jack Rosenfeld. Sorry to get you at this hour on your private line. But I need your help on a murder case."

Murder case. Uttered coldly into the phone in the middle of the night, the words hit me like exploding land mines. I clutched my chest and reeled back. With panic rising, I grabbed my bag and pulled out my cell phone.

Jack, done outlining the situation to Chauncey, looked up and furrowed his eyebrows in confusion. "You don't need your mobile," he said. "You can talk to Chauncey on this line."

Jack held out the receiver, but instead of taking it, I frantically pushed the menu buttons on my Motorola until the small screen displayed my cache of digital photos. Dan hugging me at the beach. Dan and Jimmy lying on the grass. Dan playing tennis with Ashley. Dan—my husband who couldn't be a murderer. He'd eaten lasagna tonight with me and the kids, said I looked sexy in my workout clothes, and kissed me gently before he got into our antique four-poster bed.

I snapped my cell phone shut. Next time I was able to curl up next to Dan, I'd know that according to the cops, I was sleeping with a killer.

Chapter Two

When I finally calmed down enough to take the phone, Chauncey Howell sounded coolly efficient, stunningly professional for someone asking questions of an unseen client-to-be in the middle of the night. We went over details for nearly half an hour before I hung up and agreed to meet him on the courthouse steps at 9:00 A.M.

I normally need eight hours of sleep to function, but I hit my pillow for barely two and woke up feeling alert, every throbbing muscle and nerve ready to spring. I dashed downstairs to have breakfast with Grant and Ashley before they left for school. Amazingly, despite my having woken Ashley, they'd missed all the late-night goings-on, and they were completely oblivious to what had happened. I took exactly one minute to decide that I'd leave it that way.

Ashley's outfit this morning included a purple corduroy shrunken blazer, a teeny-tiny pink T-shirt, and Citizens of Humanity jeans slung so low on her hips that jeans and tee would never have the chance to meet. She'd pulled a pink-and-purple Pucci scarf through the belt loops and snaked a sparkly pink wire bracelet around her wrist. Unlike Grant, she wasn't much at getting top grades in school, but she definitely got them in style.

"If you want a lift, I'm leaving now," Grant said to her, finishing off his orange juice and putting his empty cereal bowl in the sink. "I have a midterm and I don't want to be late."

Ashley nibbled thoughtfully at the edge of her all-natural breakfast bar and picked at the drizzled frosting with her pink fingernail. I willed her to go with Grant, but my extrasensory persuasion didn't work. "Too early for me," Ashley said. "Mom can drive me later."

Grant half rolled his eyes. "Mom's dressed like she has a meeting this morning. For the extra ten minutes, you can give her a break."

Ashley laconically turned toward me, slowly taking in my Chanel suit and estate jewelry. "That true?"

"Yes, but I can take you on my way. Though it's probably more fun to go with Grant."

"Ugh. Going with Grant is ho-o-o-r-r-ible," she said, drawing out the word with her mouth wide open. At least she hadn't pierced her tongue. "But if you're too busy for me, fine. Don't worry." In one smooth motion, she stood up, grabbed her backpack, and stormed out to Grant's Jeep Cherokee, slamming the back door behind her.

Grant unfolded his lanky six-foot frame from the chair and turned his smoky gray eyes toward me. "I do this for you, Mom, not her. You've got to admit she's a bitch."

"More like a teenage girl who doesn't know how to behave around her big brother's friends," I said. "She'll be okay. Hey, good luck on your exam."

"Thanks." He slammed the door, too, and for a moment the house reverberated with the shock of their departures.

Upstairs, I checked on Jimmy, and when I saw he was sound asleep, I told our housekeeper, Eloise, to wake him as soon as I left so he could get on the bus for kindergarten.

"He only likes when you wake him," she said disapprovingly.

True enough. But I simply couldn't face Jimmy this morning. Too young to know how to ask for explanations, he needed them provided. How could I confront the wide eyes, the puzzled look, the morning smile warped by a trace of fear? Right now, I didn't have any explanations for him about what he'd seen last night.

"I have to leave," I said feebly.

I drove to the courthouse and at 8:45 took a position on the steps with the street in view. As Jack had described him, Chauncey Howell was a one-man dream team—glib, smart, and unbeatable in a courtroom. I pictured John Roberts crossed with Johnnie Cochran and kept a lookout for a tall, handsome defender in an Armani suit who would no doubt be emerging from a white chauffeured limousine.

Which is why I never would have spotted him if he hadn't tapped me on the shoulder.

"Lacy Fields?"

I swung around and found myself face-to-face with a short, sprightly man in a seersucker suit, standing a step above me.

"I'm Lacy."

"Good. I'm Chauncey Howell."

He extended a hand for me to shake, and I noticed that his nails were nicely buffed, but his fingers were ringless and his watch looked like a Timex. His wire-rim eyeglasses had clip-on shades and the thick briefcase at his side, navy blue Cordura, sported an L.L. Bean logo. Heaven knows I'm not a snob, but I figured all top-notch L.A. lawyers were like Jack Rosenfeld, carrying their drafts and documents in butter-soft Gucci, except on days when they decided to go Coach leather casual.

Trying to get my bearings, I said, "I figured you'd be coming from the other direction. I had my eye on the street, assuming you'd be coming up."

"I came down. I've been inside the courthouse for a while."

"Have you seen Dan?" I asked eagerly.

"Not yet. That comes next. I've been chatting with the district attorney and getting a few things arranged." He patted his striped tie. "The DA hasn't given me much information, and I'll have very little time with your husband before the hearing. So you and I need to talk." He studied me carefully, taking in my pale aqua

Chanel suit with the large gold buttons, and the cream-colored silk shell that peeked out from underneath. The matching aqua sandals had seemed a bit much for the first court appearance at my husband's side, so I'd opted for a pair of Valentino taupe pumps. I knew not to carry an Hermès bag—everyone said that if Martha Stewart hadn't flashed that vintage Birkin in court, she might have gone scot-free.

Chauncey Howell pointed to a step. "Only seat I can offer you at the moment."

"I'll stand."

He shrugged and said, "Not a lot of time before I have to get back into court, so I'll get right to the point. I've gone over most of what you told me on the phone, but I'm going to ask you to repeat some of it. What I need is everything that the police did and said from the time they knocked on your door last night."

I suddenly felt overwhelmed. "I'll sit after all," I said, kneeling down to brush the grime off the edge of a step. Chauncey leaned over and handed me a yellow legal pad.

"You want me to write what happened?" I asked.

"No, I want you to tell it to me. The paper's for sitting on. The step's not that clean."

"Oh. Thank you." I plunked the pad onto the step and carefully lowered my Chanel-ed bottom onto it. Chauncey Howell perched just above. "Everything the police said," I repeated. "Well, here goes."

I tried. A few stray thoughts wandered through, but for the most part, I managed a pretty straight narrative. Chauncey seemed to be listening, but he never took the pen—a Bic Clic, as far as I could tell—from his vest pocket. Either his memory never failed or I didn't say anything worth remembering.

Still, when I finished, he said, "Nice job. You're a good witness."

"Will I have to say all that today in court?"

He smiled wanly. "No, Mrs. Fields, you're not testifying. In fact, it's just an arraignment, so there's no reason for you to be in the courtroom at all. The DA will present the charge, we'll plead innocent, and the judge will set bail. I'm trying to handle it as quickly and quietly as possible. It would be nice to have Dr. Fields out of court before the press catches wind of the case."

I nodded mutely, surprised that I was able to feel so much confidence in a man in a seersucker suit.

Chauncey reached into his bag and took out a large manila envelope. "Next question," he said. "The name Tasha Barlow. Or Theresa Bartowski. Does it mean anything to you?"

"Nothing at all," I said quickly. "I've been brooding about it all night and it might as well be Jane Doe. I have no image."

But he did. Chauncey took a picture out of the envelope and held it out for me, a standard eight-by-ten black-and-white glossy, the kind every determined young woman in L.A. takes with her on auditions.

"Is this—"

"Yes," Chauncey said quickly. "The murder victim."

I reached for the photo but Chauncey didn't let go, so I leaned over to study it. I expected a surge of emotion, but nothing came. And what should I feel anyway? My sentiments were as tangled as the rhymes in a bad Hallmark card.

"Where was she from?" I asked after a moment.

"She grew up in Idaho and moved to Hollywood about six months ago."

The picture revealed a young woman with high cheekbones, a pert nose, and straight blond hair that curled slightly toward her chin. But any suggestion of fresh-faced innocence was hidden under several layers of makeup. Her large, wide-set eyes had been doused with heavy mascara and smoky liner to make them seem sultry, and thickly applied lip gloss gave her a pouty smile. These eight-by-tens were typically called head shots in the trade, but the deep V cut of her blouse and its revealing cleavage made this more of a chest shot.

"Do you know anything about her?" I asked Chauncey.

"Not yet. I have two people on my staff working on a back-grounder this morning. They should have something in a few hours." He pushed the picture closer to me. "Nothing at all strikes you?"

Something about the face seemed almost too perfect, like an artist's rendition of a struggling young actress. "I suppose I could have met her at a party and not remembered. A lot of young women in Los Angeles look like that."

"A lot of those women see plastic surgeons," Chauncey said. His voice was mild, without much inflection, but the words knocked me back as forcefully as a thrown rock. Trembling, I looked again.

He was right that the woman in the photo hadn't achieved that all-natural look on her own. I recognized the signs, starting with the cleavage: tiny shoulders, flat chest, then breasts leaping out like over-ripe grapefruits. No Wonderbra could be responsible for that. But it wasn't Dan's style. Even in the days when he regularly did cosmetic surgery, he refused to do breast augmentation and railed against implants. He didn't think silicone was bad just for a woman's health—he worried a lot more about what it did to her self-esteem.

My eyes wandered up to the face. The lips might have had a collagen injection or two, and a scalpel had probably been involved in sculpting the tiny nose. But that wasn't my husband's handiwork, either. Dan insisted on features with character, and this nose looked like it had been stamped out from a Hollywood cookie cutter.

"You'll obviously ask Dan," I said, trying to keep my voice from shaking. "But I'd be very surprised if she were a patient of his. Anytime."

Chauncey put the picture back into the envelope and carefully slipped it inside his briefcase.

"Just a few more questions," he said. "First, you mentioned your three children. I need their names and ages."

"Grant's sixteen. Ashley's just turned fourteen. And Jimmy's five. But they won't be involved in this, will they?"

"Only in the sense that the judge will be setting bail for your husband this morning. Dan obviously has ties to the community, but it's helpful to establish close family connections. You and Dan are the parents of all the children?"

"Yes." I felt my voice quavering and stared at a crack in the step. "We got married very young and had Grant and Ashley quickly, while Dan was still in medical school. By the time Ashley was eight, Dan had a well-established practice and we decided—"

"It's okay."

I glanced up and saw Chauncey Howell smiling at me. "You don't have to justify having children," he said. "It's just that with the age difference, I didn't want to have any surprises."

"No surprises," I said. "They're all ours and they were all planned as carefully as a Carnival cruise."

Chauncey laughed briefly, then turned serious. "One more thing, Mrs. Fields. And think about this before you answer. Have you and the doctor had any marital problems lately?"

"No." I said it much too quickly, and caught Chauncey glancing at me keenly over the tops of his wire-rims. I took a breath, then said, "We've been married a long time and we still love each other. Dan laughs at my jokes and I listen to his stories. We have a good, normal family life. I mean, what happened last night is crazy. Out of the blue. It's got to be a mistake, Mr. Howell."

Chauncey adjusted his eyeglasses, pushing them back with two fingers. "I don't know enough yet to have an opinion," he said slowly, "but I'll be honest. You need to be prepared. Your husband's not a movie star, but he's a well-known, well-respected figure in the community. The Los Angeles police don't need more bad publicity. They wouldn't have gone this far without evidence."

My stomach clenched. "Don't you think it's all just a bureaucratic mistake?" I asked. "A nightmare out of Kafka? An innocent man arrested and caught in an inexplicable system. You have to untangle this."

He glanced at his watch and then stood up, a small man towering over me. "I'm going to do the best I can, believe me. Right now, I need to go inside and talk to Dan so we can get the bail hearing done." I felt glued to the concrete, too weak to pull myself up next to him, so I just shielded my eyes against the sun and tilted my head up as Chauncey continued. "With luck, nothing has been leaked about Dan's arrest. It's a bad idea for us to play this out in the press until we have a position. You can bet the police have their statements all ready for the news conference. I'd just like to put that off as long as possible."

I crossed my arms over my gold buttons and suddenly understood Chauncey Howell's understated appearance. He didn't want to call attention to Dan—or himself—today. I felt slightly embarrassed by my flashy designer suit and thought of explaining to Chauncey that I'd been trying to look the part of supportive-woman-behind-the-man-in-court. But the instinct that had seemed so on target in my bedroom this morning looked awfully foolish in the harsh, yellow-hazed morning light of the courtroom steps. This was real life. Murder. And I was acting like an extra on *One Life to Live*.

I stood up, brushed off my skirt, and handed Chauncey his legal pad. "What shall I do this morning?" I asked, trying to sound as competent as I possibly could.

"Does Dan have a passport?"

"Pardon?"

"A United States passport. For travel."

"Yes, of course."

"I may need it. The judge could ask for it as a condition of bail, to make sure he doesn't leave the country. Usually I have twenty-four hours to turn it in, but sometimes a judge wants it in his hand before the defendant is released."

"I'll go get it and bring it back." With a mission in mind, I heard my voice take on a certain authority.

Chauncey reached into his pocket and pulled out a sleek Tiffany silver cardholder (so he had one Beverly Hills affectation) and handed me his business card, which was elegantly engraved (or two affectations).

"Not necessary to come all the way back. Drop it at my office."

"What if you need it quickly to get him out?"

"I have messengers between my office and the courthouse all day. They'll have it to me faster than you could imagine."

I glanced at the address. Beverly Boulevard. More my part of town, but still. I took a deep breath. "Mr. Howell, is there a reason you don't want me in the courthouse?"

He looked puzzled. "Why wouldn't I want you here?"

I shrugged and let my hands flit from my waist down the sides of my skirt. "I can change if this isn't appropriate."

"You look lovely, Mrs. Fields."

"Call me Lacy."

"Then call me Chauncey. Look, I don't have any secret agendas. It's just not necessary to have you in the courthouse this morning. The prosecutor will present the charge, which is murder in the second degree. That's murder with intent. There'll be an affidavit from the police and I'll waive having the complaint read. That's it."

"Don't they have to say why they arrested him?"

Chauncey shrugged. "The prosecutor will promise that he has a strong case in order to get a high bail. But they won't present anything today. The police didn't have a warrant last night, but you let them in the house—which is consent—so I won't argue unlawful arrest. They had probable cause. I can take care of this end, and then we'll get to our real work, back in my office. With luck, I'll be there with Dan by noon."

We shook hands, and when he headed back to the courthouse I went to my car. I wasn't in a rush this time, but still I raced home, my heart beating so hard that I felt like I'd just gulped a pot of espresso. I always kept the passports in the second drawer of my bedside table, which happened to be a Shaker medicine chest that I'd uncovered in a flea market for $16, refurbished, and put on a gold-leaf stand that I'd had made. Okay, the gold-leaf part was wildly extravagant, but the result, incredibly creative, appeared in a feature in *House Beautiful*. What more could an interior decorator want? It got me a couple of movie moguls' wives as clients, and all of a sudden I was a celebrity decorator, with my own column in a glossy L.A. shelter magazine called *Abode*. Not too many readers, but definitely the right ones. When a normal client wondered if I was too upscale now for her budget, I just lowered my voice and murmured, "Don't worry about that night table. I bought the darn thing for sixteen bucks."

As I dashed upstairs to the bedroom, I had a sudden dread that the documents would be gone. Inexplicably vanished. I'd yank the drawer open and find nothing.

But when I pulled it open, all the important documents lay in their usual place. The world had turned upside down, but the papers hadn't moved. I got out Dan's passport and flipped through it, staring at his photo for a minute. Dan, my Dan. The man I knew better than anyone on earth. Glancing at the stamps on the pages reminded me of the exotic trips Dan and I had taken together—Paris, Panama, Machu Picchu. But no place had ever seemed stranger or more foreign than where we were right now. Forget passing through customs—I felt like I'd slipped through a wormhole to another dimension.

Trying to stay grounded, I reached for Chauncey Howell's business card, called his office number, and asked his secretary how soon I could come over.

"A couple of hours would be fine," she said. "I can't imagine that Chauncey will be back earlier. I checked, and he won't need the passport until then."

How efficient of her. But how could I get through the next two hours? I thought of calling Molly Archer, my best friend since college. Sophisticated, smart, and inexplicably single, Molly had played all the important roles in my life: maid of honor at my wedding, godmother to Grant, only person to advise me that I looked awful in yellow sweaters. We always told each other everything, but for the first time ever, I couldn't imagine what I'd say after hello. *Hey, Dan might have killed somebody, do you want to do lunch?* No, better to keep this to myself for a while. Talking made it too real.

I planted myself on the edge of my bed, trying to make sense of what obviously made no sense at all. Part of me still believed that in another week, this would just be a funny story to tell over margaritas and Mexican food. But my more rational side knew that everything had changed. In twelve hours, I'd gained a whole new vocabulary. Murder in the second degree. Murder with intent. Where did these words come from, anyway? Chauncey's legal phrases seemed to belong to someone else's life, not mine. I was a normal suburban mom-slash-decorator who worried about kids, carpools, and carpets, not dead actresses. I took yoga classes, jogged when I could, and fought off the four extra pounds at my thighs. Maybe I had fabulous clothes and a flair for design, but mostly I helped with homework, fed Jimmy's gerbils, and fussed over my family. I liked to putter in my garden, and I knew about geraniums, not jail cells.

When the phone rang, I jumped to answer, hoping it might be Chauncey with news of Dan. But it was only a client wanting to chat about the fabric samples I'd dropped off at her house yesterday. Yesterday? More like a million years ago.

"Is this a good time?" she asked. "You sound distracted."

"This is fine," I said, putting on my best business-as-usual manner. Apparently the rest of the world was still spinning on its regular axis, even if mine had slipped off-kilter. Let's see, fabric. I remembered that. We discussed thread count, nub, and durability. I steered her toward chenille, and as soon as she agreed, I switched gears and described the advantages of velvet. I wasn't being contrary—just using up time.

Once we hung up, I stared at the phone, wondering if I could use my powers of persuasion for something more important—like convincing Jimmy that everything was fine. It wouldn't be easy. Jimmy was a scared little boy, but he was also smart. When he lost his first tooth, a dollar bill appeared under his pillow. Waking up in the morning, his hair rumpled and his voice still groggy with sleep, Jimmy had clutched the money in his little fist but refused to believe in the tooth fairy. "I think Mommy or Daddy left it, or maybe Grant," he'd said solemnly. Try to tell him now that nothing bad had happened to his dad? Sure, and Easter eggs come from a bunny.

I got off the bed and went through my closet to see if I had a better talking-with-the-lawyer outfit. After a few minutes, I gave up in defeat and decided not to change. To keep myself busy, I looked around the bedroom, thinking about what I could improve. I moved a Murano mint bowl from one side of the dresser to the other, and pushed the Steuben swans Dan gave me for our last anniversary to the front of a shelf. The swans' mate-for-life symbolism used to strike me as corny, but now I felt a surge of gratitude. Only a thoughtful, kind, and caring man would buy love birds for his wife. And who ever heard of a thoughtful, kind, and caring killer?

Needing to get out of the house, I drove over to Beverly Boulevard. It was too early to barge into Chauncey's office, but his law firm happened to be located in the best design district in town. I found an expensive antique store to wander through, but it seemed about as diverting as Kmart. Not even a blue-light special could attract me now—all I wanted was to see Dan. Giving up, I made my way over to Chauncey's place, willing to wait however long it took.

But it didn't take any time at all. Chauncey had worked fast, and when I got to the office, Dan had already arrived. He was sitting resolutely on Chauncey's black leather sofa, sipping a bottle of his favorite ginger Honest Tea. When a secretary ushered me in, Dan smiled tiredly, then came over to give me a little hug. I'd planned to stay cool, but at Dan's touch, a wild mix of emotion flooded through me. I lay my head against his chest, overwhelmed with relief, confusion, and dread.

"Are you all right?" I asked, barely whispering.

"Yes, yes, I'm fine." He looked slightly paler than usual, but he had on pressed khakis and a new powder blue polo shirt with a Ralph Lauren insignia. Either Chauncey Howell had picked it up for him coming to court this morning or the prison had a Barneys in the basement.

I stepped back, reminding myself to stay strong. With everything else collapsing around him, Dan didn't need his wife crumbling, too. But imagining for the thousandth time what Dan had gone through last night, I gave a little shudder.

"Was it terrible in the . . . cell? My God, I saw a drug addict being dragged back." I looked at him with what I hoped was tender sympathy.

But Dan just shrugged and sat down again on the sofa. "There's really nothing dramatic to tell. Chauncey handled everything quickly this morning. I'm sure this will all be over soon."

"Honey, I'm scared. This can't be happening. It's just way beyond awful."

"Not so bad."

Dan crossed his arms in front of him and I pinched my lips together. So Dan was being brave and taking it like a man. When Zeno of Citium invented Stoicism in 300 B.C. and declared that males should be unmoved by joy or grief, did he realize that he was going to piss off women for the next two thousand years?

"Chauncey's just been getting some information from me," Dan said, avoiding any emotional discussions by sticking with facts. "You can probably help." He gestured toward a chair across the room, and I sat down, pulling at the edge of my slim skirt. I had to remember to tell the tailor to go an inch longer next time, though it probably wouldn't matter. I'd feel vulnerable right now even if I were bundled in a burnoose.

Chauncey strummed his fingers on his desk, not seconding the invitation. "Dan, you have complete lawyer-client confidentiality in this room, but we have some difficult topics to cover. I need you to be able to talk freely." He glanced at me, and I got the point.

"I don't have to stay. I can wait outside," I said, jumping up to leave.

Dan shook his head. "Don't do that. I want you here."

I sat down again, feeling a little like a marionette, with Chauncey and Dan pulling the strings.

Deciding just to ignore me, Chauncey turned back to Dan. "Let's go over Tasha Barlow, or Theresa Bartowski, again." He pulled out the picture that I'd seen that morning, along with several others. "You've had a little time now. What do you think?"

Dan leaned forward to look at the images, but then sat back again. "I meet a lot of women at parties and charity benefits, so it's possible our paths crossed. If that's it, she made no impression. I'll go by my office later and check my files. But I'm good at remembering patients' faces, and hers just isn't one I know."

Chauncey played with his pen, rolling it around on his finger. "Look, Dan, the prosecutor didn't give me too many details of his case this morning. We'll hear some of the evidence at the preliminary hearing, but I'd like to put that off as long as possible. He did say there's material evidence that places you at the scene of the crime."

He paused to let that sink in. Dan just rubbed his eyes.

"An eyewitness connected you with the victim," Chauncey continued, speaking slowly. "She saw you going into the apartment—and Tasha turned up dead in her bedroom less than an hour later."

His tone was so matter-of-fact he might have been talking about the price of shirts at Brooks Brothers. So maybe I'd heard wrong. Because if Chauncey had announced that someone saw Dan in the dead girl's apartment, wouldn't there be screeching violins and quick cuts of shocked faces? Hadn't anyone seen *The Maltese Falcon?*

"It's impossible," Dan said finally. "I don't even know the victim. I couldn't have been in her bedroom."

"What's the motive supposed to have been?" I asked in a small voice.

Chauncey put down his pen. "We may not hear anything about motive until the trial. But I'd say the prosecutor has a couple of ways to go. Dan's a plastic surgeon accused of killing a young actress. The obvious answer is surgery gone wrong or sex gone wrong."

"But I didn't—"

"I know," said Chauncey, interrupting Dan before he could offer another denial. "But let's think along those lines." He asked some questions about Dan's schedule, the number of patients he saw, and the amount of time he spent at home. He got the names of various doctors and nurses Dan worked with at the hospital and asked about malpractice cases.

"None that I've lost and only one that was ever filed against me. That was back when I was a resident and a woman who'd had a rhinoplasty didn't like the way her nose turned up at the end. We went to mediation, and instead of a financial settlement, the chief surgeon I'd been with agreed to do it over for her."

"Nothing else?" asked Chauncey.

Dan shrugged. "Maybe I've been lucky. But I'm also not one of those surgeons who shows up to cut and never talks before or after. I'm involved with my patients. I try to build a relationship with them."

Chauncey cleared his throat. "What *kind* of a relationship?" he asked.

Dan stared at him, getting his implication. "Professional," he said curtly.

Chauncey tapped his pen against the desk. "Fine. But when you talk about getting involved with patients—well, all I can say is you have to be careful."

Dan sat back, silent. I'd heard him explain a thousand times that he became a doctor because he cared about people, not paychecks. Medicine had changed, but he wouldn't. He took calls in the middle of the night, rushed to hospital bedsides, and worried about surgical complications at all hours. I used to tease him that if I really wanted his full attention, I should be his patient, not his wife. But it was just a joke.

"Is the risk of malpractice why you limited the cosmetic side?" asked Chauncey, moving on.

"Not really." Dan didn't elaborate. The *Vogue* editors still lined up at his door, but lately he'd pared his practice to focus on serious surgery, treating accident victims and the badly scarred. He got kudos for his global good works, but the more he said no to cosmetically inclined clients, the more they clamored, begging for his magic touch.

"Let's talk about a few personal things now," Chauncey said, adjusting his glasses. "Any particular problems in your marriage I should know about?"

I popped up from my chair. "Listen, I think I'll wait outside, after all. That way Dan can be completely honest with you."

Dan shook his head. "Sit down, Lacy. There's nothing I can't say in front of you."

I sat. This jack-in-the-box act was starting to get a little old.

"Lacy and I have an unusually good marriage," Dan said. I waited for more, but that was it. Actually, it wasn't bad.

"Just the normal arguments that any couple has?" Chauncey asked.

Dan thought for a minute. "I guess that's right. Nothing major for the neighbors to complain about." He gave a little smile. "Lacy's good-natured and even-tempered. The kids can be difficult and I can be moody, but she puts up with that and keeps all of us going."

Wow—nice testimonial. Definitely made up for not sleeping last night.

"You and Lacy have been married how long?" Chauncey asked.

"Almost eighteen years. We got married when she was twenty-two and I was twenty-five. Pretty young. I was still in medical school. My father didn't approve."

Didn't approve? Dan's father had raged against me like King Kong on the streets of New York. He fumed because I'd gone to a state college on scholarship, had loans to repay, and had a bank account balance of zero. Three strikes even before he knew I was an art major. Dan's tight-lipped mother was too cowed by her husband to suggest that a good marriage needed more than a hefty 401(k). Dan told his father he loved me because I was funny and free-spirited and opened his soul to the world. His father said to worry less about his soul and more about his surgery. Since neither of his parents would come to a wedding and my single mother couldn't pay for one anyway, Dan and I got married on a beach in the Bahamas surrounded by a few friends (including maid of honor Molly) and a crowd of college kids on spring break. In one of the wedding photos, Dan was holding a ring in one hand and a Bud Light in the other. He claimed it was the first—and maybe only—time in his life that he was raucous, rowdy, and unrelentingly happy.

"My parents softened a little," Dan said to Chauncey now, "but when I need to count on someone, it's Lacy."

From across the room, Dan caught my eye, and we exchanged a knowing smile. When Grant was born, Dan's parents sent a sterling silver baby spoon from Tiffany's—but never called. We put it in a drawer, used baby-safe plastic utensils, and always understood that our real family was each other.

Chauncey jotted a few notes and glanced up at me. If he noticed Dan's gaze locked with mine, the warmth of the connection didn't register.

Chauncey fired off a few more questions and Dan offered careful answers. I squirmed impatiently on my chair, not sure how discussing sex, social life, and surgery could solve the murder of Tasha Barlow.

When Chauncey finally finished and put down his pen, he walked us out to the lobby, saying he'd call later. He left and I tossed Dan my car keys.

"Let's go home," I said.

"Home?" Dan looked as surprised as if I'd just nominated Clarence Thomas for an honorary membership in the ACLU.

"Home. You remember the place. Spanish roof that pings when it rains. Pool in the backyard. Two flat-screen TVs with Dolby digital stereophonic surround sound, so you can watch *Star Wars* day or night."

Dan smiled. "I definitely like the place, but I thought I'd head to my office."

"Your *office?*"

"Come on, Lacy, I had to cancel my surgeries this morning, but I have to catch up on a lot of paperwork. And I need to check my files for any mention of Tasha Barlow. No reason for me to miss a whole day of work." He fingered the keys. "I guess I'll drop you off and then pick up my own car."

Here's what I've learned from almost two decades of marriage: Telling your husband he's being ridiculous (even when he's being ridiculous) doesn't do any good. Dan had gone to work in the midst of Malibu mud slides and a Richter-rocking earthquake, so a minor murder charge wasn't going to stop him—no matter what I said.

On the car ride home, we made slightly stilted conversation, sticking to safe topics that didn't involve prison, perps, or dead actresses. When we got to the house, I noticed black scuff marks on the otherwise smooth, highly polished front foyer floor and I felt a little chill. The heavy-footed cops had left their mark. What would it take to get rid of the gashes and restore the flawless finish—to our lives, never mind the floor? No amount of scraping and waxing would undo the collateral damage.

Seemingly oblivious to the metaphoric mess, Dan came over to kiss me.

"I'm off, sweetheart," he said blithely. "Thanks for being such a champ."

A champ? Right now I felt more like a chump. "I wish you'd stay home this afternoon," I said, trying not to whine.

"It's a workday," he said. "I can't think of a single reason why I shouldn't work."

"Should I give you a whole list?"

"Nope," he said and ducked for the door.

Four years dissecting corpses in medical school, five years treating the mauled and maimed during round-the-clock residency, and nearly two decades in private practice had given Dan a certain detachment. Clinical distance was necessary in an operating room, I suppose. But right now the ice water in his veins made my blood boil.

I changed into blue jeans and a T-shirt and puttered around the house for the rest of the afternoon, trying to distract myself by paying bills and making out invoices to clients. Grant got home from school and tennis practice a little before five, called out, "Hi, Mom, I'm home!" and disappeared into the kitchen. I joined him a moment later as he wolfed down a leftover piece of cheesecake then dug into a two-pound package of cherries.

"I did okay on the physics test, but I made a couple of stupid mistakes," he said, spitting a pit into his hand. "One question on quarks got me crazy because I couldn't remember if a proton has two up quarks and one down or if that's a neutron. Isn't that stupid? Who forgets something like that?"

"Who doesn't? When I was in high school, a quark was still the sound a duck made."

Grant laughed and started talking about electromagnetic

forces. When he switched to gravitational pulls, I realized that sooner or later, I had to sink his high spirits.

"Sorry if I'm boring you, Mom," Grant said, sensing my distraction. "I guess force fields aren't your favorite topic."

"It's fascinating," I countered quickly. "All that physics about positive and negative pulls makes sense. Unfortunately, I'm feeling a pretty negative drag right now."

"Bad day?" Grant asked.

"Very," I admitted.

"Stuck with a client who wanted Louis XIV when you thought Danish modern?" asked Grant, teasing.

"Danish modern didn't deserve a comeback, and I never recommend it," I said reflexively.

Grant grinned, went to the refrigerator, and poured himself a glass of Gatorade. "I was just joking, Mom."

"Right." I took a deep breath. "I did, however, have a bad day. As did your father. Who spent part of the morning in jail."

Grant put down the glass and stared at me.

Don't flinch, I told myself. Make it sound normal.

"What happened?" Grant asked, getting his composure before I did.

"A mistake or something. Some kind of confusion. We don't know what's behind this yet. The police came in last night and arrested him."

"Last night? How could that be? You didn't say a word this morning."

"You had school to think about. And that midterm. So I really am glad if you did well, despite the quirky quark."

"Dad gets arrested and you're thinking about my physics exam?" Grant looked at me in complete amazement, stunned to discover that his mother was behaving like a very unstable molecule.

"Now I'm thinking about Dad," I confessed.

Grant suddenly paled. "Where is he?"

"At his office. You know your father never stops working."

"What's the charge against him?"

Suddenly, a loud scream echoed from upstairs, followed by another and another. Grant charged for the door and I followed close behind, bounding up the back staircase as the bloodcurdling yells continued. We were storming down the hall when Ashley flung open her bedroom door and barreled out.

"Daddy murdered a girl! Daddy killed someone!" she hollered hysterically. "Oh my God! Daddy killed a girl!"

Grant grabbed her by the shoulders. "Shut up," he said loudly.

"Daddy killed her! My daddy!"

Grant shook her, not loosening his grip. "Shut up," he said, more forcefully this time.

Ashley burst into sobs, not dissolving onto Grant's handy shoulder, just standing straight and hollering and crying.

I went into Ashley's bedroom, where breaking TV news had interrupted a *Friends* rerun. Onscreen, a reporter stood in front of an office building that looked a lot like Dan's.

"I'll have more on this exclusive story of the Deadly Doctor as the information develops," she said. "I'm reporting live from Beverly Hills. Now we go to Amy Chin outside the murder victim's apartment."

Ashley had taken a breath from her screaming, but now she started again, and I couldn't hear a word that Amy Chin reported, but I was riveted to the video images that flashed on the screen—several pictures of Tasha Barlow, some shots of a slightly shabby apartment, and then the crime scene footage.

I understood why Ashley had become hysterical. Instead of *Friends*, she'd tuned into enemies.

Back in the hall, Grant had wrestled Ashley to the floor, and she was whimpering now, not fighting off Grant, who had one arm firmly around her shoulders. I remembered using the same tactic to stop her tantrums as a toddler.

They both looked up at me, but I sank down next to them on the floor so I could look Ashley in the eye. "What did you see on TV?" I asked, my tone harsher than I'd intended.

Ashley started sobbing again.

"Did you see Daddy?"

"Yeees," she wailed.

Shit, I thought.

The phone rang. I grabbed it from Ashley's desk and heard Chauncey Howell.

"My secretary just saw Dan on TV."

"So did my daughter."

"What the heck is he doing?"

"He went to his office. I assume they ambushed him outside."

"He talked to the reporter," said Chauncey, as if announcing that Dan had personally placed one of his polished loafers in a steaming pile of horse manure. "Has he gone mad? Your husband apparently claimed he was completely innocent and the police had made a mistake."

"That sounds right."

"Mrs. Fields, he's not to say anything. *Anything.* Do you understand me? Get him back home. I'll send a limousine if you want. Tell him to leave through a back door of his office, or a service entrance, or whatever it takes so he's not seen. Same when he arrives back at your house. No reporters. No pictures. No comments. Is this clear?"

"Clear," I said. "I'll page him. Or call his office."

"After this, rely on your answering machine. Don't pick up any calls. If I need to reach you, I'll use the unlisted number. Assume people are listening in on your cell phone and that your listed number is bugged," Chauncey said.

"Jimmy's playing with a friend's child down the block," I said, trying to account for everyone.

"Tell him to come home," Chauncey replied, slamming down the phone.

I called our neighbor Jane Snowdon and, giving only the scantest details, asked her to walk Jimmy to our backyard. Pushing aside the plantation shutters, I peeked out the window and saw a lone unmarked van across the street. While I watched, another van, this one bright with the logo NEWS CHANNEL 4, pulled up. I closed the wooden slats and called Dan.

"What are you doing?" I asked when he picked up the phone.

"Paperwork," he said coolly. "I have a lot to catch up on."

"Dan, the kids are hysterical. They need you. And I just spoke to Chauncey Howell. He wants you home. You ended up all over the five o'clock news."

"Did I? Well, good. I told the reporter I was innocent."

"You're apparently not supposed to say anything. Chauncey wants to send a limo to get you home."

"My car's parked outside."

"Can you get to it without being ambushed again by a reporter?"

Dan paused briefly. "You know what the parking lot's like in this building. Open. Outside. I suppose someone could come up to me when I go to my car."

"Then take Chauncey's limo," I said. "I'll have him send an extra driver. He'll come up to your office and get the keys, then drive your car home. Maybe some of the reporters will follow him instead of you."

Dan snorted. "You and Chauncey are blowing this way out of proportion. You're picturing a horde of reporters, and there was exactly one. She got her story. I'm sure she's gone."

"Dan, for once don't be stubborn," I pleaded.

I cracked open the plantation shutters again and saw two more vans pulling up, one with satellite antennae on top for live broadcasts. My husband might be in denial about the situation, but the assignment editors knew a good story.

"One reporter a couple of hours ago, maybe, but they all know about you now," I said. "Ms. Channel Five had a very brief exclusive. We've got TV crews piling up in front of the house."

I heard Dan walking across his office, probably to look out his own window, and I thought I caught a little gasp. But he composed himself well before he spoke.

"Fine. Tell Chauncey to send his driver and the backup. But give me an hour. I have work to do." Like Chauncey, he slammed down the phone.

I quickly called Chauncey back and got a "Nice work. Good idea" for my efforts, which was better than I'd got from Dan. But that didn't matter right now.

After Ashley's outburst, the hallway outside the children's bedrooms seemed empty and eerily quiet. Thank God for Grant, who could bring some sanity even to his sister. I went downstairs and found Ashley huddled on a sofa in the family room, just snapping shut her Motorola T721 cell phone. Full color, two-way radio, and custom cover, but she sulkily insisted everyone else at school had the newer model, with quad-band wireless technology that played video clips. No doubt in the middle of math class.

"I'm going to the Devil Diner for dinner," she said, twirling a strand of hair around her finger. "Everyone will be there. Mandy's picking me up."

"Mandy doesn't drive," I said, not bothering to ask if this was the same "everyone" that had the fancier phone.

"Mandy's boyfriend will pick me up," Ashley amended. "And you're not funny."

"I'm not trying to be. In fact, I'm quite serious, so pay attention. You're not going to the diner. You're not going out tonight."

"What is this, house arrest? I thought Daddy was the criminal, not me."

"Neither of you are criminals," I said quietly.

"Oh, Daddy is. Even though I had to learn about it on television. He killed someone, so I can see why he shouldn't go out. But what did I do wrong?"

The extent of adolescent self-involvement never failed to amaze me, but Ashley seemed to be bringing it to new heights. "Today, nothing. Or nothing that I know about. You'll stay home on Daddy's behalf."

"So we can have one of our fabulous family dinners?"

"I usually like our family dinners, but we'll skip it tonight. You can eat before Daddy comes home. Eloise cooked chicken with mangoes and rice."

"That sounds nauseating."

"I'll make you some pasta. Or there's pizza from last weekend in the freezer."

Ashley snorted, and as usual, I didn't quite know what I'd done wrong. I tried to live by the mandates of suburban motherhood:

1. Don't embarrass your kid.
2. Don't *ever* embarrass your kid.
3. Like, oh my God, why are you making *rules?* Don't you realize that's *embarrassing?*

For my daughter, I tried to be cool (I downloaded Coldplay even before Gwyneth Paltrow married the lead singer)—but not too cool (my low-rider jeans never rode too low). I maintained the unreasonable hope that by being thoughtful, sincere, and understanding, I would eventually win over my daughter.

"Here's an idea," I said now. "Why don't you order in from Devil Diner? Tell the delivery guy to come to the side door and I'll answer."

"You don't get it. I want to go *out*. I don't care what I eat. I just want to get out of here."

"That's not going to happen tonight."

"When's Daddy getting home?"

"An hour or so."

"Can I sleep at Mandy's tonight?"

"Only if you can manage that without leaving the house."

"You're not funny."

"I think you mentioned that."

"I hate this family!"

"I sympathize. I'm not so thrilled with it either today. But it's all we've got."

Ashley stormed out. I thought of rushing after her, but how many more futile gestures could I make today? I was pondering that when I heard a double knock and opened the back door for Jimmy.

"I think something's up in the neighborhood," said Jane, who'd walked Jimmy home. "There are news trucks outside. Any idea why they're here?"

I closed my eyes briefly, composing myself. "Listen, Jane, will you forgive me? I can't talk now."

She nodded, looking slightly baffled. "Sure, Lacy. I don't want to intrude. Call me if you need me."

Jimmy scampered off, and when I went upstairs a few minutes later, he was lying in front of the TV. Normally, I'd tell him to turn it off, but I was grateful to have him distracted. Besides, it was the Discovery Channel. Seeing crocodiles snap at each other was better than watching grown-ups with teeth bared.

I found Grant sitting at his desk. Like Dan, the boy could work through any storm. But for all his emotional strength, he was still a kid who'd just been told that his dad was suspected of murder.

"Want me to tell you what I know about Dad?"

"Uh, yeah." He sat back, not looking at me, just twisting the lead in his automatic pencil in and out. "I'm not going to get my information from television news."

"Then here goes. The whole thing. I apologize for not filling you in before." I ran through the story, just as I'd told it to

Chauncey outside the courthouse, and then added some editorial comments about how Daddy certainly didn't know Tasha Barlow and the only question was how the mix-up had occurred.

Grant nodded and kept his head down, and I was mesmerized watching him grinding the tip of his sneaker deep into the rug.

Finally, he looked up. "I think you're being brave, Mom."

"Thanks, honey. But I don't know what else we can do. Ashley's upset, but she'll pull herself together."

"Yeah. Ashley. But Mom, you're not questioning Dad at all, and I'm going to do the same thing. No waffling. No wondering what happened."

I looked at him straight on. "Are you wondering if Daddy's innocent?"

"Nope, Mom. I'm with you. Dad's innocent." He blinked his wide, intelligent eyes, and I swallowed hard.

Of course Dan was innocent. Inn-o-cent. I knew it deep in my bones. No questions, no qualms, no pangs of doubt. Inn-o-cent. That gnawing, hollow feeling in my stomach didn't mean a thing. Though it might take all the Rocky Road ice cream in the world to make the emptiness go away.

"I wish I could do something for Dad," Grant said "Help him. I just don't know how."

"Honestly, you help just by being yourself," I said. Predictably, Grant rolled his eyes, but I went over and gave him a hug, anyway. "We're all feeling pretty helpless," I admitted.

The phone rang, and I grabbed it from Grant's desk, heard Dan's voice, and asked anxiously, "Where are you?"

"In the limousine, on my way home," he said tersely. "Chauncey is with me."

"That's great. I'm glad," I said. Chauncey had made it to Dan's office in record time, completely ignoring his request for an extra hour.

"Chauncey wants to talk to you."

I heard the phone being passed, and then Chauncey said, "I think your ploy worked, Lacy. I only see one news truck following us. Now what's the best way to get into the house without being seen?"

Marveling that Chauncey had asked me for a plan rather than his client sitting right next to him, I quickly considered some scenarios. "Come to the garage, on the side of the house," I advised. "I'll put my car on the street so you can pull the limo all the way in. Once you're in the garage, I'll close the door with the remote, and there's an entrance to the family room."

"Okay," Chauncey said. "But if you take your car out to the street now, you'll be swarmed by photographers."

"Better me than Dan," I said. What would the paparazzi do with a shot of me, anyway? Sell it to *Mad* magazine? They definitely wouldn't get a buck out of *Real Simple*, because my life had become way too complicated.

I finished the conversation with Chauncey, and when I hung up, Grant put down his pencil. While pretending to work, he'd been listening to every word. "Mom, you're very brave. I mean it. I'm really proud of you."

I gave him another hug. If every murder charge had a silver lining, then this was mine—sterling praise from my husband and son in one otherwise awful day.

Chapter Three

Instead of grabbing the newspaper off the front lawn as usual in my Natori nightgown the next morning, I threw on jeans and a Fire & Ice Ball sweatshirt to impress the local TV reporters with my humanity. But the street seemed quiet, with no news trucks in view. I didn't hang outside long enough to check for telephoto lenses peeping out of the beech tree.

Back inside, I took the *Los Angeles Times* out of its plastic bag. The story about Dan had made page 1, just below the fold, with a screaming headline:

RESPECTED L.A. DOC ARRESTED

ON MURDER CHARGE

Underneath was a photo someone had snapped at a charity ball a few months ago, with Dan in his black Armani tuxedo and Harry Winston diamond studs. His blue eyes twinkled and his warm smile showed off his irresistible dimple. He looked heartbreakingly handsome—which explained why the picture filled most of the bottom of the page. So much for keeping Dan out of sight of the paparazzi last night.

Never-made-it-actress Tasha Barlow, whose goal had been to have her face in front of the world, was relegated to a tiny square on page 27. In the high school graduation photo, her nose looked obviously bigger and her breasts strikingly smaller than in the head shot Chauncey had showed me. When she moved to the coast, Tasha had paid some plastic surgeon a wad of money to make her into a different person. But that didn't mean Dan had held the knife.

The type blurred in front of my eyes when I tried to read the article, so I shoved the newspaper under the sofa and flicked on the small Sony TV in the kitchen, flipping past Matt chatting with his new mate, Meredith, on NBC and the genial hosts bantering on CBS, until I caught a mention of Dan on one of the local news reports. The story was mercifully brief, a juicy headline but no sleazy footage to draw it out. But there was plenty of video for the next story, and I watched until Grant came downstairs.

"Who's Mikita?" I asked, as soon as he came into the kitchen.

He rubbed his eyes and looked at me blankly. "What?"

"Have you ever heard of Mikita? She's all over the news this morning. Come here."

Grant joined me at the countertop television, where the slo-mo footage of a gorgeous young woman running naked down Sunset Boulevard was being replayed for at least the third time.

"She's one of those models–turned–rock singers," Grant said. "What happened?"

"Apparently she took a little too much Ecstasy and coke last night and washed it all down with a bottle of champagne. She left the Viper Room, pulled off all her clothes, and . . ." I nodded at the TV. "The rest you've seen."

Grant laughed and went to the refrigerator for orange juice. "Did she push Dad off the news, at least?"

"Mostly." I cleared my throat. "Come eat." I put Wheaties with strawberries on the table, but Grant looked around the kitchen.

"Where's the newspaper?" he asked.

I didn't answer immediately, and, misinterpreting, Grant said, "Want me to go outside and get it?"

"I already did," I admitted. I fished out the paper from under the sofa. "Unfortunately, the L.A. Times gets printed before two A.M., which is when Mikita did her strip act."

Grant grabbed the front section from me and sat down at the kitchen table, propping the paper between his cereal bowl and his glass of juice, just like he did every morning. But today, instead of analyzing the Lakers' losing streak, he was perusing a story about a dead girl and a maybe murderous doctor—who happened to be his dad. Grant's face grew paler and paler, and finally he folded up the newspaper and pushed it away.

"I didn't know she'd been strangled," he said finally, his voice so broken and soft that I could barely make it out.

"Strangled?"

"You didn't know that?"

"I didn't. It never came up."

"That's what the article says." Grant's chest heaved with emotion and he rubbed his eyes.

"I didn't read the article. I'm not as brave as you thought."

Grant jabbed his spoon at the few shreds still floating in his bowl. "All night I thought about how Dad doesn't have a gun," Grant said in a pained rasp. "He couldn't have had anything to do with the murder because he's just like you—he hates guns and wouldn't know what to do with one. But I guess now that doesn't matter."

I slid the newspaper closer, more to get it away from Grant than to look at it myself.

"None of it matters. However that girl died, Daddy doesn't even know who she is. You can't forget that."

"Sure," Grant said, but his voice was still weak.

"This is going to be over," I said, maybe a little too loudly. "The police are going to apologize to Daddy. I hope that'll be on the front page, too."

Grant nodded but didn't look at me as he stood up and went over to the sink. Instead of slipping his bowl into the dishwasher—housekeeper or not, I insisted the kids clean up—he ran the warm water for a long time, slowly running a sponge around and around his one dish. Even from the back, I could see him making a huge effort to get under control. And he did it. When he finally turned around again, his voice sounded normal. "I'm going to school, Mom. I guess Ashley's not coming?"

"School?"

"Yeah. That's what I do, remember?"

How quickly I forgot. Maybe you can make the transition from murder to math more easily at sixteen. "You're done with your midterms, aren't you?" I asked.

"Finally."

"Then stay home. The reporters can't chase Mikita forever. I don't want them to reappear and swarm you with questions."

Grant shrugged. "I'm going, Mom."

"Let me call Chauncey and see what he thinks."

"Chauncey should be thinking about Dad's problems, not mine. I don't need a lawyer to tell me I can go to school."

Grant picked up his North Face backpack and strode toward the door. He was decisive, and once he took a stance, he remained resolute. And what could I say, anyway? The only firm position I could take right now was that I was completely and totally confounded. Arguing with Grant would be like planting a flag in Jell-O.

I stood by the window as Grant steered his shiny black Jeep down the long driveway, neatly avoiding the shrubbery hedge on one side and the carefully planted beds of white irises and pink anemones on the other. The outside border of red coleus was wildly overgrown and I half hoped he'd run it over and spare me from gardening shears. But Grant pulled carefully into the street, not using his horsepower for a hedge clipper. For now, all remained quiet—nobody was waiting to follow him.

Trudging back upstairs, I heard Dan on the phone in our bedroom. I peeked in and saw him pacing across the carpet, his head down and his hand cupped protectively around the receiver. He seemed to be listening more than talking, and after he said a gloomy good-bye, I came into the room.

"Everything okay?" I asked worriedly.

"Sure, A-OK, as the astronauts say." Dan sounded disconsolate and he kept pacing across the carpet, arms folded, not looking at me.

"They also say, 'Houston, we have a problem,' " I reminded him gently.

"Call it a challenge," said Dan.

"A challenge, but not the *Challenger*," I added.

Dan gave me a halfhearted smile and I briefly felt better. Maybe if we could still banter, everything would be normal again. But only for a moment.

"That was Brandon Jackson on the phone," Dan said, bringing us both back to earth.

I waited. Jackson was the high-profile president at Cedars Medical Center, the prestigious hospital to which Dan had dedicated his life the last ten years. I knew him from Christmas parties and charity events, but this had to be the first time he'd called our house at 8:00 A.M.

"He'd already heard the whole story and he said I have his complete support," Dan said morosely.

"Great," I said hopefully, since nothing in Dan's tone suggested great, good, or even mediocre.

"One little hitch. I'm temporarily suspended from the hospital. At least until the directors' meeting in a couple of weeks. Brandon wants to get a sense of how the board feels."

If that's how Brandon defined "complete support," it was a good thing he wasn't president of La Perla.

"I'm sure he didn't mean anything personal. It's probably just standard procedure," I said, trying to sound encouraging. Though I had to wonder which farsighted hospital administrator would have written the protocol for dealing with a doctor accused of murder. Most didn't know how to handle a physician who ordered aspirin when the in-house pharmacy offered Advil.

"You know hospitals—all those crazy rules," I continued, determined to show my husband what support really meant. "You can't say a patient's name on the elevator because of privacy codes. No flower arrangements allowed on the maternity floor in case peonies make someone sneeze. And Brandon's a bureaucrat. Isn't he the one who wanted to ban balloons? I guess he's worried about allergies to air."

Dan sighed. "Nobody's planning on sending me flowers. Or balloons." He slumped down onto the bed and let his shoulders sag.

I sat down next to him, sidled close, and rubbed his cheek. "What can I do, honey? What do you need?" I asked softly.

"I don't need anything," Dan said, more brusquely than he probably intended. Being vulnerable or needy had never made it into his emotional repertoire. Still, I put my arms around him and he kissed me briskly on the cheek—less a prelude to passion than the tap of a worried woodpecker.

"Did Brandon say anything else?" I asked.

"Nope." Dan shook his head. Continuing in his stoic mode, he was done with the subject. If I wanted to indulge in extended analysis of who-said-what-to-whom and what-it-all-means, I could marry someone without a Y chromosome. Though I'd have to move to Massachusetts.

"What's going on with the kids?" Dan asked, changing subjects about as gracefully as Karl Rove discussing a CIA press leak.

"Grant went to school this morning, but Ashley didn't," I said evenly. "She's sleeping. Jimmy just got up. We need to talk to him about what he saw the other night. I think he's too scared to ask."

"I'm not up for talking. But let me drive him to kindergarten. I guess I have some time."

I knew the proper reply was "Thank you, darling"—which would make my husband feel needed and encourage his continued participation in the kindergarten carpool. But I also knew it was a bad plan. How to say this nicely?

"Oh, let's let him miss a few days of finger painting," I said sweetly.

Too sweetly. Dan looked at me, puzzled. "Why would we do that?"

I bit my lower lip. If sweet didn't work, maybe blunt would. "Because you shouldn't go out this morning and neither should Jimmy."

Dan jerked his head back, as if he'd been slapped. Maybe I should have stuck with "Thank you, darling."

"I don't go to the hospital and the kids stay home. We'll go into hiding. Is that what Chauncey wanted?" he asked sharply.

"It's the only thing that makes sense," I said softly. "We can't pretend life is normal. Everything's changed, Dan. Aren't we going to face it?"

So much for A-OK. Dan's blue eyes blackened in anger. Without an additional word, he stood, turned on his heel, and walked out of the room.

Whether or not it was what Chauncey wanted, going into hiding was more or less what we did for the next four days. Except for Grant, who refused to make any changes in his life, none of us went farther than a hundred feet from the front door. A couple of reporters kept ringing our doorbell and leaving messages on the phone, and one news truck reappeared half a dozen times. But a wildfire in the Valley that destroyed two celebrity homes, along with endless analysis of the naked-Mikita tape, filled the schadenfreude quotient for the local media.

"Which doesn't mean the attention is over," Chauncey warned us on the phone. "As soon as there's a new development, they'll be back. For now, just live your normal lives."

"We don't have normal lives," I told Chauncey.

"I understand how you feel. But just go ahead with whatever

would be on your calendar if none of this had happened."

I checked the Treo where I kept my schedule. "A meeting of the benefit ball committee at Dan's hospital," I told him. "I'm supposed to be head of the decorations committee."

Chauncey cleared his throat. "Well, I suppose with Dan banned from the hospital right now, you'll have to give that up."

Not that anybody would mind. As head of the committee last year, I'd imported thirty-five brightly colored parrots from Peru and had them perch on gilded branches during the dinner dance. A truly original touch—but nobody told me that parrots like sparkles. Or that they'd start dive-bombing for diamonds on the jewel-bedecked necks of L.A.'s wealthiest women. But I'd learned my lesson.

Dan announced that getting back to normal was just fine with him. With his usual skill at denial, he explained that being away from the hospital gave him some time to write an article on facial reconstruction for the *Annals of Plastic Surgery*.

Ashley had a different perspective.

"That lawyer can go screw himself," she said angrily on Friday night, when I told her Chauncey's advice. "I'm not going to school to have everyone insult me because my dad's a killer."

"Your dad is being questioned in connection with an event he knows nothing about," I said stoically. "That's all you have to say to anybody who asks."

"Nobody's going to ask. They're just going to talk behind my back."

"Welcome to eighth grade. Talking behind your back is the coin of the realm."

She glowered at me. "What's that supposed to mean?"

"All I'm trying to say is that kids gossip about everything. Real, made up, it doesn't matter. Don't make a big deal about this and neither will they."

"Oh my God, you're so fake!" she yelled. "This is a murder, not an acne breakout! You have no idea the crap I'll get! It's almost as big a scandal as when Sandy's father got fired from Fox!"

Now wasn't the moment to marvel that a homicide investigation reached the same rung on the mortification meter as a network shake-up. "I'll drive you to school on Monday and we'll go to Mr. Morland's office and talk about how you should handle yourself," I said calmly.

"I know how to handle myself!" she yelled. "I don't need an idiot principal to tell me how to face my friends! And I don't need your idiotic advice, either!"

She stormed out and slammed the door.

Ashley kept herself scarce all weekend, but Monday morning, I peeled her out of bed and announced that she needed to be in my car in thirty minutes, period. Twenty-five minutes later, my clothes-conscious Fred Segal–shopping daughter clomped down to the kitchen and paused in the doorway in baggy black jeans, a three-inch-wide leather belt with metal studs, and a shapeless black DEATH BAND T-shirt probably scrounged from a Goodwill drop-off box. Instead of her usual dainty pink sandals, she'd tied on scuffed Doc Martens over thick woolen socks. Her fingernails looked like they'd been polished with burnt cork and she'd lined her lips with a dark, ghoulish pencil. Some strange gel had turned her hair from blond and fluffy to murky and Goth straight.

She glared at me, daring me to say something. So I did.

"Can I get you some toast?"

"No."

"Bagel? Orange juice? A waffle?"

"Nothing. I'm not eating."

"Then let's go."

In the car, she turned on the CD player so Eminem was blaring from the speakers and sat with her arms folded, staring straight ahead. I snuck a few worried sideways glances at her. The coal-black getup was as frightening as she'd intended—much more disturbing to me than the sex-kitten couture she'd been sporting a few weeks ago. If only I'd appreciated how good life had been before it got so bad. Right now, I wouldn't mind seeing Ashley preening again in pink Pucci, and I could even cope with a bare midriff (though I still wouldn't give in on the navel piercing). In this new Goth getup, Ashley didn't have to worry about people nattering about Dan. They'd be too busy gossiping about her.

A few blocks before the school, I flipped off the CD. "Anything you want to discuss?" I asked. "Anything we should go over before you get to school?"

"Yeah," she said. "Let's go over how you can be so fucking hypocritical."

"Pardon?"

"You heard me."

Okay, I did. Fucking. Hypocritical. I couldn't criticize every word she said, so I went for the more offensive part.

"How am I hypocritical?"

"Oh God." She rapped her black fingernails against the side window. "I get sent off to school, but you haven't left the house all week. I'm supposed to face my friends but you can't face yours."

"Of course I can," I said.

"Yeah, right. You get dinner delivered every night so you don't have to see anyone at the grocery store. You skipped your stupid book club last night because you couldn't bear people asking you questions. Your best friend Molly's left ten messages and you haven't answered one. Now you complain about what I'm wearing, but look at you—sunglasses and a floppy hat and huge scarf to drive to school. Since when do you wear hats?"

"I didn't have time to wash my hair this morning. And I haven't said a word about what you're wearing," I added, wanting some credit for my restraint.

"Bullshit," Ashley said.

I pulled up near the front of the school, and Ashley jumped out of the car. "This whole family is full of bullshit."

She disappeared into a crowd of kids hanging out in front of the school and I pulled away slowly. Maybe Ashley was angry, but she was also right. The thought of going into the grocery store and encountering anyone who knew me made my stomach turn. How the heck did you march up to the deli counter and order a half pound of smoked turkey when the guy at the slicing machine knew about your husband, the murder suspect? Was I supposed to buy meat pies and start making jokes about *Sweeney Todd?*

I had to figure it out. I made a U-turn and steered the Lexus toward my favorite gourmet-food store in Pacific Palisades. I parked around back near a row of shops just as two women I knew bounced out of the exercise studio and disappeared into Bon Delice for a post-Pilates chai tea. I ground my teeth, knowing that the minute I followed, I'd be the morning's entertainment. I could just picture the pitying looks, patronizing comments, and supercilious offers of help. *Did you see poor Lacy? So brave of her to be buying arugula, with all she's been through.*

Who needed Bon Delice anyway? I wasn't on the prowl for crème fraîche and brioche today. For skim milk and Arnold's 100 percent whole wheat bread, I could zip over to the anonymous supermarket chain three miles down the road. Save face and save money at the same time. Marching through the front door at Gelsons, I grabbed a shopping cart and began checking out the Gala apples and D'anjou pears. But it didn't take long for two women across the aisle to start checking me out. I caught one of them pointing in my direction, and then they both began whispering. Embarrassed, I quickly moved away. Over by the artichokes, I got an open stare from a voluptuous woman in a green running bra, yellow python pants, and white stilettos (talk about a scandal), and when I went to pick out a fresh, runny Brie, I caught the clerk behind the cheese counter stealing furtive glances at me. I tried to glare at her, but my oversized Christian Dior sunglasses got in the way. Heart sinking, I finished my shopping as quickly as I could and rushed over to the express checkout, getting in line behind a woman in a Juicy Couture pink running suit. She turned slightly, and I realized it was my neighbor Jane Snowdon. Jimmy and her son Jared were in the same kindergarten class, and Jane had been in my Tuesday morning yoga group for years.

"Lacy?"

I nodded miserably, barely looking up. I should have called Jane after she brought Jimmy home that first day. But "should have" was never helpful. I probably should have done something about global warming and nuclear proliferation, too. Then there was that box of Godiva chocolates I shouldn't have eaten.

"I'm glad to see you," Jane said, unloading her groceries onto the belt.

"You, too," I mumbled.

"I didn't recognize you at first," Jane said, good-naturedly gesturing toward my reflecting sunglasses and pulled-down hat, and the Hermès scarf I'd wound halfway up my face. "When I spotted you over by the papaya, I thought you were a star recovering from plastic surgery."

"I'm trying to recover from something a lot worse," I said.

"Not nearly as interesting to most of us as a good eye tuck," Jane said with a laugh. "Didn't you notice everyone staring? I heard two women trying to get up the courage to ask you for the name of your doctor."

I smiled, and then started to chuckle. And then despite myself, I laughed out loud. The women who'd been scrutinizing me didn't know about Dan—they just assumed I was concealing a swollen face and surgery scars. A little less disguise would have been better camouflage.

"Today's my first time out of the house in a week," I admitted, feeling my defenses dropping a bit.

"I can imagine how hard it is," Jane said sympathetically. "After I saw the news trucks, I turned on the TV and figured out what had happened. I'm so sorry, Lacy. I didn't know what to do. I almost sent a Mrs. Beasley's basket."

"Thanks." I was genuinely moved but slightly baffled. Somehow Mrs. Beasley's mail-order food treats had become the number-one favorite gift in town. Every Christmas, Dan got half a dozen wicker sleighs filled with brownie bars, mini-muffins, and tea cakes, which we admired for a while and then threw away. Maybe that explained it. The goodies looked lovely and tasted terrible—making them the perfect present in Hollywood, the eating-disorder capital of the world.

"We're trying to get back to normal," I told Jane. "That's why I'm here—in addition to needing milk."

"Any idea what happens next?" Jane asked, moving down a few steps to pack her vegetables, soy cheese, and yogurt into plastic bags. (Not biodegradable, but plastic takes up less room in landfills than brown paper. Very confusing these days to be ecologically correct.) The cashier, preoccupied with plying an emery board around a flawless fingernail, completely ignored us.

"We find out what really happened to the girl and solve the case," I said flippantly. "Because the police have it all wrong."

"You'll solve it," Jane said earnestly.

"Maybe not me personally," I amended.

"Why not?" Jane paused in her packing and turned to look at me. "You always know when things aren't what they seem. You have an amazing eye. Do you remember when you took me to the Santa Monica flea market?"

"Of course I remember," I said, pleased. Mixed in with some wicker and bamboo outdoor furniture, I'd spotted a pair of nineteenth-century Chinese marble garden stools. I'd convinced Jane that if she arranged them next to the brocade sofa in her living room, she'd have a fabulously original end table.

"You spot an outside seat and see an inside table," Jane continued. "You're probably the one who can spot a real killer, too."

I laughed because she had to be kidding. Knowing how to track down a creative coffee table didn't qualify me to chase a clever killer. And I wasn't prepared to find a murderer just because I could make over a room.

Or was I?

I stood up a little straighter. Come to think of it, I was resourceful. Maybe I could build a case the way I created a room—start from the basics and add the frills later.

Jane put her grocery bags into the cart, ran her credit card through the machine, and blew me a kiss. I watched her walk out of the store. And right there in Gelsons on Sunset Boulevard, standing in the twelve-items-or-less checkout, it suddenly hit me. The time had come for Lacy Fields to get off her duff and on the case.

The minute I got home, I stashed away the packages and finally put in the call I should have made ages ago to my longtime best friend, Molly Archer of Molly Archer Casting. We'd been Tri Delta sorority sisters back at Ohio State, meeting for the first time during Rush Week, when we stood in the middle of campus singing "Honky Tonk Women." Molly was from a fancy suburb of Cleveland, while I'd grown up in a rural town outside Dayton, my determined mom an assistant manager at a Wal-Mart thirty miles away. Molly and I pledged the sorority and connected immediately—both of us were smart, curious about the world, and ready for new adventures. Our friendship grew tighter in the four years, and a week after graduation, we drove out to Los Angeles together to look for jobs. Now Molly's name appeared in the end credits of a couple of dozen network television shows, and she was more hanky-swank than honky-tonk.

Her male assistant answered the phone and reported that Molly was on a conference call.

"Can she return?" he asked officiously.

"Return what?" I asked him, always amused by the L.A. colloquialism. "Return the sweater I bought her last Christmas? Return to the days of our youth?"

"She'll return," he said, hanging up quickly.

Five minutes later, the phone rang, and Molly said, "Lacy, dear, thank goodness you called. I've left a million messages, but I won't complain that you've been avoiding me. I understand. If it were me, I'd be a werewolf howling at the moon."

"No hair growing on my hands just yet," I said, smiling. That was Molly—never skipping around the subject or playing coy. She hadn't built the biggest casting agency in L.A. by being reserved.

"I should have rushed over when you didn't answer my calls, but I was stuck in Copenhagen casting *Moon Over Denmark*. I'm about to sign Spike Lee as the native father. He's perfect, right?"

"Not exactly your standard Scandinavian."

"You know me. Always cast against type." She chuckled. "Anyway, this is so awful about Dan. What have you been doing?"

"Wallowing," I admitted. "But now I want to take some action."

"Good! What can I do?" Molly asked animatedly. She'd been the sorority social chairwoman for a reason.

"To be blunt, I'd like to know something about the girl who died. The victim. Name of Tasha Barlow, née Theresa Bartowski."

"Changed her name?" asked Molly with a tinge of scorn. "Don't these kids know that ethnic is in? Much better to be Geraldo Rivera than Jerry Rivers, I always say."

I laughed. "Whatever she called herself, she wanted to be an actress. I thought you might have run across her. Since the scouts stopped hanging out at Hollywood and Vine, the only place to be discovered is your doorstep."

"Oh my God, how idiotic of me!" Molly boomed. "I didn't even think of that. Hold on."

She yelled out, "Ben!" and then told the imperious assistant she needed him to check something. I heard an exchange of voices, the clattering of a keyboard, and then Molly came back.

"Apparently, we have nothing on Tasha in the computer database, where we keep everybody active," Molly said, going into business mode. "But Ben found her résumé and picture in a file folder. She'd sent it in herself. No agent. And . . . hmm." I heard Molly flipping pages and then a brief silence while she read. "I see why we didn't put her in the system. No creds—just a couple of ams in Idaho."

I did an instantaneous translation. No credentials, just amateur shows.

"For a reference, she gave a high school acting teacher. And— wow, this is strange." Molly stopped and I waited for her to go on, but the pause seemed interminable.

"What's strange?"

"The girl didn't have a single television credit, but she wrote 'Professional Contact,' with a phone number for Roy Evans."

"Who's he? The love child of Roy Rogers and Dale Evans?"

Molly laughed. "Prime-time correspondent on that network show *Night Beat*. He does puffy celebrity interviews and fawning chats with rock stars. Has no talent except toadying up to the stars."

"You don't sound like a fan."

"Oh, I admire him. Brings obsequiousness to a new level."

"What's the connection with Tasha Barlow?"

"I have no idea," Molly said briskly. "Let me call over to one of the producers at the network and find out. Can you hang on for a couple of minutes?"

"Sure, but you're busy. I feel guilty taking you away."

"Good. You keep feeling guilty and we'll find out Dan isn't."

She put me on hold, and it occurred to me that Molly still had the same go-for-broke style I'd admired when we were in college.

Freshman year, I knew I wanted to major in art history, but I couldn't afford a lot of visits to museums. For Christmas, Molly had her mom buy me a membership to the Cleveland Museum of Art. The first time we all went, I stood in front of a Fra Angelico painting from the 1420s that I'd only seen in books, breathless at how the picture glimmered with gold, the image of Christ seeming to radiate light. Then I dragged Molly and her mom over to a Robert Rauschenberg collage and explained how the visual puns bridged the gap between Abstract Expressionism and pop art.

"I think your friend has a future," Molly's mom had said.

I could always count on Molly—but not in the usual ways. Sophomore year, I'd burst into tears the night before my French final, flummoxed by the *passé composé*. Molly had spent the previous summer in Nice, so I asked her for help. Instead of pulling out a grammar book, she went out and bought me a bottle of Beaujolais and a tape of *Last Tango in Paris*.

"All you need is a little inspiration," Molly had said, tossing me the gifts. "A glass of wine and a night with Marlon Brando, and I guarantee an A."

Well, it was an A-minus, but I never forgot.

"You won't believe this!" Molly said exuberantly now, coming back to the phone.

"Tell me," I said, eager for anything. Molly's energy oozed over the phone, finally letting me feel hopeful rather than hapless.

"Tasha Barlow worked as a makeup girl on *Night Beat*. They hired her freelance for a few remote shoots, which is how she must have known Roy Evans."

"A freelance makeup girl?"

"Better pay than a waitress if you're trying to be an actress, and you get a foot—or a finger—in the door. Plus there can be good perks. Remember Noah Wyle from *ER*? He married his makeup artist."

"Must be confusing when someone yells, 'Code Red.' Wyle

thinks it's a heart attack and his wife figures there's a lipstick emergency."

Molly laughed. "I don't think Tasha was about to walk down an aisle. But listen to this. Tim, the producer I called, thinks Roy Evans is a major sleaze, and just the kind to hit on hair and makeup girls."

"You think Roy and Tasha were . . . involved?"

"Why not? Makes sense. She obviously did more than powder his nose. You know these TV guys. Roy didn't actually write a recommendation or put himself on the line, but telling Tasha she could use his name on her résumé probably got him a week of blow jobs."

I snorted. "Lovely thought. Tim have any other news?"

"The show hadn't used Tasha much, and Roy was the only one who got close to her. By the way, he thinks Roy's talent would fit in a teacup. I told him more like a thimble."

"You and Tim share the same opinion."

"Mmm, I hope we'll share even more," said Molly, smacking her lips. "I owe you big, darling. I haven't seen Tim in ages, but when we finished talking Tasha, he asked me out to dinner. Nine o'clock tonight at Spago Beverly Hills."

"Glad my little murder brought you two together," I said, a little wounded.

"Oooh, Lacy, I'm sorry. That was insensitive. I shouldn't be dating when you need me detecting."

I sighed. "Of course you should. One of us should still have a social life, and your Tim sounds good. Not even taking you someplace that serves two all-beef patties on a sesame seed bun."

Molly tittered. "Come on, darling, you're on the right track, so get moving. Pull yourself together and go talk to Roy Evans."

"How? Call him up and tell him I need to discuss a dead makeup girl he might have been screwing?"

"Tim could help," Molly said, thinking out loud. "But wait,

here's a better idea. You do that column for *Abode* about decorating for the stars, right? Call Roy and say you want to write about him—and you'll help redecorate his house."

"The magazine's not exactly mass market. Only about two thousand subscribers."

"Keep that between you and the Audit Bureau of Circulation. All these second-tier guys have first-tier egos. They think they're more talented than they are and that if they just got a little more press, they'd be on top."

"I'm starting to think your sign should say 'Molly Archer Psychology,' rather than 'Casting.' "

"It's the same thing, believe me. I'll have Ben give you the number. Call Roy. Say I suggested him for the article and let me know what happens."

She blew me kisses and hung up. Her energy was contagious, so I spoke briefly with Ben, then dialed Roy's number immediately, before I could lose my nerve. An assistant explained Roy had left for the day, but then I mentioned Molly's name, and the day must have started again, because Roy Evans picked up. Five minutes of talk and he got the gist—then invited me over to his office.

"It's silly that I'm here and you're there when we could both be here," he crooned. Not a bad line. And obviously not the first time he'd used it. I wondered if Tasha Barlow had fallen for it.

"Great. Give me an hour and I'll be there," I said with my new Molly-inspired mettle.

I quickly pulled on a gray Jil Sander pantsuit, adding only a Tiffany pin with a simple circle of pavé diamonds and pointy-toed pumps from Sigerson Morrison. Very professional and proper. By the time I was steering the Lexus down Wilshire Boulevard, I'd decided the getup was *too* proper. Roy Evans didn't seem like the kind of guy to be impressed by an understated designer cut. Maybe I should make a pit stop at Neiman Marcus for a lace camisole.

But no. I wouldn't get waylaid. How I looked didn't really matter—the question was how I'd bring up Tasha Barlow in the middle of a decorating discussion.

In the heavy traffic, it took forty-five minutes to get to the security gate outside the studio. Once there, I pulled into the visitors line and waited patiently behind a stretch Mercedes, a BMW convertible, and the ultimate cheap chic—a Prius. When I finally inched up to the glassed-in security booth, the young uniformed guard took my license and checked it against his computer. Then he looked at me curiously and asked me to pop open my trunk.

"Why?" I asked, my heart pounding. Had the computer identified me as high risk—a murder suspect's wife not allowed on the lot?

"You might have a dead body in there," he said.

I felt blood drain from my face, and I dropped my head against the steering wheel to keep from fainting. My hands trembled, making a *rat-a-tat* attack against the console.

The guard leaned his smooth, innocent face into my open window. "Uh, ma'am, we check every car. That was a joke. I was trying to be funny."

"If I want funny, I'll watch Jay Leno," I said, my voice raspy.

His thin eyebrows arched high into narrow half-moons. "I'm sorry, really. We're not supposed to make jokes at security, so don't tell anyone, please?"

I nodded. The cars in front of me had also opened their trunks, but somehow that hadn't registered. Two bouts of paranoia in one day. The world wasn't as absorbed with my story as I was.

I made my way from the sunny parking lot to the main building, trying to calm down and let the network aura work its magic. In the lush lobby, posters of the prime-time stars lined the walls, and I noticed that Roy Evans wasn't among them. His fluff appealed to the audience, but probably not to the network image-makers.

A chic, excessively slim receptionist sent me up to the eighth floor, where another chic, excessively slim receptionist told me to take a seat. I perched self-consciously on an upholstered bench and flipped through two issues of *Variety* and one *Hollywood Reporter* before a miniskirted blonde with a cleavage-revealing shirt and thigh-high leather boots minced over to me.

"Mr. Evans can see you now," she said importantly, draping a well-manicured hand on her hip. "I'm his assistant, Spring."

I wasn't sure if Spring was her name or the only season she worked, but I followed her as she flounced down the long carpeted hallway. She definitely had a spring in her step, and maybe one in her hips—the only explanation for how they swung so vigorously from side to side.

"Ah, La-cy Fields."

A broad-shouldered man in a sleekly cut three-button suit stepped out of his office, pronouncing my name slowly in an alluring baritone.

"Ms. Fields, let me introduce you to Roy Evans," said Spring somewhat pointlessly, sidling a little too close to her boss.

"I'm so glad you're here," said Roy, oozing charm as he reached for my hand with both of his. His fingernails had been manicured and he had an oversized gold signet ring on his little finger. His face still bore traces of bronze pancake makeup. Giving him the benefit of the doubt, I assumed he'd recently been on the air.

"Come in," Roy urged, taking my elbow and steering me into the office. He gave his assistant a wink that I wasn't supposed to see, then firmly closed his door. As I sat down, I realized he had the blinds closed, the lights dimmed, and a CD playing softly in the background. He'd set the scene—though I wasn't sure for what.

"Do you like this song?" he asked, pausing to listen. "Norah Jones, brand-new. She let me hear it last week when I interviewed her. That's what I most love about my job, if you want to know—I get to meet everybody."

I didn't really want to know, but I nodded anyway.

"And now I get to meet you," he said, with a sincere—or maybe not—smile.

I cleared my throat. "I'm delighted to finally meet you, too," I said, as if instead of learning his name a few hours ago, I'd been a fan forever.

"I can't blame you," he said, without any trace of irony. "I talk to people and they never forget me. Courtney Love. Sting. Madonna. I interviewed them, and now they're all chums of mine. Real buddies. They send me Christmas cards every year."

No finer proof of friendship. I wondered if he ever got a lemon cake from Mrs. Beasley's, too.

"I know some of the greatest talents in the world," Roy continued, sounding thoroughly impressed with himself.

I nodded admiringly. My fears about what I'd say during this meeting had already disappeared, because clearly I wasn't going to have to say anything.

"Let me show you this interview," Roy said, grabbing a tape from his desk and strutting over to pop it into the VCR. "Have a minute to watch?"

"Of course," I said. The screen flickered on, revealing a scratched image of Roy interviewing Jennifer Lopez, who was dressed in a simple white shirt, her long hair tumbling over her chest.

"You looked beautiful at the Golden Globes last night," Roy was saying to her, sounding more like an infatuated boy than a network reporter.

"It was nice to see you in the press tent," Jennifer said. "You gave me such a warm smile."

Roy stopped the tape and turned to look at me. "That's Jennifer Lopez. *J. Lo.* Talking about my warm smile. How's that? Should I play it again?"

Without waiting for an answer, he hit REWIND and then PLAY, crossing his arms and staring triumphantly at the small screen. I could swear his lips moved this time when J. Lo was talking.

"I've been seeing stars at awards shows for years," Roy said now, clearly pleased with himself. "When a beautiful actress walks by, I grab her and whisper, 'You're going to win tonight. I know you are.' The losers never remember what I said, but the winners always come back later and say, 'Oh, Roy! How did you know!'"

I laughed. He laughed. Okay, we'd bonded. Roy Evans wanted to talk about himself and I was willing to listen.

Roy regaled me with two more stories about fabulous moments in his career (one involved being hugged by John Travolta, who, as far as I knew, hugged everyone), and then he finally paused for breath.

"Enough about my career. We should talk about you. And what you want to write about me." Coming from anyone else, that would have been a bad joke. But Roy was serious. He could move the spotlight only so far. "I understand you're a star decorator and a decorator to the stars."

"I'm a decorator, but my clients are the only stars," I said, knowing immediately what Roy needed to hear. "*Abode* has me write about famous people with great style."

Roy nodded, unfazed at being put in the "famous people" category and probably pondering his great style. Since his office looked like it had been furnished at OfficeMax with a little help from Staples, I was pondering it myself.

"I'd love to be in the magazine," he admitted, in what seemed like his first spontaneous comment so far. "But I'm in a new condo and it's pretty empty."

"Empty is perfect. Just what I was hoping for," I said, improvising. "I can help you decorate, and then we'll reveal the wonderful results in the magazine." The fact that I'd come up with this plan on the spot didn't make it any less brilliant.

"A before-and-after?" he asked dubiously. "Isn't that about you, not me?"

"All I do is take your personality and express it in your surroundings," I said, catching the tone in his voice. "For you that might be *rich* leathers and *handsome* accessories." I paused to let the *rich* and *handsome* sink in. "When your friends visit, they'll admire your great taste and never dream you had a decorator—unless you want to tell them about me, of course."

He nodded. "I like your style. Let's do it."

I stared at him for a moment, startled by what an easy sell this had been. But then I nodded and said, "Well, good. When do you want to get started?"

"Right now works for me," he said. "Only one condition. We have to do this fast. When I see something I want, I have to get it immediately."

That obviously applied to more than furniture, but I said, "Not a problem. I know a lovely store on Robertson Boulevard that delivers fast. We can go tomorrow, look around together, and I'll get on track."

"Sounds like a plan." Roy banged his palm against the desk to seal the deal. Our conversation was almost done, and I'd gotten so absorbed in the decorating discussion that I hadn't managed to bring up Tasha Barlow. No smooth transition now. Oh well, we still had tomorrow.

Roy stood up and came around to the other side of his desk. "You're terrific, Lacy, I can tell already. We'll enjoy working together." He took my hands in his again and gave me the warm, J. Lo–approved smile. Ah, yes, he was good.

"We'll have some fun," I said.

An obvious exit line, but Roy didn't let go of my hands. Instead, he looked down thoughtfully and wrinkled his brow ever so slightly. "Lacy Fields," he said, as if thinking about my name for the first time. "Are you by any chance related to the Dan Fields I read about in the paper? The murder suspect?"

I took a quick breath. "He's my husband, actually."

"Really?"

"Unfortunately, yes. I mean, not unfortunate that he's my husband, but unfortunate what's happened."

"I knew the victim," he said, dropping his silky voice almost to a whisper. "She worked here."

I gulped, stunned that we'd hit on the topic that had driven me to visit Roy Evans in the first place. I pulled myself together. "It's an awful situation, but Dan had nothing to do with it. I'm sorry about the victim. Was she . . . a friend of yours?"

"Not really. I just knew her. We worked together sometimes." He finally let go of my hands and looked carefully at me. "What's going on with the investigation?" he asked casually.

"The police are pulling together all their evidence—whatever that may be. Our lawyer has detectives trying to get to the real story. At the moment it's all kind of hazy. I just know Dan's innocent."

"How did your husband know Tasha?"

"I'm not sure he did."

Roy didn't say anything. That was an old trick of interviewers—leave a long pause and somebody would rush to fill it in. But I didn't have anything to add so the silence lingered in the room. Finally I put out my hand and said, "I hope you're still willing to work with me. I'll see you tomorrow?"

"Tomorrow," Roy said.

I left his office and managed to get down the elevator, through the lobby, and into the parking lot before I started trembling. However anxious I'd been about being recognized by the deli clerk and the security guard, it never occurred to me that Roy Evans, network reporter, would know who I was.

Had he made a lucky guess? Or was it more than luck?

I suddenly felt my knees wobble and grabbed onto a red Porsche convertible to keep from falling over. Sure, Molly Archer's name carried a lot of weight and, yes, Roy Evans seemed so publicity-hungry that he'd eat a *People* magazine on rye for lunch. But he'd asked me to be his decorator in a heartbeat, and while I had a good reputation, I wasn't exactly hosting *Extreme Makeover: Home Edition*. Roy Evans, master manipulator of conversation, had steered our talk around to Tasha Barlow. Maybe the stunningly self-involved star had the same motive for the meeting that I did—he wanted to get information about the murder.

Because possibly we both knew the police had arrested the wrong man.

Chapter Four

On my way to the showroom on Robertson Boulevard the next morning, I stopped for a morning smoothie at Jamba Juice. The line snaked out the door, giving me time to stare at the posted nutrition guide and learn that the Orange Berry Blitz offered 390 percent of the daily allotment of vitamin C—which seemed to be 290 percent more than I needed. Tasty concoctions like Mango Mantra or Berry Pizzazz could strengthen my immune system, promote brain cell activity, and give me a healthy heart and eyes. I wasn't sure if the drinks came in a tall cup or an IV tube.

"Strawberry Nirvana," I said to the young girl behind the counter, when it was finally my turn. Probably practicing for her afternoon acting class, she pursed her heavily collagened lips and flicked her long black hair, revealing a dragon tattoo that wound around her upper arm. If Angelina Jolie called in sick to a set one day, Jamba Girl could be a fast fill-in.

"Are you trying to promote peak performance?" she asked dramatically, leaning forward on the counter.

"Actually, I'm just trying to get breakfast," I said.

She rolled her purple-gray color-contact-enhanced eyes. "If you need an additional energy boost, we have ginseng and ginkgo biloba to fight fatigue and increase stamina."

"Not fattening, is it?"

She gave a deep sigh. "If you're worried about weight, you need the Burner Boost with chromium and thermogenic herbs to control appetite and increase metabolism," she said, proving that she could at least learn her lines.

"Put in whatever you like," I said, giving up. I blamed Starbucks for starting it all by insisting that "tall" meant small, and that a "barista" made the coffee. Now we'd moved on to the stage where you needed a medical degree to get breakfast.

The Angelina-wannabe spent an inordinately long time mixing and stirring, and when I finally took the cup, I tossed a dollar into the tip jar, knowing the bonus she'd really like was Molly Archer's private email. Back outside, I settled into a café table, flipped through an *Architectural Digest*, and watched the morning bustle of shoppers. With the sun drenching down and the frothy drink (whatever it was) tickling my tongue, I could almost forget that I had more on my mind than whether crimson or persimmon was the color of the moment. I felt calmer than I had in days. Maybe Angelina had slipped me some Valium instead of the ginseng.

Ready to face my client, I sauntered over to the chic showroom and told the sullen receptionist that Roy Evans would be coming in soon. She brightened at his name, tossed back her curly blond hair as if all of life were an audition, and agreed to send Roy back as soon as he arrived. In the private display area, I milled around, pondering which of the rosewood dining tables newly imported from Milan would be right for Roy. He definitely couldn't handle what I'd commissioned for a French director's mansion in Malibu—a gleaming slab of sinuous steel that reflected the sunlight and sea. It got endless *oohs* and *aahs*, but Roy wasn't secure enough for cutting edge.

I checked my watch, then moved into the next room, which spotlighted chairs so gloriously modern they couldn't possibly be comfortable. I sat down. Right. Forty-five minutes later, I was considering the comfort level of a suede Armani sectional when my cell phone rang.

"Lacy, can you forgive me?" Roy's mellifluous voice on the line was sweetly pleading. "I had a long interview with that young singer Abby Jean. What a body."

"I'm still at the showroom. I can wait for you," I said.

"You shouldn't," he said. "But if you have a second, listen to this song from Abby's first album. She's going to be big." He must have held out the phone to his CD player, because I heard the distant, moaning sounds of a female pop singer.

"Sexy, isn't she?" he asked, back on the line. "I think she was hot for me. Once I told her she was going to be a big star, she didn't want to leave."

So Roy had been trying to score with his interview subject. The man had no shame.

"We should reschedule our appointment," I said, sticking to decorating.

"Absolutely. By the way, how's your husband doing?"

"Pretty well, thanks."

"What's new with the murder investigation?"

So here we were already. If I were suspicious about Roy Evans, I'd think that was the crux of this conversation. And, okay, I was suspicious of Roy Evans.

"I've been getting a lot of information on your friend Tasha," I said carefully. I wouldn't lie, but maybe I could get him worried. "I'm sure you've heard all the talk about her at the network."

"I haven't heard anything." Roy's voice suddenly had a slight edge to it, as if some of the polish were being chipped away. "Tell me the gossip."

"Just the rumors you'd guess," I said, hoping he'd fill them in for me.

"She slept around?" Roy asked.

"Something like that."

"Well, she was a cute little piece of pie. Not a surprise if a lot of men wanted her."

"I guess not," I said.

Brief silence and then he said, "Is there a list somewhere?"

"Of what?"

"The men. Do you think the police have a list of the people she slept with?"

"Could be, but I really don't know."

"Fine," he said, much too sharply. His voice had gone from edgy to angry, and I pictured him struggling to get back in control.

"I guess if we're going to do this decorating thing, you should see where I live," he said finally. "Can you come over Saturday?"

I hesitated. I had to see his place if I planned to furnish it, but why did the idea of going over there make me so uncomfortable?

"Um, sure. Give me your address."

"That's a big commitment. I haven't given a woman my address since my last divorce became final." He chuckled, pleased by his own little joke. But he reeled it off, and I had a feeling that this time, he wasn't going to miss our meeting.

I headed out of the showroom, pausing by the front door to look at a neo-Victorian mirror with inlays of polished metal. I glimpsed myself in the glass, and my hands reflexively flew to my face.

"Awful," I gasped loudly.

"Everyone hates that piece," said the receptionist, misinterpreting. She closed her *InStyle* magazine—which was the only place she'd see celebrities today. "I don't know why it's right in front."

The mirror frame looked a lot better than I did. My skin seemed mottled, I had bags under my eyes, and what was going on with my hair? Maybe I couldn't do much about my dark mood, but I could definitely fight back against my dark roots.

Outside, I pulled out my cell phone and hit *11 on the speed dial. Like most of the moms I knew, once my kids grew up enough that I could take the nursery school number off speed dial, I replaced it with my hair colorist's. Who wants to get older when you can just get blonder? So many of us worshiped at the peroxide altar of youth that an appointment with Alain was harder to get than a private audience with the Dalai Lama.

I decided to give it my best shot. When Alain's assistant, Andre, came on the phone, I outlined my problems. All of them. Hair crisis and personal disaster. I felt a little guilty gossiping about myself, but better me than anyone else.

"So it's an emergency," said Andre sympathetically.

"Dire emergency," I said. "If you're doing triage, consider me the equivalent of a massive heart attack on Oscar night."

Andre laughed. "Come right over. I'll try to squeeze you in."

Bless the man. Next holiday season, I'd upgrade his gift from a wool Polo sweater to cashmere. Alain himself took the guesswork out of saying thanks—he stayed registered at Barneys year-round.

I made my way over to North Camden Drive in Beverly Hills and slipped inside, past the usual cast of power clients. Instead of being a hairdresser to the stars, Alain worked for the women behind the stars. For Hollywood networking, his salon was the estrogen-laced equivalent of Monday nights at Morton's. I spotted a chair-hopping talent agent chatting up a studio development exec, and a screenwriter advising a Warner Brothers vice president to go brunette. "Much more dramatic," she said in a low voice. "And trust me, *I know drama.*" Amid the streaking, peroxide applications, and wholesale highlighting, more movie deals got made at Alain's than on the ninth green at the Bel Air Country Club.

I changed into a thin robe and sat down in a soft chair that faced a wall of mirrors. Good lighting, so I didn't look nearly as terrifying here as I had in the showroom. Alain came up behind me dressed in blue jeans and a crisp black shirt, his own hair crewcut short and light brown. The style changed regularly but always stayed understated. Alain didn't do flamboyant.

"I'm glad you came in," he said, putting his hands on my shoulders. "Are you all right?" He knew what was going on, of course. He knew everything.

"I'm fine. Just my hair's a problem. Murky in the middle and brassy on the ends."

"Oh, dearest, it's never just about the hair," he whispered. "You can confess to me."

I caught his eye in the mirror and suddenly felt tears welling up. For unloading emotion, a session with Alain beat a private appointment with Dr. Phil any day.

"Everything's awful," I admitted. "I'm frightened for my family, and for Dan. It's all so sinister and scary, and I have this sense of danger around every corner. Plus it doesn't make any sense. Dan has a generous heart and he's a good man. He really is a good, good man."

I had a feeling I'd picked up that last line from a bad Lifetime movie (are there any good Lifetime movies?), but I didn't care. I sniffled and indelicately wiped a finger across my nose.

"Dan's practically the last honorable guy in Hollywood," I said. "He doesn't deserve this. He spent years building his reputation, and I can't bear what people must be thinking about him now."

Alain handed me a tissue. "Nobody's thinking about Dan. They're too focused on their own affairs. You know what it's like in this town."

"He's accused of *murder*," I whispered.

Alain snorted. "A juicy extramarital affair with a B-list star trumps murder any day."

I laughed and blew my nose, almost at the same time.

Andre came out of the back room, holding a tray with enough little tubes of color to keep Mondrian happy. Alain pulled on thick plastic gloves and began methodically mixing.

"I never heard details. Do you mind? Who was the girl who died?" Alain asked, taking a brush and painting the new color carefully onto my roots.

"A would-be actress who never acted, as far as I can tell," I said. "Not exactly a power player. She worked as a makeup girl for Roy Evans."

"Roy Evans? Omigod." He pinched his lips tightly and stared intently at the back of my head as he continued wielding his brush. Alain heard about everything but didn't repeat much—which is why we all confided in him. But finally he murmured, "I happen to have a client who knows Roy Evans *very* well."

"Personal friends?" I asked, trying to be discreet.

"She works with him," Alain said, easily outdiscreeting me.

"I'm going to work with him, too," I said, a little too quickly. "Decorating. Isn't that a coincidence?"

"So you've met him? What'd you think?"

What *did* I think of Roy Evans? Self-involved. Untrustworthy. Fake as a two-dollar bill, as my mother used to say. "He struck me as having all the depth of a puddle," I admitted, "but maybe I missed some mud underneath."

Alain laughed loudly and set the timer for twenty minutes. "I've heard all sorts of big Roy stories from my client. Her name's Julie Boden, by the way. You might want to talk to her. I'll get you two in touch, if you want."

"Alain, you're too wonderful."

"I know," he said with a sweet grin, then flitted away.

I opened up a *House & Garden*, but I couldn't focus on "Ten Ways to Use Paisley" when I was thinking about Julie Boden and Roy Evans and Tasha Barlow. Sometimes L.A. seemed like the ultimate small town. Everybody knew everybody. And somebody probably knew the real killer. Molly had me call Roy. Alain said to call Julie. The Hollywood game of telephone tag, continuing.

Alain came back, peered at the color under the foil, and clucked approvingly. He sent me off for Andre to wash my hair, then told him to apply undercover cream conditioner, secret-formula shine enforcer, and Code One glaze. Getting glossy hair apparently required as much covert action as joining the CIA. I leaned back against the hard ceramic sink as Andre smoothed on the products. Though my neck started to stiffen from the awkward position, it was soothing to have someone taking care of me. I wasn't in any rush to leave the cozy salon and get back to the real world.

Cell phone reception in Beverly Hills was terrible—one of God or Pacific Bell's little jokes—so I didn't get a message from the headmaster at Ashley and Grant's private school until I was heading home. I pulled over and dialed with trembling fingers. Headmasters like Mark Morland didn't usually call with good news. I'd have been surprised if he wanted to report that Ashley had scored a field hockey goal or been unexpectedly elected class treasurer.

"I know this is a difficult time for your family," Mr. Morland said when he picked up. "I spoke to Grant, but since Ashley's still out, I wondered if I could help her in some way."

"Ashley's been back a couple of days. Maybe you just haven't run into her yet," I said, glad to be more in the know than he was.

He hesitated only briefly. "Actually, Mrs. Fields, I checked the attendance records before I called." I should have figured that. "And I spoke to her teachers." Ditto. "None of them have seen her or heard from her."

He sounded confident, but it took a minute for the information to sink in. Monday morning at school, I'd watched Ashley disappear into the crowd. But it never occurred to me that she'd actually evaporated.

"I don't even know what to think," I said, suddenly panicked. "I'll come right over."

Half an hour later, I sat perched in his office, staring at a bulletin board studded with varsity sports schedules, Students Against Drunk Driving banners, and faculty phone lists. Mr. Morland himself looked slightly rumpled and distracted. He had a PhD in philosophy from the University of Chicago, and his air of absentminded professor appealed to the parents who could buy everything for their kids except a few extra IQ points. A placard on his desk said:

There are no facts, only interpretations.
    —NIETZSCHE

I wondered if I should write down the line for Chauncey to use in court. *There are no facts in this case, your honor. Only interpretations.*

"A terrible situation with your husband," Mr. Morland said now, rubbing his hand across his forehead. "Has Ashley been taking it hard?"

Did hysterical screaming count as "taking it hard"? I thought of her crashing to the floor, wailing and bellowing when she first heard the news.

"Ashley's sensitive," I said, "but this is tough for everyone. We've all been pretty shaken."

"What happened when you brought her back on Monday?"

Normally, I'd put on a happy face about my kids for the principal. But why pretend now? "She was miserable. She didn't want to come to school or face her friends. But everyone said we had to get back to normal, so I dropped her off and . . ." I shrugged.

"She came home after school?"

"Pretty late."

"What did she say?"

"Nothing. She went into her room and I assumed she had homework." I felt myself edging into Bad Mother territory here. Everyone knew that the key to dealing with a teenager was Communication with a capital C. And I'd just earned a D.

"Girls at this age are emotional in the best of times," Mr. Morland said soothingly. "When they're feeling vulnerable, they can really disappear. It's not your fault."

Of course it was my fault. Forget Nietzsche, hadn't he read Freud? When you're the mother, everything's your fault.

"So what do we do now?" I asked.

Mr. Morland sat back in his chair. "Sometimes the students know more about what's going on than we do. They confide in each other. Is Ashley still close with Mandy Bellows?"

I nodded. So that's what you got for outrageous tuition payments at a fancy private school—a principal who kept track of your kid's friends.

Mr. Morland excused himself and stepped outside to talk to his secretary. He'd barely returned when Mandy Bellows swooshed into the office, her long golden hair flying, her perfect heart-shaped mouth pursed into an expression of surprise.

"Did I do anything wrong? My English teacher told me to rush right over," she said, panting slightly, either from the exertion of running to the office or the anxiety of being here.

"Why don't you sit down, Mandy," Mr. Morland said, gesturing for her to take the chair next to me.

Mandy shimmied into the seat, crossing her long bare legs in front of her and patting her floral skirt, which barely made it to the middle of her slim thigh. Last year, when Mandy was struggling through her parents' loud and nasty divorce, she'd appear at our door almost every night, bedraggled and with her face streaked with tears, then hole up in Ashley's room for hours. Ashley remained a loyal friend—not to mention therapist and advisor—and never left her side. Now that the divorce was final, Mandy's anguish had vanished. Her skin shimmered, her made-up eyes glimmered, and her tiny tight clothes clung to every curve of her nubile body. Mr. Morland had already banned tube tops in the classroom, but Mandy remained the best argument I'd ever seen for sending Grant to an all-boys' seminary.

"I asked you to come by because we need your help with Ashley," Mr. Morland said to her now, jotting down a note to himself—probably to consider a mandatory uniform of burlap sacks.

Mandy blinked her long, thick lashes a couple of times but didn't say anything

"I'm not asking you to betray any confidences Ashley's shared with you," Mr. Morland continued, "but she hasn't been getting to her classes, and if she's in trouble, we need to help her."

"I, um, don't know anything," Mandy said quickly.

"Have you two talked much since her father was arrested?" Mr. Morland asked.

Mandy flushed, her face turning an appealing shade of pink. "No. No. We haven't talked at all. I, um, should have called but, um, I, like, didn't know what to say and I, like, thought Ashley would want to be left alone and I, like—"

Mr. Morland interrupted, sparing all of us.

"That's okay, Mandy. I'm sure you wanted to do what was right. Have you seen her at school at all?"

"Um, no. I, um, didn't know she'd come back."

"You haven't seen her at all?" He sounded only slightly incredulous.

"Nope. Not at all."

"Her mom dropped her here the last couple of mornings, but if you didn't know and none of her teachers saw her, then she must have gone somewhere else."

"I can understand it," Mandy blurted. "She probably didn't want to face her friends and hear about her dad being a murderer and stuff."

"But he's not," I said.

Mandy just shrugged

"Where would Ashley go if she wanted to avoid her friends?" Mr. Morland asked.

"I don't know."

"Can you take a guess?" he asked. "If she's putting herself in danger, we have to help."

"No place dangerous," Mandy said. "Ashley's not like that. I mean, with the black nails and the scary hair and stuff it might look like she's rebelling and becoming a freak or something. But it's just an act. Kind of a protection. I totally get her not wanting to be humiliated in the lunchroom, so, like, getting out of school makes sense. But I'm sure she's hanging out someplace safe."

Mandy looked at Mr. Morland and blinked her long lashes.

"We'll hope you're right," Mr. Morland said. "If you hear anything from her, please let us know. And let her know that we're concerned."

"Sure," Mandy said.

She got up to go with a little wiggle and started to stroll out. She had her hand on the door before my epiphany hit.

"Mandy?"

"Yeah?" She turned around, one hand still on the door. She'd made it through the conversation with Mr. Morland unscathed, and she was all confidence now.

"If you haven't seen Mandy, or even talked to her, then how did you know about the black nails?"

"Pardon me?"

"You said her black nails could make it look like she's rebelling. How did you know she had black nails?"

Mandy seemed to deflate right in front of our eyes. Her hand fell off the doorknob and she slouched slightly. A moment passed as she slowly rubbed the toe of one espadrilled foot against the heel of the other.

"I just knew," she said, looking down at her own nails, which were polished with a pale pink shade from Hard Candy.

"Ashley hauled out the black nail polish for the first time on Monday, the day she came back to school." I stood up, staring hard at Mandy. "Same with the scary mousse on her hair and the baggy clothes. Before that, she was dressing"—I paused, trying to be discreet in describing the girls' usual flirty style—"dressing just like you," I concluded mildly. "You wouldn't know about the whole punk thing if you hadn't been in touch with her."

Mandy ran her fingers through her silky hair, twirling a strand around and around.

"I have to believe you know exactly where Ashley is," I announced, pointing my finger at Mandy and strolling toward her with high-heeled authority. "In fact, you've probably taken her to some secret hideaway."

"You're crazy," Mandy said. But the assurance was gone from her voice and I heard a little tremble in it. Ah, yes. She was starting to crumble like a Lay's potato chip.

"Not crazy. Ashley didn't abandon you during your tough time last year, and you're much too loyal to disappear on her now." That could have been a compliment, but I was still jabbing my finger at her, as confident as Candice Bergen on *Boston Legal*.

"Someone had to be on her side, because you're not!" Mandy said angrily, her voice getting louder. She squinched her face furiously, reducing her big, wide eyes to narrow slits.

"I'm her biggest supporter!" I said, heatedly.

"Then I'd never want you supporting me!" Mandy screamed, her eyes flashing. "Like, oh my God, her dad's a killer and you expected her to be at school! This is a million billion times worse than what I went through last year! Ashley would die if she had to be in class all day! You're just mean and stupid not to know that!"

She took a step closer to me so we were almost nose to nose. It must have looked to Mr. Morland like we'd start punching each other, because he came from behind his desk. Taking a swing at Mandy would probably feel pretty good right now, but I struggled to keep my composure.

"Where is she, Mandy?" I asked, dropping my voice almost to a whisper.

"I don't know," she said, seething.

"Of course you do," I said.

"I said I don't!" she yelled.

Now the annoyingly calm Mr. Morland put a comforting hand on her elbow. "I know you're trying to protect her," he said, "but we're worried about her safety."

"I told you she's safe," Mandy said furiously. "Why don't you believe me?"

"Because we need to know where she is," I said softly. "And you knew about the black fingernail polish."

I thought Mandy might throw a fit or burst into tears—but instead she made a quick calculation that the jig was up. "She's at my dad's house," she said tersely, her teeth clenched. "Ashley's at my dad's house."

I looked at Mr. Morland, who remained expressionless. I turned back to Mandy.

"Your parents know about this?"

"Nope, the house is empty. My dad's on a business trip and I'm staying with my mom this week." The obvious upside of divorce for a rich teenager: two parents, two houses, and lots of room to maneuver in between.

"How about if I drive you there and we pick her up?" I asked.

"She's going to hate me," Mandy said, shaking her head.

"She'll understand. You're doing the right thing," said Mr. Morland sanctimoniously. The man was getting on my nerves.

We headed out to my car, and I let Mandy call ahead to warn Ashley we were on our way. By the time we pulled up at the gated Spanish-roofed house, Ashley was sitting sullenly on the grass outside. She exchanged a look with Mandy, slung her faux-Prada bag over her shoulder, and started to walk wordlessly toward us. I raced over to hug her.

"Honey, I'm so glad you're okay," I said enthusiastically. Ashley didn't say anything—though her sneer spoke volumes.

"I'm not angry," I promised her. "I've just been so worried about you since Mr. Morland called."

More silence. So that was her strategy. I couldn't fight with her if she turned mute.

"Look, Ashley, I understand your wanting to run and hide. I know how awful this is for you," I said, trying to commiserate.

Ashley rolled her eyes and got into the car. This was like having an argument with Marcel Marceau.

I slipped into the driver's seat next to Mandy, who hadn't moved.

"Should I take you to your mom's, Mandy?" I asked.

"I'll go to your house," she said. "No way Ashley should be alone."

I didn't point out that Ashley wouldn't be alone—she had me and Dan, her two brothers, a bed full of stuffed animals, and a lizard named Ralph. I looked into the rearview mirror, catching Ashley's eye with my unasked question.

"I'd like her to come," Ashley said, uttering five full syllables. Progress, but I wasn't throwing a victory party.

At the house, the girls scurried off to Ashley's room while I hung out in the hallway, straightening towels in the linen closet and listening to the gentle drone of their chatter. Once in a while I caught a distinct word or two, but I didn't want to get caught eavesdropping, and when I heard footsteps (one of the girls coming?) I left quickly. The conundrum of every mom: you're desperate for information, but even more desperate for your kid's trust. No reading diaries or checking email messages. Unless you were sure nobody would ever know.

After about an hour, I poked my head in the room. From the wet cotton balls, streaked tissues, and colorful bottles scattered on the floor, I realized they'd been having a pedicure party.

"You two need anything?" I asked.

"Nope, I'm gonna go," Mandy said, unfolding herself from the floor. "My boyfriend has been waiting for me, like, all afternoon." The nails on her bare feet gleamed a shiny shade of Petulant Pink, and she wiggled her toes.

Ashley stayed on the bed, and when Mandy scooted out, she stared down at her own peachy-pink toenails. At least the punk/Goth phase had been short-lived.

I hesitated for a moment, then sat down on the Aeron desk chair and scooted it closer.

"Want to talk about what's going on?" I asked, forgetting that you never ask a teenager a yes-no question unless you want to hear . . .

"No." Ashley sat back and crossed her arms in front of her chest.

I tried again. "Your teachers said they'd meet with you if you need any help catching up."

"Tell them not to bother," Ashley said, flopping down on her pillow. "I'm never going back. I hate everything about that school. All my classes suck. The kids are the worst. I hate all of them— even the ones who are supposed to be my friends. The teachers are awful. Mr. Morland's a jerk. I can't stand my swim coach. Or his assistant. Or the secretaries. Or even the lunchroom ladies." She somehow skipped over the custodial staff.

"Then we'll get you out of there," I said, trying reverse psychology. "You can get a fresh start. We'll switch schools. I bet we can do it by next week."

"I'm not switching schools!" Ashley shrieked, flipping her position faster than Olga Korbut on a balance beam. "How can you suggest that? Daddy's a killer, my life is shit, and now you want to take me away from my friends at school? Why not just kill me right now?"

"What would you like to do?" I asked, still thinking I could reason with a fourteen-year-old whose mood was swinging like the trapeze at Cirque du Soleil. "You know the circumstances, and those aren't changing right now. How can we make the best of them?"

"We can't," she said.

I ran my fingers through my hair. I hadn't been able to help Grant with math problems since about sixth grade. "I have no idea."

"Try."

I looked at the sheet where he'd been scribbling notes and took a wild stab. "Okay, six feet. As tall as you."

He grinned. "Try again."

"Bigger or smaller?"

"Much bigger."

"A hundred feet."

"You're not in the ballpark."

"As tall as the Empire State Building."

He pushed the paper toward me. "Want some help?"

"Yup."

"The pile would go well past the sun. Roughly one hundred twenty-five million miles high. Cool, huh?"

"I don't get it," I said.

"It's a geometric progression. You're doubling every time and that gets big really fast."

"Cool," I agreed, even though I still didn't get it. How could piling up paper get you to the sun?

"Double it one more time and you come right back from the sun," Grant offered. "Want me to show you the calculations?"

I laughed. "I'll trust you." I couldn't do the math, but I was starting to grasp the concept: Small things could balloon out of hand pretty quickly. Keep doubling your troubles and pretty soon your whole world could burn up. Is that where our family was headed?

I kissed Grant on the top of the head, a good-night ritual that he didn't mind, and headed—finally—to my own bedroom. Dan was sitting on the bed in his soft gray Loro Piana robe, reading an issue of *JAMA*. So he'd come home at some point and hadn't bothered to say hello. I hesitated for a minute, then pulled on a peach silk nightgown and sat down on the edge of the bed next to him.

Since his arrest, Dan stayed out late most nights or worked in his study, coming to bed long after I was asleep. This was as close as we'd come to intimacy.

"What are you reading?" I asked, looking for a neutral subject.

"Another article about stabilized hyaluronic acid for augmentation of facial rhytid ablation," he said, turning a page.

"Which means what?" My house seemed to have been taken over by pod people. I couldn't understand what anybody said anymore.

"Oh, it's just about reducing wrinkles. This study says some of the injectables—like Hyloform—actually work. Particularly on filling in the nasolabial fold."

Unwittingly, I traced a finger along the line between my nose and mouth.

"Think I should try?" I asked my plastic surgeon husband. Given his usual bias against vanity procedures, I'd resisted joining the Botox-and-filler flock, but maybe the time had come.

Dan peered at me over his rimless reading glasses. "You look good to me," he said.

I made a face. What woman can ever accept a compliment without challenging it? "Thanks. But I've got worry lines everywhere, and they're only getting worse."

"I don't see any."

Well, he would. Someone who read medical journals should know that cops, killers, and callous headlines were prime causes of crow's-feet.

Dan put down his journal and ran a finger along my arm. "Any headlines today?" he asked, the shorthand we'd used for years when we needed to catch up.

I sighed. "Let's see. Today's crisis was that Ashley's been skipping school. Mr. Morland called and we talked to Mandy, who said she didn't know anything about Ashley. Mandy is so good at playing clueless she could give Alicia Silverstone a run for her money. But she knew about Ashley's black nail polish, and that gave her away. Honestly, I was proud of myself for figuring it out."

"Oh." Dan hesitated, obviously not sure he'd completely followed my story. Or followed it at all. But then, satisfied that he didn't have to get further involved, he added, "I'm proud of you, too. As long as you took care of it. Thanks."

Took care of it? Back in the days B.A.—Before the Arrest—Ashley's behavior would have shaken the family to the core. We'd have consulted teen therapists and family counselors. I'd have called Dr. Laura, Dr. Phil, and Dr. Joy Browne. But now teen angst could barely compete for our attention. We had bigger problems and more absorbing mysteries that even the finest Midnight Red nail shine from Chanel couldn't solve.

Dan took off his robe and lay back, pulling the pillows away from the hard-edged rim of the steel bed. I carefully got under the covers next to him, tucking back the silky pale ivory sheets and longing for the days when I actually cared that 600-count Yves Delorme linens felt softer than Frette. The two of us lay stiffly on our backs, staring at the ceiling, like an old married couple in a *New Yorker* cartoon.

Finally Dan rolled over and touched my arm again.

"Lacy, I never saw that Tasha woman before," he said softly, almost whispering into my ear. "I don't know who she is. I went through all my records at work, and her name doesn't mean anything to me. No matter where I try to place her, I come up empty."

His voice was plaintive, quietly pleading. He needed me to believe him, and of course I did. Dan was my husband, the man I loved and admired. Together, we had made love and made children and made a whole life. If I didn't trust Dan now, what did the last eighteen years add up to?

"We'll solve this," I whispered. "I know we will. I'm going to help."

Dan stroked my shoulder. "Please. I need you on my side," he said.

"There's no place else I want to be," I said.

Dan draped his arm around me, and I felt his body relaxing into mine, but I was too tense to respond. I closed my eyes and in a few minutes I started breathing rhythmically, pretending sleep. Before long, Dan dozed off, his chest rising and falling against mine. I lay still for a while, then slid gently away to the other side of the bed. I glanced at Dan over my shoulder, but he didn't stir and I felt a tinge of relief. No way I wanted Dan to wake and think I was trying to escape from him. No way I wanted to think that myself.

I tiptoed across the hall to my own little office, convincing myself that eleven thirty at night was the perfect time to catch up on paperwork. If only I had some to do. Fortunately, the light was blinking on my answering machine, and I congratulated myself on having been responsible enough to check. Sammie, the assistant to Julie Boden, had called earlier, suggesting I come to Ms. Boden's office at 9:00 A.M. Thursday morning. She left an address and phone number, and the information that if the time wasn't convenient, I could call anytime. They worked late.

I fiddled at the desk for a few minutes, then went back to bed. Dan wanted me at his side, and here I was. I tried not to think about Dan and Tasha as I put a hand on my sleeping husband's chest. In the old days, when we could never get enough of each other, we used to joke that sex was always the solution. Now I didn't even want to wonder if sex was also the problem.

Chapter Five

Julie *Boden's office* was in a large glass tower on Westwood Boulevard. I pulled into the underground parking lot, gave my car to the valet, and took an elevator directly to the Briggs & Briggs advertising agency on the eighteenth floor. Ushered into Julie's office, I felt like I'd dropped into her country house. She had an antique pine desk, a soft white muslin sofa, flowered down pillows, and a coffee table made from an old trunk. Then I got it. Julie didn't need the usual trappings to exude power.

"I love what you've done here," I said after Julie and I had shaken hands. Looking again at the sweet pine desk, I realized it was English, circa 1890, and the coffee table was a British steamer trunk with authentic decals from Her Majesty's Navy. "These are fabulous. So original. Where did you ever get them?"

"Here and there," she said with a shrug, glancing around the room. "Some at antique stores on Melrose, I think." Then in case I'd guessed that her decorator had found the rare pieces and simply sent them over, she added, "I buy what I like."

"Oh." Just what I'd told Roy—the best designers let you forget all about them.

Done discussing decorating, Julie gave a loud bark for her assistant.

"Sammie!"

The young woman hurried into the room, dressed in slim khaki slacks and a pretty white shirt. She seemed friendly and energetic, with light brown hair and tortoiseshell glasses. I'd noticed a decal on her cubicle from Vassar, which probably meant she'd come to California with her BA in English, in search of a glamorous job. Someone should have told her it might have been more glamorous staying in Poughkeepsie.

"Get me a green tea with fresh mint, no sugar, and lemon on the side. And I want it from the Healthy Drinks on the corner," snapped Julie, who apparently didn't know that Jamba Juice had more antioxidants.

"What about your guest?" asked Sammie.

"Nothing, thanks. Maybe just some water," I said.

"Ice or room temperature?" she asked, turning to me.

"Room temperature." Why was getting a liquid in L.A. always so complicated?

Sammie stepped into the hall and came back quickly with a small bottle of Evian, then left on her errand. Julie gestured for me to sit down. I immediately sank into the extra-soft sofa cushion and felt myself engulfed by the pillowy material. Bad choice for an office since all I could do was gaze up at Julie, who, perched in a firm, straight chair behind her desk, peered down at me imperiously. Come to think of it, maybe not a bad choice. Probably just the way Julie wanted it.

As an executive at one of L.A.'s hottest ad agencies, Julie Boden knew all about image. Her black, elegantly cut Versace suit announced her powerful position, and the funky Dolce & Gabbana red leather boots with four-inch needle-thin heels worn underneath established her as a creative type. Once she knew I'd taken it all in, she pulled off her jacket, and her sleeveless camisole revealed firm, tanned, Nautilus-sculpted arms. One framed photo behind her desk showed Julie in a low-cut sweeping gown posed on a red carpet outside the Kodak Theatre. Another had her in white martial arts garb, her lean leg raised against an opponent in an impressive kick. The complete woman.

"I got a call from Alain about you," Julie said. Unwittingly, she glanced at my hair. "He said you need information about Roy Evans."

"Roy's a new client. I'm going to do some decorating for him."

"Really." Julie's inflection was flat. "I'm impressed you do this much research on your clients. Alain also mentioned something about a murder, but I didn't catch the connection."

"There may not be one," I admitted honestly. "My husband's being investigated for a murder. It turns out Roy knew the victim."

Julie raised a perfectly arched eyebrow. "Who was it?"

"A makeup girl who'd worked with him."

Julie looked at me in vague disbelief, scanning my face as if trying to decide whether I was joking. When she realized I wasn't, she gave a loud guffaw that ricocheted across the desk.

"A makeup girl? That's perfect," she said.

"Why?"

Julie waved her hand dismissively. Her fingernails were short, round, and shiny, and a large topaz ring—the kind a woman buys for herself—flashed on her finger. "Doesn't matter. Just fits his personality. Roy thinks he likes strong, interesting women, but they end up being too much for him." She shook her head. "A fawning makeup artist. Perfect. What was her name?"

"Tasha Barlow."

Julie looked up sharply, the amusement on her face at Roy's dalliance now more like shock. She grabbed for an unopened Diet Coke on her desk and swirled it in her hands. I noticed three empty cans already in the wastebasket. In another era, tensely coiled Julie Boden would have been a chain-smoker, but in postmillennium Los Angeles, swigging serial sodas would have to do.

"Tasha Barlow?" she repeated softly.

"Did you know her?"

"No, of course not." She snapped open the soda and took a long sip. Then she cleared her throat. "Roy never mentioned her. And I don't think she worked on any of our shoots."

"This probably sounds silly, but what shoots?"

"You really don't know?" She looked at me oddly. "I'm the creative director here. I produce television commercials for our clients. Roy has been in the latest ones."

I nodded encouragingly, but she glared at me, insulted that she had to explain her lofty job.

"You probably saw my ads on the Super Bowl," she said, obviously deciding it was better to brag about her success than brood about my ignorance. "A spaceship lands on Mars and morphs into a blue Buick. Suddenly a rock star jumps out of the car and there's music everywhere. Very postmodern."

It clicked. "My gosh, I loved those. Everyone loves those. Didn't you have Paul McCartney in one? And Bon Jovi?"

"We did."

"And Roy? I guess he didn't make much of an impression on me."

"You only see him from the back, holding out a microphone when the star appears. No lines."

"I didn't notice him."

"As long as you noticed the commercials," said Julie, deciding to give an inch. "We have three airing now and Buick sales are soaring. We're deciding whether or not to renew Roy for the next two we shoot."

"If they've been so successful, you probably don't want to change anything," I said.

"Roy's not exactly the make-or-break, as you just pointed out. First round, he was thrilled just to be on the same set as McCartney. But now he wants a paycheck to match his ego, and he's not getting it."

Julie took another swig of soda, then slammed the can on the desk. I tried to decide if her defiance was personal or professional.

"So tell me more about Roy," I said. "What's he like to work with?"

"You've met him, haven't you?"

"Just once."

"Then what do you think?"

I'd spent under an hour with Roy Evans and suddenly everyone wanted my opinion. "He's charming," I said.

"No kidding. And the sky is blue," said Julie, who clearly wasn't vying for the "charming" designation for herself.

"He seems to have a lot of famous friends," I said, trying again. "He told me some good stories."

"Let me guess. You heard how Jennifer Lopez adores him."

"He showed me the video."

She snickered but didn't sound amused. "He's moving fast on you. Be prepared, because there's lots more to come. He has at least two weeks' worth of stories before he starts repeating himself. You'll be completely enamored of him and he'll make you laugh. Mr. Sunshine. You'll feel warmed by his attention. But don't go too deep, because you'll get disappointed quickly."

Julie's hard eyes and pinched lips said she'd already hit the disenchanted stage. I wanted to ask what Roy had done wrong, but Sammie arrived just then with a shiny paper bag from Healthy Drinks and placed it neatly on the desk.

Instead of "Thank you," Julie said, "Sammie, don't forget to listen to my voice messages."

"I'll do it right now."

"Tell me if there's anything important."

Sammie left quickly and Julie took her iced tea out of the bag. She gave me a small smile. "I'm a heavy drinker. Tea and Diet Coke. My only vices."

"Not the worst I've ever heard."

"Certainly not in this town."

I smiled and tried to readjust myself on the sofa, but it was like being plopped in a pile of marshmallows. "Anyway, we were talking about Roy. The man who doesn't go too deep. You don't seem to like him very much."

"Really?" asked Julie, raising an eyebrow. "Some people would say I like him too much. I gave him the job on the commercials. He wasn't the obvious choice, and I spent a lot of time convincing the client why he'd be right."

"And now you're ready to convince the client that it's time to switch."

Julie moved her mouth back and forth, then blurted, "Maybe."

I thought about it for a moment. "I take it Mr. Sunshine has a dark side."

Julie started to say something, then stopped herself, pulling the lid off her oversized cup of green tea. Opening a packet of Splenda, she stirred it slowly into the tea. She was being careful now, making sure that her personal feelings didn't get in the way of business.

"Let me put it this way," she said. "If I get new talent for the next round of commercials, we'll talk about a dark side. Otherwise, he's my guy. Mr. Sunshine. And that's it."

Julie Boden's gamesmanship was starting to grate on my nerves. And I wasn't even sure what we were playing. "Why'd you invite me here if you weren't going to be honest with me?" I asked, not caring anymore what she thought of me.

"A favor to Alain," she said airily.

"Oh, for heaven's sake. Alain is a hairdresser. We all adore him, but you're a busy woman. You didn't see me just because he called you."

"If you want to leave, you may," she snapped.

"I don't want to leave. I want to know why Alain's saying the words "murder" and "Roy Evans" in the same sentence got you to call me."

She shifted in her seat. "That's obvious, isn't it? I'm running a multimillion-dollar ad campaign for a major client. If there's going to be a scandal involving the talent, I need to know about it."

"And it wouldn't surprise you if Roy was involved in a murder."

"Don't put words in my mouth," she barked, getting up from her chair and coming around to the front of her desk. "I didn't say that."

"Then let me ask. Would you be surprised if Roy were involved in a murder?"

She leaned against the edge of the desk, inches from where I was sitting, and crossed one leg in front of the other. "I'd be shocked," she said, clearly talking for the record now.

"Tasha Barlow was strangled," I said, for no particular reason.

She looked startled, and her boot skidded against the hardwood floor. She managed to steady herself. "Accidentally, you mean? During sex?"

"I don't know. Could be. Does that sound more like Roy?"

"Sounds like a lot of men."

She moved away from the desk and walked toward the window, gazing for a moment at the panoramic view of the hills, which was only partially obscured this morning by the hazy smog. Then she turned around to me.

"Look, Roy's beat is heavy music and he fits the stereotype. Sex, drugs, and rock and roll, right? I won't try to tell you otherwise. He drinks too much and smokes pot more than he should. Cocaine now and then and some crystal meth. He has enough good qualities that I overlook his human failings. Everyone has an addiction."

"He does coke, you do Diet Coke."

Julie contorted her mouth into what should have been a weak smile but turned out closer to a grimace.

"How about his sexual interests," I said. "Crystal meth is what you take to give a wild edge to your orgasms, isn't it? Makes you feel uninhibited. Do you think Roy is the kind of guy who might get high and take a sex game too far?"

"I have no idea. Is your husband?"

I ignored the gibe at Dan. "You must have been on location with Roy, shooting those commercials. Staying in the same hotel and all."

"I don't do bed checks on my talent."

"Of course." No reason to check on the talent if she was already lying next to him in bed. Alain had hinted that Julie and Roy were pretty close. Julie and I looked at each other, but I bit my tongue. No reason to say something that would get me thrown out.

Too late. Julie must have felt she was treading on dangerous territory. Her heels clicked smartly on the floor as she strode back to her desk and sat down. "It's been interesting talking with you, but I have a commercial to prepare. When you leave, you can close the door behind you."

In case that wasn't blunt enough, Julie swiveled her chair away from me and picked up her phone. Our conversation was over. I walked out, shutting the door with a loud click.

Sammie looked up from the computer in her cubicle. "Did your meeting with Julie go all right?" she asked. She seemed genuinely concerned—a bright young woman who'd obviously seen more than one person leave Julie's office in tears.

"I don't know. You have a tough boss. I hope I haven't made her tougher for you today."

"I'm used to it," Sammie said. "Anyway, do you need to be validated?"

Of course I needed to be validated—who didn't? I needed someone to validate that I was on the right track to solve this mystery. That I'd be able to help my husband and hold my family together. But the validation Sammie had in mind was more limited, so I started digging through my Furla bag to find the valet parking stub.

"Check your pockets," Sammie advised as I continued fumbling for the ticket, which seemed to have vaporized.

"I'm sure I tucked it inside my bag," I said. But I stuck my hand in the side pocket of my black Prada pants and pulled out the ticket. Sammie grinned and efficiently slapped two validating stamps on the back.

"That should get you out of the parking lot for free," she said, handing it back.

Maybe she had some stamps in her drawer to get Dan out of jail free.

As Sammie got up to lead me toward the elevators, I thought about Julie's snapping at her to pick up the voice messages. If that was their routine, Sammie knew a lot about office goings-on. In fact, she'd probably taken the original message from Alain.

"Listen, Sammie, I came here hunting for information about Roy Evans," I said, talking quickly since we'd almost reached the end of the hall. "I'm guessing Roy and Julie had some kind of fling, right? One of those that everybody knows, but nobody mentions. But Julie sounds pretty pissed now. Do you know what happened?"

"Not really." Sammie bit at the edge of her middle finger. "Roy still calls a couple of times every day, but now Julie tells me to say she's in a meeting. Used to be she'd talk to him for hours. With her door closed."

"When did that change?"

"A week or two ago." Sammie pushed the button for the elevator, which opened almost immediately. Damn. If I'd been in a rush, the elevator would have been stuck on the fortieth floor.

I handed Sammie my business card. "Anything you hear would be helpful," I said. "You can call me."

Sammie glanced at the card, but didn't look like she'd be rushing to the phone anytime soon.

"Well, don't let Julie ruin your day," she said with a rueful smile, as if she'd had a few ruined days of her own.

Downstairs again, I paid for parking with my validated pass and drove away carefully, my mind whirring. Maybe my meeting with Julie wouldn't win either of us a congeniality award, but at least I was getting somewhere. A few calls, a few questions, and I already had some new facts in hand. The picture wasn't clear yet, but I had a start.

When I got home, I changed from Prada pants to Gap sweats and sat down in the kitchen, scribbling some notes on a legal yellow pad. But the more I looked at my evidence, the more my excitement began slipping away. Let's say I was right on all counts. Tasha Barlow hadn't just done makeup for Roy Evans, she'd slept with him. Meanwhile, Roy Evans was busy having a fling with his boss, Julie Boden. Three points of a triangle. Julie was sufficiently smitten that she'd hired Roy for a big commercial, but the passion ebbed in the past couple of weeks when he did something to upset her. Something significant, since she wouldn't even talk to him. But it would take a longer jump than even Carl Lewis could manage to assume that his affront involved killing Tasha Barlow. Could be nothing more than he forgot her birthday. Or even worse, remembered and sent a Whitman's Sampler.

I munched a few grapes from the refrigerator, then spit one out, a bitter taste in my mouth. Sex and scandal didn't really come as a surprise in Los Angeles. Pick any three random people in this town and there was a good chance I could come up with similar scuttlebutt. Did my information add up to anything that would help Dan?

Frustrated, I went over to the pantry and tugged at the smooth-glide shelves. I hadn't eaten breakfast this morning, which justified my gulping down a chocolate-glazed Krispy Kreme doughnut. Make that two. And since it was well past lunchtime, I went back to the silver-paneled Sub-Zero and devoured a piece of cold chicken and a hunk of Brie without bothering to sit down. I was just eyeing some leftover tiramisu when I caught myself short. I needed an outlet for my anxiety other than eating.

Which is how I ended up in Dan's study with a can of Pledge in my hand.

Cleaning could work off my energy, and this was the place to do it. Dan didn't let our housekeeper into his study, insisting he'd handle the vacuuming and polishing himself. He didn't do a bad job, keeping medical journals stacked in leather baskets, papers filed in color-coded folders, and books arranged alphabetically on the built-in mahogany shelves. I felt uncomfortable invading Dan's personal space, but I reminded myself I was doing him a favor. Neat, sure, but dust bunnies might be growing under the desk.

Dan's digital answering machine flashed red, showing three new calls from this morning. While I dusted, I must have accidentally hit the PLAY button because all of a sudden ...

Oh, heck, who was I kidding? I was so desperate for information that if I'd found a tube-locked Sentry safe with an anchor bolt, I'd have nabbed a jackhammer to pry it open. A measly PLAY button wasn't going to stop me.

The first message, recorded at 9:21 A.M., was from an assistant in Chauncey Howell's office, saying Chauncey wanted to meet with Dan as soon as possible. The second message brought ten seconds of silence, followed by a hang-up. The third message, which had come in less than a minute later, offered a man's voice, speaking in a husky whisper: "Nothing has changed, Doctor. I know what you did. You've just got more reasons for silence."

And then an abrupt hang-up.

I shakily hit the PLAY button again, skipped over the first two messages, and steeled myself as the husky voice resounded once more, filling every corner of the room.

This time I heard a slow intake of breath before the words. And then the same threatening message: "Nothing has changed, Doctor. I know what you did. You've just got more reasons for silence." And the click as the mystery man hung up.

My hands trembled violently, but I managed to hit the PLAY button one more time and listen as the low, rhythmic voice offered its mesmerizing message. Whoever was speaking was a master of the game: his three simple sentences sounded subdued but threatening, quiet but terrifying. I couldn't make any sense of them. I felt like a kayaker caught inside a wave, bouncing along with the sensations but way too disoriented to spin my head out of the water. I walked around the study trying to calm down, then went back to the desk and hit the button to listen again.

My brain was numb. If there was a key to understanding this message, I didn't have it. I stared at the answering machine, as if I could unearth some meaning by concentrating hard enough on the radio waves. But nothing was coming through to me, not even static.

I needed to have a conversation with Dan. Whatever was going on, I couldn't get it by guessing.

After dinner, I read Jimmy three bedtime stories about a happy rabbit family without letting on that our happy human family could split at the seams any moment. When he fell asleep, I went to my study, turned on the computer, and spent an hour paying bills. Someone had bought four pairs of outrageously expensive shoes at Charles Jourdan earlier this month, using my credit card. I sighed. Must have been me. But the days of carefree shopping on Rodeo Drive seemed a lifetime ago. I put my head down on the desk, trying to figure out what had happened to us.

"Are you doing anything tomorrow?"

I jumped up. I hadn't heard Dan come in and I swiveled around abruptly at the sound of his voice.

He was leaning in the doorway of my office, dressed in gray slacks and a pale blue polo shirt, and holding his navy blazer on one finger at his shoulder. His hair was slightly rumpled and there was the faintest hint of sunburn across his nose. He had all the elements for a Ralph Lauren ad—but his attitude wasn't right. For once Dan looked defeated. I felt my heart breaking for him.

I took three steps across the room and kissed him on the cheek, determined to be cheerful.

"Hi," I said brightly. "Did you have dinner?"

Dan shrugged. "Don't worry about it. I'm fine."

"I'll get you something to eat," I said. No crisis could keep me from being the good wife and hostess.

Dan nodded and then asked, "So what are you doing tomorrow?"

"Taking the kids to school, and then I'm supposed to meet a new client." I'd been surprised when the new third wife of a hot Hollywood producer called. I reluctantly told her my situation and she didn't care—she had a new mansion to furnish, and apparently a minor murder didn't matter as much as finding the perfect Ming vase.

"Oh." Dan looked around the room, glancing at the Warhol lithograph over my desk as if he'd never seen it before. And in a way, he hadn't. The huge black-and-white flower once had a yellow wash over it, but the color had faded, leaving only the stark lines of the drawing. Warhol's studio offered to repaint it and authorize it as an original, but I hadn't bothered. So much for the lasting value of modern art.

"I have a meeting with Chauncey at ten, and I thought you might come," Dan said.

"Sure. I'll change my client to the afternoon. Nothing's more important than you," I said quickly. I kissed him again. "Come to the kitchen."

Dan tossed his blazer over the banister. I tried to be nonchalant as I bounced down the stairs, but I could think of only one thing. Had Dan stopped in his study on the way up? Had he listened to the messages on his machine?

Message number one had been about setting up a meeting with Chauncey for tomorrow, and he'd done that. But most likely the assistant in Chauncey's office had tracked Dan down directly this morning, calling his cell phone or beeper number after she'd called here. If Dan hadn't heard the messages yet—including the one from the mystery man—I could be there when he listened for the first time. I could watch his face and judge his reaction.

I pulled out a pan and placed it on the front burner of the Garland cooktop. No, that wasn't fair. Dan was my husband, for heaven's sake. We were on the same team. I didn't have to trick him or track him or sneak around hoping he'd reveal himself. I could be direct.

"Dan?" I turned full square to face him across the counter island. He had opened a new Sharper Image catalogue and was flipping intently through the pages of robopets, massage recliners, and air purifiers. I've never quite figured out why men are mesmerized by air purifiers—and why the same ones who ignore the lingering reek of Montecristo Cuban cigars are absolutely determined to own an Ionic Breeze Quadra.

"What is it?" he asked, looking up.

"Um . . ." I stopped. My husband. Same team. Could ask him anything. I cleared my throat. "Um, honey, would you like the leftover pasta salad from dinner or should I just make you an omelet?"

"Either." He closed the catalog, giving up his fantasy of ozone guards and cleaner air. "Whichever's easier. Thanks for doing this, honey."

I cracked three eggs into a bowl, then whisked in chopped onion, red pepper, and chunks of Jarlsberg. "Anything special happen today?" I asked. I was a wimp, no two ways about it.

"Not really. I saw some patients. Mostly, I worked on that article for the *Annals of Plastic Surgery.* Almost done."

"What's it on again?"

"Post-traumatic reconstruction. Giving a patient his face back after an accident. The editor says the work I've been doing is unprecedented. Genuine breakthroughs." He sighed, and despite the compliment he sounded as deflated as the Big Bird balloon a week after the Macy's parade.

I poured the eggs into the Calphalon pan and watched the

cheese I'd mixed in beginning to melt while the eggs began to harden. That's what happened when the heat was on. Some of us melted and some turned hard.

"Anything new with the . . ." I let the sentence trail off because we didn't have a way to talk about this yet. Anything new with your murder? Anything new with your life sentence? Anything new with the girl you say you didn't brutally strangle but someone did?

Dan didn't need conversational arrows to follow me. He slumped deeper in his chair. "Nothing," he said. "We'll see what Chauncey says tomorrow, I guess."

I flipped the omelet, slipped it onto the dish, and decorated the plate with fresh strawberries and blueberries. If interior decorating dried up, I could work at IHOP.

"That's pretty," Dan said when I put it in front of him. "Thanks."

"Some toast?"

"Sure. If you wouldn't mind." My, we were being polite with each other.

I escaped back to the safety of the counter and got busy toasting, buttering, and cutting. Safer to talk when we didn't have to look at each other.

"I know this sounds crazy," I said, "but I was thinking today about whether somebody might have framed you for the murder."

"Why would anyone do that?"

"I don't know. Because they could. Because they wanted to prove something. I have no idea."

Dan continued to stare at his plate, eating slowly. "We'll see what Chauncey says," he repeated, without looking up.

I took the carefully arranged plate of toast over to the table, put it in front of him, and sat down.

"You must be thinking about this as much as I am," I said, my face close to his. "You must have thoughts."

Dan put down the fork. "Thinking, yes. Thoughts, no. I don't know what's going on, Lacy. I really don't."

For the first time in my life, I wondered if my husband was lying to me. Was I being influenced by the message I'd heard, or was this really a wifely intuition?

I cupped my chin in my hands. "We have to get through this together," I said softly. "No secrets. I'm not going to turn on you, no matter what you tell me."

"No secrets," Dan said. But he didn't look at me, and I wasn't sure what could be so interesting about his empty plate.

When we got to his office the next morning, Chauncey didn't have any breakthrough news for us, but he did have six forms for us to sign, which made it seem like we were closing on a house rather than coping with a murder. Then he showed us some of the documents he'd collected—including police reports and a backgrounder on Tasha Barlow.

After we studied them for a while, he took them back, put them neatly into piles on his desk, and folded his hands.

"We need to talk legal strategy," Chauncey said, leaning toward us. "It's still early, but I want you to understand some of the options."

And he laid them out. Plea bargains. Pretrial deals. Judicial decrees. I tried to follow, but it all seemed beside the point, and after a while, I got impatient.

"Shouldn't we be trying to find the real killer instead of going through all this?" I asked.

"That's never a solid legal strategy," Chauncey said. "It can backfire in a dozen ways."

"So someone gets away with murder while we strategize?" I was seething and trying not to show it, but Chauncey had dealt with upset clients before.

"My focus is getting the best advantage for Dan," he said.

"Which would be what?"

"Too early to say. But we have to be realistic. For example, we might be able to plea bargain to manslaughter, with a sentence of ten to fifteen years. Dan could be up for parole in as little as three years. I think the DA would listen to an approach from us."

"Dan's not guilty. Why would he plea bargain?"

"Because the alternatives are grim, Lacy. If he's convicted of murder it's a mandatory twenty-five years to life. Don't forget that."

"But he's not guilty."

"I understand that."

I stood up and took a step closer to Chauncey, my voice getting louder. "No, you don't understand that. If you understood, you wouldn't be telling Dan to go to jail just for the fun of it."

"You can know he's innocent and I can know it," Chauncey said gently. "But once a case goes to a jury, there are no guarantees."

"But he's not guilty," I repeated again. I wanted to jump up and down to make him listen. Instead, I banged my fist hard against his desk. "Not guilty, okay? Do you hear me? Not guilty. That's where we start."

"Of course."

I turned around and looked at Dan, who had slunk down into the sofa and wasn't getting involved in my tirade. I took a deep breath and went and sat down next to him. Chauncey looked at me sympathetically.

"I'm sorry, Lacy."

I took another deep breath. I wasn't going to cry. "No, I'm sorry. I'm not trying to be difficult, I just want this to go away. And I keep thinking there's a link to someone else that we're missing. Some piece that Dan hasn't connected."

"Well, let's start connecting," Chauncey said.

We were all silent for a moment.

And then it occurred to me that facts were important, but so was getting to the essential truth about Dan.

"Okay," I said finally. "Here's what I'd like you to connect. A tank of gasoline."

"Gasoline?" Chauncey opened a folder as if expecting to find some mention of fuel—diesel, premium, or regular—in the police report.

"I'm always rushing in the mornings, and one day a few years ago I came downstairs to drive the kids to school, and I noticed my gas tank had mysteriously gone from almost empty to full."

I looked over at Dan, who gave a little smile, despite himself.

"Dan had filled it for me early in the morning, before he went to the hospital," I explained. "I'm not much on taking care of cars, so he'd done it as a little surprise to cheer my day. He didn't want any credit. It just made him happy to know he'd done something nice for me."

Chauncey took off his glasses and rubbed the bridge of his nose. I could tell he wasn't following, though for what we were paying, he'd let me rant about trains, planes, and automobiles if I wanted.

"Men don't always say things straight out," I said, trying to make my point. "They forget to bring flowers on your birthday. They don't know that Valentine's Day is in February. But they have different ways of expressing themselves. If you want a good marriage, you have to hear what your husband's really telling you. With Dan, a tank of gas can say "I love you" better than any bauble from Buccellati."

Chauncey glanced over at Dan, who looked slightly embarrassed.

"Lacy and I do things for each other. No big deal," he said.

I sat back. It *was* a big deal. Any husband could call 1-800-Flowers. How many would drive to a Shell station at 6:00 A.M.? Chauncey needed to understand what Dan was really like. He needed to listen better. And so did I.

Chapter Six

I *didn't know I was heading* to Tasha's place until I was almost there. After I left Chauncey's office, I drove around aimlessly for a few minutes, then discovered I was on Pico Boulevard, heading west. The address I'd seen on the police report Chauncey showed us had stuck in my head. Living near the ocean seemed pretty swanky as the first stop for a girl from Twin Falls, Idaho, and I wondered how she'd afforded it. When I was a couple of blocks away, I stopped at a red light and looked around—a Jack's 99 Cent Store, a 7 Eleven, a couple of bodegas selling fruit, and a tiny sign saying PUBLIC BEACH: 2 MILES. So that was it. No oceanside mansions here. Tasha might have liked telling her friends that she lived on the water, but the only whiff of ocean she'd get was from the fish market next door.

I parked in the open lot next to her building and noticed shreds of yellow police tape hanging limply from the wire mesh fence. Another damp remnant inscribed POLICE LINE DO NOT CR was flapping on a telephone pole nearby. The police had come and gone, apparently figuring their investigation was over.

At the front door of the building, I studied the name cards next to the buzzers. Number 4C said BARLOW/WILSON. Without thinking, I pushed the buzzer. Nothing happened, and just when I was about to leave, I heard a scratchy, "Who's there?"

"Hi, I'm Lacy," I said. "I wanted to talk to you about Tasha."

"What about her?"

Well, that was a good question.

"Um, I'm a friend of Roy Evans."

The intercom went silent. And then a moment later, a buzzer sounded to let me in.

I gathered my courage, pushed open the door, and made my way down a dark, dingy hallway. Ahead was another door, and as I passed through it, the grim tenement feel of the building suddenly dissolved and I stepped into an outdoor courtyard, complete with a large swimming pool. The water was murky and most of the lounge chairs on the cement deck seemed broken, but streams of sunlight flooded the courtyard and brightened the scene. I had to laugh. After growing up in flat, rural Ohio, I always found that even the tackiest apartment buildings in L.A. weren't bad. The five-story complex formed an L shape around the pool, with a staircase at the middle point. Not seeing any other way to get upstairs, I started climbing, stopping after four flights to walk along the outdoor corridor.

But 4C didn't exist.

What was going on? The numbers in the corridor went from 3D to 4D to 5D.

I paused and then headed back down a floor. Sure enough, even the numbering system in Hollywood had to be creative: 1C, 2C, 3C . . . At the next door, I knocked.

The woman who opened the door was probably in her midtwenties, but she was fat—no polite way to say it—with stringy black hair that needed to be washed. Her bulging stomach made ripples in her white T-shirt, and pale, flabby legs stuck out beneath her black shorts.

"So?" she asked. "Roy has something to tell me?"

I must have been too slow formulating an answer because the woman glared at me and then shook her head impatiently.

"I've packed up his tapes," she said. "Come on in. You can take them to him. I don't want to see him again."

The sunlight that filled the courtyard didn't make its way to the apartment, and it took my eyes a minute to adjust to the gloom. Then I had to adjust to the gloomy decor. A ratty brown sofa adorned with glittery red-and-orange throw pillows teetered on a standard-issue tweed carpet that must have come with the rent. A matching brown love seat was oddly angled away from the wall, probably in an effort to hide a dark, ominous stain creeping along the carpet. A rickety bamboo stand from Pier 1 held a small television, and some random lamps and a chipped Formica table finished the scene. Nobody had painted in a long time, and the dull beige walls were cracked and peeling.

"The tapes are in Tasha's bedroom," my guide said, continuing on.

She pushed open the closed bedroom door—and I unwittingly gasped. The sense of going from Hades to heaven was even more startling than in the courtyard downstairs. Tasha's private sanctum was a glowing palace, shimmering in shades of white and gold. Center stage was a king-sized brass bed, covered with a gold moire duvet and a pile of intricate, expensive, silk-tasseled European squares. A thick, plush white carpet was the background for a delicate Persian rug, and the walls were draped in a subtle silk-patterned wallpaper. A wafting, diaphanous fabric—I'd swear it was Scalamandré—fluttered gracefully from the windows. I could have done without the six-foot-long plasma-screen television and the heavy brass Medeco lock on the door, but even that couldn't distract from the overall opulence.

"Wow," I said. Then, guessing, "Gifts from Roy?"

She snorted. "No way. Your Mr. Roy pretends he's generous—big tipper and stuff—but he has a cheap heart. And you can tell him I said so." Her eyes welled over with tears. "Terry knew it, too."

Going over to the closet, her thighs trembling, she pulled out a Whole Foods shopping bag and thrust it at me. Some clothes and a jumble of tapes and DVDs were crammed inside—some in neatly labeled boxes and some just jammed in.

"Give these to him," she said. "Tell him they're from Nora. And tell him they all suck."

"What are they?" I asked.

"Him," she said. "On the air. He liked to watch himself on TV when he was in bed with Terry. Disgusting, huh? Terry thought it was funny, but I thought it was sick. I told Terry, 'Why does he need you when he gets off on himself?' "

She looked at me for a reaction, and when I didn't have one, she said, "*Celebrity Jeopardy!* was his favorite. Know the show? He'd been on once and won nine thousand dollars. Big deal." She dropped her voice an octave, offering a good imitation of host Alex Trebek's monotonous singsong. "Final Jeopardy category: Rock Bands. Answer: 'It gathers no moss.' " She slipped back to her own voice again. "Whoo, whoo. 'What's a Rolling Stone?' He got it. So would my great-grandmother. But he made Terry and me watch it so many times you'd think he'd won the Nobel prize."

I snickered. Lying in bed watching tapes of himself. Even in Hollywood, that scored pretty high on the narcissism meter. An easy bet said that the interview with Jennifer Lopez had landed in the bag, too. Roy Evans was definitely more fascinated by himself than by anything else on the planet.

But Nora had veered from fascinated. "Tell your friend Roy that I think he's a sleazebag," she said, blinking back tears. "And he's just lucky they pinned the murder on that other guy."

I took a second to register that the other guy—the one they'd pinned the murder on—was Dan.

Nora marched back into the living room, and when I followed her, I noticed a half-packed suitcase shoved into a corner.

"Are you moving?" I asked.

"Not right now." She followed my gaze. "You mean the suitcase? I haven't managed to unpack yet. I was away when . . ." She hesitated because, like me, she didn't have a way of talking about the murder yet. "When . . . *it* happened, I was visiting my parents in

Twin Falls. I'd seen Theresa's parents, too. They gave me her Idaho Potato Queen crown to bring back." The tears welled again. "When Terry got famous, I'd be her posse. Protect her. But I couldn't even protect her now."

I was getting the picture. Theresa, the prettiest girl in Twin Falls, Idaho, had gathered her money and courage and escaped her small town, moving to Hollywood to try her luck. Nora, her loyal hometown best friend, had come along for support.

"Do you think the police got the right guy?" I asked.

"You mean do I think Roy did it?" She looked at me, almost for the first time. "Are you his new girlfriend?"

"Um, no. Not really."

"Well, watch out. He starts out all sweet, but he's a perv if you ask me. Always trying weird stuff. Made her wear high heels to bed. Said he liked women in killer heels. Brought over dirty magazines and triple-X videos and liked to tie her up and stuff. Plus watching the tapes of himself. Theresa said it was all compensation because he had a little dick. Really little."

We were getting out of my league.

"When I first heard about . . ." Nora gulped. "About . . . what happened, I didn't think it was Roy. My thought was, 'Johnny. Oh my God. Johnny got violent again.'" She shrugged. "Pretty ironic. Theresa gets involved with a weirdo and an ex-con, and then it's a doctor who did it. And he did. He was the one who was here that night."

I felt my chest tighten.

"Was she involved with the doctor, too?" I asked, trying to sound nonchalant and probably failing.

"I don't know." She sniffled loudly and wiped her nose with the back of her hand. "She was involved with too many people. This is a mean town. It makes girls do bad things. But Johnny was the one she loved, you know? And Johnny loved her. Roy was just using her. I'd always say, 'Terry, he's using you for sex.' And she'd say,

'Yeah, but I'm using him, too.' She figured he'd help her with her career. But he wouldn't. I knew he wouldn't. All he cared about was himself."

Nora sat down on the ratty sofa, scrounged for a tissue that was half buried under one of the pillows, and blew her nose loudly.

"I want to tell Johnny how much Terry loved him," she said. "I have a lot of things to tell him. But he hasn't called or anything. I guess he's scared."

"Is he the ex-con?" I asked. Now that could be interesting.

"Yup, but he was completely reformed. Johnny DeVito. Six years in jail, I think. Or maybe eight. He told Terry everything. Bought her everything she wanted. Everything in that bedroom came from him. He told her how beautiful she was all the time, and he couldn't believe she loved him because he's so . . ." Her voice trailed off and she rubbed at her nose with the tissue.

"He's so what?" I asked.

"Ugly," Nora said bluntly. "He's ugly. And the one thing he wouldn't tell is how he got all the scars on his face."

I put down the shopping bag of tapes that I was still holding and plopped on the sofa next to Nora. Since she needed to talk and I was handy, she wasn't going to send me away.

"Have you told all this to the police?" I asked.

She shook her head. "I was in Twin Falls, remember? By the time I got back, they had the guy. The doctor guy. My friend Tony says once the police know who did it, they don't care about anyone else. They just build the case. Like with Robert Blake. Or O.J."

Did Nora think that the cops had the right guy or wrong guy in those cases? Guilty or innocent? Well, we weren't going there, as Ashley would say.

"If the police are building a case against this doctor, what've they got?" I asked instead, trying to keep my voice steady. Chauncey had said the prosecutors didn't have to share their information with him yet. Maybe I could provide him some details.

"Everything," Nora said, biting at the cuticle on her thumbnail. "Eyewitness identification. Fingerprints. DNA. Gracie Adler next door saw him coming into the apartment. Gracie heard her screaming at the top of her lungs—" Nora paused, then, raising her voice half an octave to imitate Tasha, said, " 'Stop it, Dr. Fields, stop it! Stop it, Dr. Fields, stop it!' "

I felt myself trembling from head to toe. "There must be more than one Dr. Fields in L.A.," I said, just to say something.

"But there was the car," Nora said importantly. "Gracie had noticed it in the parking lot two or three times—a navy blue Mercedes 520 with the license plate BESTDOC. Can't really miss that, can you? Gracie had asked me about it before. She says she wasn't being nosy, but at her age she could use the Best Doc, so when she saw him pull in, she watched where he went."

The vanity license plate had been a gift to Dan from his office staff one Christmas. He'd been embarrassed at first, but they'd kept renewing it—and now it was his calling card.

"Maybe someone else was driving the car," I said, my voice raspy. "Someone other than the doctor."

"The police artist made a sketch from Gracie's description, and it turned out that the doctor looked *exactly* like the picture. Plus his fingerprints were on a wineglass." She pointed to a dilapidated buffet littered with liquor bottles and beer cans. "They found two glasses right there—one had his fingerprints and the other had Terry's."

"DNA?" I asked weakly.

"He'd thrown a tissue in the wastebasket. That matched, too. He was here. He killed her. And if only I'd been around . . ." She started crying again, and I stood up and walked over to the window, just to make sure my limbs were functioning. The rest of me was numb. I'd heard enough.

"I'm sorry for your loss," I said, my voice barely registering now. "I'll let myself out."

Nora tried to pull herself together. "Wait," she said. She sniffed loudly and stared down at the thumb she'd been biting. "Could you ask Roy one thing for me? Ask him if he ever gave Terry any money."

"Money?" I repeated the word dumbly. "For what?"

"I don't know exactly. Maybe for some weird stuff he liked. The cops found an envelope from the doctor that was stuffed with cash. A lot—like five thousand dollars. Now they think that all the men paid her and Terry was . . . a professional, if you know what I mean. For all that money, the doctor must have wanted something really kinky. Even kinkier than Roy. And probably that's how she ended up strangled."

I staggered back, feeling as if Nora had just delivered a hard punch to my head. Everything went black for a moment, and I grabbed dizzily for the sofa, trying not to fall over.

"I couldn't bear it if Terry became a whore," Nora continued, not noticing that I was reeling. "She pierced her tongue and she showed me the gold stud. But that doesn't mean she was being paid for blow jobs. The men loved her for herself. Probably even the doctor. She used to say she had to do what she had to do but—"

I didn't wait to hear the rest. I took the Whole Foods bag and left.

Devastated, I drove up the coast and got out at the Santa Monica Palisades, joining the parade on the promenade path. Taut young women in spandex jogging shorts and paunchy middle-aged producers walking well-groomed dogs eased by homeless men sprawled on the park grass, where they'd been welcome ever since Jerry Brown was mayor. I turned down the long staircase carved into the cliff, crossed under the Pacific Coast Highway, and came out on the beach. Kicking off my shiny Sigerson Morrison sandals, I made my way across the hugely wide beach, avoiding skateboarders, bikers, and volleyball players, and didn't stop until the chilly Pacific was lapping at my ankles.

I stood staring out at the ocean. Suddenly, everything had changed. Nora's information wasn't pretty—but it was probably pretty accurate. How could I keep pretending that Dan had nothing to do with Tasha Barlow? Despite his whispered protestations and hang-dog eyes, I had to face facts.

I took another step into the water, watching a leaf drift back and forth on the gentle surf. What was I supposed to do now? I was the wife of a man who might have committed a murder. I rubbed my foot back and forth, creating small eddies of water and sand. The good news was that I could kill myself. Just swim straight out until the ocean engulfed me and I reached oblivion. Like Virginia Woolf, though maybe without the stones in the pockets. Or answer the call of the seductive sea like the heroine in Kate Chopin's *The Awakening*. Great novel. And boy, I'd had an awakening from Nora.

But no, I'd lost the right to that kind of self-indulgence (even in fantasy) long ago. I had three good children. I'd want them to know that bad news wasn't the end of the world. No matter what happened, you had to pull yourself together and keep going.

I took a few steps back and plopped down on the sand, oddly satisfied to feel the wet muck seeping through my silk Escada skirt. Dan had been at that apartment the night Tasha Barlow was killed. Been by with a wad of cash. Had a glass of wine. Spent time with a woman who—according to the police report—was found naked except for a pink marabou-trimmed robe. Tasha Barlow was willing to indulge a man's fantasies if she could get something for it, whether that meant a reference on a résumé or an envelope of cash. If Dan had come to Tasha's place for kinky sex, a lot of the pieces of the puzzle started to fit together.

The waves splashed rhythmically onto the beach, little peaks swirling in and out, in and out. A few boats sailed gracefully in the distance, but mostly the sea remained calm and uninterrupted, a deep blue expanse stretching on forever. For some reason, it reminded me of a day a month after I arrived in Los Angeles. Dan and I had met at a party and just started dating. As we strolled together in Malibu, getting to know each other, Dan had stretched his arms out and murmured, "Looking at the endless ocean always makes me ponder the vastness of the universe."

The vastness of the universe? Young and perky, I'd thought about that for the briefest moment then teasingly responded, "Really? I'm from Ohio. Looking at the endless ocean always makes me ponder whether I could learn to surf." Dan had paused and I'd felt my heart stop, worried that I'd been too flippant for this handsome, brilliant man who could be serious even on a sunny beach day. But he'd smiled and said, "That's probably a much better thought." Later that night we went to a tiny room in the Sunset Vue Motel and made love for the very first time. When we finally lay wrapped in each other's arms, well sated and newly in love, I whispered, "Whatever you just did, I'm suddenly feeling the vastness of the universe."

It became our joke ever after—the vastness of the universe. Life and love were infinite, boundless. So many options, so many grains of sand. I scooped up a handful of the smoothly glittering particles now and let them glide through my fingers. How many of those possibilities was I considering right now?

Okay, try again. Maybe Dan had been to Tasha's place, but that didn't mean he'd come for kinky sex. Or that he had killed her. Accepting that scenario meant discarding everything I knew about my husband. When Dan said at the beginning of this mess that he didn't know Tasha Barlow by name or face, he meant it. He'd been genuinely baffled. No DNA evidence the police could gather was as compelling as the truth a wife knew.

Or was it? How many men led secret lives that their trusting spouses didn't suspect? I'd watched *Jerry Springer* a few times. I knew about men who liked to cross-dress or visit the local dominatrix now and then. I'd read the article in *Vanity Fair* about the married English lord who died of asphyxiation after hiring a prostitute to bring him to new orgasmic peaks.

But those wives didn't know their husbands like I did.

I left the beach and made my way back to my car. I wanted to go home and talk to Dan, but I had something else to do first. I turned east, retracing my route down Pico, and drove to Beverly Boulevard, to the now too familiar law office. With my wet and sandy skirt sticking to my legs and my makeup streaked from the beach mist, I took the elevator directly from the parking garage, called out, "Just seeing Mr. Howell," as I sauntered by the receptionist, then smiled brightly at Chauncey's assistant as I walked in his open door. So much for security.

Chauncey looked up, startled, but ever the implacable lawyer, he quickly got his expression under control.

"Lacy, come on in," he said cordially, as if he'd invited me over for afternoon tea and was happy I'd finally arrived. He took off his reading glasses and gestured for me to sit down. But instead I kept my ground, standing sturdily in my dirty sandals on his antique Tibetan rug.

"Jimmy wet his bed last week," I said, not bothering with hello. "He hasn't done that since he was two."

Chauncey opened his mouth—maybe to point out that he was a lawyer, not a child psychologist—then closed it again.

"Ashley's turned punk and started skipping school," I continued. "Grant's trying to remain sane, but God knows how he'll focus enough to take SATs next month. My family's falling apart."

"This is a difficult time, and it doesn't get easier for a while," Chauncey said evenly.

"Is that why you suggested a plea bargain this morning? To keep us from self-destructing during a trial?"

"I wasn't *suggesting* a plea bargain. I was presenting options for you to consider."

"And maybe you considered it a good option because you know

what I know," I said. "That Dan had gone to see Tasha Barlow the night she died."

Chauncey put the cover on his Mont Blanc pen—about six hundred dollars more expensive than the Bic he used in court—and looked at me. "You know for a fact Dan was there?"

"Pretty much. And you knew that, too, didn't you?"

After the briefest pause, Chauncey said, "I'd surmised."

"Why didn't you say so this morning? Why didn't you ask Dan about it?"

"I don't have all the official reports yet. The DA doesn't have to provide them, but he and I have known each other a long time. When I find out more about his case, I'll present it carefully to Dan. Right now, I don't want your husband saying anything—to me or anyone else—that he may need to change later."

"So you'd rather not know if he's guilty."

"This morning you were incensed that I didn't feel strongly enough about his innocence. What I've learned in twenty years as a lawyer is not to jump to conclusions. Much of life and law is subject to interpretation," he said, as if he were reading from Mr. Morland's bulletin board.

"Okay, interpret this," I said, walking toward him. My skirt swirled damply, sprinkling sand like fairy dust at every step. "I think Dan's innocent. I don't care where he was that night. Maybe the killer's Johnny DeVito. Ever hear of him? He's an ex-con who Tasha hung out with and he used to be violent. He gave her a lot of presents and she was in love with him. Doesn't it make more sense to think he killed her than Dan?"

Chauncey made a note on the pad in front of him.

"A violent ex-con hangs out with a woman and she ends up dead," I said, persisting. "Suspicious, isn't it?"

"It could be," Chauncey said noncommitally.

"Did you know about Johnny DeVito and Tasha? Does anybody? Are the police investigating him or are they just focused on

Dan? Really, Chauncey, I think we need to know all this, don't you?" I spit out my spiel too fast, my voice so high-pitched it could have shattered the Baccarat crystal clock on his desk.

Chauncey just sighed. "Look, Lacy, I don't know where you got all your information. I'll check him out. But you have to take tips like this with a grain of salt."

"It comes from a good source."

"I'm sure," Chauncey said. But he didn't ask what it was.

"Something else for you to check," I said, louder now, and raising the pitch yet another octave. Maybe I could at least crack the crystal candy dish. "I'd like to know if Johnny DeVito's fingerprints were on the envelope that the police say came from Dan."

Chauncey wrinkled his brow. "What envelope?"

"The one with the money in it."

"I have no idea what you're referring to, Lacy."

I felt a surge of triumph. Chauncey didn't know all the facts the police had told loyal roommate Nora. Suddenly I was the one in the know. Someone had to be.

"Dan left an envelope stuffed with money in Tasha's apartment," I said authoritatively, tossing back my salty, stringy hair. "The police theory, I guess, is that Dan had gone to . . . um, buy favors from Tasha Barlow. But that's crazy. Come on, Chauncey, you've seen Dan. He's the last man in Hollywood who needs to pay for sex."

As the words tumbled out, I knew how pathetic I sounded— the deceived suburban housewife who didn't understand that if handsome Dan shelled out for kinky mistress maneuvers, he could count Hugh Grant, Charlie Sheen, and scores of other shouldn't-have-to-pay-for-it guys as his comrades.

Chauncey rubbed his temple. "There's definitely been some talk that the victim might have died during sexual activity."

"Dan wouldn't—" I stopped and bit my lip. Dan wouldn't pay out to have some woman put out. Wasn't his style. But I couldn't discuss Dan's sex life with Chauncey Howell or anyone else.

I turned and walked out of the office.

Back home, I slunk upstairs, flicked on the computer, and Googled Johnny DeVito. Sixty-three thousand references. I scanned the list, but the search engine wasn't on my side. Nothing about Johnny DeVito, ex-con. Or Johnny DeVito, gone missing. I clicked on the third site, and suddenly my computer flashed "*Johnny Dangerously.*"

I sat back, stunned. Is that what I was facing—a man known as Johnny Dangerously? Then I got it. Google was a search engine, not a psychic. *Johnny Dangerously* was a 1980s movie starring Danny DeVito and the searching software had juxtaposed the two names and sent me to this site. Still, looking at the name gave me a chill. Johnny Dangerously. What if the name really did describe him—and nobody else but me realized it?

"Hi, Mom."

I jumped, hearing Grant's voice at the door of my study. Before I could turn off the computer, he ambled into the room and looked over my shoulder.

"*Johnny Dangerously?* Whoa, Mom. What are you up to?"

"Nothing," I said. "At least, the wrong thing. I tried to get information on a Johnny DeVito, but I got the movie, not the man."

"Next time put quotation marks around the name," said Grant knowingly.

I nodded, still getting used to the idea that my son was grown up enough to know more than me about something. Or when it came to computers, iPods, and Xbox, more than me about everything.

"So who's the guy?" Grant asked, moving from the tech topic to the touchy one.

I shrugged. "I'm not sure."

"Something to do with Dad?" Grant asked, zeroing in immediately.

"Could be. Johnny knew the . . . victim. And he'd been in jail."

Oh, damn, why was I discussing this with my teenage son? Probably because he was here and cared and was smarter than any of us. "Anyway, I was looking for some background on him."

"Let me try."

I stood up and Grant slid into the chair in front of the iMac. He hit buttons on the keyboard, leaped quickly through websites, and then hit PRINT. A couple more minutes and he printed again. For Grant, the computer wasn't any more intimidating than a number 2 pencil. And why should it be? He'd been weaned directly from Beech-Nut applesauce to a Pentium PC.

"I found some newspaper articles," Grant said, taking the pages out of the printer. "Archives of the *L.A. Times*. Two stories from when your guy went to jail."

We looked them over together. Johnny Dangerously (as I now thought of him) had gone to prison for selling drugs. One of the articles hinted about a tie to organized crime and the possibility that he'd gotten away with murder a few years earlier. There weren't any pictures and not a lot to go on.

"Makes sense if he's the guy who did it," Grant said. "That'd be cool."

I looked carefully at the dates on the articles. Something was nagging at my mind, but I couldn't place it.

A little after midnight, I fell asleep waiting for Dan to come home. Under the goose-down comforter, I dreamed that I was lying at ocean's edge in Malibu, watching Johnny Dangerously ride the waves on a Spyder surfboard. He did a double half-pipe and skidded up onto the too sunny beach next to me. I glimpsed his scarred face and my heart pounded a drumbeat of recognition. I knew this man. I'd seen him before. I tried to memorize the features, but he got back on his surfboard and paddled into the swirling ocean. I ran into the water, but the sun—too bright— glared in my eyes, and in the scorching light, Johnny's face began to fade, replaced by a blazing halo. Johnny Dangerously had disappeared in a scrim of dazzling white light. The face—mysterious, half forgotten—was gone. I made a visor of my hand, trying to protect my eyes and see into the radiating mist, but it was too late.

I woke up abruptly and blinked hard, trying to eliminate the bright red dots that were bursting behind my eyelids. It took a few moments to realize that I wasn't on a beach. Nobody was surfing. The dazzling sun in my dreams must have been a mental transposition of the halogen spotlights above the bed, which were now blazing directly into my eyes.

I sat up and squinted, trying to get my bearings.

"Dan?" I called out hesitantly. Shading my eyes against the brightness, I saw my husband standing by his dresser, an intricately carved nineteenth-century Fujian province chest, tugging off his socks. That wasn't an activity that typically required a thousand watts of illumination. Usually when Dan came home late, he undressed by the soft glow from the bathroom light. But tonight he'd blasted on the overheads—and not bothered about the Auto-Glo dimmer dial, either.

"What's going on?" I asked groggily.

Dan turned around, his face a frozen mask of anger. "You went to Chauncey's office this afternoon. Why the hell did you do that?" His voice was icy and deadly soft. I could hear the steel edge of rage under the coldly modulated tone.

"I wanted to talk to him," I said lamely.

"We all talked together this morning. Then you charged in on him later, looking like something the cat dragged in."

Is that how Chauncey had described me? One wet Escada skirt and suddenly I was challenging Courtney Love for top spot on the world's worst-dressed list? But that was beside the point.

"Chauncey needed to know some things," I said stoically. "I just wanted to help."

"Don't." Dan spat out the word like a bullet. "Don't help." His face was rigid with anger, deep lines etched into his cheeks. He slammed the dresser drawer—not a way to treat a nineteenth-century original—and as he stormed toward the bed, I recoiled against the pillows, reflexively raising my hands to my chest as if to protect myself.

Dan stopped. "Scared of me?" he asked.

I tried to recover quickly because I hadn't meant to cower. Hadn't meant to act like I was afraid of my husband. But Dan had seen the panic.

"Of course I'm not scared of you." I got out of bed, knees shaking. "You just startled me, that's all. Turning on the lights. Acting so angry. That's it. I'm sorry if my going back to Chauncey annoyed you. But it wasn't a big deal. I don't know why you're so upset."

"You don't?" Dan picked up a pillow handmade from the remnant of a Tunisian rug and threw it against the headboard. "This is my case and my problem and Chauncey happens to be my lawyer. If you have doubts, tell me, not him."

"No doubts," I said.

"Bullshit, Lacy. That's bullshit." He stood on the opposite side of the bed, glaring across the huge distance that separated us. "Chauncey told me exactly what you said. You've been checking up on me. So what's the real story, Lacy? You think I did it? You think maybe the police are right?"

"Of course not." I should have gone over and taken his hand. Given him a hug. Anything to make the assurance seem real. But instead I stood where I was, my arms folded tightly in front of my chest.

Dan hesitated, staring at me like he barely knew who I was. Or maybe that's how he thought I was looking at him.

"Do you want me to move out?" he asked.

I teetered slightly. "Why would you do that?"

"If you think I'm guilty, I should get the hell out of here. Leave tonight. Right now. Okay? Let's decide." He folded his arms in front of his chest, unconsciously mirroring me.

We stood there facing each other. Is that what eighteen years of marriage got you? Doubts, anger, guilt—and a husband storming out in the middle of the night? I bit my lip and felt tears stinging my eyes. No, we also had love and friendship, three kids, good sex, and an original Jasper Johns hanging in the foyer. That had to add up to something.

"There's nothing to decide. I want you here," I said. Whatever my doubts, he was my partner. For life. "All I was trying to do was get some evidence for our side. For your side. That's all." The tears splashed against my cheeks, and I wiped at them furiously with the back of my fist.

"I hate thinking that I'm ruining your life," Dan said, but the anger had ebbed out of his voice. He couldn't bear it when I cried.

"You'll ruin my life if you leave. I was a silly girl from Ohio when we met. You were a smart boy being bullied by your father. Everything we have we've built together."

"Oh God, Lacy." Dan sat down on the edge of the bed, and I saw his lip trembling. My stoic husband, who never revealed emotion. Dan the Doctor, who'd learned to keep his feelings under control and never admit vulnerability to anyone, including me. A trembling lip wasn't much after all this, but it pierced my heart as surely as if he'd thrown himself at my feet, begging for love.

"I want everything to be right for us, don't you know that?" I asked, coming over to sit next to him. "I'm sorry if I upset you today. That's not what I had in mind."

"Then stop playing detective. Don't check up on me."

"I promise," I said softly.

Dan wrapped his arms around me, and when I buried my head in his chest, he held me even tighter. Just like in the old days. I leaned into him, clenching him fervently. I didn't want him ever to leave me. However embattled we were, we had to trust in the other's devotion.

"Kiss me," Dan whispered, and I didn't need any encouragement. His anger and my fear had turned to mutual desire. I slipped my bare leg over his and inched my hips closer, trying to erase any space between us.

"Hold me, I need you close," I said. Then, meaning it devoutly, I added, "I love you."

"I love you, too." He leaned into me, pushing me back onto the pillows. Then he was lying on top of me and we were kissing and groping so hungrily we could have been back at the Sunset Vue Motel. Dan tugged at the blue silk camisole I was wearing, yanking it over my head, and for the first time in all these weeks, I felt the heat of my husband's naked chest searing into mine. He dropped his head to my breasts, gently kissing them, then painted circles with his tongue, faster and faster, until my whole body was aching for him.

"Oh God, I want you," I said, pressing hard against him, and he said, "You have me."

Dan's lips lingered on my skin, and his hands moved from my back so he could continue massaging my breasts. Then he turned his attention upward, his fingers slipping slowly toward my neck. . . .

My neck.

I froze. All the eager passion drained from my body and I felt myself turn to stone. *Don't touch me there*, I thought. I tried to sit up, but Dan's full weight was pressing against me and I braced myself not to flinch as his fingers flitted at the suddenly overly sensitive, soft space under my chin.

"Come here," I whispered to him urgently. "Come kiss me." If he moved away from my neck, maybe I could lose myself in his embrace.

Dan stretched his long body over mine and our lips connected and our eyes locked. But instead of my husband's face, all I could see was Tasha Barlow—alive, then dead. Dead and strangled and pale. Thumbprints left at her neck.

I closed my eyes, willing the images to go away but not able to make them disappear.

"I want to make love to you," Dan said, not yet noticing that my lust had drained away and that I was suddenly cold and tense.

For an answer I swayed my hips, avidly pretending an ardor that I didn't feel. I couldn't push Dan away. Not now, when we fervently needed to connect. Dan wanted to know his wife loved and trusted him, and I was desperate for proof, any proof, that my husband hadn't changed from the caring, honorable man I'd vowed to love and cherish. If a little married sex could make us believe in each other again, I was all for it.

I dug my fingers into Dan's back. He slid into me, and a moan escaped my lips—a mix of passion and panic as I wondered what would happen next.

Chapter Seven

I *woke up the next morning* with Dan asleep next to me, his arm gently encircling my waist and his warm breath tickling my ear. I lay still for a while, staring at the luminescent digits on the Bose clock radio, hoping they'd be hypnotic enough to put me back to sleep. No luck. By the time they'd changed from 7:01 to 7:09, I was as tense as a violin string and ready to pop.

I got out of bed because even though it was Saturday, I had to get to work. Roy Evans had left three messages to confirm that I'd be coming by at ten that morning to look at his apartment and lay out floor plans. I slipped quietly into the bathroom and turned on the water in the granite shower, swiveling the oversized nozzle that promised to make you feel like you were frolicking in a tropical rain. Seventy-five jets of water releasing three gallons per minute to rejuvenate body and spirit. Or at least get you wet really fast.

I adjusted the spray from AERATE TO MASSAGE and let the water throb against my back. Dan had made it pretty clear last night that he saw my role in this drama as supportive wife. He didn't want me checking up on him or acting like an extra on *Law & Order*. But as I scrubbed my elbows with the Guatemalan loofah (much gentler than the regular ones), I convinced myself that visiting Roy wasn't a problem. Even Dan would understand that was decorating, not detecting.

Still, I didn't mention where I was going when I left to meet Roy at his apartment in Venice, just a few miles from where Tasha Barlow had lived. Once Venice had been the funky, eclectic beach

town where outcasts and druggies drifted when they had too
many tattoos, too little money, and too much interest in bongs.
Now the boardwalk was a mecca for tourists to visit on a sunny
Sunday so they could marvel at the weird collection of fire eaters,
crocodile walkers, and Muscle Beach boys who still gathered.
Shops offering tongue piercing or full-body tattoos lined the
beach, but incense was no longer as popular as T-shirts and cheap
jewelry. It was Disney on the Pacific.

Away from the water, Venice was a charming jumble of neigh-
borhoods. Twenty years living in L.A. and I'd never actually seen
the canals, but now I drove down some narrow, one-way streets,
admiring the '20s and '40s Spanish bungalows, Craftsman-style
cottages, and stately, turn-of-the-century homes. Maybe decorating here wouldn't be so bad.

Though I should have known. When I got to Roy's address, the
building was recent vintage, white brick and nondescript, teetering
unattractively a few blocks from the beach. I made my way upstairs and rang the bell. The door was answered so quickly that the
woman who opened it might have been standing there waiting for
me.

Instead of saying hello, she just stared at me, and I returned the
favor. I tried to keep my eyes on her face, but it wasn't easy since
her plunge-neck lace shirt revealed a cleavage so enormous that it
must have put a serious dent in the world's supply of silicone.
Some unnatural substance had been injected into her lips, too,
which were puffy and painted with sparkling gold gloss. I worried
that if she stepped outside into the sun, she'd start to melt.

Apparently she wasn't too impressed with my looks, either,
since she glanced at my Lilly Pulitzer capris and Gucci flats with
undisguised distaste.

"I'm looking for Roy Evans," I told her politely. "I'm Lacy
Fields."

"I know who you are," she said snappishly, her low voice whiny and irritated. "Come in. Don't worry, I was just leaving." She blinked her eyes, thickly streaked with purple kohl liner top and bottom and enhanced with too-long fake lashes. Maybe the right makeup for a porn video but a little much for a morning at home.

"You don't have to go," I said, but she bumped against me as she sashayed into the hall, the four-inch spike heel on her orange-jeweled strapped sandal grazing against my ankle. If I hadn't just seen those shoes for five hundred bucks at the Helmut Lang store, I'd have figured she'd found them in a Hollywood dumpster outside Trashy Lingerie.

She strutted away down the hall. Her ample, well-toned butt swung from side to side with each step, every curve evident through her leopard-print Spandex skirt. I wasn't the only one watching her grand exit.

"Some body on that woman, don't you think?" purred a mellow voice next to me.

I jerked around to see Roy standing in the doorway, a contented smile on his face. He put a solid arm around me and then, looking me up and down lasciviously, added, "And some body on this woman, too."

I gave a little smile but quickly erased it, not wanting him to see that I was briefly grateful for the compliment. Falling for Roy's flattery would be like confusing a wolf whistle with a love song.

With a firm grip on my elbow, Roy propelled me over the threshold and closed the door with a decisive snap of the deadbolt. I noticed that he was freshly shaved and showered and smelled lightly of Burberry aftershave.

"You look gorgeous," he said, giving me a half hug.

Once flattered, twice prepared. I stepped away from him, not returning the affection. "I didn't mean to scare away your friend," I said.

"Nothing scares her away," Roy said with a laugh. "That was Deanna. The woman who expects to be the next Mrs. Roy Evans.

And whose antics ended my marriage to the last Mrs. Evans."

"Oh, well then, all the more reason. I mean, we're decorating, and if she's going to be spending a lot of time here—"

"She'd like to spend *all* her time here," Roy said, interrupting me with a chuckle. "Great va-va-voom body, don't you think? And great party girl. PAR-TEE. But not much heft in the brains category."

"Generous heft in other categories," I offered.

"You bet." Roy chuckled again. "I've lusted after her tits and ass for years."

"Known her a long time?"

"Since high school," Roy said. "She wouldn't go out with me because I wasn't cool enough. Her breasts weren't quite so big in those days. But lately my bank account's gotten as inflated as her breasts—and bam. We meet again."

"Best reason to be on television," I said. "You finally get the girl who ignored you in high school."

Roy laughed. "Once I hit the network, she started waving her booty at me. And wavin' and wavin'. That snagged me pretty fast."

Booty and breasts sounded like the perfect basis for a Hollywood marriage. I gave Deanna good odds. Plenty of women had made it down the aisle on a lot less.

"Is she in the business?" I asked.

"Dirty business," Roy said with a wink.

Okay, I was pretty much done with Deanna. "Well, time to get to work," I said. "Let's look at this condo of yours."

I started walking around, taking it all in, even though there wasn't much to see. Boxy rooms. No charm. Decent windows and good light, but not much else. Roy had moved into a building that had nothing to recommend it. Through the living room windows, the Pacific was just visible in the distance, and Roy had probably picked the place figuring the ocean view would impress his friends. And it might—if they had high-magnification binoculars.

"Great views, huh?" Roy said predictably, trailing behind me.

"Great," I echoed.

I strolled around the living room, trying to get inspired. Not much to do with the green velveteen sofa. Or the worn and slightly chipped wood-framed mirror that had vague pretensions of being early American.

"I bought that in an antiques store in Vermont," Roy said, when he saw me looking at the mirror. "Very classy, don't you think? Very expensive."

So that was it. He wanted to buy some class but was clueless about quality. Or value.

"Classy as long as we stick with originals," I said. "No more reproductions."

"But that is—"

"A reproduction," I said firmly. "We need to think about getting a few terrific pieces. Maybe a Louis XVI console with a marble top for the entryway. I just saw one at Sotheby's. If you don't mind the price, it definitely makes a statement."

He nodded. "I'd go for that. What else?"

"We splurge on a few good pieces and save by using items you already have."

Roy pointed to the sofa, but I shook my head. Green velveteen wasn't in my plan. Nor was the leather ottoman with a switch on the side in front of it.

"Massaging chair," Roy said, flipping the toggle. "Sit down and you'll see how good it feels."

I shook my head. "No thanks."

"Women love it," Roy said.

I shook my head again. But Roy took a step closer and leaned against me. His motion was so quick and natural that I couldn't really say he pushed me down—but suddenly I was sitting on the vibrating ottoman, and when I tried to stand up again, his hands on my shoulders were just heavy enough that I stayed where I was.

"Tell me what you know about Tasha Barlow's murder," he said. His tone was no longer that cozy conversational singsong he'd mastered, and his eyes boring down on me had turned mean.

"Not a thing, really." I sat very still—or as still as I could with a square of leather throbbing under me—trying to stay cool.

"But you're trying to find out. Snooping around. Thinking maybe you'd like to pin it on me instead of your husband?"

"It's not my job to pin it on anybody," I said shakily. "I just came over here to help you decorate."

He snorted but let go of my shoulders, and I stood up.

"Then let's decorate," he said, his voice back to normal. I wondered for a moment if I'd imagined the threatening tone. "Come see my bedroom."

Normally, that offer would have been easy to resist. And given what had just happened, maybe I should have escaped while I could. But no, I shouldn't be melodramatic. I'd come here for a reason, and something told me that the key to Tasha's killing was as likely to be found in Roy's king-sized bed as anywhere else.

I took a deep breath. *He likes kinky stuff,* Nora had said. And sure enough, instead of a welcome mat, the doorway to the bedroom boasted a pair of upended spiked sandals, the heels so long, sleek, and sharp they might have been miniature daggers. Next to them, a shiny purple garter belt with a sheer stocking dangling from it hung tantalizingly over a knob. Roy obviously hadn't bothered to clean up from his long night with Deanna, and the remnants were everywhere. On the imposing mahogany four-poster bed, a tangle of twisted black satin sheets trailed off the side like an overturned trellis, and heaps of pillows lay piled at odd angles. Two empty bottles of Mumms champagne and a half-empty bottle of Absolut Citron vodka littered the floor, along with a couple of shot glasses and a wine flute stained with crimson lipstick. Another wineglass—which had seemingly been shattered against the wall—lay in a thousand pieces on the blue carpet. The sweetly pungent, acrid smell that hovered in the room was partly explained by the burned-down nubs of expensive candles and cheap incense. The discarded butts of hand-rolled weed flung carelessly around probably accounted for the rest.

It took me a minute to notice a woman's stocking flying proudly from one of the posts of the bed, and a long, pale pink scarf waving like a flag from another.

Roy gave an evil chuckle when he caught me staring at the suggestively decorated posts. "Deanna likes it rough. And I want my Deanna happy, you know? Because she's a nasty girl. And I like my girls nasty."

Unwittingly, I took a step back. What was going on here? Roy had worked so hard to seem smooth and sophisticated in our first meeting, and now all pretense was gone. Did he have some reason for letting me see his lustful side—or was he just feeling invincible from his night of drinking and pot smoking and wild sex?

"So," I said brightly, standing solidly on my flat pink Guccis. "Decorating ideas. Let's think about what you need." I paused. My standard question to clients, "What do you do in the bedroom?," usually got a laugh. But that was from my usual roster of suburban wives who sometimes wrote their thank-you notes in bed (they could use a small desk) or liked to read the newspaper there (ditto a comfortable chair). But I didn't dare raise the topic with Roy, whose boudoir behavior clearly included more variety acts than an old Ed Sullivan show.

"Let's see, what do I need in here?" Roy asked in a deep, suggestive voice. "Well, let me show you what I collect."

"A collection is wonderful!" I said eagerly, as if he'd just produced a dozen Fabergé eggs. "I know one house that has a whole room just for Elvis mementos. A client of mine had every *Sports Illustrated* swimsuit issue—so I framed them and displayed them in a glass-fronted case." I grinned wickedly to let Roy know that whatever he collected, he couldn't shock me.

"Then can I interest you in a little S-and-M display?"

My heart thumped a little harder than I wanted it to. *He likes to tie people up*, Nora had said. And where exactly could that lead?

"Historical S-and-M artifacts can fetch thousands these days," I said primly. "They're treated as serious antiques."

Without a word, Roy reached under the bed, felt around in the mess of sheets and soiled tissues, and pulled out what looked like a dog collar.

I swallowed hard. Maybe I could be shocked. This was a long way from Elvis in sequins. Roy held the piece out for me as if he were displaying the Hope diamond, but in this case it was a pale blue circle of leather, encrusted with colored stones in gaudy shades of purple and turquoise and yellow. A slim piece of leather—a very short leash, in dog terms—was attached, and ended in an odd metal ring.

"So what would you do with something like this?" he asked. "A little too nice for a display case, I think. It needs to be used."

I looked at it again. Definitely not a Fabergé egg. "I don't really know what it is," I admitted, though I had a pretty good idea.

He turned it around and around in his hands—he had delicate fingers for such a big man—then sauntered over to the far wall and snapped the metal hook into a grommet I hadn't previously noticed. The collar hung there like some odd, ugly necklace.

"I have more, lots more," Roy said. "Better than a Picasso for decorating, if you ask me. Though with all the naked women in his pictures, I'd bet the old boy liked S and M himself, don't you think?"

I didn't really have an opinion, though I'd definitely check out *Les Demoiselles d'Avignon* a little more carefully next time I went to the Museum of Modern Art.

"Come here," he said. "You have to look at this closely."

I took a few hesitant steps, and I was just saying, "So what do you think—" when he put his arm around me again and I felt his warm skin rubbing against my bare arm and then all of a sudden—

SNAP.

I felt like I was gagging and I gasped for air, not completely sure what had happened. A second ago I'd been examining the gaudy collar and now my face was pushed against the wall, the collar nowhere in sight, and I couldn't move.

And then I got it. The collar was around my neck.

Behind me, I heard Roy laugh. "Some people like it forward and some like it backward," he said. "I think it's quite attractive on you this way."

I tried to turn around but there wasn't any give in the leather, and the ugly, cheap stones cut sharply into my neck. I reached up to feel if there was blood and tears popped into my eyes.

"You okay?" Roy asked.

"Take this off me." I thought I was screaming, but my voice came out in a throaty whisper.

"Of course I will," Roy said heartily. "But I want you to get the whole picture. You believe in originals? This is original. And historic. Very nineteenth century. King Charles the Fifth was quite involved with sadomasochism, I've heard."

"Charles the Fifth was fourteenth century," I whispered. "Hundred Years' War and all that. You're probably thinking of King *George* the Fifth."

"Thank you for correcting me."

"It could have been Henry the Eighth," I said, babbling on. Maybe if I kept talking, I could pretend that nothing so awful was happening. "He was sixteenth century, but he had a lot of wives, so he probably liked—"

"Sex," Roy said, interrupting. "He liked sex. And so did Napoleón. What century was he?"

"Late eighteenth," I said, even though I knew Roy was mocking me now. Why was I discussing the kings of England when I was bound to the wall?

"How come you know so much?" Roy asked. He was standing too close, breathing into my face, and I thought I could smell the alcohol on his breath, barely masked by a haze of peppermint Altoids. "You're just a smarty-pants, huh?"

"Roy," I said softly, trying not to panic. "Take this off me. Right now. It's not funny."

"Not until you tell me how you know so much," he said, hissing through his teeth. I had a feeling he wasn't talking about the kings of England anymore. "In fact, not until you tell me everything you know."

"I don't know much at all," I said.

"Oh, you do. Or you think you do. And you're hiding something from me. Which makes you a bad girl who needs to be punished."

Just like Tasha was punished?

My teeth chattered, even though the room was hot.

"This hurts. You've got to get it off me," I said. I heard an edge of desperation creeping into my voice—which might be exactly what Roy enjoyed. I tried to change tactics, sound less scared. "I'll find you more antique collars, if you want. Charles, Henry, Napoleón. We'll go to Sotheby's." Calm, calm, calm. "We could go this afternoon." Was I really trying to get out of this bind by promising him expensive antiques?

"This afternoon? Maybe. Depends what happens before then." Roy made a show of looking at his watch. And then he was gone. Out of the room.

"Roy?" I called.

But there was silence. I thought I heard the front door open and close again.

"Roy!" I tried to scream, but my throat was dry. I couldn't see anything except the wall in front of me. I was in a bind—quite literally. *Don't panic*, I thought, but I was already gasping for breath, hyperventilating. If I collapsed, I would probably strangle on this horrible contraption. My whole body trembled in terror. I felt like a fish flopping helplessly at the end of a line—shocked, sensing the end.

Pull yourself together, I told myself sternly. *There has to be something you can do.*

I raised my hands above my head, feeling for the connection that bound me to the wall. The hook was solid metal, and no matter how I twisted and turned, I couldn't budge it. I ran my fingers carefully along the length, hoping for a loose link. Nothing but a tiny keyhole. And I definitely didn't have the key.

I could start screaming. There were probably six condos on this floor, and somebody would have to hear. Didn't people in condo buildings always complain about noisy neighbors? I strained at the collar, trying to look around the room. Despite the drawn shades, small patterns of sunlight peeked in from the corners of the three big windows, offering a dance of color in the center of the otherwise darkened room. Three windows. Three walls with windows. That meant none of those walls was shared with neighbors. And the only other wall, the one where I stood, abutted Roy's living room.

If Roy was an S-and-M freak, he'd picked his apartment well— a back bedroom where nobody could hear you scream.

Somebody had to live downstairs. I stomped on the floor as hard as I could, but the beige wall-to-wall carpet underfoot muffled the sound, and my flat heels weren't making much of an impact. I tried one additional blow, but my foot landed so hard that I slipped and the collar snapped against my neck with whiplash force.

"Owwwwww," I heard myself howl, as tears began running down my cheeks.

Is this how Tasha Barlow had died? Victim of some sick practical joke? Or had she been a happy participant in Roy's deviance, only to have something go dramatically wrong with their bizarre sex play? Strangled on a dog collar. That was a headline the newspapers would like.

I closed my eyes, trying to be rational. Roy wouldn't leave me here to die. Whatever drugs had stoked him this morning had to wear off. Tasha had been strangled in her own apartment, and Roy was barely willing to admit knowing her. My turning up dead in his silent back bedroom would be worse. A definite crimp in his network career.

How long would I stand here? Time stopped meaning anything. Five minutes passed, maybe, or twenty. I heard the door open and close again, and then Roy was standing beside me.

"What are you still doing here?" he asked, with a big smile.

I didn't say anything.

He looked at my red eyes and tear-streaked face and said, "Oh no, Lacy, I'm sorry. You didn't realize this was a joke?" He leaned over to the ledge that was easily reachable from where I was standing and stood up, holding a key in the palm of his hand. "The key was right here. I figured you'd get it in a minute."

He unlocked the chain and I was free. I stood there rubbing my neck, backing slowly away from him and into the living room. The key hadn't been there. No way. I'd examined every inch of the room that I could see or reach while he was gone.

"Hey, I didn't mean to scare you." He touched my fingers and smiled ingratiatingly, the charming network guy again.

"Then what were you doing?" I asked. I sat down on the sofa, too traumatized to leave. I knew I should run out of the apartment and never seen Roy Evans again—but part of me needed to hear his explanation.

"Oh, one of those candid camera things. Reality TV's very popular these day. I thought I'd try it out for my show. I figured you'd ace this 'cause you're such a smarty-pants."

I knew he was lying. And he knew that I knew. It would be easy to dismiss Roy Evans as a psychopath. But he was something much more frightening. A clever and careful manipulator, in complete control of his own game.

"Well, anyway," he said easily, "you should be careful. You don't want to get yourself into any more bad situations."

So he was trying to scare me off something. With Dan, that made two men who didn't want me snooping around. Had Roy set up this scene with collar and lock? Planned it? Or was it spontaneous—sparked by his coked-up conscience?

I couldn't stand this. I jumped up and walked to the door. "I've gotta go," I said.

He looked casually over at me. "Not yet," he said. "You have something to give me. Something of mine. I'd like to get it."

"I don't have anything of yours," I said. I tried the door, but it was bolted, and I fumbled with the locks.

"The package Nora gave you. You didn't know I knew about that, but I know a lot, Lacy. I know what you've been doing." He was walking toward me, slowly, stepping closer and closer. "Now, the package. A shopping bag, I think she said. I'd like it right now."

I held on to the door handle. "I don't have it," I said.

"Where is it?" His voice had taken on its threatening edge again.

"I threw it out," I said, going for the bald-faced lie.

The shopping bag. After I'd left Nora yesterday to drive to the beach, I'd been so upset that I'd forgotten all about the bag she'd given me. *Roy's things*, she'd said. What he'd left behind in the apartment. There'd been some clothes, as I remembered, and his tapes. I was supposed to deliver them to Roy. And I could, since the bag had to be in my car trunk still. I hadn't thought about it again until this moment.

"I put it out for garbage," I said, suddenly realizing that if Roy wanted his things this badly, there must be a reason for me to hold on to them. "You know, at home in Pacific Palisades, where I live. They pick up on our street on Tuesdays and Fridays, so it's gone by now. We have recycling, too, but that's on Wednesdays—and half the time I forget, anyway." I'd read once that if you were lying, you should keep the story simple. No elaborations. But I couldn't stop myself.

"Dan hates it when I don't separate the plastics and the metals and sometimes he'll go through the garbage to make sure I didn't throw out any recyclable newspapers," I said, ranting on. "But I'm pretty sure he didn't search this time. He's stopped. I mean I probably convinced him that one trashed Diet Pepsi bottle isn't going to cause global warming, you know?"

I'd gotten the bolt unfastened, and now I opened the door. "Sorry about the package," I said hastily. "I didn't want it and didn't think you would. I only took it because Nora insisted."

And I fled down the hall, following the path that Deanna had taken what seemed like hours ago, and hoping that once again Roy wouldn't bother to follow.

I drove recklessly up the Pacific Coast Highway, wanting to get far away as fast as I could. My hands shook so violently on the wheel that I knew I should pull over and try to compose myself, but I didn't bother because I figured it might be months before I could calm down. A few miles up, I saw a sign inland that must have registered on my subconscious the last time I drove by here on the way to Malibu, and I pulled off at the next exit, making my way through unfamiliar streets in a warehouse district. I stopped in front of a long, rectangular cement structure with the huge blue lettering above it that I'd noticed from the highway—SELF STOR-AGE. I drove around a couple of times, not seeing an entrance, but then I spotted an asphalt path and figured there had to be a door at the other end, so I abandoned my car and ran inside. An old Korean man in a tiny front office barely looked up when I asked about the facilities. He pointed to a hand-printed cardboard sign on the peeling wall that outlined storage-room sizes and prices. I picked the smallest and cheapest and handed him cash in exchange for a key.

"Pay each month by third day or items thrown away," he said in broken English.

"Sure," I said.

I dashed back to the car to retrieve the shopping bag, and when I walked in again, the Korean was doing a crossword puzzle and never glanced at me. Did he ever wonder what was hidden away in this storage? Stolen diamonds? Desiccated corpses? An ill-gotten Louis XIV chair with matching ottoman? Maybe he kept duplicate keys so he could prowl through when everyone was gone.

Hurrying down the dank cement hallway made me think of the L.A. jailhouse, and I envisioned the circle of hell reserved for designers of jails and storage facilities. The dark, labrynthine corridor was cracked and uneven, and was it my imagination or were there odd, squealing sounds emanating from behind some of the lockers? No, the noises were coming from the ceiling. I looked up and a dark, swooping shadow seemed to lurch down from the rafters. Bats. It had to be bats. I instinctively swung up my arms to protect my face, forgetting that I was still holding the shopping bag, and the hard-edged tapes on the bottom smashed into my rib cage.

"Owww!"

For the second time that day, I uttered a shrill bark of pain, and this time it reverberated in the concrete corridor—"*Ow! Ow! Ow!*" With adrenaline surging, I started to run, the sounds of my own terrified breaths echoing obtusely in my head. The Whole Foods bag had been ignored, lost from both my memory and sight, but now at every step I expected to confront an enemy desperate to grab it away.

Finally reaching my three-by-five cubicle, I fumbled with the key until the door creaked open, then shoved the parcel inside. Safe. Bitter saliva filled my mouth, like I might throw up, and I leaned my forehead against the cold concrete, trying to calm down. I rubbed a tentative finger on my rib cage. Sore but not broken. Without my hysterical sounds, the corridor was quiet, and no bag-snatching specters lunged from the shadows. Emboldened, I unlocked the storage safe again and pawed through the bag. Unlikely that Roy had risked his reputation this morning to get back a pair of Cole Haan shoes and a couple of suits—even if they offered pretty good evidence that he'd spent a lot of time at Tasha's. Most of the tapes and DVDs were neatly marked with the date and the name of a segment from *Night Beat*—presumably one featuring Roy. But anything could have been taped over. And at least three of the tapes had had their labels ripped off and looked a little more beaten up than the others.

Then something chewed at the back of my mind. Nora had said that Roy liked to watch videos of himself. Liked to watch them in bed with Tasha. But maybe all the tapes he screened weren't network quality. I thought of Deanna, who paraded out this morning looking like a porn queen. Is that how Roy Evans chose his women? Could it be that he made his own hardcore videos? And what if one of his home movies costarred Roy Evans with Tasha Barlow?

I considered lugging the tapes back home so I could watch, but there was no way—not right now, with my promise to Dan. And not with the kids around. Roy's secret—if he had one—would have to stay in this cubicle for now, protected by a flimsy key that I dropped in my Fendi wallet and by a Korean who couldn't care less.

Chapter Eight

When I got home, all I wanted was a hot bath. I felt chilled to the bone. The sleek brass Brookstone barometer-thermometer-hygrometer by the front door reported that the temperature was sixty-two degrees—nippy for L.A., but probably not an explanation for why I was trembling like a six-year-old in a spelling bee.

Grant clambered down the stairs to the front hall when he heard me come in, then paused a few steps from the bottom.

"You okay, Mom?" he asked, looking at me, concerned.

I tried to stand up straight and not sway like a flag in Dodger Stadium—even though my eyes were red, my face was white, and my mood was blue. All I managed was a little nod.

"You sure?" he asked. He'd started to hold out a paper to me, then pulled it back, probably figuring I didn't have the strength to take it.

"I'm fine," I said firmly. If I didn't have kids, I'd probably have collapsed into a mewling heap about now, but in front of my son, I couldn't/shouldn't/wouldn't fall apart. No way I'd make Grant face a weeping woman when he needed a mature mom.

I gestured toward the paper. "What have you got there?"

Grant took a moment, seemed to decide I must be fine, then jumped down to the landing with a thud. "I found the guy you wanted," he said.

I hadn't put down my keys yet, but I took the picture he held out for me and looked at it. Nothing too striking—just the blurry image of a man walking out of a courthouse, holding a sweater at an odd angle in front of him. Then I realized it was draped over his wrists, probably to hide handcuffs.

"Johnny DeVito?" I asked.

"Johnny DeVito," Grant confirmed.

I looked again. So there he was—the ex-con lover boy. The man Nora claimed had loved Tasha—and who had definitely bought her some darn nice bedroom furniture. He had his head cocked down, but I could see the outline of his face, which seemed puffy and slightly distorted. Not ugly, the way Nora had said, but not quite right, either.

"Found it online, and I blew it up so you could see him better," Grant said. "It was a really distant shot. Sorry about the bad quality."

The picture was fuzzy, the features slightly blurred. Grant's sophisticated laser printer could definitely spit out a better image than that—I knew because I'd paid for a lot of pixels—so the problem had to lie with the original source. Probably a newspaper, which meant that at some point, Johnny DeVito had made news.

I held the picture up to the light. "I wish I could make out more," I admitted. "Looks like someone whitewashed his face."

Grant shrugged. "I know, kind of strange, isn't it. But it was the only picture I could find of him anywhere. And I spent a long time looking."

"I didn't mean for you to do that," I said, suddenly back in suburban mother mode. "You have so much else to do that's important. Your SATs. Your math test . . ." I let my voice trail off because I couldn't get up my usual anxiety about Grant's calculus grades.

"I'd be glad to *flunk* math if it would get Dad cleared," Grant said, with more emotion in his voice than usual.

"An F won't help anything," I said, but then I let it drop. School might have been important on a planet long ago and far away, but since the murder investigation, we'd all been transported to another galaxy, where the old rules didn't apply.

Grant shoved his hands into the pockets of his cargo pants. "So can you find out more about this guy?" he asked. "Prove he did it?"

"I wish," I said with a sigh that came out louder than I'd intended. "I have some pretty good information, but Daddy's mad that I'm playing detective and he wants me to stop. I think he's wrong, but you know Daddy. He can be pretty stubborn."

Grant looked down and shuffled his feet, and I realized I shouldn't have said that. The family needed a united front. Dissing his dad wasn't part of the game.

"Does Dad know this DeVito guy?" Grant asked.

"I doubt it," I said, but then I paused and added, "You should ask Daddy." But we both knew he wouldn't.

Towering above me, Grant leaned over my shoulder to study the picture again. "You've gotten taller again," I said, turning around to eye him. "Did you shoot up another inch in your sleep last night?" I smiled and Grant just shrugged, briefly embarrassed. How disorienting to be a teenage boy, your life changing so fast you couldn't keep up with yourself. I could relate.

"I'm tall enough to beat up your Johnny if I find him," Grant said, flexing his arm, lean and muscular under his Fila tennis shirt. Facing DeVito across a net, Grant definitely had an edge. But all bets were off if the weapons were more powerful than Prince rackets.

"So tell me about the stuff you've gotten," Grant said, taking a step back and folding his arms. "The evidence that will help Dad."

Was there ever stuff I could tell. And wouldn't that be nice. I could reel off all the bizarre details of my detecting escapades, starting with Roy's dog collar, and get my intelligent son's perspective. With his scientific mind—he did get a 98 in physics, after all—he could analyze all the details and maybe come up with theory and proof. But for once, I stopped myself. Grant was already more tangled in this mess than he should be.

"The evidence is clear that Daddy's innocent," I said, going for the bottom line.

Grant sighed and rolled his eyes. "Lame, Mom."

Yup. Lame mother-talk. "But we're on the verge of a break-through," I said, trying to stay optimistic. "I have a good feeling."

"Last time you had a good feeling, I got hypothermia," Grant grumbled. "Remember that day at Bear Mountain? You told me I could leave my Polartec in the car and ski in a T-shirt. Only it snowed."

"This is different," I assured him. "Clear skies coming up."

Grant looked at me dubiously and I didn't blame him.

"By the way, a guy from FedEx delivered a couple of boxes for Dad. They're in the garage. I told him to put them there in case they were bombs or something and shouldn't be in the house."

He glared at me, daring me to challenge him, but I didn't. Given the way things had been going lately, who was to say they *weren't* bombs? Couldn't blame Grant for trying to keep one more thing from exploding in our faces.

Grant's friend Jake pulled into the driveway in his new blue Subaru Outback—finally, an L.A. kid with an appropriate car—and when the two of them left, I wandered out to the garage. Three cardboard boxes were piled in a corner, with a return address from Dan's office. I peeled the packing tape away from one of them and peeked inside. Dusty manila covers and stacks of scrawled papers gave them away as old patient files. Grant had clearly been watching too many late-night movies. Nothing here that was going to detonate.

I went back inside and escaped to the bathroom, finally able to wash away my morning with Roy Evans. I filled the deep Jacuzzi tub and poured in a few drops of Jo Malone French lime blossom bath oil, then lit the Fresh Yuzu candles I had around the ledge, fragrant with Japanese grapefruit and Sicilian lemons. It was like taking a bath at the United Nations.

By the time I got out, I smelled like a fruit salad and had managed to forget that my situation stank. Maybe that bath oil really was worth a hundred bucks. At six o'clock, I decided to give a family dinner a try. I'd always been convinced we could save civilization if every family sat together once a day, eating a meal and talking. That I didn't feel like eating and definitely wouldn't be talking wasn't going to stop me. Not up for cooking, I called Pacific Hunan and ordered a dozen dishes of Pan-Chinese food. When the delivery came, I dragged the bags to the family room and plopped the food into cheerful Fiestaware red bowls, which I arranged on the palazzo-stone table (expensive but indestructible, as I always explained to clients). I set out big linen napkins and brightly colored twisted-glass chopsticks at each place, then checked the logs in the fireplace and flipped the switch so the gas ignited and the fire came to life. Not bad. I dragged three oversized kilim pillows out of the closet, arranging them in front of the fireplace, then stepped back and took in the scene. Low-key and cozy. Very *Elle Decor*.

I called everyone in for dinner, and the stage set seemed to work. "Looks nice, Mom," Ashley said, her first pleasant comment in weeks. Grant turned on the sound track from *High Fidelity*—one CD all of us could bear. The mood was right, and in between the spring rolls and the kung pao chicken, Ashley and Grant started singing along to the Kinks' "Everybody's Gonna Be Happy." If only. Jimmy got into the spirit by showing that he could eat lo mein one strand at a time with his fingers. And I didn't even look at Dan when John Wesley Harding sang "I'm Wrong About Everything."

I brought out dessert and Jimmy grabbed a tangerine and energetically dug into it, sending the peels flying all over. Dan went for a fortune cookie and snapped it open, putting the little paper aside as he bit into the hard dough.

"Anybody want to hear my fortune?" Dan asked with a smile. "My *good* fortune."

Well, that got our attention.

Ashley put down her chopsticks and paused in midchew.

Jimmy, sensing an important moment, squeezed tangerine juice all over his bare foot.

"My future is looking very bright," Dan said, playing with the slip from the fortune cookie. "That's what it says. Or what it should say."

Ashley gave a little gasp—a quick intake of breath—and the expectation etched on her face was easy to read: *It's over. Daddy's going to tell us this horror is finally over.*

On the CD, Bob Dylan was crooning about his head being on straight and being strong enough not to hate.

I tried to swallow, but could hardly breathe, waiting for Dan's next words. One sentence and our lives would return to normal. Someone else had been arrested. The police had issued an apology. Tasha Barlow wasn't even dead.

"Tell us," I said, my voice shaking and small. "Tell us."

"Good news is good news," Dan said.

We waited.

Dan looked around at us proudly, enjoying his moment. Then he spoke. "Some important people saw my article on facial reconstruction and want me to write a textbook. It'll be the definitive one in the field. For Harvard University Press, no less."

Ashley uttered a loud wheeze of disappointment, and I felt like the air had been sucked out of the room. Bob Dylan was pretty pissed off himself.

I don't cheat on myself, I don't run and hide,
Hide from the feelings that are buried inside

he wailed from the CD in protest.

Ashley stood up abruptly, kicking the kilim pillow so hard that it flew into a half-eaten bowl of prawns foo yung. The shellfish slammed onto the stone table and the thick sauce oozed onto the carpet, dripping down like blood.

"We don't care about your stupid book!" Ashley yelled, her bitterness bursting back. "Who do you think will read it when you're on death row?"

She stormed out of the room, and the chain reaction that followed went pretty much as would have been expected. Jimmy burst into heaving sobs, Grant muttered an apology and excused himself, and Dan said nothing but set his lips into a firm line and started to clean up the prawns. I stood open-mouthed, unable to move. As usual, the whole disaster had been my fault. I never should have served fortune cookies.

I called Nora first thing Sunday morning.

"You talked to Roy," I said, trying not to sound accusing. "I thought you weren't planning to see him."

"Yeah, well, he called. He wanted his stuff back, but I'd already given it to you. And he told me you're not his girlfriend." She said it triumphantly, as if we'd been fighting for him, and she'd won. She could have him.

"Have you heard from Johnny DeVito?" I asked.

"No." She sniffled. "But I really need to talk to him. I left him a couple of messages, but now he changed his phone number. I found a card he sent Tasha. It probably was a long time ago because I found it with some dried flowers. I remember he'd sent her roses for her birthday. Anyway, it had a return address and I was thinking of checking it out. Seeing if I could find him. But my car's in the shop."

"Want me to drive?" I asked. Whoa. Where had that offer come from? But it was too late for me to take it back, because without hesitating, Nora said, "Sure."

An hour later, I pulled up and waved to Nora, who was waiting outside, sprawled across the top step of the apartment building. She got up slowly and ambled over to the car, wearing pale blue nylon sweatpants that stuck to her thighs and a matching jacket that hung down loosely and still managed to reveal a roll of fat at her waist. Grief hadn't made her lose her appetite.

We exchanged brief hellos, and she pulled the door closed on the Lexus, then reached for the seat belt.

"So where are we going?" I asked, ready to take off. I put the car into DRIVE and checked the rearview mirror. Nobody had followed me here. Though, come to think of it, who would?

Nora held out a slip of greasy paper and read me the address, mentioning a town I'd never heard of before.

"Is it near here?" I asked.

She shrugged. "Dunno."

I didn't ask how she'd planned to get there. Instead, I typed the address into the Direction Finder GPS on the dashboard and waited for a map to appear. I studied it for a minute. The town was in a valley on the other side of the hills and in territory I didn't know. "It'll be a long drive," I said, but neither of us was changing her mind, so I took off.

We didn't say anything as we drove, just listened for the synthetic voice on the GPS to call out directions every couple of minutes. We followed it onto a freeway. During a weekday rush hour, the eight lanes would have been packed, but this Sunday morning the road could pass for the track at Le Mans—a smattering of cars, all of them roaring at eighty-five miles per hour. I stayed in the right lane and didn't go much above sixty—okay, sixty-five—but Nora clutched the edge of her seat and looked like she might start screaming any minute.

"You okay?" I asked.

"I hate freeways," she said. "We don't have these at home."

"We're not in Kansas anymore," I said, veering around a Honda that thought the speed limit sign meant something.

"I'm not from Kansas, I'm from Idaho," she said. Either she didn't like my joke, or she hailed from the one town in the world where *The Wizard of Oz* hadn't opened yet.

We exited the freeway, following the electronic voice into a nouveau riche suburb of oversized McMansions crammed onto tiny lots. They looked cheaply built, but screamed with flamboyant flourishes like Corinthian columns, Doric arches, bulging balustrades, and Victorian finishes. Often all on one house.

"Ooohhh," said Nora, nose pressed against the window like she was on the Swingin' Safari Ride at Disneyland, "look at these. Aren't they fancy?"

More folly than fancy, but why argue? Bad taste could be purchased at any price. We turned another corner onto Hillman Drive, and I slowed down in front of number 17, the numerals visible on a small mailbox in front. The house itself sat far back on the lot, high up a steeply pitched incline. I might have loosely labeled it American Colonial (crossed with English Tudor) if not for the terraces with swirled white railings. A nice touch—if the house were perched on the edge of the Mediterranean.

"Have you ever seen anything more fabulous?" asked Nora, her hot breath making little circles of condensation on the window.

"Never seen anything like it at all," I said truthfully, pulling up next to the curb and turning off the car. Decorative brass fencing circumnavigated the house, but the driveway and the main walkway remained open. Still, no way would I try to navigate my Lexus up the steep driveway.

"Can't you get closer?" Nora asked.

"We can walk from here," I said, getting out.

She glared at me—maybe they didn't walk in Twin Falls, either—but then marched ahead. I hung back slightly as she trudged up a steep staircase, panting and puffing. Finally, on the front porch, Nora rang the bell. After a long wait while nobody answered, she rang again. And again.

"You coming up?" she asked, looking down the staircase at me. Her face was red from the exertion.

"I'll wait here. It doesn't seem like anyone's home."

"We came all this way. Someone *has* to be home!" She took a few steps back to get a view of the upper levels of the house. In an old episode of *Murder, She Wrote*, a curtain on the second floor would part just about now and then drop down again. But CBS hadn't approved this script and nothing happened. The house was quiet.

"You watch too many detective shows," I said with a wry smile. In real life, people didn't come to the door just because you showed up.

I started back down the driveway, but Nora kept her eyes on the house.

"Helloooo," Nora called out. "Hellloooo. I'm looking for Johnny. I have to talk to Johnny. I know he's there!"

Silence, silence, silence. Not even a leaf moved.

But now Nora began acting like a complete fool. "Helloooo, Johnny!" Yodeling, she leaned back to give her words more volume. "It's me, Nora! I have to talk to you! Tasha loved you! I have something important to discuss!"

I crossed my arms, waiting for her to give up. But instead I saw the front door open a crack. I caught only the vaguest glimpse of the person who answered. He stood six inches shorter and fifty pounds heavier than the man in Grant's picture. Even if Johnny DeVito had done some jail time, he couldn't have emerged that changed.

And then suddenly the door was closed again and Nora wasn't on the landing anymore.

Shocked, I started moving back toward the house, feeling as if someone had pushed a button for slo-mo replay. But in fact someone inside had pushed a different button—because as I approached the driveway, the decorative fencing groaned to life and a heavy metal gate started to close. With the two sides of the brass gate sliding together faster and faster, the passageway narrowed by the second. Once it sealed, there would be no exit.

Where did I want to be standing when the gate slammed shut?

I waited just a moment too long to make my decision—or maybe my subconscious had an opinion, because I stayed bolted to the ground. Bad choice! A second before the gate locked into place, I changed my mind and tried to dash through. But the space was so narrow even Kate Moss wouldn't fit.

"Nora?" I called out as the gate slammed shut. "Nora? Everything okay?" But my trembling voice wouldn't scare the squirrel scampering on the front yard, never mind scare up Nora.

Futilely, I pounded against the hard metal bars, then paced behind them as if planning a prison break. Only I wanted to break into the jail, not out of it. What to do? I didn't have Nora's cell phone number, so calling her was out. No way to contact the occupants of the house, either. I didn't know who lived there, and unless it was a police emergency, Pacific Bell wouldn't give a listing by address. Police emergency. Now there was an interesting option. And what exactly would I say to the police? *We came to this house and rang the bell—and now that my friend's inside, I think something must be wrong.* That would make a lot of sense.

I began walking around the perimeter of the property, my Miu Miu mules snagging on the muddy grass. The tall fence, sturdy and impenetrable, was definitely too high to climb. Not that I could anyway. High-jump over? No, I'd never quite perfected the Fosbury Flop. I glanced from the fence top to the property next door, wondering if I should venture over and attempt to talk to a neighbor. I tried to peer across the yard—but, not paying attention to where I was walking, I tripped over a tree root. My left sandal flew off my foot, I stumbled hard—and then fell, sprawling headfirst across the wet ground.

"Ouch!"

I lay still for a minute, hearing my own cry echoing, then slowly pulled myself up, trying to assess the damage. A bloody knee, mud everywhere, throbbing ankle. I rubbed it anxiously and decided it was twisted, not broken. Tentatively, I stood. Sore, but I'd live. I hobbled back to the Lexus and slid into the front seat.

And sat there. I didn't really want to abandon Nora, but how long should I stay, hoping she'd come out? In college, as I remembered, you waited fifteen minutes for the professor to show up for class, then picked up your backpack and left. In a bar on Sunset, you hung out twenty minutes expecting the blind date before bolting. Chewing through breadsticks at a fancy restaurant, you'd bide your time for half an hour before a business associate was toast. But what would the new etiquette books say about this one? *Wait forty minutes for the roommate of a murder victim to emerge from a mysterious house. If she doesn't, you're free to go home to the husband and kids!*

My swollen ankle throbbed and I wanted to get out of there. I stared out my slightly streaked driver's side window, memorizing every detail I could about the house where Nora had disappeared. Maybe I should write a note and limp over to slip it through the gate, so Nora could call me when she got out. If she got out. I shuddered. Something didn't feel right.

The passenger door opened and someone slipped into the seat next to me. I spun around, relieved to have Nora back.

"Where were you . . ." I started to ask, but the words died on my lips.

The person sitting in my car wasn't heavy, wasn't a woman, wasn't Nora. A thin, tallish man in worn blue jeans and a white shirt faced forward, not looking at me. He had an L.A. Dodgers baseball cap pulled down low over his forehead and his shirt collar was tugged up high. As I stared at him, he turned slightly toward me, but I couldn't really see his face—just my own, reflected back in his hugely oversized mirrored sunglasses.

"Drive," he said quietly.

"Who are you?" I wasn't sure whether to be confused or scared. For an answer, he flipped something in his left hand, and immediately a silver knife blade flashed in the sunshine. I gasped, but I had my answer. Scared.

But not too scared to know I had to get out of the car. One swift yank of the door, a roll to my left, and I'd be on the ground. Kick off my shoes, jump up, and run away. Fast thinking. Ready to go. One, two—kick, yank, roll . . .

"OUCH!" I screamed for the second time.

A searing pain snapped through my arm, and I lurched back against my seat. I instinctively rubbed my stinging right shoulder.

What the hell had happened?

My hand burned, and when I looked down, I gasped again. However fast I'd moved, my visitor had been faster—clamping a metal handcuff around my right wrist, chaining me to the steering wheel. I stared in disbelief. First the dog collar, now this. Was I the only one in Los Angeles County without a mania for manacles?

"Who are you?" I cried. "What do you want?"

"I want you to drive," he repeated quietly.

The sunglasses had jerked to the side and I could see gruesomely raised scars around his eyes and thick, irregular lumps along the side of his face. And then I got it. Ugly Johnny DeVito was sitting next to me.

"Start the car and let's go," he said in a low, intimidating voice that was oddly familiar.

I didn't turn the key. "Where's Nora?" I croaked. Of the fifty thousand questions in my head, that's the one that popped out.

"Doesn't matter," he said. And then in the same calm, terrifying voice he said, "Just do what I tell you."

My head was spinning, trying to formulate an escape plan. Something better than I'd managed with Roy. Driving off, maybe I could holler out the window or honk my horn to attract attention. On the other hand, safety articles always warned to kick and fight and resist right where you were. Once you'd moved to a new location a killer would be more likely to attack.

And I was pretty sure that Johnny DeVito was a killer.

He also had a knife in his hand—and now he held it flat against my bare arm. I struggled, trying to shimmy away from him, but he pushed the blade down harder until I felt the sharp edge starting to slice into my skin. Small drops of blood popped out in an even line on my upper arm.

"Stop!" I screamed. "I'll drive!"

Amazingly, he took the knife away, holding it calmly in his hand, inches away from my oozing arm. I awkwardly started the car and put my foot carefully on the gas, crawling away from the curb at five miles an hour.

"Drive normally," he said.

I didn't normally drive with a swollen ankle, a knife wound in my flesh, and my hand chained to the steering wheel. But I just nodded and increased my speed. Then it occurred to me that I was in control of the car. I could keep upping the speed—maybe smash into a telephone pole or roll the car down a hill.

No, I wouldn't do that. Not when I was chained to the steering wheel and couldn't escape. Johnny DeVito had outsmarted me. I sniffled and looked at my arm. He'd stopped before creating any real damage. Only one streak of blood had dribbled down and was pooling at my elbow.

He directed me to turn left, and I did. Then two rights and another left. Otherwise he stayed silent, still holding the knife. But at least it was in his lap, not at my face.

Human contact. Maybe that's what we needed. Make a personal connection with the killer. A while ago, it had been all over the news when a woman calmed a kidnapper by reading him *The Purpose-Driven Life*. I didn't have a book handy, but I did have a purpose—to save my life.

"I don't know this neighborhood at all," I said, trying to sound calm. My voice broke just a little, but I could do this. "Very nice. Interesting houses."

He didn't say anything, but from the corner of my eye, I saw his thumb playing with the knife blade. Not a good sign. What else could we talk about? A neutral subject.

"I see you're a Dodgers fan. Great team, don't you think? You know, my dad was originally from New York and he loved the Dodgers when they were the Brooklyn Dodgers and he refused to watch them play in L.A. Couldn't forgive them for moving. Isn't that something?"

Johnny DeVito stayed expressionless, unmoved by my dad's charms. He probably also wouldn't care that my dad had died when I was twelve—even though I cared a lot. But I didn't plan to discuss death with a man holding a knife.

New topic. Something so he wouldn't think I posed any danger to him. Which at the moment—let's face it—I didn't.

I took a deep breath. "You might be wondering how I ended up outside your house. I mean, I don't really know it's your house. It could be anyone's house. I only came because Nora wanted to. And we got here by the GPS, so I really couldn't find the place again if my life depended on it."

I gulped. Maybe my life did depend on it.

But I had no reason to stop now. I wanted to keep going. I did keep going. Without trying to look at him, I just babbled on.

"Now that you're telling me where to go, you're the GPS, if you know what I mean. Ha ha," I said. Very funny. But he didn't laugh. "Anyway, if you want me to drop you off someplace, I can do that, and then I'll just flick on the direction program and get home. We can forget all about this. Of course you'll have to take off this little handcuff." I wriggled my wrist. "Not that it's bothering me or anything, but if you get out, it would help if you take it with you."

He stared straight ahead. "Shut up," he said softly.

"Pardon me?"

"Shut up."

I clamped my mouth tight. Maybe I should have talked about the weather.

A few more minutes passed as I drove down a fairly bleak street that seemed just this side of deserted.

"Turn right at the next corner and pull over to the side. Right next to the Dumpster."

I brought the Lexus to a stop right where he told me. If he planned to murder me and throw my body into the garbage, I'd just made it very convenient for him. My mind whirled as I tried to come up with options, but I didn't see any. Johnny held the knife at the ready again.

With the motor off, the silence was startling.

"I saw what your husband did to my Tasha," Johnny DeVito said, in his low, growling voice. "I should do the same thing to you." He suddenly swatted his right hand across my face—not a strike so much as a full-on push, as if he were throwing a banana cream pie at me. He crushed his fingers—surprisingly smooth— against my nose and ground his palm into my lips. I tried to bare my teeth and bite him, but he gave a final angry shove and pulled back his hand. My pink twelve-hour-formula lipstick was now smeared on his palm, and that seemed to infuriate him. He slapped me twice hard across my chin and cheeks. I felt tears spring to my eyes.

With a deep, vile sneer, Johnny sat back and brandished the knife.

"He humiliated her. Exposed her. Same for you. Take off your pants," he said.

I stared at him in shock but didn't move.

"You never listen the first time," Johnny said, and he slashed at the edge of my Donna Karan capris with his blade, slicing through the thin fabric—and grazing my skin.

I screamed—and once again, he stopped.

"Take them off or I cut them off," he said. "The top, too."

Shaking and crying, I wriggled out of the bottoms and fumbling with my free left hand, started to unbutton my blouse.

Johnny stared at me, open-mouthed. The black silk embroidered La Perla bra with its sheer netting underneath was meant to cause exactly that expression on men, but right now I would have been happier wearing a Hanes T-shirt. He hadn't noticed the panties yet, which were sheer in the back and had a matching lace ruffle across the front.

I tried to look businesslike, as if I weren't stripping for a man with a knife.

"I can't get the shirt off over the handcuffs," I said.

"Do the best you can."

I took off one sleeve, then let the other drop down until it was caught at the steering wheel. Johnny nodded, then leaned over and with a small key snapped open the lock. He threw the shirt and pants in the backseat and held the knife at my leg.

"Get out of the car," he said. "Now."

This time I decided to listen the first time. I flung open the door and jumped out. Without looking back, I started running away from the car, moving as fast as I could on my aching ankle, ready to set another personal best despite my kitten-heeled mules. I would have kicked them off, but I could feel hard bits of gravel digging into the thin soles, and bare feet wouldn't make it better. So I ran. If Johnny DeVito had a gun, let him shoot me from behind. I had to get away.

But he didn't come after me. When I finally dared to look over my shoulder, the car was gone. He'd left.

I stopped running and tried to catch my breath. At first, all I felt was relief. I was out of the handcuffs and out of his clutches. He hadn't killed me. But as I kept walking, the weirdness of the new situation finally struck me. I was walking through an industrial street in five-hundred-dollar lace underwear, without a cell phone or a penny to my name. I was still half terrified that Johnny

DeVito would reappear and wreak whatever vengeance he thought I deserved for Tasha's death.

I walked in the middle of the street, waving my arms wildly at the few cars passing by. Two of them just swerved around me, one beeping loudly. Then a swarthy Hispanic man in a beaten-up white van slowed down and called out, "You okay, lady?"

"No!" I screamed to him. "I need help!"

He leaned out the window, staring at me. Maybe he'd never seen French lingerie up close before, but he didn't need to leer quite so insistently. Then the leer turned to a big grin and, sounding pleased with himself, he asked, "You competing in one of them reality shows? If so, I'm your man. Ready for the next challenge."

I shook my head. "This is real life!"

He looked up and down the street, checking for cameras, and seemed disappointed when he didn't spot any. I started walking over to the van, but he put out an arm to stop me. If he wasn't going to be on TV, he wasn't wasting his time. He drove off.

Exhausted and shaking now, I kept walking, teetering from side to side like a drunk. The slash mark on my arm had started bleeding again, but I didn't have any way to stop it. No way was I taking my bra off to use as a tourniquet.

I turned a corner and ahead of me saw a long Silver Star trailer, the kind actors use as dressing rooms on a movie shoot. Usually four or five are lined up amid miles of curling cable and glaring lights, the center of a buzz of activity. But here it was quiet. No union workers scarfing coffee and glazed doughnuts while ogling clipboard-carrying assistants in tight Seven jeans. No actors' stand-ins waiting patiently on their marks, pretending to be stars. No studio executives loitering by their limos, trying to look like they were paid to do more than show up. No sounds at all. Just a double row of orange cones that might be marking the site for future frenzy.

I walked slowly over to the trailer, carefully climbed the rickety metal steps, and knocked on the door.

A heavyset, jowly security guard in a blue-and-gold uniform opened it, and when he saw me, he laughed.

"They're not starting to shoot for another week," he said. "Mr. Clooney hasn't even arrived yet. If you want to write him a fan letter, I'll put it in his pile."

"I don't want to meet George Clooney," I said. "Actually, I've met him. Twice. But that's not why I'm here. A couple of hours ago, I was abducted and driven over here and forced to take off all my clothes. I need someone to help me."

The security guard looked mildly amused. "Abducted by aliens?" he asked.

"No. By a scarred man with a knife. A former convict."

"Aliens would be a better story," the guard said thoughtfully. "Might interest Mr. Clooney, but probably not. He seems to prefer serious topics these days. But I give you credit for trying. Once the movie starts, we get three women a day in underwear showing up trying to meet him."

"I was attacked," I said, pointing to my bloodied arm.

"Laser gun or light saber?"

"Neither. Knife."

The guard sighed. "You're not trying." He started to shut the door, but I stuck an elbow in just in time.

"Listen, my name is Lacy Fields. My husband is Dan Fields, the plastic surgeon. The alien stole my Lexus, too, and I need a car service to get home. Can you call for me? We use Royal Wheels when we're going to the airport, so I have an account with them. But any one will do. Really."

The guard looked at me in disbelief, then firmly shut the door.

I sat down on the metal trailer step. The weak sun hadn't done much to warm the plating, and I was suddenly chilled. I wrapped my arms around my middle, wondering if I could ask the guard to borrow a shirt. But he'd figure I just wanted a George Clooney souvenir to sell on eBay.

I sat for a very long time, hoping he'd made the call and waiting for a Royal Wheels Lincoln Town Car to pull up. But when a car finally glided toward me, it was a blue Chevy. And instead of a capped and uniformed limo driver, two men in slacks and shirts got out. One dough-faced, one handsome with hard eyes.

"Mrs. Fields," said one of the men, just a trace of irony in his voice. "We meet again. I'm Detective Reese. Looks like you need some help here."

But not this kind of help. Reese and Shields were the cops who had arrested my husband.

Chapter Nine

I'd been at the station house for three hours when Reese came in to say they'd found my stolen car.

"Located it around the corner from where we picked you up," he said, swinging one leg around a chair next to me. He straddled the seat, sat down, and then folded his arms over the backrest. He lowered his head so his chin was propped in his hands and his penetrating green eyes were staring into mine. A nice maneuver that he'd learned either in detective school or watching *Law & Order*.

"Was it damaged?" I asked.

"Nope, it seems to be in perfect condition." Reese blinked once, his long lashes fluttering up and down. "But given your story, it's pretty strange that we found it there, don't you think?"

"Not at all. It fits in exactly with what I told you." I tugged at the sleeve of the shapeless, vomit-green shirt Reese had given me to wear, along with matching pull-on pants that wouldn't stay up on my hips. The only other option had been an orange prison jumpsuit and I wasn't going for that. "I guess DeVito drove away after he dumped me and then got out himself."

"Getting home how?" Reese asked.

"How would I know? He got out and called someone, obviously. Didn't want to get caught in a stolen car."

"He's a thoughtful kidnapper," Reese said slowly. "He left the keys under the mat in the front seat."

I took a sip of the flat Diet Coke Detective Shields had handed me an hour ago. It was the only nice thing he'd done, other than throwing his jacket around me when I got in the backseat of the squad car. I'd asked them to take me home, but instead they'd brought me to this interrogation room in police headquarters. The gist was that if I cooperated, they wouldn't bring indecency charges.

"I was threatened. I was kidnapped. I was knifed," I explained indignantly. "That's what's indecent." By L.A. standards, my outfit wasn't shocking, anyway. A bra? Please. At least I was wearing one. Something you could rarely say for the starlets who strolled around Melrose Place on Saturday afternoons. You could see more nipples on the streets of West L.A. than on the baby-supply shelf at Walgreens.

Now Reese sighed and stretched his legs straight out in front of him. The move would have been better with a pair of cowboy boots, since all he could show off were slightly scuffed oxfords.

"Mrs. Fields, let's run through this one more time," he said. He glanced down at the yellow pad where he'd been taking notes. "You drove in your Lexus to visit a man named Johnny DeVito, but you used a GPS so you don't know how you got there. You went with Nora Wilson, the former roommate of Tasha Barlow, but she's not with you anymore. You don't know where she is. You don't know where Johnny DeVito is. All you know is you didn't like the neighborhood you visited. Badly designed houses."

"Number seventeen Hillman," I said. "I told you the address. An architectural abomination."

Reese made a little check mark on his paper, then continued. "You get to the house, which may or may not belong to this De-Vito fellow. Who, by the way, you want us to find because you think that it was him, not your husband, who killed Tasha Barlow."

"Correct," I said, nodding.

Reese looked at me for a long moment and shook his head. But he went on, this time not bothering to consult his notes. "So the woman you're with goes inside and doesn't come out. You go back to your car and a man gets in beside you. He handcuffs you to the steering wheel and makes you drive to a deserted street. Then he gets you to take off all your clothes by threatening you with a knife, but he doesn't touch you."

"Exactly," I said.

"Oh, for God's sakes," said Shields, coming into the room then. "Are we still playing this game? Hasn't she given up yet?"

"Given up what?" I asked.

"Lying," said Shields. He leaned his elbows on the table and put his doughy face close to mine. His breath smelled of garlic pizza and half-moon sweat stains darkened the underarms of his pale blue shirt. If Reese and Shields were playing good cop–bad cop, I was getting confused, since they kept switching roles. Better just to think of them as ordinary men doing their job.

I looked over to Reese, who shrugged. "It does sound strange, Mrs. Fields. Rather suspicious. Almost like you made the whole thing up."

"Right," said Shields. "Because she did make it up. She drove herself to the movie set, stripped to her underwear, and concocted the whole crazy story."

"If I made it up, how do you explain this?" I asked, pointing to my bloodied arm, which was now neatly bandaged. I'd had to sign half a dozen forms before the nurse at the police station would give me an alcohol wipe and gauze pad, and another half a dozen for a Band-Aid to put on my leg, where Johnny's knife had nicked me.

Shields gave a short laugh. "Superficial wounds," he said. "You could do them to yourself. Draw a little blood for sympathy but not cause any damage."

"And why would I do that?" I asked.

"Damned if I know," said Shields. "Maybe you're a psychopath. Or an exhibitionist. Or you just want some attention for yourself. But I can tell you this. I'm going to figure it out. And when I do, I have the feeling your husband won't be the only one behind bars."

I sat back and folded my arms. They weren't going to intimidate me. "I'm the victim here, not the perpetrator," I said.

Shields raised his eyebrows.

"You gave it a good try for an amateur," he said. "A lot of details, which is risky, and you haven't changed your story. But you want to know what gave you away? Without being rude, let me just say it. The bra and panties."

I looked at him in surprise. "What about them?"

"They match."

I blinked and sat up a little straighter. "You think I'm lying because my underwear matches?"

Shields wiped an imaginary crumb off his sleeve and then nodded. "I've been married nineteen years, so I know about ladies' underwear. And that's one fancy set you were parading. What is this, Valentine's Day? I see my wife get dressed every morning. She puts on whatever's clean, and the lacy bits get saved for a special night. So I gotta think that if that's what you put on this morning, you knew people would see it."

"I always wear nice underwear," I said staunchly, feeling a little color rising to my cheeks, "and it's usually La Perla. Sometimes I buy Cosabella, but their bikinis can be a bit tight. I almost wore a Chantelle bra this morning, but it had too much lace and you could see the pattern right through my shirt." I looked down at my chest and then back at the detectives, who probably didn't have an opinion on unsightly bra lines. "My mother always said that a woman in cheap underwear feels cheap all day. So, Detective Shields, tell your wife to get rid of the mismatched Maidenforms, and then buy her some French lingerie. If La Perla's too expensive, they make a lower-priced line called Malizia. It's usually not silk"—I lowered my voice as I revealed the secret—"but you can hardly tell the difference. And it's sexy, so you'll probably rip it off your wife pretty fast, anyway."

I stopped talking and the room fell silent. Shields shoved his pudgy hands into his pockets and took a few steps away from me. I saw Reese trying to hold back a smile.

I stood up. "So that's it. I've told you everything I know. Do you think I can leave now?"

Reese looked over at Shields, who gave a barely perceptible nod. Maybe he was afraid I'd start lecturing next on panty protectors.

"Thank you for being so forthcoming, Mrs. Fields," Reese said, standing up. "We'll go over this with our superiors and get back to you. But for now, you're free to go. Do you want to call your husband, or should I drive you home?"

Neither was a good option. All I wanted right now was to keep my misadventure quiet. Pretend it never happened.

"If you've found my car, I'll drive myself home," I said. And then, flashing what I hoped was a winning smile, I added, "I'll send you back the clothes I borrowed. And call me anytime if you have questions about lingerie."

My story stayed under wraps for barely twelve hours. First thing the next morning, my friend Molly Archer called me in a flurry.

"Lacy, if you wanted a showbiz job, you should have told me," she chided. "I would have helped. I think your escapade was just clever as could be, though I must say I was surprised you'd be doing something like that now."

"What escapade?" I asked cautiously.

"Going to George Clooney's trailer in your undies."

I swallowed. "Where'd you hear about that?"

"Hear about it? I'm looking at it. *The National Enquirer* online edition has the scoop today, and I'll bet they have it in the print edition next week."

I slipped over to my desk and typed in the site on my computer. Two clicks and there it was—a picture of me at Clooney's trailer with almost nothing on, and the headline DESPERATE HOUSEWIFE.

"Oh my God," I said.

"What's wrong?" Molly asked cheerfully. "You look to die for. Great leg definition. You must be doing yoga. Who took the picture?"

"I have no idea," I said. "The only person around was the private security guard. He must have had a camera hidden in his pocket or something when he opened the door."

"Oooh, that's who's been selling all the inside pictures to the tabs!" Molly crowed. "Darling, I'll call you right back. I want to phone George to warn him he has a mole on staff."

She hung up and I quickly read through the article, which claimed I was an older actress desperate for a part in Clooney's new movie. Standard tab tactics—start with a picture and fabricate a story. It would have been funny, but a lot of people other than Molly were going to recognize me. Last night, I'd managed to get home and change my clothes without Dan or the kids seeing me—and I still wanted to keep my misadventure to myself for a while.

"What am I supposed to do?" I asked Molly in a panic, when she called back.

"First of all, be flattered," she said. "Some editor looked at the picture and decided you were an actress. At least they didn't decide you were a stalker."

"No place I could have been hiding a gun. But what do you think happens when the papers figure out who I am and link me to Dan?"

" 'Killer Doc's Wife Goes Crazy With Stress,' " said Molly, quoting a fake headline. She'd obviously been around tabloid stories a few times before. But now she paused, a worried tone creeping into her voice. "But what were you really doing at Clooney's trailer, anyway? Showing up in your underwear?"

I didn't answer, and Molly suddenly took a sharp breath.

"Oh gosh, this isn't funny, right?" she asked, her tone changing abruptly from her previous banter. "Did something awful happen?"

"Pretty awful," I admitted. "To tell you the truth, I'm scared out of my mind."

"Come right over," said Molly. "I haven't seen you in too long. We need to talk."

I'd already promised to meet a client at the Pacific Design Center, so I told Molly I'd stop by after that. My client, the wife of a movie producer who'd just had his first hit, met me dressed in a black embroidered miniskirt, four-inch-heeled Christian Louboutin sandals, a white James Perse T-shirt, and a pink fur bolero shrug. The perfect outfit to wear when picking out a light fixture for your mansion on Benedict Canyon. We spent an hour admiring various options, but my usual persuasive powers failed me. She fell in love with a hand-forged three-tier iron and bronze leaping stag chandelier and couldn't be convinced to consider a simpler Verona style.

"I need iron and bronze to make a statement. I've heard Russell Crowe is moving into the neighborhood," she said, as if that explained the choice. Maybe the stud liked stags. Hey, it was her thirty thousand dollars, not mine. The excess made me slightly nauseated, but I doubted I could convince her to spend less and donate the savings to Children's Relief Services.

Since I was already in West Hollywood, I didn't bother with the freeway and just drove up La Cienega, past the Hollywood Bowl, to get over the mountains to Burbank. Molly had her casting office in a cottage on West Olive, a quick drive from NBC, ABC, and Warner Brothers. Molly could cast an actor and have him on the set in an hour. Not the usual system—but network execs trusted her enough that it had happened.

When I walked in, the corridor outside the casting room was packed with a dozen gorgeous male actors in their twenties, all with broad shoulders, blond hair, rippling abs, and tight Levi's that showed off their buff buns. I grabbed a mini poppy-seed muffin from the overflowing tray of goodies by the front desk, untouched since nobody else here would dream of eating a carb. Total body fat percentage in the room was about 5 percent.

A minute later, Molly herself bustled out and, seeing me, raced over with a hug.

"You're here. I'm so glad. I've missed you."

She took my hand and pulled me around the corner to her sleek office—all black and chrome furniture and shiny surfaces. She had an original Marcel Breuer Wassily guest chair by her desk, with slanted leather seat straps guaranteed to cut into your thighs and nudge your knees into an uncomfortable angle. The chair belonged in a museum. Preferably behind a red rope where nobody would have to sit on it.

Molly perched on a swirly faux-leopard couch and patted the cushion next to her. I came over and sat down.

"I hope I'm not dragging you away from something important," I said, twisting my neck so I could look directly at her. Given the sofa's curvy line, eye-to-eye conversation wasn't easy.

Molly flipped her curly dark hair back from her round face and gave a little laugh. She was beautiful in a non-Hollywood way, with sparkling eyes and clear skin that she'd gotten from God, not Lancôme. She wore less makeup than any woman I knew, and even though we were exactly the same age, the tiny laugh lines around her eyes somehow made her look younger, not older.

"We're casting a Fox reality show," Molly said with a grin. "The spec sheet says we're looking for a California surfer type. Extra requirement is that he has to bare his butt. And here's how old I am, darling. I asked two of my young girls to do the auditions and I'm not going back in at all. I figure that either I'd be turned on by those young naked buns, which would probably be illegal, or I wouldn't be turned on, which would officially qualify me as middle-aged."

I laughed. "So you're not even going to peek?"

She winked. "Not unless you want me to." She went over to the flat-paneled mirror on one wall and flicked a switch—and all of a sudden, we had a window into the audition room.

I looked at Molly in surprise. "One-way mirror?" I asked.

She nodded. "I just had it put in. Isn't it too much fun? It makes me feel like Molly Archer, Detective."

I grimaced. "I've been trying the whole girl-detective thing myself. It isn't that much fun, believe me."

Molly cupped her hand to her mouth, as if pushing the words back in. "I'm so sorry, darling," she said, closing the switch and coming over to sit next to me again. "I wasn't thinking. Now tell me what's going on. And how you ended up almost naked on a movie set."

"It's a pretty long story," I said.

"I want every word," said Molly firmly.

I settled in—which wasn't easy on a backless chaise—and outlined the basics, leading neatly to the day in question, which I described in detail from the moment I picked up Nora until I snuck in my own front door. Molly shook her head a few times, and when I finished, she whistled softly.

"Wow," she said, "I don't even know what to think."

"Neither do I." I took a deep breath. "And are you ready for something equally bizarre?"

"Probably not," Molly said. "Another day like that one and you qualify for your own reality show. Ozzie Osbourne was never this interesting."

I launched into my adventure with Roy Evans. At the part with the dog collar, Molly stood up and started pacing across her glossy bleached-wood floor. By the time I'd finished, her face was red with anger.

"Chaining women in his bedroom. Least I can do for you is get the asshole fired." She shook her head. "I wonder if he's been behaving weirdly at work. Someone else must have noticed if

he's . . . off. I'll call Tim," she said, picking up the phone to dial
her friend, the producer at *Night Beat*. I suddenly remembered
that the last time they'd connected because of me, they'd made a
dinner plan.

"How'd your date go with Tim?" I asked as she punched in the
number.

"We never managed it. He got busy and then I got too busy."
She shrugged, and instead of lamenting the sorry social life of a career woman in L.A., she slammed down the phone. "And now I'm
getting his voice mail. Shit."

She paced up and down a few more times then, trying to calm
herself, opened the switch at her mirror window to watch the casting session. Another would-be surfer boy strolled across the stage
into a spotlight. Unlike the other candidates, this one was dark-
skinned and dark-haired, with a crinkly smile and Schwarzenegger
biceps. Molly looked at him appraisingly, then flicked on an intercom, which rang on the floor. We watched the assistant handling
the auditions pick up the receiver.

"Can this one talk?" Molly asked her.

"He's great," said the girl, making an obvious effort not to look
toward the one-way mirror. "Funny, charming, and he passes the
test you taught me—I'd like to sleep with him. I'd also love to give
him the part. Too bad he's not blond."

"We're casting a reality show," Molly barked. "Half the state's
Latino now and if I see one more OC blonde on TV, I'm going to
throw up. That's reality. So hire him."

The girl giggled and Molly disconnected and turned back to
me. "I'm sorry. Just a little distraction while I try to think." She
stood still for a moment, staring at the one-way mirror, then shook
her head and grabbed her bag. "Tim works with Roy, so maybe he
knows what's going on. If he doesn't, I want him to hear your story.
And hear it from you. Let's head over there."

I might have protested, but Molly in motion was like a tornado—once she was whipped up, she wasn't going to change course. It was safer to be inside the whirlwind than face it down.

In the gloomy underground parking garage, Molly announced we should take my Lexus to drive over to the network.

"I want to sit in the same seat that Johnny Dangerously did. Maybe I'll get a clue. I'm pretty good at picking up auras."

"If you can figure out this one, you should start telling fortunes on Sunset," I said. But I opened the passenger door for her and whisked away a big box of fabric samples from the Design Center that I'd tossed on the front seat. "Let me put these in the trunk so you have some room."

Molly slid into the car, and I quickly opened the trunk and dropped in the box. I was just shutting it when something nagged at my brain, an unexpected image penetrating, and I stopped and peered in again. My heart leaped so hard I could hardly breathe.

The entire back half of the trunk was taken up with a bulging black garbage bag, the heavy, oversized kind that gardeners use for leaves. A neat twist sealed the top. I reached out to push my thumb against the thick plastic and feel the contents, but then I drew it back. If this was evidence, I shouldn't touch it. And I didn't want to, anyway. I grabbed a couple of the fabric samples from the box and draped them over my fingers—Pierre Deux country check in one hand, Pindler & Pindler pale peach silk in the other. Expensive fabrics definitely had nice give. I untied the twisty without any trouble.

The smell should have told me everything I needed to know. But I peeled back the top of the bag and stared inside. Maybe my mouth dropped open, but I didn't scream. I was in denial. Or shock. In the dim garage, I had only the vaguest impression of a bloated face staring up at me through a clear plastic bag knotted at the neck, swollen eyes bulging as if the bag still contained a bunch of grapes. I had a vision of tangled hair and a blood-spattered sweatsuit. With all the nice fabrics in the world, she shouldn't have had to die wearing blue nylon.

"Need any help back there?" Molly called from the front seat. She'd cracked open her door. The car must have been steaming hot.

"No, I'll be right there," I said. My voice sounded surprisingly normal. I lifted my arms over my head and slammed the trunk door shut. And with the decisive *thunk*, the full horror hit me. It was like that moment after a car crash when the air bag suddenly explodes in your face so you can't move and you can't breathe and you're not sure if you're still alive. All you know is that something too awful to describe has occurred.

I grabbed my stomach and leaned forward, retching all over the bumper. I wiped my mouth with the peach silk, then retched again.

Molly was on her cell phone and she'd walked away from the car, probably to get better reception. She didn't know what was happening, and I was suddenly too weak even to call out to her. I pictured us driving over to the network and pulling up at the lot, where the security guard would check my trunk. Maybe I'd get the same kid who'd made the bad joke about finding a dead body. Only it could end up as a good joke. He'd find one.

Molly came back to the Lexus. Her aura-sensing powers must not have been working, because she was looking jubilant. "I reached Tim," she said cheerfully, tucking her slim Motorola camera phone back into her bag. "He ran into Roy a few nights ago in one of the VIP rooms of the White Lotus. The hottest club in Hollywood and Roy Evans was in the inner sanctum. Where's the justice in the world?" She laughed. "It turns out Roy was snorting coke and making an ass of himself. Tim's ready to build a case to get him fired."

She paused, and I sat there miserably, holding the keys, my hands clenched in my lap.

"Anyway, Tim wants to talk to you," Molly said finally. "Should we go?"

"No," I said. I started to cry and put my head against the steering wheel. "I'm feeling kind of sick."

I flung open the door and started retching again, doubling over as snot and puke and tears puddled at my feet and splashed over my lime green ballet flats.

"In the trunk," I sputtered, coughing and thinking I might collapse right there, so Molly might as well know. "Nora's dead. Someone put her in my trunk."

"My God. No," said Molly. She reached over to hold my head. "Who do you think? Johnny Dangerously? Someone else? Who?"

"Not Daaaan," I wailed, the thought rising from nowhere and coming out as more plea than proclamation. My body went limp and Molly grabbed my waist to keep me from falling over into my own vomit. Somehow, she hustled me out of the car and back inside to her office, where I fell on the leopard sofa, keening and crying in grief. Maybe Nora hadn't been my dearest soul mate, but her murder cut me to the core. How could I believe in goodness and justice when my trunk was crammed with a girl whose only sin was eating too many ice cream sundaes?

After letting me sob for about three minutes, Molly, woman of action, grabbed my hands.

"We need a plan," she said. "Do we call the police?"

I shook my head. "Reese and Shields already think Dan's a killer and I'm a crazy woman. What do you think they're going to do with this? They know I was with her yesterday. I'll end up in jail."

Molly shuddered. "Okay, then, how about this. We drive the car to South Central and leave the keys in. It'll be stolen in an hour. You report it missing, the cops find the car and the body, but you're off the hook."

I grimaced. "They won't buy it. Especially since they already think I made up the whole thing with Johnny DeVito." I curled up on the sofa, drawing my knees practically to my chest like a scared six-year-old. "But we're stuck. You've watched enough TV shows. It's not easy to get rid of a body."

"Nonsense. It's only a problem if you don't want the body found," Molly said. She walked briskly to her desk and seemed to make a decision. "Look, Lacy, you're sick. You can't deal with this now. I'll have my assistant drive you home. Leave me your key. The garage is locked, so your car is safe."

She gave me a look that said I shouldn't argue. So I didn't. Having someone tell me what to do right now was what I needed, anyway.

At home, I avoided Dan all night, and when he fell asleep in the den watching an old movie, I covered him with a light blanket instead of nudging him to bed. Upstairs, I was on pins and needles all night, half expecting the police to show up again at our doorstep. I tossed in bed until almost two, then fell asleep, wracked by nightmares of mangled cars dripping blood, and bloated bodies climbing the stairs and dancing on my bed. I woke up screaming.

And my screaming woke up Jimmy.

"MOOMMMY! MOOOMMY! I'M SCARED!"

Jimmy's terrified cries jarred me from my dreams and, jolted to consciousness, I raced to his room.

"It's okay, honey," I told him, stroking my little boy's sweaty forehead and hugging him tightly. "It's just a nightmare. You're okay."

I lay down next to him, rocking him like I did when he was a baby. The closeness calmed both of us. Jimmy whimpered for a while, then fell asleep with his head tucked into my chest, clutching the duck-decorated blue blanket he'd had since he was born. He'd given up his security blankie months ago, but after the night with Reese and Shields brandishing their guns, he'd begged for it back. My poor baby. Would he ever feel safe again? Would I?

When the telephone rang two hours later, I tiptoed out of Jimmy's room, too drained to face another middle-of-the-night emergency. But I steeled myself for bad news. Could someone have broken into my car? Maybe it was just Mandy calling with gossip for Ashley that couldn't wait for daybreak.

I gave a shaky "hello" and a familiar voice whispered, "Darling, it's me, Molly. Sorry if I woke you, but you have to hear this. The police found a dead body outside the White Lotus. Draped over Roy Evans's car."

I let the news sink in. "Molly, how did you—"

"Always assume your phone is tapped," Molly said quickly. "Isn't that what you told me?"

I fell silent for a minute, and then Molly said, "I'm going to run. I'll talk to you in the morning. Actually, the afternoon, because I won't be in before then. But look outside your house before you go back to sleep. And if you want to know, I did all of this to impress Tim, not you."

She hung up and I anxiously peeked through the pleated shade in my bedroom. Nothing interesting out front, so I went to the side window that looked over the circular driveway. Grant's car was there because he never liked to put it in the garage, and Jimmy had left his bicycle—the new one with the training wheels—leaning against a tree. And farther down the dark driveway, I could just make out the hulking shadow of my Lexus. Now emptied, I had to assume, of its previous cargo.

By now, I couldn't have gone back to sleep even if I wanted to. At 6:00 A.M., I turned on my computer and checked one of L.A.'s entertainment bloggers—ClubGirl.com, whom everyone read because she was out all night, every night, getting the scoop. And boy, did she have one. Police had been waiting outside the White Lotus to question Roy Evans about an unidentified body. But

Evans came out of the club with an ounce of coke in his pocket and turned violent at being confronted by the police. He was held overnight on drug charges. According to network executive Tim Riley, Roy Evans was being suspended from his on-air job, pending an investigation.

Chapter Ten

At *breakfast, Grant began* quoting philosophy to me, a welcome change from his trying to make me understand quantum physics.

"We're studying Aristotle in my world civ class," he said, between gulps of grapefruit juice. "You know, the dude who said ethics is all a matter of context. What's wrong in one situation might be right in another."

I took a sip of coffee. In college, I'd had a crush on the professor in my senior philosophy seminar. The good side of that was I'd done all the reading. The bad side was that my mind tended to wander in class.

"Aristotle's the one who said being virtuous is more important than specific actions, isn't he?" I asked, trying to remember something other than the exact shade of the professor's eyes. "Not like Kant, who believed in the categorical imperative. Absolute behavior with no exceptions. None of that ends-justifies-the-means stuff."

Grant squirmed in his chair. "So which guy do you believe?"

I considered the circumstances—something Kant wouldn't have done—and realized Grant had some ulterior motive for raising the subject in the first place.

"Both have their merits, I guess," I said. I poured some more juice into his glass. "If you've done something that feels shady, I guess Aristotle gives you a better excuse."

"Not shady given the situation," Grant said. He pulled a thick sheaf of papers out of his backpack, looked at them briefly, and then handed them to me. "Jake and I had been talking about what we could try that might help Dad. Anyway, this was Jake's idea. He did it, not me."

"What'd you guys do?" I asked. Since Jake was his best friend, I was guessing Grant had some part in the plan.

Grant leaned down and scratched the back of his head. Either he hadn't washed his hair this morning or he didn't want to look at me. "We got Tasha Barlow's cell phone records. It wasn't so hard. Jake found this awesome program that lets you steal a user name and password. So he was able to hack into her Pac Bell account." Now he did look at me. "Jake's taking AP computer science and he's getting an A," he added, as if that explained it. "Maybe an A-plus."

"Was hacking on the midterm?"

Grant shrugged. "No, but it's not such a big deal. Everybody does it. I mean, not everybody hacks as well as Jake, but he's a genius at this."

"The genius could end up in jail. Hacking's not a joke."

"Dad being charged with murder's not so funny, either," Grant said adamantly. "So that makes it okay, don't you think? You've got to figure it's like stealing bread to feed a starving child. Maybe it's against the law, but it's the right thing to do."

I tried not to smile. Grant was smarter than he had a right to be. And given my own little escapades in the past few days, how could I quibble with him about ethics? Maybe you had to act badly sometimes to do good. Just like that dude Aristotle said.

"So what'd you find?" I asked, shuffling through the pages and looking at the computer-printed lists of phone numbers. "Who did she call?"

Grant looked pleased to be on practical ground again. "She called a lot of people, including Johnny DeVito about a million times. But here's the thing, Mom. She never called Dad. Not a single phone call from Dad or to Dad, for as far back as Jake could find."

I tried to be thrilled that Dan hadn't chatted regularly with a dead girl whom he said he didn't know. At least phone sex wasn't part of the equation. Grant leaned over the table and pulled out the last page of the pile. "Don't get mad, Mom, but once Jake had Johnny DeVito's numbers, he figured out how to get his records, too. And are you ready for this?" He grinned at me triumphantly. "A while ago, Johnny called Daddy three times. He called Dad's cell phone and his office phone. Dad called him twice. Most of the calls were short, but there were a lot of them."

I looked at Grant helplessly. "Honey, I don't know if that's such a good fact to know."

Grant shrugged. "Facts aren't good or bad. They're just facts. You know Mr. Morland's credo—it's all interpretation." He got up from the table and grabbed his backpack. "But I think it's really something, don't you?"

With a little wave, Grant blew out of the house to head to school, and I sat at the table, stunned.

So Dan and Johnny DeVito had talked on the phone. One way or another, Dan knew Johnny and Johnny knew Dan.

And then something clicked.

Johnny DeVito, sitting next to me in the car, holding his knife and growling at me. *I saw what your husband did to my Tasha. I should do the same thing to you.* His low, threatening tone had sounded familiar. It was as if I'd heard his voice before. I had—and now I knew where. On the answering machine in Dan's study.

Without so much as a bottle of Windex for a cover story, I raced down the hall and burst into Dan's private office. The digital readout on the answering machine showed zero messages, and when I hit the PLAY button, I got silence. Dan had erased everything. But it didn't matter, because I heard the tape again, playing in my head. Johnny's voice. *Nothing has changed, Doctor. I know what you did. You've just got more reasons for silence.*

Doctor. Anybody might call Dan that, but the title would come naturally to a patient. And wouldn't that make sense? The scars on Johnny's face had been nagging at the edge of my brain. Maybe Johnny had come to Dan, hoping to be healed. Who better to remake a disfigured face than the man world famous for facial reconstruction?

I opened a closet and found the boxes of patient records Dan had sent home, shoved to the back behind a pile of newspapers. Grant had worried that they contained a bomb—but I was hoping for a bombshell. Without much hesitation, I fell to my knees and ripped into the cartons, cutting my finger on the cardboard and breaking a nail on the strapping tape. Who cared anymore. The first box didn't turn up anything, nor did the second. I was just giving up on the third box, too, when I noticed some manila envelopes lying on the bottom, each sealed with a red tab that said PRIVATE: DO NOT OPEN. I rifled through, then snapped off one of the seals. Wow. "Private" didn't begin to describe it. Had Dan really done a face-lift on famous alabaster-skinned movie star Naomi Kind? And done it when she was only thirty-five? Forget the murder mystery, I could sell this little tidbit to the *Star* and make a fortune.

I broke open a few more of the DO NOT OPEN packets and gasped at the names. One famous actress after another. Julia Ross. Helen Holmes. Christy Thames. They could have paid him in Oscars. In between the facial reconstructions that had made his reputation as the Saint of Hollywood, Dan had been busy doing a breast lift here and an eye nip there. Who knew? Certainly I didn't. Did the AMA really mean doctor-patient confidentiality to include wives? It was hard to know which was more impressive—my husband's surgical skill or his skill at keeping secrets.

But I'd had enough of secrets now. I threw all the red-sealed envelopes on the ground and tore into them. Either I'd find the information I wanted or I'd gather plenty of good gossip to tell Molly. She deserved it. After what she'd done for me last night, a scoop on secret surgery was the least I could offer.

The file I wanted wasn't there. No matter how many times I pawed through the pile, I couldn't find any envelope carefully labeled with Johnny DeVito's name. I sunk down, looking at the mess I'd made, and tried to calm myself. New theories started swirling in my head. If Dan had done little nips and tucks on all these other actresses, might he also have treated Tasha Barlow? She didn't seem famous enough to make the list. But ten minutes ago I wouldn't have believed that Dan knew Naomi Kind from anyplace except the Doctors of Courage charity ball, where she'd presented him with an award. Pretending she'd never met him before that night made her an even better actress than I'd thought.

I tossed a few of the files back in the box but didn't bother putting them neatly away. Resolutely, I marched up the stairs, fingering the phone lists that I'd shoved into the pocket of my robe. Time to stop pretending.

I heard the shower running and slipped into the bathroom, which was thick with steam.

"Honey?" I called out.

No answer. Dan couldn't hear me over the rushing water.

I waited for a moment, then untied my Hanro wrap robe and let it drop to the floor. I didn't need an interrogation room to talk to my own husband. I pulled open the beveled frosted-glass door and stepped inside the shower.

Dan looked up, startled.

"Hi," he said, uncertainly.

"Hi."

I tried to smile. "Um, want me to wash your back?" I asked. Wasn't this cozy. Husband and wife lathering up together. Well, maybe not cozy, since the shower stall was about the size of a standard room at the Hilton.

Dan looked at me like I was crazy, but I took the washcloth from its hook, rubbed it over the thick cake of L'Occitane verbena soap, and stepped around so I was standing behind him. I stroked the washcloth in firm, wide circles around the ropy muscles in his broad, tensed shoulders.

"Feels good," Dan said, rolling his head as if trying to ease a crick in his neck.

"It's supposed to," I said. It was going to be easier to unsnarl the knot in his neck than the knot in my stomach. I put down the washcloth and used both hands to massage his back, pivoting my thumbs along his spine and spreading my fingers over his trapezius muscles. Or maybe those were the latissimus dorsi. Good thing he was the doctor, not me, since I could never remember anatomy.

But I knew enough about body parts to realize that with the warm water beating down, Dan was getting heated up. That hadn't been the point, but if his excitement was rising, maybe his defensive instincts would start dropping.

"I have a question for you," I said, still ministering to his firm flexors.

"Shoot," Dan said.

"What do you know about Johnny DeVito?"

The name landed like a shot of cold water—the ultimate anti-Viagra. From my position behind, I couldn't see Dan's face, but his back stiffened and he pulled away from me.

"Why do you care?" he asked.

"Because something's going on with you and Johnny DeVito," I said, "and because I'm afraid of him. He left a menacing message at our house. He threatened me with a knife—a long story that I'll tell you later. He might have killed Tasha Barlow. He might have killed her roommate. If he's a friend of yours, I don't think he's a good influence."

Dan took a few steps over to the granite ledge that ringed the shower and sat down.

"He's not a friend," Dan said, looking stricken. "I met Johnny DeVito many, many years ago. It was ancient history. Then he called me out of the blue."

Dan stopped.

"Why did he call?" I asked.

Dan shook his head and rubbed the back of his hand against the morning stubble on his chin. "Lacy, I know things are tough but talking about this isn't going to help. Forget about Johnny De-Vito. Let's just try to preserve our relationship, okay?"

I flipped my now wet hair back from my face. "You can try to preserve it, but if we don't talk, it's a little late. Sort of like trying to save the Parthenon. Haven't you noticed? It's already crumbled."

Dan gave a wry smile.

I came over and sat next to him on the ledge, thigh to naked thigh. In other circumstances, it might have seemed sexy, but right now we were both stripped bare of anything but fear and uncertainty. Maybe there was something intimate about that, too.

"A lot of people are risking their lives for you," I said bluntly. "Molly dragged a dead body out of my car. Grant and Jake hacked into two Pac Bell accounts. I've been tied up twice. All that, and you can't risk telling me what happened with Johnny DeVito?"

Dan blinked his eyes as if I were spouting Swahili, but instead of asking what I was talking about, he said, "It was many, many years ago."

"You mentioned that."

Dan pursed his lips together, and then he seemed to make a decision. "Okay, here goes." He took a deep breath. "Johnny DeVito showed up at my office very late one night, maybe fifteen years ago. I didn't know who he was, but his face was a bloody pulp. Chunks of skin were hanging down, his nose was practically cut off, and his scalp was ripped away from his forehead. I told him to go to a hospital, but he wanted me to sew him up. He figured the police would be checking hospitals."

I made myself stay quiet, even though I was stunned.

"I kept saying I wouldn't help him," Dan continued, "but he threatened me with a gun. And then he waved a huge wad of cash at me. Back in those days, all that money meant something, Lacy. My parents weren't giving us anything. You were pregnant and I was just starting out in my practice. I took it and did the best I could."

"That doesn't sound so awful," I said in a small voice. "Maybe you wouldn't do it now, but it was a tough situation." Aristotle again.

"I shouldn't have done it then, either," Dan said. "I figured out pretty fast that Johnny DeVito had been in a knife fight. You know the old joke about someone leaving a bar brawl with a black eye and saying, 'Yeah, but you should see the other guy'? Well, in this case, the other guy was dead."

"Who was it?"

"Some drug dealer. They were both high and who knows what they fought about. I told Johnny to come back in a few days so I could change the dressings, but he never did. A week later, he called to say that one side of his face was dripping pus. No big surprise that it was infected. He needed massive doses of antibiotics." Dan slammed his right fist into his cupped left hand. "I could have done something if he'd come in. I told him it was going to scar."

Dan seemed more upset about the surgery taking a bad turn than anything else.

"Keep going," I urged.

"Not much more," Dan said. "I wanted to call the police at that point, but I'd have been arrested as an accomplice. Eventually, the whole thing faded away. Johnny went to jail on some other drug charge years later. Frankly, when I heard about that, I felt better. But then he got out. We'd never had any contact until he called me. He wanted his money back from the surgery."

Despite myself, I laughed. "Had you given a lifetime guarantee? I thought only L.L. Bean did that."

Dan looked down, his face a study in misery. I stood up and turned off the water, then got a soft Turkish towel for each of us.

Dan draped his across his knees, and I tucked the fluffy fabric around my waist.

Dan shrugged. "What was I going to do, Lacy? Johnny DeVito's a skank, but a smart skank. He knew how far my career had come. Knew about my reputation. And I was worried that he wanted to destroy all of it. I couldn't prove that he'd killed someone, but he was ready to spread the story that I'd ruined his face."

"You had an explanation."

"Which wasn't going to play out very well in this town. Not with my clients."

I nodded. I couldn't argue with that.

"I arranged to give him back his thirty thou," Dan continued. "All cash. He didn't position it as blackmail—just that he wanted to go straight and it was tough getting work the way he looked. He said this was cheaper for me in every way than a malpractice suit. I should have known better, because instead of going away, he just ratcheted up the pressure."

"To do what?"

"Give him more money. After the first time, he started sending emails telling me where and when to show up with cash. I went twice more. God, Lacy, I should have told you. Or called the police. Or someone. I think I would have, but then this wild murder charge came up. I didn't think that announcing I was paying off an ex-con was going to help anything."

I thoughtfully raked my fingers through my wet hair, tucking a clump behind my ears.

"Where did you meet Johnny? For those drop-offs?" I asked.

"His place," Dan said.

"A fancy house with a Mediterranean patio?" I asked.

Dan shook his head. "More like a dive of an apartment in West L.A. One of those standard cheap rentals you despise."

"Brown tweed carpet and ratty brown sofa with bright orange pillows," I said. "Bamboo TV stand and a chipped Formica table."

"Good description. I guess those places all look alike," Dan said with a small smile.

"They do look alike," I said, feeling my heart pounding. "But this particular one—any chance it was apartment 4C in a building that figured that number belonged on the third floor?"

Dan looked at me in surprise. "Exactly."

I put my arms around my husband. My eyes were filling with tears, and I buried my face in the crook of his shoulder. Ironic that Dan had done his best to avoid a minor scandal—and ended up with a major one. "This explains everything, honey—including all the evidence in the murder case about how you were at the victim's place more than once. Now I get it. Don't you see? You were meeting Johnny in Tasha Barlow's apartment. She was his girlfriend."

By midafternoon, Dan and I were plopped on the couch in Chauncey Howell's office, holding hands and smiling secretly at each other. Finally an explanation that made sense. Confession was good for the soul, and it had also been good for loving sex on the shower floor.

But Chauncey wasn't nearly as excited.

"Interesting story, but I'm not sure what it gets us," Chauncey said. "Do you have any proof Johnny DeVito was blackmailing you?"

"He didn't give me any receipts," Dan said briskly. "But let's see. I made some transfers from my account and then took it out in cash. I guess that should do it."

"You took out cash?" Chauncey asked scornfully. "All that proves is your wife was buying big-ticket antiques again and trying to avoid the sales tax."

"I haven't bought anything in months," I protested. "Or weeks, anyway." At least days. Was he counting the 1940s Dresden dessert dishes I'd bought on eBay? They hadn't even been shipped yet.

"I'm just giving you a sample of what a prosecutor might say," Chauncey explained.

"I have the emails telling me where to go and how much to bring," Dan reminded him.

Chauncey grimaced. "Emails telling you to bring money to Tasha Barlow's apartment, including the night she died. The DA could say it was the price you were paying for the night."

"But that's not true," Dan said.

Chauncey shrugged and I rolled my eyes in frustration. To me, it all added up as neatly as Bill Gates's checkbook. But Chauncey was seeing holes bigger than the Bush deficit.

"Thirty thousand is a lot for a tryst," I said, finding a flaw in Chauncey's objection.

"There was only five thousand in the envelope the police found," Chauncey said, consulting his notes again. In Dan's Hollywood circle, five thousand was what a producer might spend at Spago for a night of truffled pasta and vintage Dom Perignon with a few friends. And the fee wouldn't be out of the question for a night of wild but discreet sex.

Dan nodded. "Five thousand's all he'd asked for. The previous two times were the same."

Chauncey drummed his fingers on his desk. "I can understand why you might have kept the blackmail quiet at first—hoping it would just go away. But why didn't you tell the police about it the night you were arrested?" Now Chauncey wasn't pretending to be the prosecutor—he really wanted to know.

"Because the connection didn't occur to me." Dan covered his eyes briefly with his hand, then rubbed the bridge of his nose in chagrin. "I'd brought cash to Johnny DeVito in a scuzzy apartment in West Los Angeles. A young actress died in a place near the ocean. It didn't click until Lacy realized it was the same place."

Chauncey nodded and then, softening his tone slightly, said, "Look, I'm not saying this can't help. The case against you is circumstantial. And given your blackmail story, we can at least suggest different circumstances. Let's go through it one more time."

Dan grimaced but plunged in. At the first payoff, Johnny De-Vito had met him in the apartment and counted the envelope of cash before letting Dan go. He'd promised Dan they were even now. But then came the demands by email. Dan was instructed that someone would buzz him into the building, and he should come up to apartment 4C. The door would be open, and he should leave the envelope of cash on a table in the front hall. At the last drop-off, he found a note on the table when he got there, asking him to wait for about twenty minutes. He should have something to drink while he waited and make himself comfortable. If nobody came, he could leave. Dan paced around the apartment and flipped through a newspaper. He got a glass of water and blew his nose a couple of times. After about thirty minutes, he left, figuring Johnny would just come by later to get it.

"So Johnny was in Tasha's apartment that night, too," I said to Chauncey, in case he hadn't thought of that.

"Or else he wasn't," Chauncey said, frowning. "The envelope was still there when the body was found."

"My God, Chauncey, isn't this obvious?" I was practically shrieking. Why didn't he get this? "Johnny was blackmailing Dan. He knew Dan would be at the apartment that night for the pay-off. So he killed his girlfriend—for whatever reason—and framed Dan. It's obvious. End of story."

Chauncey looked at me solemnly. "I hear you, Lacy, I do. And I wish it were that easy. But we've checked out Johnny DeVito very carefully. He has an alibi for that night. He wasn't even in town."

I looked down and smoothed my softly pleated Zac Posen skirt. It might have been a little young, so just to be safe, I'd paired the pastel print with a sophisticated white Celine jacket. But right now I wouldn't have felt protected in a snowsuit.

"Dan, let me point out something else," Chauncey continued, tapping his fingers on the desk. "If the prosecutor buys your story of the pay-offs, his scenario goes something like this: You got to the apartment and Johnny DeVito wasn't there but his girlfriend was—waiting in a skimpy peignoir. You were angry at Johnny and wanted to send a message, so you killed her."

Dan and I looked at each other, but this time neither of us was smiling.

"Whose side are you on?" I asked Chauncey.

"Yours," he said. "Unequivocally. But a defense has to explain the evidence. All of it. Dan's story gives him a reason for being at Tasha's apartment, but if he continues to claim he never saw the woman, we're stuck. For example, how do we explain the neighbor who heard Tasha scream, 'Stop it, Dr. Fields, stop it!' "

I felt my spirits sinking faster than a Chicago Cubs fan before the World Series. I stood up. My head was hurting and I'd had enough. "By the way," I said to Chauncey, putting my Fendi bag over my shoulder, "if Johnny DeVito has an alibi for that night, where was he?"

"Working," Chauncey said. He glanced through a thick file of papers, then closed it and pulled out another one. Finally he found what he wanted. "Since he got out of jail, your Johnny's been picking up jobs as a stagehand. Or a grip, I guess it's called these days. This was a commercial for Honey Twists cereal and they were on location in a small town in Nevada for most of the day and night. Plenty of people can confirm. Including a hotshot producer named Julie Boden."

Chapter Eleven

When *I called Sammie,* she said her boss wouldn't be in all week—
she was out in Rainbow Basin, just north of Barstow, producing
another Mars-lander Buick commercial.

"Julie's a genius," Sammie raved. "She got Jessica Simpson as the
talent this time."

Calling Simpson "talent" seemed like a stretch to me, but then
Sammie was young.

"How about Roy Evans?" I asked. "Is he doing this one?"

"No. Julie fired him." Sammie hesitated then cleared her
throat. "Did you know the police identified the body that was on
Roy's car? It's really strange, Lacy. She'd been roommates with
that other girl who died. The one you asked Julie about. How
weird is that?"

"Odd," I said, not adding that the whole situation had become
even odder than Sammie knew.

"But the police say someone dumped the body there while Roy
was in the club," said Sammie. "Julie triple-checked that. Roy's off
the hook."

"Except for the little matter of the drug charge."

"Oh, that." Sammie sighed. Then, parroting what she'd no
doubt heard from Julie, she said, "It was just an ounce and this is
Hollywood. Everyone does it. Roy's famous—or semifamous—
and he has a good lawyer. He'll get off." Good thing Sammie came
to California, because she'd never have learned all that at Vassar.

"So have you and Julie been busy with a lot of shoots?" I asked, changing the subject.

"You bet," said Sammie enthusiastically. She reeled off the names of three products they were promoting, including Honey Twists, and I asked when they'd shot the commercial for that one. She gave me two dates—one of them the day Tasha had died.

"I heard that was a long day of shooting," I said carefully.

"Day and night and part of the next day," said Sammie brightly. "Can you imagine trying to get six five-year-olds to say 'Twists are my favorite tweat!' without spitting up their cereal? I'm surprised the whole crew's not still there."

"Do you know if a guy named Johnny DeVito was working as a grip?" I asked.

"I haven't heard of him, but I'll check."

I heard her clacking on her computer, and in a moment she said, "The director didn't have his name on the crew list. But Julie must have hired him separately, because she put him on the credit sheet."

That was a new one—an executive producer handpicking her grips. I thanked Sammie for her help, then hung up and called Molly.

"The police say Roy's not a suspect in the notorious White Lotus murder," I said when I got her on the phone.

"Who knows?" Molly said quickly. "My friend Tim's still conducting his own investigation. Ever since Rathergate at CBS, the networks don't believe anything unless it's signed by Ruth Bader Ginsburg."

I laughed.

"After what happened to you, I hope Tim finds a reason to keep Roy off the air for good," Molly said loyally. Then, lowering her voice, she asked, "Did the cops question Dan about the body?"

"Not yet. I keep waiting for Reese to show up, but he hasn't."

Since we were on the phone, I didn't add that I'd taken the Lexus to a car wash in a busy section of downtown L.A., asking to have every inch cleaned, shampooed, and deodorized. Instead, I gave Molly a brief recap of what I'd learned about Johnny DeVito being on Julie's payroll.

"It's fishy, but I don't think Julie would make up that alibi, do you?" Molly asked. "Too easy to check. With that face, people would remember if they saw him on the shoot or not."

"Okay, so let's say it's legit. What's the possible connection? Why would Julie Boden hire a scarred ex-con as a grip?"

"I'm clueless," Molly said. "Let's see, even assuming Julie was sleeping with Roy and Roy was sleeping with Tasha and Tasha was sleeping with Johnny, that's still three degrees of separation. I don't see where it adds up, unless they were all screwing together in a happy foursome."

"Too nauseating even to consider," I said. "But Julie Boden's shooting in the desert this week. She knows something. I'm going to track her down."

"You're not going alone! Way too dangerous."

"The only thing dangerous about Julie Boden is her withering glance."

"Not so," Molly parried. "She's a star in an ad agency, so she's a master at stabbing people in the back. Ruling with an iron fist. And don't forget her killer instincts."

"She can't hurt me with a metaphor."

"Forget it, darling. I'm coming with you."

We argued back and forth, but I knew Molly always got her way. This was the woman who'd just convinced HBO that the sexy young tabloid queen Lindsay Lohan was the right actress to play a wizened, toothless Aztec warrior in the new series *Cortez*. I didn't stand a chance.

I called my friend Jane Snowdon to ask if she'd mind picking Jimmy up after school.

"Not a problem," she said. "And Jared's dying to have someone for a sleep-over. Can I keep Jimmy until tomorrow?"

"Deal," I said, not sure if I should feel relieved or guilty.

By late afternoon, Molly and I were settled into her Range Rover, heading east on I-10. By the time we turned north onto I-15, I relaxed a little, secretly glad to have Molly with me. We drove through Barstow, a town built in 1886 by the Santa Fe Railroad to house a train depot and hotel. Nothing much had changed—now the town had a train depot and a lineup of cheap hotels. As we sped past, I noticed two vans and an array of expensive cars in the parking lot of the Best Western and guessed the advertising team was staying there. Either that, or the hotel had the finest dinner buffet in town.

Just a few miles farther on, we hit the real desert and the scenery changed dramatically. The paved road ended and layers of sandstone and sediment rose in mysterious shapes around us. Huge slabs of stone tilted at precipitous angles and brilliant colors splayed across the wavy terrain. In the tumultuous landscape, a spectacular upheaval of rock cut by millions of years of wind and water, I looked around for a gift shop or information center, but we were alone.

I gazed out on rocks that were a stunning blaze of orange, red, and green in the setting sun.

"It really does look like we're on Mars," I said.

"That's because every sci-fi movie you've ever seen was shot here," said Molly, slowing down a little on the dirt road. "The Mojave Desert is Hollywood's idea of the Red Planet."

I laughed and looked around. "Who needs the Hubble telescope when we have all this?"

"Much cheaper to get here, anyway. You're supposed to be able to find a lot of fossils, too," Molly said. "The sixteen-million-year-old kind. The place was once teeming with mastodons and camels and rhinos."

"Now it's not even teeming with ants," I said. The only signs of life were a few far-off Joshua trees growing like sentinels on the canyon walls.

And two Homo sapiens sitting underneath one of them.

Molly spotted the couple, too, and she pulled the car over to the side and stopped. "I don't see any commercial shoot going on," she said.

"Maybe they finished for the day. I noticed the equipment vans in the parking lot back at the Best Western."

"We've come this far, we might as well enjoy the scenery," Molly said, getting out of the car. "You see things much better around here if you hike instead of drive."

We trudged slowly up the steep hill, the slippery soil giving way under the rubber soles of my Tod's moccasins. Despite the stunning and vast terrain, both of us kept our eyes focused on the couple under the tree.

"Julie Boden and Roy Evans," I confirmed to Molly in a whisper, as we got closer.

"I thought he'd been tossed off the commercial. Ego bigger than his talent."

"That's what I heard."

We approached the twosome from behind, and we'd maneuvered within shouting distance when Julie finally sensed someone coming. Startled, she swiveled around and seemed to shove something into the sand behind her back.

But Molly strode up to her with a friendly smile. And then, of all the unlikely openings for a desert rendezvous, she extended a hand as if she were table-hopping at Spago and said, "I'm Molly Archer of Molly Archer Casting."

Julie scrambled to her feet and, against all odds, looked vaguely impressed. She hesitantly reached out to shake Molly's hand. "Nice to meet you."

"I'm here to tell you that I should have cast this commercial for you," Molly said. "Hire my agency and I'll get Sting to star in your next round."

If Julie was baffled that Molly Archer had traveled to Rainbow Basin trying to drum up business, she didn't show it. Getting a gig in Hollywood was never easy.

"We have Jessica Simpson starring," Julie said.

"You're doing a car commercial, not the Radio Music Awards," chided Molly. "Jessica's fans are too young to drive."

"Buick wanted to hit a younger demographic."

"Haven't they heard about Boomer power? Forty to sixty is the new eighteen to thirty-four."

Julie paused to ponder that one. But Roy Evans, annoyed with shop talk, stood up now, too. He looked even bulkier than I had remembered, his eyes meaner. He sniffed the air like a black bear sensing trouble, then took a lumbering step forward.

"What the hell are you two doing here?" he asked.

In the odd acoustics of the desert, the deep growl of his voice resounded across the rocks, bouncing across the canyons and echoing angrily back at us.

"We're hiking," Molly said, thoroughly unruffled. "Isn't this a beautiful place? And since we all ended up here together, we might as well talk."

"I don't want to talk. To either of you. Get the hell out," Roy said. Behind him, the sun was sinking fast, and the spot where we stood suddenly fell into shadow.

"Thanks, but we'll stay. This is a public preserve," said Molly mildly.

"Get out," Roy repeated, his voice jagged. "It's dangerous to hike here. Especially for your friend. Her."

And to prove it, he pulled out a gun and shot once into the distance.

I screamed, then screamed again. But the earsplitting report of the bullet overpowered my shrill shrieks of terror. I jerked back, planning to run away, but instead I tripped on a rock and stumbled. Molly grabbed for my arm and pulled me back to my feet. She held me tightly and I figured we'd hot-foot it down the hill together, but instead she squared her shoulders to face Roy and stood unbudging.

"What do you think you're doing?" she asked him, with just the slightest tremble in her voice.

"Come closer and you'll find out," Roy said. He moved the gun in a slow arc in front of him then pointed it at me, the barrel on an even line with my chest. If he pulled the trigger, at least I'd die fast.

Julie took a few steps toward Roy and reached out to stroke his shoulder. "Put it away, Roy," she said softly but firmly. "Put the gun away. You don't need any more trouble."

"She's the troublemaker," Roy replied, staring at me across the barrel of the weapon. "Little Miss Goody Two-shoes. I fucked Tasha, so that means I killed her, huh? Is that what you're trying to prove?"

"I . . . I don't know," I said, my voice croaking as badly as a first-round failure on *American Idol*.

"Why would anyone think you killed Tasha?" Molly asked boldly. Despite the gun, she hadn't stepped away from my side.

Roy snorted. "Did you tell her about the tapes yet?" he asked me. "The ones you said you threw away?"

I shook my head. I hadn't mentioned them and, dammit, I still hadn't watched them. I should have, because for Roy, real life was reel life, best played out on a screen.

"Then let's clear the air," Roy said, his nostrils flaring. He looked at Molly. "Two kinds of movies get made in L.A. and Tasha only had a chance in one of them. But even that's tough. She was lousy at threesomes and just ordinary for straight fucking and blow jobs. But she was made for S and M. She still had that scared look when she got tied up."

"So you were helping her get into porn," Molly said coolly.

"Not a crime," said Roy, even though it was. "We made some audition tapes the day she died, right after I took her to get her tongue pierced." Roy snickered. "I should've had a camera there. She screamed so loud I swear the queer tattoo artist got a hard-on."

"What happened to the audition tapes?" Molly asked.

"Your friend the bitch has them." He turned to me with a leer. "What do you do, watch them every night before you fuck that killer husband of yours? He get off on seeing Tasha tied up?"

"If I had the tapes, don't you think I'd have given them to the police by now?" I asked tremulously, ignoring both his sordid question and the queasy feeling in my stomach.

The sun had dipped behind another peak and darkness was setting in quickly. Roy stroked the gun in his hand.

Julie touched Roy's shoulder again. "Stop worrying about the tapes," she said to him almost in a whisper. "Even if they show them to a jury, it'll just be evidence of Tasha's bad character, not yours."

"I was helping her," Roy hissed. "I got her to wax her bush. Pierce her tongue. Every time I advised her, she was grateful. Made sure to thank me regularly. Why would I kill her?"

"You wouldn't," Julie said briskly. "Ms. Molly Archer of Molly Archer Casting understands that Tasha must have appreciated you. She knows what people will do for a break in this business."

"I've never dealt with the porn business," Molly said evenly.

"It's all the same," Julie said, smoothing out the bangs around her face. "You know what they say: the difference between a movie star and a porn star is the size of her tits."

Roy laughed and slipped the gun back into his pocket. He seemed normal again—Mr. Hyde gone and Dr. Jekyll returned.

Just like that day at his apartment, a switch flipped to change him from star to psychopath—and back again.

"We need to leave. The crew is expecting me back at the hotel," Julie said. She turned her back to us and kneeled down, digging out the vial that she'd shoved into the sand and slipping it into her bag. We gathered belongings and walked down the hill together, as if we'd just finished a late-afternoon picnic.

"How's the commercial going?" Molly asked Julie when we got to her Range Rover.

"We should finish tomorrow," Julie said, in producer mode. "We start at dawn to catch the sun rising over the desert. Amazing light at that hour. The whole place gets an eerie pink glow."

For mimicking the Red Planet, pink was apparently close enough. Right now, though, everything around us had dissolved into shades of gray.

"It's beautiful here," Molly said. Then, turning to Roy, she added casually, "So pretty I guess you couldn't stay away, even after Julie fired you off the commercial."

I tensed, half expecting Roy to grab for his gun again. But Julie gave him a little kiss on the cheek and linked her arm through his.

"Roy came out to visit and cheer me up," she said. And there was something like affection in her voice when she added, "He's always full of surprises."

Molly drove the Range Rover slowly down the now dark Old Fossil Road. Roy followed closely behind, his headlights beaming bright in the rearview mirror. When we hit the highway, Molly picked up speed and Roy did the same, zipping past her and disappearing into the black night. Eventually, we spotted the neon lights of the Best Western sign glowing against the dark sky, but Molly didn't slow down. Like me, she wanted to get away.

We chatted idly, not quite ready to analyze the bizarre scene that had just occurred. But then there was a long silence and Molly finally said, "You okay?"

"I guess so." I sighed. "This gets weirder and weirder, doesn't it? At least Roy cleared up the mystery of the tapes. Now I'm just pissed that we came all this way and didn't get any information on Johnny DeVito."

Molly shook her head. "You're like the cops. You get a theory and then you only want evidence that'll support it. A few minutes ago you were up close and personal with Roy Evans's handgun. Aren't you a little curious about the psycho with the Saturday night special?"

"Is that what it's called?" I asked. Not that it made much difference. Whether he was a bozo with a Beretta or a freak waving a forty-five, I didn't want anything more to do with him.

Molly shrugged. "I didn't do a ballistics test, but I can tell you it wasn't a prop. He had a gun in his pocket, and he wasn't happy to see us."

I nodded. "Roy's scary. But he seems more desperate than dangerous. Johnny, on the other hand, is an ex-con and a blackmailer. And probably a killer."

"But Roy's just a charter member of the Sierra Club, looking for unspoiled places to hike?"

Instead of replying, I peeked out the window to check where we were, but the landscape disappeared into inky blackness just a few feet away. All seemed calm, but I half expected a coyote or a jaguar to leap out from the murky depths and claw at our safe, sealed car. Isn't that what had happened with Dan and me? We'd been gliding along, cozy and secure in our idyllic suburban life, when inexplicable danger suddenly menaced.

"Hungry?" Molly asked me suddenly.

"Starved," I admitted, grateful for the change of topic. "Or maybe it's just that huge hole in the pit of my stomach."

"At least it's not from a bullet," said Molly, with black humor.

We pulled off the road at the next exit, and for once in my life I would have been happy to see a Burger King or some golden arches. But instead of fast food America, we'd exited into last-century Americana. The town boasted a general store (closed) and a gas station (ditto). The only light glowed dimly from a small aluminum-sided diner, and Molly pulled up next to a sign outside promising MEATLOFA SPECIAL, $7.99.

"It's been a while since I've had meatloaf," Molly said as we went inside and settled into a booth with red vinyl seats and a speckled Formica table. The glass salt-and-pepper shakers and the sugar dish looked like they'd been there since about 1965, and a television set over the counter blasted the Classic Sports network. The two old men sitting on stools in front of it drank beers and futilely hollered for Dallas to win Super Bowl V. On the set, Curt Gowdy talked about quarterback Johnny Unitas and mentioned the college band that would play at halftime. No multimillion-dollar production with klieg lights, screaming fans, and the Rolling Stones? Even I was feeling a little nostalgic.

"They don't have meatloaf—they have meatlofa," I said, pulling myself back to the moment. "Which could be made out of almost anything."

"Got to take a chance once in a while," Molly said. "Here's hoping it comes with mashed potatoes."

The waitress came over and Molly ordered her meatloaf special. This was a place to watch a zone defense, not order a Zone diet, but I asked for an omelet with no toast, no French fries, and no cheese.

"And egg whites only, please," I said.

"Can't do that," said the waitress, taking my menu. "You ever seen an egg that came without a yolk?"

Molly grinned at me, and when the waitress walked away, she

said, "Good lesson. Sometimes you have to take things as they come. Appreciate what's in front of you."

I sighed. "I know you're not talking about meatloaf. Or even meatlofa. So what's in front of me that I'm not appreciating?"

"Do I have to tell you again?" Molly leaned forward, her eyes glinting with excitement. "Think about it. The same Roy Evans who'd been kicked off a commercial was sitting in the middle of the desert with Julie Boden, the woman who'd kicked him off. And then, just for the fun of it, he started waving a gun. He at least deserves to be on your list of suspects."

I took a piece of white bread from the basket and began tearing it into small pieces. "So Roy's crazy, I get that. He's a creep. But if every creep in L.A. had also killed someone, the highways wouldn't be so crowded."

"Agreed. But we didn't know this whole porn angle before." Molly paused to take her own small piece of bread, then squished it between her fingers into a doughy square. "Here's the thing. Roy said Tasha's talent was for S and M and he was helping her make an audition tape. We can pretty well guess that he tied her up for the camera. Now here's the question. What if he liked the panicked expression on her face so much that he went a little too far trying to get it?"

I squirmed on the vinyl seat. "Every actress's dream, to die for her art. If you think Roy's a killer, why were you so stoic out there? Did you notice the gun waving at me?"

"Sorry." Molly smiled sheepishly. "I came to the quick conclusion that Roy wasn't firing it, he was just stoked on crystal meth. Julie told you he uses. Sex, drugs, and rock and roll, she said, right? I've seen actors snorting in the bathroom before a casting call. Word on the street is that it's as good for acting as for sex because you lose all inhibitions. Dangerous, though. The stuff's damn addictive."

I took a sip of water and crunched on the ice chips. "That doesn't answer your first question—why Julie and Roy wandered into the desert together."

Molly shrugged. "You saw the same vial I did. I figure he's supplying her."

I blinked a few times, trying to open my eyes to the evidence. "First time I met Julie, I'd decided that she and Roy had been lovers—and the affair went sour. But I could be wrong."

"Or you could be right," Molly said generously. "Let's say she hired him for the first round of commercials because they were screwing. A few obsessive weeks together with wild sex and crystal meth. Then the passion cooled and she got disillusioned."

I tugged at a corner of my scratchy paper napkin. "Or maybe she was still in love but heard about Tasha and decided to get rid of her rival," I said, playing out an idea. "She wanted Roy for herself. Who needs competition from someone half your age?"

"Hell hath no fury like a forty-year-old woman who's been bested by a bimbo," said Molly. "Is that your new theory? Julie instead of Johnny or Roy?"

I rolled some bread between my fingers, making a white gummy ball to match Molly's square. "I don't know. Does Julie strike you as a killer?"

"I think anybody could be a killer, given the right circumstances. If the motive was money or power, Julie would be on top of my list. But I don't see her risking her career—never mind her life—for a second-rate star. Remember, she fired him. It makes more sense to me that the love affair ended, and the drug affair began."

The waitress clattered over and dropped off our plates. Molly looked at her meal—the hoped-for mashed potatoes and a brown square of what in college we called mystery meat. She stabbed the lumpy mess with her fork, then tentatively took a bite. My yolk-yellow omelet featured a glob of fat congealing on the top and a huge scoop of greasy hash browns towering over the side of the plate. Maybe the chef was trying to drum up business for the local Jenny Craig. I played with the decorative orange peel, wondering if I could make it a meal.

"Okay, so let's think about Roy," I said. With no blood redirected to my stomach for digestion, at least my brain was working well. "Your theory is that he was making a porn tape with Tasha, tied her up, had one of his mood swings, and went too far. End of story. Simple enough for a jury to understand. I'd buy it. But then, I'd buy anything that doesn't involve Dan."

Molly nodded. "Want to run it by Chauncey Howell?"

I rolled my eyes. "No, I couldn't bear to hear him be polite but patronizing again. To have him thank me for my nice opinions but note that the only real evidence still points to my husband. Any solution involving Roy doesn't fit in with the evidence of the neighbor who heard Tasha screaming, 'Stop it, Dr. Fields, stop it!' "

Molly pushed aside her plate, motioned to the waitress for a check, then left twenty dollars for the four bites we'd eaten between us. She didn't say anything more as we strolled back to the car and she slid into the driver's seat. We cruised silently through the grim town, then got back on the dark highway, with a Ray Charles CD providing the only sound.

"Lacy, I have a question," Molly said finally. "What if Roy didn't kill Tasha, and it wasn't Johnny DeVito or Julie or a masked stranger? Are you going to be able to cope if Dan was somehow . . . involved?"

"Why would you even ask me that?"

"Well, we can make fun of Chauncey all we want, but he's a pro. You hired him because he's the best. If he says the evidence is against Dan, maybe it really is."

So far I'd had some day. I'd traveled to this godforsaken part of the country, gone one-on-one with a gun, and risked dysentery to eat dinner. Now I felt a blinding migraine coming on, and I shut my eyes, trying to block out the whole world. Molly's question was more than I could bear.

"I told you about Johnny's blackmail and why Dan went to Tasha's in the first place. Doesn't that explain enough?" I asked

"Sure, but I thought of a problem. Dan said he went upstairs and into the empty apartment. You've been to that building, Lacy. How do you get in the main door?"

"There's no doorman, just an intercom," I said. "Somebody has to buzz you in."

"But who?" Molly asked. "Roommate Nora had decamped to Idaho and Johnny DeVito's got an alibi that puts him far away. An intruder or killer in the apartment wouldn't welcome a stranger."

Molly paused, as if she couldn't get herself to finish the thought. But she managed it anyway. "So the somebody who buzzed Dan in was probably Tasha Barlow. Which means they would have been alone together in the apartment."

I stared out the window, then bit my lip, suddenly furious.

"You're supposed to be my friend, Molly. I can't believe you'd say something like that."

She sighed. "Sorry, honey. I'm your *best* friend. That's why I said it."

Lashing out at Molly wouldn't get me anything but agitated. I leaned forward and adjusted the volume of the CD player, turning it high so we wouldn't have to talk anymore. The car filled with the sounds of Ray Charles crooning his classic "Here We Go Again." "*I'll be her fool again . . . One more time,*" he sang soulfully.

Okay, one more time. Was I a loyal wife or a fool? A fool for love, a meddling fool, a fool rushing in where angels feared to tread. Dan had fooled some of the people some of the time—could it be that he'd fooled me all the time?

Outside the car window, I heard a coyote howling. In the mournful wail, I felt danger lurking, unseen forces moving closer. I needed to be the shield that protected my family from all threats. But how could I do that when the real menace might already be inside?

Chapter Twelve

Late the next afternoon, Chauncey called, and I found myself clenching my teeth to get through the conversation. Lately, talking to Chauncey was like going to a bad masseur at a pricey spa—you spent a fortune and hurt more than ever when he was done.

"The district attorney shared Tasha Barlow's bank records with me. He didn't have to do that, but we have a good relationship," Chauncey said, letting me know just how well connected he was.

"Anything interesting?" I asked.

"Well, yes, Lacy, something very interesting. Tasha had made two five-thousand-dollar deposits recently. They were just around the dates Dan said he had made two blackmail payoffs. Though he claimed the money had gone to Johnny DeVito."

"So Johnny gave Tasha the cash. That's not a shock," I said starchily.

"All I'm saying is that it doesn't help our case," Chauncey said mildly. "If you follow the money, it just makes another connection between Dan and Tasha, not Dan and Johnny DeVito."

I slammed down the phone. I knew Chauncey lined up on our side, but he sometimes felt like a scout for the other team. Still, Molly was right when she said he was a pro. And he had a reason for giving me the report about the bank records. It could be that just like Molly, he was he trying to prepare me for the worst. I didn't want to be prepared—I wanted to fight.

I went to Grant's room and found him huddled at his computer with Jake, playing online poker.

"Hate to interrupt if you're winning," I said, "but I've got a question. I have an email that's kind of important. Do you think you can trace the source?" Why follow the money when we could just follow the email?

Jake hit FOLD on the computer screen, ending his hand, and then adjusted his glasses. "I can try, Mrs. Fields."

I went to Dan's downstairs office and found the last email from Johnny. Dan and I had studied it together when he first told me about the blackmail, but it was curt—two lines telling Dan to show up at apartment 4C with five thousand dollars and giving the time and date. I erased the message—too much information to share with our son—and forwarded it to Grant's computer, typing in "This is what I need traced." An hour later, I wandered back down to Grant's room.

"Got anything on the email from Johnny?" I asked them.

Grant cleared his throat and rubbed at his eyes. "Well, Mom, you don't really know it was from Johnny. Anyone could have sent it."

Since I'd printed out the page, I looked at it now, studying the text as if it were the Book of Job.

"The address line said johnnydevito@yourmail.com," I said. "That kind of sounds like it's from Johnny."

"Or from someone who wants you to think that," said Jake, pushing back his wire-framed eyeglasses. "You can alter the name on the FROM line pretty easily. This is one of those free sites, so I tracked it and found who signed up."

"Who?"

"Drew Barrymore."

"What?"

Grant gave a little smile and Jake sniggered. "Not a lot of security on these sites," explained Jake. "It's easy to register under any name. Johnny DeVito could have been trying to hide his tracks by using a fake name. Or someone else could have registered and been sending emails under his name."

I couldn't think of a single reason anyone would do that.

"Since the registration didn't prove anything, I figured I'd try to track down the actual computer it came from," said Jake. "It's pretty easy."

Jake exchanged a look with Grant. If he'd done something else illegal, I didn't want to know about it. But I was curious.

"How do you do that?" I asked.

"Every computer has a unique signature, which can't be changed. It's called the IP address," said Jake.

"It's like tracking someone down by a fingerprint instead of a name," added Grant helpfully.

Jake nodded. "So I tried to find the IP address that was used to register on the site. If you know which server it's on, you can then trace it to the individual computer. That's the hard part, but I happened to get lucky."

"Not luck. More like all you computer nerds know each other," said Grant.

"That, too," admitted Jake. "Anyway, I know someone who has a friend at the server company who was able to find what computer had that IP address."

I looked at him expectantly.

"The computer belonged to Tasha Barlow."

The name fell hollowly into the room.

"So the email you gave us—that you thought was from Johnny—was written on Tasha's computer," said Jake.

I swallowed and looked at the boys, whose faces were both contorted in concern. "That doesn't mean Tasha wrote it," I said, trying to sound unworried. "Johnny visited her apartment a lot. Makes sense if he used her computer, doesn't it?" I smiled, because the two of them were still staring at me. "Listen, guys, thanks for all the help. I'll stake you in the next poker game. My treat."

I left, trying not to be shaken by the news. Not information I'd share with Chauncey. I could already hear what he would say about Tasha sending emails to Dan telling him to show up at her place with money.

Over a pizza dinner with my kids that night, I made a proposal. Friday was Teacher Enhancement Day at their school (general rule: the higher the tuition, the more days off) so we had a long weekend free. While the teachers were enhancing, we could be enjoying.

"I have a great idea," I said, flipping open the box and serving a plain slice to Ashley, a pepperoni to Jimmy, and the rest of the pie—mushroom and onion—to Grant. "How about a family ski trip?"

Grant stared at me as surprised as if I'd just suggested he spend a little less time on homework and a little more time on MySpace.

"You're nuts, Mom," he said. "You hate skiing, remember? Last time we went to Tahoe, you said you'd rather hop one-footed across the Grand Canyon than go up a chairlift again."

"I can hop," said Jimmy, standing up from his seat. He tucked one foot behind him and began bouncing around the room. When he got to me, I gave him a big hug.

"Maybe it's not my favorite sport," I said, thinking fast, "but we should go because Jimmy loves skiing."

"He does?" asked Grant.

"He does?" asked Ashley.

"I do?" asked Jimmy.

Everyone stopped for a moment.

"He cried for an hour last time you took him to ski school," Ashley said. "I don't think he ever got on the mountain."

"That's because he was a little boy then. Now he's a big boy." I kissed Jimmy on the top of his head. "Right?"

Jimmy nodded solemnly. "Right," he said, just a little uncertainly.

I crouched down into the snowplow position, knees bent and toes pointed inward.

"You can do this a lot better than me," I said.

Jimmy imitated my stance.

"Let's race," I said, leaning forward and pretending to be moving forward. "I bet you're really fast now. Whoosh!"

"Whoosh!" said Jimmy. He slid across the kitchen in his neat snowplow and grinned excitedly. "Whoosh! Whoosh! Whoosh!" He looked back over his shoulder at me. "I'm faster than you. I *win*!"

"You win," I conceded. "You're going to be the champ on the slopes."

"I can't wait to go skiing for real!" Jimmy said, throwing his arms above his head, clearly elated now.

I smiled. Like everything else in life, parenting was all about spin. All Jimmy needed right now was a boost of confidence. He'd been through a lot in the last few weeks, but maybe something positive could come out of it. Compared with seeing cops running through the house and guns being pointed at his daddy, throwing himself down an icy mountain wouldn't be such a big deal.

"If we're going, I need a new ski outfit," Ashley said.

"Your jacket's practically brand-new," I reminded her.

"But it's so last year. Hot pink—and this season everyone has baby blue. And I'm thinking maybe a one-piece Gore-Tex jumpsuit with a racing stripe down the side. And a little fur at the hood."

"How much do you care?" I asked, looking for a way to avoid a fight.

"I care *desperately*," Ashley said dramatically. "I'm *desperate* for a new one."

"In that case, you can use your birthday money to buy it, instead of getting the new cell phone," I said evenly. "Of course, another possibility is to use the money for a contribution to the Make-A-Wish foundation. Give a day of joy to a sick child. Probably more worthwhile than either a new Razr or a baby blue ski suit, if you ask me—but it's your decision."

Ashley glared at me, not blinking, and I expected another typical teenage tantrum. But instead, she suddenly relaxed. "Okay, I get it," she said, sounding only slightly grumpy. "There are worse things than last year's ski outfit."

I nodded and gave her a little smile, which—miracle of miracles—she returned.

"So skiing it is. Tahoe, I guess?" asked Grant.

"I thought we'd try Sun Valley this time. Someplace new and a little more adventurous," I said carefully, not revealing my real motive for this trip.

"Oh, cool!" said Ashley. "My friend Caroline has a house there, and she says there's a private landing strip."

"I'll rev up the Gulfstream in the garage," I said. "But just in case it's not there, Delta has a direct flight. We can leave Thursday after school."

"Will Daddy come?" Ashley asked warily. Her face was blank, and I suddenly realized I didn't know what answer she wanted to hear.

"I hope so," I said.

I spent the next day digging around closets, collecting snow pants, parkas, sweaters, long underwear, ski boots, skis, poles, helmets, neck warmers, leg warmers, hand warmers, gloves, glove liners, wind masks, face masks, mufflers, and a few pairs of après-ski slippers. Stuffing it all into duffels, I suddenly remembered why I'd never wanted to go skiing again. But we made it to the plane, retrieved our luggage on the other end, rented a car, and drove to the condominium I'd rented online. I held my breath as we pulled up, but for once, it was as perfect as promised—gleaming new and huge, with floor-to-ceiling windows in the family room that looked directly out at Baldy, the big mountain where we'd ski.

I had my own reasons for coming to Idaho, but my plan couldn't wait a day. Friday morning I took Jimmy to ski school, and he cheerfully waved good-bye, saying only "Whoosh!" when I gave him a kiss. Instead of leaving, I planted myself at the bottom of the beginner slope, and a few minutes later watched Jimmy snowplow down. When he noticed me, I gave a thumbs-up, and he happily headed back to the chairlift. Since it was much more satisfying to watch Jimmy improve than to hit the trails myself, I stayed where I was. By the afternoon, he kept his skis parallel on the straightaways and made neat turns.

"Can we race for real, Mommy?" Jimmy asked me after one run, his face flushed red far more from excitement than from the cold.

"You'd beat me, no question," I said, wiping his dripping nose with a tissue.

"Probably," he said, newly puffed with pride as he headed back to the chairlift line.

Ashley and Grant insisted on having Dan ski the expert trails with them, even though he couldn't match them for speed.

"We don't mind hanging back for him," Grant said, when we all sat down in the base lodge for late-afternoon hot chocolate. "Dad always waited for us when we were little. Payback time."

"He won't have to wait for me," Jimmy said, licking whipped cream off the top of his cup. "I'm fast."

Maybe this confidence thing had gone too far.

If watching Jimmy kept me from skiing the first day, something else got in the way the next day. My back hurt. Or at least that's what I claimed. Truth was, I'd been planning this backache all week.

"You didn't do anything yesterday, so how could you be stiff?" Ashley asked the next morning, when I explained why I wouldn't join them.

"Maybe from standing on the slope watching," I suggested lamely. I rubbed my hands into the small of my back. If only I were better at acting.

"What will you do all day?" Dan asked.

"I'll go exploring, or shopping. It's beautiful here. Don't worry about me."

Dan and the kids got busy collecting equipment, all of them eager to take advantage of the perfect ski conditions—warm and sunny with a forty-two-inch base. I tucked two Kit Kat bars in the pocket of Jimmy's parka to assuage my guilt for not joining him today.

After dropping my family at the mountain, I drove back toward the town. But instead of stopping, I kept going on the two-lane highway that provided the only access in and out. Traffic in the opposite direction stacked bumper to bumper, with skiers trying to make their way to Sun Valley, but my lane remained almost empty. Why would anyone be driving away from the slopes on a day like this?

I glanced at my watch: just after 9:00 A.M. When they finished skiing, Dan would take the kids on the shuttle bus back to the condo—probably getting there about four. That gave me seven hours. If I allowed two hours to drive to Twin Falls and two hours to drive back, I still had plenty of time. Nobody had to know I'd done anything other than shop for sweaters and get a massage.

If anyone in my family somehow found out I'd gone to Twin Falls for the day, I'd explain it as a spontaneous, spur-of-the-moment inspiration. Not the whole reason we'd come here. Sure, I'd been a little deceptive in planning this family vacation for my own secret motives. But who could complain when skiing the gorgeous mountain had improved everyone's mood?

I stayed straight on the highway for about an hour, then turned onto Highway 93, heading south. Before we came, I'd done some research online and written down the phone numbers of all the

Barlows in the Twin Falls phone directory. Three of them. Not until I was leaving did I remember that Tasha Barlow had once been Theresa Bartowski. A quick check—only one. I hadn't called ahead.

When I reached Twin Falls, I pulled over and unfolded the slip of paper from my pocket. Hesitantly, I took out my cell phone and dialed the first Barlow number. Voice mail. Second number, ditto. Third number, no answer. Fourth number—the one for Bartowski. Disconnected.

Not meant to be.

I hung out for about an hour, poking around town and reading a magazine left in my car. Then I tried the numbers again. Still no answer anywhere.

Discouraged, I drove to a gas station and asked the man at the small convenience store inside if I could use a bathroom. He handed me a key. A big sign on the door said CUSTOMERS ONLY, and, feeling gripped by the sanctity of small-town morals, I grabbed a Diet Sprite as I left and handed the man behind the counter a twenty. He took another bite of his jelly doughnut, then put it down and looked at the bill.

"Have anything smaller?" he asked, leaning over the counter. In the process, his pilled woolen sweater curled up over his stout center, exposing a fleshy-white expanse. He hefted the waist of his baggy jeans, trying to pull them up, and finally got sweater and pants to make some kind of accommodation over his bulging belly.

"How much is it?"

"Dollar even."

I fumbled in my bag, but I didn't have any singles. I dug into my change purse and carefully counted all I had. "Eighty-seven cents," I said ruefully.

"Deal," he said jovially, handing me back the twenty and taking the change. "That's good enough."

"Well, thanks so much," I said, suddenly grateful to be getting a thirteen-cent discount on a soda I hadn't wanted anyway.

"Where you from?" he asked, ringing up the sale on an old-fashioned cash register. So old, in fact, it looked antique and interesting. What a find for that movie producer's house I was decorating on Benedict Canyon—a perfect conversation piece in the high-tech entertainment room.

"Uh, I'm from Los Angeles," I said. What would he think if I asked him to sell me his cash register?

His face fell. "Los Angeles. Too bad. You seem like a nice lady. And that's a mean town." He shook his head. "Mean town, Los Angeles. Makes good girls do bad things."

Something about his words sounded familiar. Then it struck me. Nora had used almost exactly the same phrase when she was talking to me about Tasha. I tried not to overreact.

"I heard the folks around here have had some tragedies in L.A. lately," I said slowly.

He nodded. "Two girls dead. Theresa, she was the most beautiful girl you've ever seen. I don't mean just in Idaho—anywhere. But pretty isn't everything. She went to L.A. and turned bad. Our Nora did everything she could to put that girl's head back on straight. And then Nora ended up dead, too." He put a pudgy thumb to his eye to wipe away a tear.

Oddly enough, I felt a little lump in my throat.

"Neither of them deserved to die," he said, his voice shaky. "But Nora, she'd always been the good one. Too good to die."

"I knew Nora," I said softly. "Kind of a coincidence, but I'd met her twice. I didn't know the other girl."

The man blew his nose. Then he wiped his hand against the leg of his jeans and held it out to me. "I'm Bill Wilson, Nora's stepfather."

"Nice to meet you, Mr. Wilson," I said. "I'm . . ." Who was I? In these parts, I couldn't say "Fields" because Dan's name must be inscribed on the dartboard in the local bar. But I'd had an identity before I got married, too. "I'm Lacy Montgomery."

"Pleased to meet ya."

"You, too."

And then I shook hands with Nora Wilson's stepfather.

I expected him to ask how I knew Nora, but another customer came up with a six-pack of Coke and a king-sized bag of Fritos, and I stepped aside to let him pay. Then a woman with Nevada plates on her car shouted from outside that the gas pump was stuck, and Mr. Wilson excused himself and plodded out to fix it. A minute later, he came back in.

"Ain't stuck if you just lift the damn lever," he muttered. "Tourists."

I gave a little smile. "We're everywhere," I said.

"I don't actually mind," he said, running a not-too-clean cloth across the counter to wipe up some coffee stains. "Keeps this place going. Right now, keeps me going, too."

He looked sad, and I nodded sympathetically. I'd spent days on end thinking about the two dead girls, but I'd never considered them quite this way—as the lost daughters of loving parents. However bad my situation right now, it didn't compare with the pain Bill Wilson must be feeling. You never knew how you'd been blessed until the treasure was lost. Never take it for granted. I closed my eyes and said a silent prayer for Grant, Ashley, and Jimmy.

"This must be horribly difficult for you and your wife. And for Theresa's parents." After all my half-baked planning, the encounter with Bill Wilson had been unexpected. And it wasn't even the meeting I'd wanted. I'd come here hoping to get some information from the other set of grieving parents.

"My wife's pretty strong," Bill Wilson said. "Her faith gets her through. She always spent a lot of time at church, and now I tell her the priest should name a pew after her." He gave a little smile. "I don't mind all her praying. We got married when Nora was thirteen, but she took my name and we were family. Her own dad had never been much—he killed himself when Nora was nine. How do you do that to a little girl?"

"My God, that's awful," I said. But we couldn't discuss it, because business picked up again. A truck driver whose sagging jeans made Bill's look like they'd been custom fit on Jermyn Street strutted in, demanding two slices of pepperoni pizza. An excessively tanned woman in form-fitting black ski pants and white Ugg boots sidled up to pay for gas and ask where she could get a double skim decaf cappuccino.

"Closest place'd be Sun Valley," Bill said.

The woman huffed out, and I gave a little laugh. I could start to like Bill Wilson. Too bad we weren't meeting under different circumstances.

When the store cleared and I had his attention again, I decided to give it one more try. "Do you see Theresa's parents much?" I asked.

He shrugged. "The Bartowskis moved away a few weeks ago. All the gossip was getting to them, and they wanted to go someplace where they could start fresh."

"What was the gossip?"

"Oh, you know. What I said before—Terry wasn't the same sweet girl anymore. She'd had her head turned. Become a whore, if you ask me." He reached for the half-eaten jelly doughnut that he'd put aside before and scarfed down the rest of it. He dug another one out of the box and wiped the sugar off his fingers with a crumpled napkin. Couldn't really blame the man for getting pleasure where he could find it right now.

"Nora visited us right before Terry died. She said evil things were going on, and Terry didn't even want her around. She'd told her not to come back. You could see it was hurting Nora. She went to church with her mother a few times and talked to the priest. They decided the devil was in Tasha and Nora had to go back and save her. But she never got the chance." I was afraid he'd start to tear up again, but he didn't.

"So Nora was here in Twin Falls when Terry died," I said.

"I wish," Bill Wilson said. "Then I would have kept her home. Never let her go back to that hell place and she'd still be alive. But she'd driven home in her old Jetta, and she said she was going to take her time getting back. She left here a day before the murder. I don't know exactly when she got there. Maybe the next day after."

"And then . . ." I paused. "What do you think happened to her? How did she end up . . ." End up dead in the trunk of my car. Tough question to ask.

"That hell place," Bill Wilson repeated. "She got sucked into it. Nobody would want to murder Nora, unless it was same person who killed Terry. That doctor, the police say. Or maybe one of the people who'd been corrupting Terry. Who knows. Nora was a saint, but you can't be a saint in a city of devils."

If you believed the newspapers, Dan was the Saint of Holly-wood, and if you accepted her stepdad's word, Nora was the saint of roommates. Now one was dead and one was accused of murder. Maybe saintliness wasn't all it was cracked up to be.

I ate a couple of slices of Bill Wilson's pepperoni pizza and swallowed some lukewarm coffee, just to hang around the store a little longer. In between customers, Bill told me his wife worked in the church office every afternoon. "If she keeps busy, she doesn't think about Nora every minute," he said. He didn't suggest I stop by. "She cries whenever she talks about what happened. So I say—don't talk." His simple solution made a certain amount of sense, though it wouldn't go over big in L.A., where the answer to every-thing was three-times-a-week therapy at two hundred bucks per hour (now down to forty-five minutes) for endless talking about what hurt. Of course you could select the mode of treatment—emotive, cognitive, behavioral, analytical, attitudinal, interven-tional, or hypocritical. No, that was something else. But I couldn't argue with Bill. God had given us defense mechanisms, so we might as well let them come to our defense.

I finally got back in my car and cruised around for a while, passing a simple church that might or might not have been the one Nora attended. Little children scampered around a school playground, and a few blocks away, clusters of teenagers hung around a parking lot smoking. The small, well-kept houses on the side streets seemed meager and unimportant compared with the lavish estates in L.A. But basically, we all lived the same life—a house, some schools, children growing up for better or worse. When you lived inside one of those houses, it was the center of the world.

Growing up, Theresa Bartowski had been one of the little girls on the playground, clambering to the top of the jungle gym and fantasizing about a future where she flew even higher. But pig-tailed reveries of Oscar-night speeches and Harry Winston jewels ended in a sordid double death. Nora's stepdad said Terry wasn't the same girl once she got to L.A., and I didn't doubt that. Tasha Barlow breathed her last in the poolside apartment, hoping for a shot at a porn flick. Beautiful, innocent Theresa Bartowski had disappeared from the world long before.

I sighed. Metaphysical musings wouldn't carry much weight in a courtroom. Nobody was murdered for a metaphor. Terry/Theresa/Tasha Bartowski/Barlow didn't die because her dream died. Somebody smothered the life out of her. Maybe she'd abandoned her past, but somebody else had decided she wouldn't have a future.

I pulled a U-turn and headed north out of town. A mile up Highway 93, signs directed me to Twin Falls' big tourist attraction—the site of one of Evel Knievel's motorcycle jumps. Actually an aborted jump—he'd never done this one. I dutifully stopped in the parking lot and looked down the five hundred-foot-deep gorge, now irrigated and bright green. More notices directed me down the road where I could apparently gaze at the dirt pile that had been planned as the launchpad. Amazing. A monument to something that hadn't happened.

I arrived back in the Sun Valley condo before the rest of the family. Half an hour later, clattering in with wet clothes and high spirits, they found me lounging in the living room. Dan stuck his skis against a rack in the foyer and walked stiffly to the sofa. Only the satisfied smile on his face kept me from immediately offering Advil.

"The best day in the history of skiing," he said happily, settling in with the hot chocolate I held out for him. "But we missed you on the mountain."

The kids cuddled around him, filling me in on their exploits— Grant soaring over moguls, Ashley and Dan cutting perfect turns together, the whole family taking Jimmy down his first intermediate slope.

"I fell twice, but it's okay to fall when you're skiing," Jimmy said, clearly parroting what the others had told him.

"You just get up again and keep going," said Dan.

"And I kept going," said Jimmy proudly.

Ashley's day had been improved by a dark-haired sixteen-year-old boy who had flirted with her in the lodge during lunch.

"His name's Nick, he's from Manhattan, and he goes to a private school called Dalton," she reported. "I might visit and go to the junior prom with him."

"Dream on," said Grant, who was leaning against the back of the sofa.

"No dream. He already text-messaged me," Ashley said smugly, as if the memo on her Motorola was just the first step to a lingering kiss, a BCBG charmeuse prom dress, and—God forbid—a post-prom breakfast on the beach. I shuddered, wondering when teenage dreams improved life—and when they turned dangerous.

Grant bent forward to stretch out his skiing-constricted

quadriceps, then nimbly touched his toes. "I'm going to shower," he announced, bouncing upright and doing a couple of waist twists before heading to his room.

"Good idea," said Dan. He stood up with just a little creaking in the knees and, despite obviously aching muscles, scooped up Jimmy from the sofa and swung him onto his shoulder. "Come on, champ. Let's get you into dry clothes."

Jimmy giggled happily as they went off, and once all the testosterone had left the room, Ashley took a sip of hot chocolate.

"Think it'd be okay for me to call Nick? And maybe see him tomorrow?" she asked, swirling the cinnamon stick.

"It wouldn't do any harm," I said slowly. "But just keep it in perspective. If he's from New York, you're probably not going to see him very much after that."

"Yeah, I guess you're right," said Ashley. She licked some whipped cream off the edge of her mug and sat back, curling her legs under her like a contented kitten. Maybe reality didn't have to be that painful, after all.

"So it was fun today?" I asked, going for the open-ended question.

"Almost felt like we were a regular family again." She sighed. "I wish we could just stay in Sun Valley and forget all the awful stuff in L.A."

I nodded sympathetically.

"Daddy seemed happy skiing," Ashley continued. "You know what I figured out? He wants us to be proud of him. He's always been the one who saved people and got charity awards and stuff. Everyone admired him. Now all that's gone. He must feel like less than zero."

"He does want you to be proud," I agreed.

"I was remembering that night a while ago when we were eating Chinese food and he made a big deal about getting a book contract. I shouldn't have gotten so mad at him," Ashley said ruefully.

"Mandy says that whenever a boy's being a jerk, it's usually because he's even more insecure than you are."

"Mandy's probably right."

"You know, it's not so easy being me these days," Ashley said, not quite ready to lose the sympathy vote, "but it's got to be even harder being Daddy."

I shimmied over on the sofa and put my arm around her. Fourteen wasn't famous as the age of empathy. But she was doing pretty darn well.

"You're a great kid," I said, giving her a hug. "And you're really growing up."

"Think so?" Ashley took a final sip of hot chocolate and looked at me over the rim of the mug. She gave a little smile. "Then maybe I'll meet Nick tomorrow, after all."

Chapter Thirteen

Tim Riley agreed to talk to me about Roy Evans and suggested we meet at Club L.A. at 6:15 A.M. If that was the only time during the day that a big-time TV producer didn't get disturbed, I was game. But five minutes after I dragged myself into the gym, Tim's Blackberry started beeping. He apologetically thumbed through the e-mails already pouring in, then quickly called a reporter in Las Vegas to say that, yes, he needed his story edited and mixed immediately. He might use it in that night's show.

"I know it's at a strip club, but keep it clean or it'll never air," Tim said to the producer. "Network Standards and Practices is now being run by two celibate monks and a kindergarten teacher."

He took two more calls, then hung up and looked at me with an abashed smile. "Sorry. I guess we should have met at five thirty. Sometimes it's quieter then."

"Definitely quieter for me," I said. "The only sound I make then is snoring. Don't you ever sleep?"

"Not on this job." Tim flashed an appealingly lopsided smile. "The geniuses on the East Coast can't seem to figure out the three-hour time difference. I should have sent them calculators at Christmas. I just flew back from New York, and I swear I'm not even going to reset my watch."

"You don't have to," I said, taking his arm to study the oversized chronographic timepiece on his wrist. "This Concord could probably monitor ten time zones. And I bet it keeps ticking a thousand feet underwater. Long after your heart has stopped."

He grinned, then climbed onto a True treadmill and set the digital display for a CARDIO-FIT workout. "For now, at least, my heart's still ticking. Mind if we talk and walk?"

"Sure." I'd come prepared in Nikes and workout garb, so I got onto the treadmill next to his and glanced at Tim out of the corner of my eye. He was tall and lean, with firm-as-steel calf muscles, dark, curly hair, and small rimless glasses. I knew he was smart as a whip, and he looked more New York intellectual than L.A. producer. No wonder Molly adored him. Maybe I could convince them each to stop working for an hour and go out on a real date.

"So I hear you have Roy Evans's homemade porn tapes," Tim said, almost immediately adjusting the speed on his treadmill from warm-up walk to jog. A few drops of sweat popped out appealingly on his gray tee. "Do you want to come over to my office and watch them?"

From the elliptical machine across from us, a studly young guy laughed. "Hey, Tim, is that your pickup line now? Come watch porn with me?"

Tim didn't bother looking up, he just flipped a finger at his friend.

I cranked up my own speed. "I have the tapes but I haven't seen them yet."

"Just one more illicit activity in the pathetic portfolio of Roy Evans," said Tim.

"I know you're doing an internal investigation. Have you found much on him?" I asked, panting slightly from exertion. Since the night of Dan's arrest, I hadn't been exercising—unless you counted endless spinning on a psychic treadmill.

"I don't want him back on the air—but I'm trying to be fair," Tim said. "I feel like one of those special prosecutors, because more and more turns up every day. I guess if you look hard enough, you can sink anybody."

Is that what was happening to Dan? The police were looking hard and working hard to make sure he sank.

"What's the word on the body they found by Roy's car?" I asked, surreptitiously lowering the speed on my treadmill. I'd have to count on anxiety to keep me thin.

"The police ruled it foul play. But off the record, the coroner thought there were some indications of suicide."

"How could that be?" I asked, remembering the horror in my trunk. "It'd be a pretty good trick to kill yourself, jump into a black garbage bag, and then tie the top from the outside. Even Houdini would have been impressed."

"True," said Tim, adjusting the incline on his machine to mimic running uphill. Frankly, I'd go for a downhill button about now. "But the report says the body appears to have been moved several times after death."

Give the coroner credit for getting that right. Move one: someone had put Nora, dead Nora, in the trunk of my car. Move two: someone else dragged her body from my car into the parking lot of the White Lotus. I still wasn't sure how Molly had managed that little trick, though it wouldn't have been too hard for her to get the club attendant to look the other way. Maybe she promised to cast him as an extra on *One Tree Hill*. Being a casting agent in L.A. was better than being the pope at a nursing home. Everybody was willing to kiss the ring now for a heavenly payoff later.

"For Roy, I've got deviant conduct on and off the set. Plus drugs and more drugs. I can't decide if he's a manic-depressive, a psychopath, or just a badly behaved addict."

"All nice choices."

Tim turned up the treadmill speed again, running so fast now he seemed ready to cross a finish line on the other side of the gym. "I'm going to my office after this," Tim panted. "Come on by and we'll watch the tapes. I'll provide the popcorn."

* * *

I didn't really want to go back to the storage warehouse myself, but I didn't see a choice. Molly had done enough. Grant had done too much. Ashley and Jimmy were out of the question and Dan wouldn't want to know. Chauncey Howell was out of my budget. I didn't need an escort who charged five hundred bucks an hour.

A different Korean sat at the front desk this time, and he simply nodded when I waved my key in his direction. The corridors seemed better lit than before and no bats flew down at me. I wandered uneasily toward my cubicle, realizing that I'd half suspected the first time I was here that I was hiding porn tapes. Maybe I'd never wanted to see them.

I found the shopping bag in the storage space just where I'd left it and I pawed through, tossing Roy's suit and shoes and shirts back in the cubby. If I forgot to pay by the third of next month, the Korean would be slightly better dressed.

I arrived back at Tim's office and found him huddled with two other producers, trying to put together the final cut on the night's show. He took one look at my overflowing bag of tapes and shook his head.

"All from Roy?" he asked.

"Yes, but not all of them are . . . well, you know. Some are just his show segments. Tapes of interviews he'd done. All the things he liked to watch in bed."

One of the producers in the room, a youngish woman with form-fitting jeans and bright-orange Pumas, giggled.

"My boyfriend watches golf in bed," she said. "Not a great aphrodisiac."

"Unless someone scores a hole in one," offered the guy next to her.

Tim shook his head, then got up and led me down the hall to a cluster of high-tech digital edit suites. He poked his head into one after another, but all of them were full.

"Find me a plain old VCR and I'll look at them by myself," I said.

"It'll take you forever," Tim said. "You've got more hours of film there than in *Doctor Zhivago*. Talk about slogging through."

He made a call to another part of the building, and when he hung up, he said, "Good news. One of the best editors we have is free for a couple of hours. Corey. He's quick—and he won't blab, either."

Ten minutes later, I paced around the back of Corey's editing room while he fast-forwarded through the first tape, the start-to-finish recording of an endless interview Roy had done with some third-rate *Survivor* contestant.

"Raw footage," Corey said, popping the tape out. "But not the kind of raw we're looking for."

The second tape was boring but aboveboard, as was the third. The fourth and fifth were segments that had aired on *Night Beat*, and the sixth was Roy's favorite—himself on *Celebrity Jeopardy!* Corey moved quickly but carefully through the tapes, scanning half a dozen more.

"If this is what he watched with Tasha, I'd guess he murdered the poor girl with monotony," Corey said finally.

"We have more," I said, looking into the bag, which was beginning to feel bottomless.

"Hand 'em over," said Corey wearily. "Though if the union hears that I had to screen this Roy Evans film festival, I'll qualify for hardship pay."

I laughed. But eight tapes later, the bag was empty, and the dirtiest trick we'd seen involved Roy pushing aside a reporter from *Entertainment Tonight* to interview Usher at a press conference.

"I don't get it," I said, bewildered. The tapes were all as harmless as a network-censored night at the Bellagio.

Corey started piling the tapes back into the bag and I sat back thoroughly befuddled, staring at the bank of now blank monitors.

Somehow, the day had disappeared and the clock in the window-less edit bay pointed to 6:05 P.M.

"So what did you find?" asked an excited voice behind us.

I turned around to see Molly and Tim striding into the edit room. Tim must have finished his show and sent it via satellite for the prime-time airing on the East Coast. That was the good side of L.A.'s functioning on New York time—not much sleep, but everybody got dinner.

"Nothing interesting," I reported. "Nada, naught, zero, zilch. Closest we got to sex was Roy leering at Beyoncé's booty."

"Don't forget when he got on his knees in front of Lindsay Lohan," said Corey. "Though that didn't turn pornographic until he explained he was bowing before acting greatness."

Molly laughed and grabbed a snack-sized Snickers bar from the well-stocked candy bowl on the table. The best part of television was the unending supply of junk food in every edit bay. Or maybe that was the worst part. Tim reached into the dish and filched a single cinnamon Altoid. Given his running this morning, he could go crazy and take two.

"I don't get it," Tim said, sucking thoughtfully on the mint. "From what Molly said, Roy admitted that he'd made porno tapes with Tasha."

I nodded. "Yup. And he was sure I had them."

"So if you don't have them, who does?" asked Molly.

"Question of the day," I admitted.

Molly scanned the room, her eyes finally resting on Corey. "Are you sure you didn't miss something on one of the tapes? I mean, you could have skipped right over a bad blow job without even re-alizing it."

"Wrong and wrong," said Corey, rocking back in his swiveling seat. "First, you can't have a bad blow job. Second, I'd never skip one." He grinned. "Nope, we screened every single tape and didn't miss a thing. I'd bet my last Emmy on it."

"Corey's won three Emmys," Tim said, as if that settled it.

Molly plopped down in the chair next to me, and Tim leaned against the table, his long, outstretched legs brushing against Molly's.

"Let's try to figure this out," Tim said, pulling out a yellow legal pad. He made a couple of notes with his Sharpie pen, then raised a finger. "Point one. We know Roy made S-and-M tapes featuring himself and Tasha. Point two"—two fingers up now—"we also know he was so desperate to get them back that he tied up Lacy in his apartment and then threatened her with a gun in the desert." Tim made a couple of arrows on his pad, and then he looked from Molly to me. "Add points one and two and you get to point three. Which is that given what we know about Roy, it's just possible he recorded more than bad sex. I'm willing to consider whether the missing tape shows the S and M gone wrong—and Tasha dying."

Molly reached over and rubbed her hand against Tim's knee. "Darling, you're the most brilliant man I know. You got to that one fast."

She looked at me and I nodded. We'd come up with that theory in the diner, over bad meatloaf and omeletes. But now that I'd rolled it around for a while, I saw a problem.

"If Roy were rolling tape while he accidentally killed Tasha, don't you think he would have taken the evidence with him?" I asked.

"Unless he panicked and forgot about it," said Tim.

"In which case he would have left the incriminating tape in the video camera and just run out," I said. "I've read the police reports and seen the crime-scene photos. No video camera that I can remember."

"If he took the camera, he took the tape, too," Molly said, coming quickly to my point of view.

"Fair enough." Tim ripped the top sheet off the pad, crumpled it up, and threw it away. "So you're thinking the tape's not a smoking gun—just a smoky one. If a girl's been strangled, you don't want the cops to know you once liked tying her up."

"I'll buy that," said Molly. Her hand was still on Tim's knee.

I fished around in the candy bowl and pulled out a silver-wrapped chocolate Kiss.

"So where are Roy's porn flicks?" I asked.

"That's the question," said Tim, picking up his Sharpie to scrawl a four-sided form on the new sheet of paper. "We're right back to square one."

"The tapes must have been in the apartment somewhere, which is why Roy thinks I have them," I explained. "Nora had told him that she gave me all his stuff."

"Maybe they're still there," suggested Molly.

"Or maybe the police took the tapes at the very beginning. And buried them as evidence because they're only looking to make a case against Dan," I offered.

Tim raised his eyebrows. "Corrupt cops? I guess this is L.A."

"Corrupt's one thing, but clever's something else," said Corey, suddenly entering the conversation again. "You're giving the cops way too much credit." He flung the contents of the now ragged Whole Foods bag back onto the floor. "Look at all these tape boxes. They're mismarked and badly labeled and they were probably scattered all around the apartment. It took us hours to scan through them. So how the hell would the police have known which ones to seize? You can bet Roy didn't plaster the pornos with triple-X stickers."

I put my head into my hands. I wanted everything to be the cops' fault, but Corey had a point. There had to be a different explanation. I just didn't know what it was.

Tim glanced at his watch, checking the time in whatever world zone he'd settled on using. "Anybody want to go to dinner?" he asked. "We can continue this over some food."

Corey quickly declined and I said I had to get home. We both stood up to leave.

"I'd love to come," Molly told Tim with a big smile. Then she leaned over to the candy dish and rifled through.

"What are you looking for?" Tim asked.

"A chocolate Kiss like Lacy took. I'm starved."

Tim grabbed her hand and pulled her to her feet. "Come on, you can do better than that. How about if I promise you a kiss after dinner?"

"Chocolate?" Molly asked coyly.

"Nope," said Tim. "It'll be fewer calories. And much tastier."

When I got home, Ashley met me at the door and announced that the police were in the living room, asking questions about the murder of Nora Wilson.

"Shit," I said.

Ashley's mouth twitched and she tried to keep herself from smiling. "Since when do you use language like that, Mom?" she asked with faux disapproval.

"Since today. Sorry. Who's with them?"

"Daddy. And Chauncey Howell."

So Dan had called Chauncey. That was a relief, anyway. "Have they been here long?"

"Yup. And you're right, Mom—it's shit. Bullshit and double bullshit. I can't stand this place. Why don't we just all get on a plane and get out of here? Move to Australia."

"New Zealand might be better. We could pretend we're in *Lord of the Rings*."

"I'm serious," Ashley said, furrowing her brow. "Daddy's being persecuted. We have to leave. Just like that scene in *The Sound of Music* where the family climbs into the mountains together to escape the Nazis."

"That was Austria, not Australia."

"Who cares? As long as we're together, we can go anyplace." She looked at me with blazing eyes, thoroughly serious about her plan. She wanted to protect her dad, whatever it took.

I put my arms around her. "You're right. A family's pretty strong. *Our* family's strong." I hugged her. "For now, we'll keep fighting for Daddy right here. But if it doesn't work, we'll consider every option. I'm perfectly willing to be Julie Andrews."

"Or Frodo," said Ashley.

She went upstairs, and I contemplated joining the crowd in the living room, then decided there wasn't any point. I slid open the double-glass doors to the patio and went outside. Darkness was settling in, and the early-evening stars peeked across the sky. I lay down on the padded chaise lounge and stared straight up, spotting a shooting star. I closed my eyes and made a virtuous wish upon a shooting star that involved Dan being cleared and his anguish being over. Then I threw in a little fillip for the whole family. Somehow, this bad time had been bringing us together, and I hoped the connections would continue in good times, too. Not too much to ask of a fireball in the firmament, was it? I opened my eyes, and the glowing point was still moving across the sky. Damn, that meant my star was really a satellite. Well, who said you couldn't wish on an orbiting space station?

I untied the sweater from my shoulders, but didn't move from the chaise. The evening air felt warmer than it had been lately, signaling spring coming soon. I sensed a vague tingle of anticipation at the thought of the lilacs blooming and the roses opening. I was ready for rebirth, a new start, life leaping forward again.

A few minutes later, Dan opened the glass doors and came outside to join me, holding a bottle of wine, opener, and two long-stemmed glasses.

"Are they gone?" I asked.

"Gone," he said. He carefully lowered himself to the edge of my lounge chair, and I slid my legs over to give him more room.

"So what now?" I asked.

"Now I'm going to get drunk." He pulled the foil off his 1993

California Cabernet, then popped out the cork with the Rabbit wine bottle opener I'd bought him years ago as a Valentine's gift. Hmm. Valentine's Day had come and gone this year and I'd forgotten all about it.

"You never get drunk," I said.

"I've decided to make an exception." He poured the wine into the two glasses and handed me one. "Maybe all the coffee I drink is causing blackouts. That would explain how I killed one girl I'd never heard of. And now, apparently, I killed another one I never knew existed."

"Are you really a suspect again?" I asked, horrified.

"No, probably not." He took a large gulp of the wine. "Chauncey says they had to question me since she was the other girl's roommate. You kill one, you kill them all, I guess."

A little black humor to go with his black mood. I swirled the wine and took a small sip. If he planned to get smashed, excellent idea to do it drinking a Simi Reserve at a hundred bucks a bottle.

"And what was supposed to be the motive?"

"Let's see, Nora saw me strangle Tasha, so I offed her to get rid of her as a witness. Fortunately, there's a big hitch. Nora was in Twin Falls, Idaho, visiting her parents when Tasha got killed."

"Who says?"

"Nora said. The apartment had been sealed off, so a plain-clothes detective was there when she got back. She turned hysterical when she found out what happened. The cops confirmed that she'd been at home."

"Yes, she'd been home. But she'd already hit the road back to L.A. by the time Tasha got killed."

"How do you know?" Dan asked, refilling his glass.

"You need to be a little more inebriated before I tell you."

"No, tell me now. Then I'll drink to forget."

I looked up and found my satellite, or maybe a different one, orbiting smoothly in the sky. Maybe it was my lucky night. Dan's mood seemed different than it had in weeks, and I was done dissembling. I launched into a long explanation about my excursion south from Sun Valley and encountering Bill Wilson at the gas station. I described what Nora's stepdad had told me about good-girl-turned-bad Tasha and about good-girl-wanting-better Nora. When I stopped, Dan ran a finger around and around the rim of his glass.

"You went to Twin Falls just to find him?" he asked, hitting what seemed to him the important point.

"Not necessarily him. I was really looking for Tasha's family. I thought someone might have information that would help."

Dan didn't have much reaction. Then he asked mildly, "What else have you been doing?"

I took another swallow of wine. "Really want to hear?"

Dan nodded.

"Okay, here's another story." I started reporting on my trip with Molly to the desert. When I got to the part about Roy's waving a gun at me, Dan put down his glass and reached for my hand, holding it tightly and stroking my thumb with his. I felt light-headed, either from the Cabernet or from the relief of finally confiding in Dan. Why stop now? I described finding Nora's body in my trunk and outlined everything I knew about Roy Evans and Julie Boden. I told him about the porn tapes we couldn't find and about Johnny DeVito's alibi—which I still needed to unravel.

I finally paused. Dan brought my hand up to his lips and kissed my palm over and over. Then I felt my fingers getting wet, and I realized tears were spilling from his eyes and splashing down his face. He tried to wipe them away, but our fingers were still interlaced, and I accidentally poked his nose—which made him laugh, but didn't stop the tears.

"You've been doing all this for me," he said, still clenching my hand and dabbing at his eyes with the back of his other arm.

"Because I love you," I said.

"And you think I'm innocent. You want to find who really did it."

In the darkness, I nodded. "Are you angry? Should I get another bottle of wine? Or do you need something stronger? Glenlivet?"

"No." He dropped his head into his hands—actually, three hands, since he was still gripping mine. "I got angry that night a while ago when I thought you were checking up on me. When you seemed afraid your husband was a murderer. But all this—"

He stopped, his voice breaking. In eighteen years, I'd never heard my husband cry. And I had no idea what to do. I gently stroked his very wet cheek.

"I was never afraid . . ."

"Yes, you were," he said. "You didn't know. And how could you?"

"I knew in my heart. I didn't care about the police evidence and I still don't. Screw Chauncey, screw the cops, screw anybody who doesn't know you like I do."

"I love you, Lacy. Having you believe in me means the world," Dan said softly. Unconsciously, he started playing with the wedding ring on my finger, twisting the solid band back and forth.

"I love you, too," I said. I kissed his cheek, tasting the salty tears, and licking them away from the corners of his eyes. But instead of letting the lovely moment pass unsullied, I added, "I just wish you'd told me a few things earlier. Like about Johnny De-Vito."

Dan leaned back and closed his eyes. "I plead guilty on that."

I punched him lightly on the arm. "Don't even say that word in this house."

He smiled. "Okay, I plead being a typically arrogant man who figured I could handle everything on my own. Real men take action. They don't lie on lounge chairs in the dark, crying to their wives."

I kissed Dan's smooth chin and slipped my leg over his. "You seem more real to me now than you have in a long time," I admitted. "Real men make mistakes."

"I've definitely made mistakes," Dan said wearily. "Letting my-self be blackmailed doesn't put me in the Good Guy Hall of Fame."

"But it shouldn't put you in jail, either."

Dan sighed deeply. "I haven't been so innocent. You know that."

"I do?"

"I saw that you went through the patient files in my study. And I don't blame you, by the way."

"I didn't find anything incriminating," I said, not sure where he was going.

"It's okay. I can finally admit it," he said, as grimly as if he were about to confess that he'd personally caused the blast that sunk the *Hindenburg*. "I was making payoffs to Johnny DeVito to protect my saintly image—when all the time I was doing what I said I wouldn't do anymore."

"Which is what?" I asked, worried.

"Face-lifts on famous actresses."

"Ah yes, your covert operations," I said, stroking his muscular arm. He was so solemn that I had to stifle a giggle. "Most surgeons would be bragging about them. Or calling Liz Smith to deny the rumors. Which, of course, is how you start the rumors."

Dan sighed. "I couldn't play that game. It didn't fit my image of myself. But this is Hollywood. The more often I said no, the more in demand I became."

"You think your surreptitious surgeries had anything to do with the murders?"

"Not a chance," said Dan ardently. And of course he was right. "But they had a lot to do with making me feel like a fake."

"So are all the secrets out now?" I asked.

"All of them," said Dan.

"And I still love you."

"Which amazes me," he said softly. I thought he was going to start to cry again.

"Ashley would die to hear about your Very Famous Actresses. Makes her as cool as the boy in her class whose father won an Academy Award for sound mixing. You should get one for face fixing."

In the darkness, Dan gave a little chuckle, and I felt him finally relax, leaning his body into mine. "I'm grateful to have you, babe. My world is falling apart, and you can still make me laugh."

"We're going to put it back together," I said, kissing him softly on the lips.

Dan was quiet for a long time. Then he asked, "Do you think Johnny DeVito could have killed his girlfriend then framed me?"

"I don't know," I admitted. "Tasha Barlow was involved with a lot of sleazeballs. But Johnny Dangerously was definitely near the top of the list."

Chapter Fourteen

Chauncey *announced that* the judge had scheduled the pretrial hearing for April 13. The good news: we'd finally get to see the witness list and hear the full outline of the case. The bad news: the date was sooner than he'd hoped. The awful news I discovered for myself when I went to mark my calendar. Our lucky day was Friday the thirteenth.

I had a couple more people to talk to before then.

Gracie Adler, who lived in Apartment 5C, next door to Tasha and Nora, sounded a little shocked when I identified myself on the phone to her as "the wife of the Best Doc in L.A."

She hesitantly agreed to meet—but didn't want me in her apartment. "For obvious reasons," she said, in a slightly high-pitched tone.

"Then I'll buy you coffee," I said. "How about the Starbucks that's around the corner from you?" There was a Starbucks around every corner.

"You can never get a seat in there," she complained. "Too many screenwriters. One cup of coffee and they think they've rented a table for the day. What are they doing on those laptops, anyway? They all want to write the next *Titanic*. I tell you, it's a disaster."

I laughed, but Gracie had missed her own joke.

"I don't know how the place makes any money," Gracie added ominously.

Rather than discussing the java company's business plan, I offered another suggestion. "How about meeting at Holistic Haven?" I asked. "It has a nice tea lounge."

I gave her the address in Santa Monica, and when I arrived five minutes early, Gracie was already seated at one of the blond-wood tables—even the furniture in L.A. was bleached—negotiating with the waiter.

"A plain Earl Grey," Gracie requested, putting down the two-page menu of teas, which outlined their country of origin, herbal contents, and benefits for vigor and vitality.

"Ours is an unusual Earl, with a trace of bergamot," said the swishy young server, as pompously as if he'd picked and dried the tea leaves himself. "Some people find it a bit smoky."

Gracie looked at the menu again. "So what's good?"

"I'd recommend the Lotus, which provides the inner radiance and essence of lotus flowers. Or Zen Zinger, the rarest green teas and herbs in an enlightening blend."

"Enlightening blend or enlightened blend?" Gracie asked.

"*Perdón?*" asked the waiter, who didn't look particularly Spanish. Maybe he was hoping to costar with Salma Hayek.

"I just wondered if it's the tea that gets enlightened or me."

I smirked but the waiter looked confused. Good bet that he hadn't aced the grammar section of his SATs.

"I'll have the Lotus," I said.

"Make it two," said Gracie, handing back the menu. "I could use some inner radiance." She'd caught my smirk and now gave me a little wink. "Some outer radiance, too."

In her midseventies with slightly stooped shoulders, Gracie Adler was probably a couple of inches shorter than she'd been a decade or two ago. But she still had a zesty spirit about her and a sparkle in her eye. She looked like a woman who enjoyed life instead of worrying about it. Her arms were lightly tanned from hours outdoors and her face looked comfortably lived in, with smile lines around her lips and expressive crinkles on her brow.

"How'd you know about this place?" she asked me.

"I come here for the spa treatments once in a while," I said. "The tea lounge is just to get you in the mood."

"I've never had a spa treatment," Gracie admitted. "Think I'd like it?"

"Let's find out," I said, inspired. "We can talk while we're being rubbed with honey and wrapped in apple-and-milk paste."

"Sounds like something I cook for Easter," Gracie said, but she followed me to the back room and didn't object when I asked to charge two facials. The treatment menu was even longer than the tea list, but Gracie settled on the oatmeal-jalapeño exfoliating scrub followed by the cucumber-cream skin-moisturizing special.

"Better food here than most restaurants I go to," she said.

We sat on comfy chairs across from each other while the attendants rubbed our faces with the scrub—I had a feeling it wasn't Quaker Oats—then put on soft sitar music, telling us to relax for ten minutes while the beautifying mixture did its magic.

But calming down wasn't part of the plan for today.

"Do you mind talking about the night Tasha was killed?" I asked Gracie when the attendants had left us alone again.

"You paid for this, so you've got me for the next twenty minutes," she said, leaning comfortably back.

"Look, I'm a little desperate," I said. "My husband didn't kill Tasha Barlow. He was at the apartment for a reason, and it wasn't to see her. We can explain all the evidence, except for one thing. The screaming you heard."

Gracie didn't say anything. She started to scratch her nose, but came away with a handful of all-natural, all-organic scrub.

"How come you noticed him that night?" I asked.

"I had a cold, so I was home, feeling sorry for myself," Gracie said slowly. "I'd forgotten to send back my Netflix and I didn't have a movie to watch. And what rubbish on TV. How do people sit through that garbage?"

I laughed. "I agree. You just don't seem like the type to be spying on your neighbors."

"No, I'm not. Stay busy and you can't feel sorry for yourself, is my motto," Gracie said. "I was resting in bed, but I had on a tape of a concert from my grandson in New York. He plays the trumpet in his middle-school band. *Fanfare for the Common Man.*"

I laughed. "Listening to middle-schoolers massacre Copland has to qualify you for extra points in heaven."

"He's very talented," she said loyally. "Though I told my grandson I didn't really like the drummer. It sounded to me like there was a lot of banging that didn't belong."

"Was that before or after you saw Dan's car?" I asked, remembering that Gracie had identified the BESTDOC license.

"Before," said Gracie. She shifted uncomfortably in her chair. "Something about all that banging made me get up. I looked out the living room window, and that's when I saw the car, with your husband just getting out. He walked to the front door of the building, hit the buzzer, and came in. I couldn't see him after that, of course. I turned off the music and went back to bed. I think I fell asleep then."

"Tell me more about the banging," I said. "Do you think it could have been something from next door mixing with the music? Not the drummer?"

Gracie started to answer, but the attendant came in then to gently rub our faces and then remove the mixture. My face was tingling and I noticed that Gracie's was flushed red. I hoped she wasn't allergic to jalapeño. Fortunately, the cucumber application was cooling—even though Gracie was getting heated up.

"I hadn't thought about the banging that way," she said, slightly agitated, once we were waiting in our soothing soaks. "But you could be right. It sort of didn't make sense to me at the time, and I guess it's been nagging at the back of my mind."

"You could listen to the tape again when you go home," I said mildly.

"I will," she said firmly.

"Was it a long time before you heard the screams?" I asked.

"I think so," she said. "As I said, I fell asleep. My phone rang, and when I answered, nobody was there. And a couple of minutes later I heard someone screaming, 'Stop it, Dr. Fields, stop it!' Then, 'Stop it, Dan!' and 'Stop it, Dr. Fields!' again. Maybe three or four times."

"Did she sound hysterical?"

"She sounded loud."

"You knew it was Tasha?"

"I knew it was a woman next door. When the police told me Tasha had been murdered, I was able to identify the voice."

I paused for a long time. "Would you say Tasha was an extremely polite young woman?"

Gracie shrugged. "You know girls today. They're so wrapped up in themselves and how they look that they can't even remember to say hello. Her roommate, Nora, was a little friendlier. She'd ask how I was doing. Once or twice when she was going to the grocery, she knocked on my door to see if I needed anything. I'm not so old I can't take care of myself. But it was nice of her."

I thought about it. "I don't know, Gracie. Maybe growing up in Idaho gives you good manners, but it doesn't make sense to me. 'Stop it, Dr. Fields' is what I'd yelp if my husband were tickling me too much. Here someone is strangling the girl, and she's saying his name over and over? It's like a bad script in a made-for-TV movie."

"Are you suggesting I'm making this up?" Gracie asked. She picked up a soft white chamois cloth from the counter and started wiping her face. "An old lady looking for attention and pretending to hear things?"

"Not at all," I said. I hoped my voice was more soothing than the cucumber mask, which was starting to make my nose itch. "But imagine you were being attacked. What would you do?" I jumped out of my chair and lunged at her, hands tensed in front of me like I was ready to grab her neck.

"HELP!" she shrieked.

"Exactly," I said, stepping back.

"HELP! STOP! NO! DON'T DO IT! HELP! *FIRE!*" Gracie screamed, still terrified by my attack. She leapt up from her chair and started to rush across the room.

"Gracie, it's okay!" I hollered. "I was just pretending! I didn't mean to scare you!"

She stopped and looked at me like I was crazy. And then she got it. She walked slowly back to her chair just as two attendants and the swishy waiter hurried into the room.

"What's happened?" asked one, panting slightly. "Something wrong?

"Our facial masks are all-natural and chemical-free," said the other attendant hastily. "You couldn't be having a reaction."

"I'm fine," said Gracie. "We were just reenacting a crime scene."

They hesitated, but then shrugged. Clearly this wasn't the strangest thing that had ever happened in a treatment room.

The waiter looked around. "I thought I heard 'Fire!' That's why I rushed."

"You did," said Gracie, pleased with herself. "An old trick. It's supposed to get people's attention better than 'Help!' Apparently it works."

The waiter stamped his foot, gave a little snort, and marched back out. I whispered to the attendants that they could go, too— we'd take off the moisture masks ourselves.

I wiped the cucumber off my face, then splashed on some cool water. Gracie did the same, then sat very still in her chair. She was a smart woman. Enlightened and enlightening, in fact.

" 'Stop it, Dr. Fields,' " she said softly to herself. She stared at the cloth in her hand, then looked at me. "You think somebody wanted to make sure I heard the name."

"Could be," I said.

Gracie nodded slowly. "Here's something else. My bedroom shares a wall with her living room. The screaming was clear as day. Not as muffled as it might have been if Tasha were a room away, being strangled in her bedroom."

"Gracie, what did you do when you heard the screaming?" I asked.

"I called 911," Gracie said. "I wasn't going to go over there myself, you know."

"And did you look to see if Dan's car was still outside?"

"Not immediately," Gracie admitted. "I was making the call, pulling on a robe, and trying to figure out what I should do. I was pretty panicked and not exactly thinking clearly."

"But you checked again at some point?"

"When the police arrived, I looked out because I heard the sirens. I was impressed that they'd gotten there so fast."

"And you saw Dan running to his car?"

"I never said that."

"Was the car gone?"

"I think so. I'm pretty sure. Another car was parked in the space."

I took a deep breath. "Gracie, how long would you say it took the police to come?"

She shook her head. "It seemed like forever. Time does slow down when you're scared, you know? But it was quick. Maybe three or four minutes."

"That is quick," I said.

Gracie glanced at her soothed and smoothed face in the mirror and ran a finger across her newly soft cheek. Then she gave a little gasp and looked at me like she'd had a sudden revelation from above.

"I can't even say that your husband was still in the apartment when I heard the screaming," she said.

I nodded, and Gracie got up and started pacing around the room.

"What if it wasn't even Tasha who was screaming?" I suggested. "Maybe she'd been killed earlier—which could explain the banging noises you heard. Now the killer was trying to set up Dr. Fields."

Gracie grimaced. "My God, do you think the call I got was from the killer? Making sure I was up and paying attention?"

"Possible. Pretty easy to check if the call came from next door," I said, an authority on phone records ever since Grant had taught me about them.

Again, I saw the spark in Gracie's eye. "Look, I don't have anything against your husband. I never even met him. I was just telling the police what I'd heard. I don't mind admitting if I missed something."

I smiled. "Thanks. That helps."

Gracie looked at me and headed for the door. "Whatever I can do. We should talk again. But next time, let's eat lunch instead of wearing it, okay?"

When I got home, Ashley was in the kitchen with Mandy. Open containers of flour, sugar, and baking powder were strewn across the counter, along with a spilled container of Hershey's cocoa and a half-eaten bag of Ghirardelli semisweet chocolate chips.

"Baking?" I asked in surprise.

Mandy turned to Ashley with a big grin. "See? I told you that your mom's amazing at figuring things out. She's a good detective."

I laughed. "Let's see, the Mixmaster's on the counter, the oven is turned to three fifty, and there's a mess of ingredients. If I were a really good detective, I'd know what you were making and why."

"Chocolate chip brownies for the French class bake sale," said

Mandy helpfully. "Madame Pierre said we had to make something *très français*."

"Brownies are *français*?" I asked.

"The Champs Élysées has a McDonald's," Mandy said firmly.

Trying to figure that one out, I popped a chip into my mouth. "Help me out. I thought McDonald's sold Big Macs."

Mandy stood a little straighter. "The point is that cultural boundaries don't exist anymore. You can eat brownies in Paris and sushi in Seattle and croissants at Burger King. We're making a statement about our global interconnectedness."

"Not bad, Mandy," I said, impressed. The girl was growing up and getting glib. She could probably run for Congress.

"Yeah, really impressive," said Ashley. "But the truth is we didn't know how to make anything else."

"Keep that to yourself," I advised. "People only know what you tell them."

"Anyway, back to your detecting," said Ashley, cracking an egg into a cup. "Mandy thinks you'll come up with something to get Dad off."

"You will," said Mandy brightly, turning to me. "Remember the black nail polish clue? How you figured out that I'd seen Ashley because I knew what color her nails were? I was really pissed at you that day, but now I think it was pretty cool."

"Thanks," I said. I hadn't been cool when I was fourteen, so it was nice to have a fourteen-year-old think I was cool now.

"I bet there's a clue just like that in this case," she said.

"I'm looking," I said wearily.

The girls went back to baking and I went upstairs to my study. I didn't even bother to turn on the computer. I just stared at the blank screen and strummed my fingers on the desk. Mandy was right. I should be able to figure this out. Unfortunately, nobody had shown up yet in punk nail polish to give the story away.

But Gracie Adler had given me a new perspective.

From the way I figured the timetable now, the killer had been in the apartment when Dan was there. My earlier theory that Tasha had buzzed in Dan didn't work because what Gracie saw and heard made sense under one condition: Tasha was already dead.

I suddenly remembered the Medeco lock I'd noticed on Tasha's bedroom door. Strange touch for an inside room, but it made sense if she'd been making porn flicks and wanted to make sure she wasn't disturbed. Now the killer used the lock to make sure Dan didn't wander into the bedroom and find the dead body.

Once Dan was in the apartment, the stage was set. Wandering around the living room for twenty minutes, Dan would almost certainly leave fingerprints and DNA tracks. Not to mention the envelope of money. The only trick was making sure the police thought of him.

Which was where the screaming came in.

The killer waited until Dan was gone, then acted out the scene, repeating the words "Dr. Fields" and "Dan." Smart. Dan wasn't known in the building, so the killer was safe on that score. It wasn't likely that another tenant would tell the police that the panicked shouts had occurred after Dan himself had already left.

Maybe the killer was just lucky. He'd murdered in a moment of passion, then found someone handy who could take the fall. Or maybe the killer knew Dan was coming—and he'd cleverly planned the murder around him.

A cunning killer pointed to Johnny DeVito. Murder wasn't beyond him. He'd slashed someone before and gotten away with it. He was blackmailing Dan and probably didn't have any scruples. On the other hand, I couldn't really picture him as the person Gracie Adler heard screaming. The problem wasn't that he was a man. Any guy could pull off a pretty authentic falsetto, especially when the sounds were being distorted by the apartment walls. But

Johnny was the silent, skulking type. Yelling into the night didn't fit his personality.

Roy Evans? He was on television, so faking a voice wasn't much of a stretch. But I'd already been over this ground with Molly and Tim. It didn't add up that he was the killer.

My mind whirred. Julie Boden? She was involved with Roy Evans, and probably in love with him at some point. She'd hired Johnny DeVito—for reasons that I still didn't know—and given him an alibi. But what if Johnny was providing *her* with the alibi? She'd slipped out of the Honey Twists shoot that night and driven to Tasha's apartment, getting back before anyone noticed. Not likely. An executive producer was always making decisions. She couldn't risk a director or writer complaining that she'd been available only by cell phone that night.

But say she'd pulled it off. She'd been fortunate enough to pick a night when Dan showed up. The timing was auspicious. Miraculously, she found out his name and decided to risk screaming it. That didn't explain how she knew to phone Grace or position herself in the living room. And most of all, it didn't explain a motive. Had Julie killed for love? Oh, please. Roy should be so lucky. She just wasn't that into him. Besides, Julie had seemed stunned when I mentioned Tasha Barlow's name the first time we met. She might have suspected Roy was screwing around, but she didn't know he was with Tasha.

I was so frustrated that I slammed my fist onto the desk. Goddamn, it shouldn't be this hard. Every *Law & Order* episode got settled in under an hour.

The sweet smell of baking chocolate wafted up from the kitchen. Eating might help. I rifled through my top drawer and found a Healthy & Natural caramel fudge granola bar. I ripped into it happily. More calories than a bag of almond M&Ms, but at least it sounded virtuous.

With the caramel trickling down my throat, I relaxed a little and thought about my mini-detecting with Mandy. Someone knowing something that she shouldn't.

Yes!

I sat bolt upright, my heart pounding. The answer was as obvious as a fistful of black nail polish. Whether it was the stress-free moment or the shot of sugar, suddenly I knew.

Nora.

She'd given herself away by the slip—or the slit—of a tongue.

I felt a swift surge of excitement. Like the thrill you get when you finally unscramble 5 Down on the crossword puzzle and realize the answer for "*Sex and the City* network" isn't HBO—it's TBS. Suddenly everything else fits.

According to Roy, Tasha had pierced her tongue the day she died. He'd taken her himself and enjoyed her screams of pain. But Nora had described the gold stud to me, and she couldn't have done that unless she'd been with Tasha before the murder. So why had Nora lied and told everyone that she arrived back the next day? Maybe it was like Mandy's dissembling, which had been to protect her friend. But no, Nora's duplicity was different. Her double-dealing served to protect only one person—herself.

I turned on my computer, waited for it to boot up, then quickly went to MapQuest.com. Directions from Twin Falls to Tasha's came up in seconds, reporting the distance as 932 miles with an estimated driving time of just over fourteen hours. Bill Wilson had said that Nora left the day before the murder. Even in a poky old Jetta, she could have gotten back long before Tasha was strangled.

I knew the setup. Nora had been in Twin Falls and told her parents and her priest about Tasha. They agreed that the devil was in Tasha and saintly Nora had to save her. But Tasha didn't want to be saved. She didn't even want Nora to come back. Nora, on a mission, returned anyway.

I tried to picture the scene. Nora arriving unexpectedly, finding

Tasha making a porn tape. Tasha prancing around in a marabou nightie. Flashing her newly pierced tongue so she could give better blow jobs. They'd had a fight and Nora tried to shake the devil out of her—but shook a little too hard.

My heart was beating hard, and I stood up and started pacing around the room. Nora knew about Dan because he'd been up to the apartment before. So she buzzed him in, locked herself in the bedroom with her dead roommate, and waited. The rest was a cinch. Calling Gracie Adler, who'd told her before about spotting the BESTDOC coming to visit. Yelling as if she were Tasha, so Gracie would know who was attacking. Then all Nora had to do was get out before the police came. All these apartment buildings had fire exits, usually a back staircase with a door from the kitchen. So she went down and into the night. Maybe she hid away in a cheap hotel for the night. Or more likely she drove back toward Twin Falls so she could turn around and arrive the next day in the guise of innocent and anguished friend.

"Mom?"

I spun around and saw Grant at the door with his friend Jake. I opened my mouth to blurt out my breakthrough, but Grant's face was a mask of worry, so I just asked, "What's up, guys?"

"Dad told us about the court date," Grant said tensely. "We've been trying to get more information on Johnny DeVito before then. Didn't get that much."

Jake nodded. "I went into some online chat rooms and found someone who knew him in high school. Apparently his dad was a thug and so was he, but he had a smart sister. They lived in the Valley, by the way, if that helps."

"Everything helps, but I think we're going to be okay." I leaned back with a smile and they looked at me, mystified, since until now I'd been as edgy as a Todd Oldham table.

"I'm pretty sure we were focused in the wrong place," I continued calmly. "Johnny DeVito blackmailed Dad, but he didn't have anything to do with the murder. He didn't kill Tasha. Now I know who did."

Jake's cell phone rang. He took the call and walked out of the room, not riveted enough by my coming revelation to stay around. I had to remember that this case wasn't the center of everybody's world. Just mine.

And maybe Grant's. "You know who killed her?" he asked, his laser focus on me.

"Yes, I do." I smiled at him triumphantly. "Are you ready? It's kind of a surprise." I paused for effect and then said, "Her room-mate Nora."

Grant's jaw dropped. Literally. He stared at me open-mouthed. "Didn't she end up dead, too?"

"Very much so."

"Then it doesn't make sense," said Grant. "If Nora killed Tasha, who killed Nora?"

I hadn't gotten that far yet. "Maybe she killed herself," I said, warming to the idea. "After she strangled Tasha, she didn't want to live anymore. Her own father killed himself when she was little. So she had a family history of suicide."

Grant crossed his arms and rocked back and forth on his Nikes. "Proof?" he asked finally.

I turned back to my computer and quickly Googled "family" and "suicide."

"According to a Swedish study, people are twice as likely to kill themselves if there's a family history," I said, scrolling down the screen. "And an American study says it's three times."

"I mean real proof," said Grant, dismissing the sociological studies as being as scientific as Tarot cards. "Wouldn't the autopsy show if it was suicide?"

I nodded. "Apparently there were some indications. But the body had been moved a couple of times, so the medical examiner ruled foul play."

"Then how are you going to make your theory stick?" Grant asked.

"I have a feeling it's going to stick like flypaper," I said with a smile.

He looked at me through furrowed eyebrows, and I realized the kid had probably never heard of flypaper. Probably thought it was something to replace the button fly on Levi's 501s. Didn't matter. One way or another, I was going to zip up this case.

Chapter Fifteen

"*So then Nora destroyed* the porn tapes to preserve her friend's good name," Molly said early the next morning, when I called her at home with my theory. "Or whatever was left of it."

"Exactly," I said. "She would have known about the tapes and known where they were. You can bet she wasn't giving them back to Roy."

"Well, that part adds up," Molly said slowly. "And so does the rest of it, frankly. The killer definitely knew her way around that apartment. And knew that Dan was coming."

Molly didn't answer, and I realized she'd covered the phone and was chatting to someone on her end. A moment later, her companion grabbed the receiver.

"Lacy?" asked a man's voice.

I was confused. "Um, yeah. Who's this?"

"It's Tim. I'm lying next to Molly, so I heard everything you said. And I think you might be off base."

Off base? I could have been in the outfield for all I cared. "You're lying next to Molly?" I asked, focusing on the more important point. "You mean like in *bed*?"

"No, on her divan. We never quite made it to the bedroom."

Did I want to hear this? Of course I did—even in the middle of a murder case.

I could hear Molly giggling and snatching the phone back.

"Lacy, dear, we have you to thank for hooking us up," Molly said. "Remember when you called me that first time and I checked with Tim to see what he knew? Turns out he knows everything. Anyway, we finally managed to go out for dinner, and once we started talking, we connected in a big way."

"Very big," Tim bragged in the background.

Molly snorted and ignored him. "What can I tell you? If you spend a lot of time talking about porn tapes together, you get ideas."

"On the divan?"

"It was divine," chirped Molly.

The sound on the phone changed as Tim hit the SPEAKER button to turn our call into a conference. Oh, great. Now Molly and Tim could have their hands free—or not free—while we talked.

"Back to your solution for the case," Tim said. "I think it's too pat. If I were on Dan's jury, I'd think you were just trying to make a scapegoat of the dead woman."

I swallowed hard. Dan's jury? If I could help it, nobody was ever going to be sitting in judgment of my husband.

"And bereaved friend as the killer?" asked Tim, continuing. "I don't know. The image is all wrong."

"I don't mind Nora as killer," said Molly spiritedly. "I'd easily cast her for the part. She fits that whole against-type look that I like."

"Except this is one of those rare jobs you're not casting," teased Tim. "It's reality."

"I love reality," countered Molly. "I cast it all the time. Much more surprising than anything from Jerry Bruckheimer."

"Nice woman turns killer bitch?"

"Happens more than you'd think," said Molly.

"Then I better get out of here," joked Tim.

"Come back!" called Molly in a sweet squeal, halting his faux exit from the divine divan. Whatever Tim did next—I guess he found a place for his hands—Molly gave a yelp and broke into a tinkling laugh.

I hung up quickly. They could finish their bedroom scene without me. Tough-minded Molly seemed to have morphed into a giggling girl overnight, but she'd be okay. Tim seemed like a good guy and it was time my friend found someone special. Especially someone who knew his way around a casting couch.

Predictably, Tim was in an excellent mood when I showed up at his office later in the day. But the smiles and hugs faded away when I told him what I wanted.

"A miniature recording device?" he asked warily. "You mean like a hidden camera?"

"Just something small that I can put in my purse," I said. "Your investigative reporters must use them, right?"

"Sometimes," said Tim carefully. "The law on making recordings without the second person's knowledge is a little unclear. But I can almost guarantee you won't be able to use it in court."

"Still, I can play it for the judge at the preliminary hearing," I said, having no idea whether I really could. "That's three days from now, when the judge gets to look at evidence and decide if the case goes to trial. Our lawyer says the determination is based on whether or not there's probable cause. I want it crystal clear that there's not."

Tim managed a little nod and went out of the room, coming back with two electronic toys. "The camera's a little complicated and you have to think about where you're going to put it. If you'll be okay with just audio, I'd go with this." He held out a flat device the size of a credit card.

"Perfect," I said, fingering the shiny, smooth surface. "You're sure this actually works?"

"Sure. Press the button, drop it in your bag, and record for an hour. But you can have it only if you promise that you don't do anything stupid," he said, touching one of the flat buttons.

"*Don't do anything stupid.*" This time his voice echoed loud and clear from the digital mini-machine. I grinned and made the promise.

"So what's the mission?" Tim asked, persisting.

"To talk to Johnny DeVito," I admitted. "Dan says he hasn't heard from him since the murder, except for one message that he left on the machine. Since then, silence. No calls, no emails."

"Is that bad?" asked Tim.

"It's odd," I said. "And I'd like to find out what it means."

Sammie was in an even better mood than Tim—but for a different reason.

"I'm leaving," she told me exuberantly when I called. "I gave Julie my notice yesterday."

"Better job?" I asked, thinking she deserved it.

"Not really a job, but I just sold my first screenplay. Even if the movie never gets made, the option is decent. I understand now why screenwriters call it 'fuck you' money."

I laughed. "You told Julie to take her job and shove it?"

"No, I'm a proper Vassar girl, so I decided to leave on good terms. You never know who you'll need again."

"Well, I need you again," I admitted. "I'm trying to track down that Johnny DeVito guy I asked you about last time. Think you can help me?"

I told her briefly what I wanted and Sammie said she'd try. "I don't mind twisting the rules a little since I'm out of here," she said, "but it's probably better if I just leave him a message."

"Fine," I said. "Tell him I want to meet as soon as he can. But in a public place."

"Will do," she said.

"By the way, what's your screenplay about?"

"An English major from Vassar who comes to L.A. and works for a bitchy boss," Sammie said brightly. "I know, not much of a stretch. But when you started asking questions about Roy, I realized the twist. The boss has an affair with one of her stars. And then the young, dazzling assistant has an affair with him, too."

I gasped. "Sammie, you and Roy didn't—"

"Of course not!" she interrupted. "I had to make up *something*, didn't I?"

I laughed, and after we hung up, I went back to fiddling with Tim's recorder. Anything to make the time go. But I kept looking at my watch, counting down the minutes to the preliminary hearing. Why didn't Sammie call back? All I really wanted to do was drive over to 17 Hillman Drive again, knock on the door, and confront Johnny DeVito.

And why not? I had to take action. I changed into low-slung black jeans and a pair of Pumas, to avoid the kitten-heel-mules problem of last time. Boy, I was learning a lot. If I didn't become a private detective after this, at the very least I could be a costume designer on *CSI*.

Halfway to the garage, I stopped myself. This wasn't a movie— or even a TV show. Maybe in Sammie's next screenplay, the heroine would jump in her blue roadster and return to the mystery house to solve the case. But I'd promised Tim I wouldn't do anything stupid. And going back would definitely qualify as stupid.

I marched back inside and checked in with Sammie.

"I've left two messages at the number Julie gave me," she reported. "It's just an anonymous voice box, so I don't even know if it's his number."

But finally at about six, she had a different report. "He called when I was out buying Julie an iced tea," she said. "He'll be at Sanford's gym at seven thirty tonight. You can meet him there."

I got directions off MapQuest rather than relying on the GPS, then popped the recorder into my Michael Kors clutch. The bag was much too dressy for jeans—even a pair that cost two hundred bucks at Barneys—but I didn't think Johnny would care. And the clutch would be less noticeable than a big purse when I put it on the table to record.

Traffic was heavy and I crawled along the thruway, chiding my-self not to tailgate. An accident wouldn't help anything. When I got off, the roads looked familiar, but it wasn't until I saw three huge silver trailers and a road sealed off for a movie crew that I knew where I was. The George Clooney set—and the very streets where I'd wandered around in bra and panties. I felt a flush of em-barrassment, but then decided I didn't have to worry. Anybody who saw me then wouldn't recognize me now. My face wasn't what they'd noticed.

Sanford's gym was tucked back toward the industrial part of town. In the gathering dusk, the area looked more decrepit than I'd remembered, the streets rattling with a few trucks leaving ware-houses. The gym itself had a faded sign over the metal door and pitted aluminum siding along the front. Through the streaked windows, I could see some bare bulbs hanging inside and a rack of old metal dumbbells lining the gym wall. Unless retro-chic had moved from furniture to fitness, Crunch didn't have to worry about Sanford's snagging celebrity clients. This wasn't the place for the latest in vinyasa yoga.

I pulled into a parking space out front, turned off the motor, and nervously called Molly to tell her where I was. Somebody should know.

"Do you see any other people around?" Molly asked after she listened to my quick synopsis.

I squinted, trying to see what was going on inside the gym. "A few," I said. "And there's someone at a front desk, I think."

"Any way I can convince you to turn around and come home?"

"My husband goes to court in seventy-two hours," I said softly. "If I can prove Nora killed Tasha, we could get the case dropped. I'm convinced Johnny DeVito knows something."

Molly cleared her throat. She knew not to argue. "Then here's the deal. Call me every fifteen minutes to say you're okay."

"I can't. With luck, I'll be in the middle of an important conversation."

"A text message that just says 'OK,' " said Molly firmly. "You get five minutes grace. After twenty minutes, I call the police."

I turned on the recorder and tried to look sure of myself as I strode toward the gym, but I doubted I was doing a very good job. The man at the front desk looked up at me without any curiosity. He was short and heavyset, his belly gone to flab but his arms bulging with the muscles of someone half his age. His black hair was slicked down and his white T-shirt unaccountably crisp for someone who'd been in a gym all day.

"I'm supposed to meet someone here. Johnny DeVito," I said, with as much poise as I could muster.

He nodded, still unsurprised. "Nice to meet you," he said, extending a hand. "I'm Jerry DeVito. His father."

Whatever composure I'd gathered fell away. I hadn't known what to expect in Sanford's gym, but I definitely hadn't expected this. I didn't want to take his offered hand, but I did anyway, and instead of a simple handshake, he squeezed my fingers so tightly that I almost cried out. When he pulled back, I could still feel the impact of his potent grip. Either he was stronger than he realized or he wanted to make an impression.

"Johnny's not here," he said.

"Do you know if he's coming?"

"No." He looked across the gym as someone walked out from the back. "Why don't you talk to my daughter."

I turned to follow his gaze and saw a woman striding toward us, dressed in a perfect Prada pantsuit with a diamond pendant glinting at her neck. I let out a loud gasp. The outfit was nice, but that's not what shocked me. It was the woman herself. Julie Boden.

"Th—that's your daughter?" I asked, stuttering to get out the words.

Jerry nodded. "She's a good girl. Helped me buy my new house."

"On Hillman Drive?" I ventured.

He nodded again, and suddenly I realized I'd seen him once before. He was the man I'd glimpsed at the door, letting in Nora.

While I tried to get my bearings, Jerry DeVito ambled away and Julie pulled up short, inches away from me.

"You're always turning up," she said.

"I wasn't . . . um, expecting to see you," I said.

"Isn't life interesting." She started to walk across the gym again, expecting me to follow her. And of course I did. We went into the women's locker room, which had the dank smell of a high school gym and about as much style—a couple of showers with flapping plastic curtains, two toilet stalls, and some metal lockers. A cracked mirror hung crookedly over a sink. Julie pointed to a wooden bench, and I sat down, too stunned to stay on my feet.

"So what did you want from my brother?" she asked bluntly. We weren't making small talk. Not that I could, anyway.

"He'd been blackmailing my husband," I said, "and I thought maybe we could make a deal."

"What kind of deal?"

"Dan didn't kill Tasha Barlow. I think her roommate Nora did. And I also think Johnny knows that and could help prove it."

Julie raised her eyebrows. "I thought Roy Evans was your favorite suspect. Or Johnny." She folded her arms and paced a few steps away from me, then came back. "Nora. Good for you."

"You think I'm right?"

"I know you are. Nora killed Tasha."

I swallowed hard and unwittingly glanced at the Kors clutch next to me. Julie caught the fleeting look and grabbed for the bag. I tried to snatch it back, but she quickly dumped the contents on the bench. Everything fell out—except the digital recorder, which I'd tucked inside a zippered compartment. She flipped open my cell phone, apparently thinking someone was listening on the other end. Then she saw the I'M OK message I'd already prepared, along with Molly's number. She hit SEND.

"Let me correct you on something," she said coolly, as if nothing had happened. "Johnny asked your husband to give him back the money from his operation. Your husband complied. That's not blackmail."

"I saw the emails asking for money. That's blackmail," I said, trying to keep my voice as calm as hers.

"Yes, it is, but Johnny didn't write them."

"Who did? Drew Barrymore?"

Julie looked at me blankly, then snorted. "Tasha sent them. Though she didn't do anything alone. Nora was the brains in their operation."

Now I was the one with the blank look. "What are you talking about?"

Julie opened and closed the cover on my phone a few times, then tossed it aside. "Johnny had confided everything in Tasha. I don't know why. She had that Idaho innocence that made him trust her. She came up with the idea of getting money from your husband. When Johnny didn't want to, she threatened to leave him. So he did it and gave her the money. She spent every dime."

I thought of the fancy bedroom. A thirty-thousand-dollar job easily. She must have instinctively known she'd be working from there.

"So Johnny needed more cash from Dan to keep Tasha happy," I said.

Julie snorted. "Only this time he talked to me. He didn't want to end up back in jail. We hadn't exactly been pals, but he's my brother. I pulled some strings, got him into the union, and gave him work as a grip. I knew he was giving most of his salary to Tasha, but at least he was keeping straight."

His alibi had been real. He'd been miles away the night Tasha was killed, and so had Julie.

"So how did you find out that the blackmail was still going on?" I asked.

Julie looked away, and suddenly I got it. I felt my throat tightening.

"Nora told you," I said softly. "The day I dropped her at your father's house."

Julie played with her pendant and picked an imaginary piece of lint off her jacket. "It happens we were all there that day. Johnny was living with my dad and I'd come by to visit. I saw you outside and told Johnny who you were. He ran out before I could stop him."

In the car, Johnny hadn't been trying to scare me away—he was taking his vengeance because he thought Dan had killed the woman he loved. The one woman who had pretended to love him.

"Blackmail's easy, isn't it?" asked Julie bitterly. "You learn the technique and you just keep going. Nora would get all the money from your husband now. Five thousand every month or so. But she had a bigger idea. She knew Johnny had killed someone years ago. No statute of limitations on murder, and she thought fifty thousand was a fair amount to keep him from going back to jail."

I stood up and started backing away from the bench. I suddenly understood. I had the story right—but the motive wrong. Dead wrong. Nora wasn't a good girl who'd killed her friend and then committed suicide in a moment of remorse. She was an angry girl—an overweight Midwesterner in cheap clothes who barely existed in the glamorous world of L.A. Overlooked and ignored, she'd tried to find her place attached to Tasha. But Nora had come with dreams, too. She wouldn't be a famous actress, but she would be the one pulling the strings. The one raking in all the money. She wasn't beautiful, but she wanted to matter.

Now I could imagine the fight in the apartment in different terms. Nora demanding a bigger cut from Tasha. They were partners, after all—so why was Tasha taking all the cash? Fifty-fifty on the blackmail. Fifty-fifty on the porn tapes. When Tasha tried to flick her away, as she always had, the loser friend had had enough. Her turn to be in the spotlight.

The need to find some significance to her life wasn't new. Nor was the anger at being marginalized. There was even a good chance Nora had planned the murder while she was still in Twin Falls. Talking about how long it would take her to drive back so she'd have an alibi. Sending a flurry of intimidating emails to Dan to assure that he'd be at the apartment that night. Leaving the note in the front foyer telling Dan to wait so the scene would seem more realistic.

Nora didn't need Tasha anymore. She was better off on her own. She could try to keep getting payments from Dan. She could blackmail Johnny. She could use the sex tapes to connect to Roy. She wasn't appalled by the porn—she just wanted to get her part of it. Maybe she could cut herself into his business, selling drugs and porn. Much better than what Tasha offered.

I continued shuffling backward towards the door. Because now I also knew what had happened in the DeVito house that day.

"You didn't plan to kill Nora," I said quietly, inching slowly away. "But you didn't have much choice. She was a threat to your brother. Blackmailing him and blackmailing on behalf of him. It had to stop."

"She'd killed Tasha and she was a dangerous bitch," said Julie.

"Not to mention incredibly grating," I added, almost in sympathy.

"I'll say," said Julie, with a little laugh. For a moment, I could imagine that we were two friends in the locker room, blow-drying our hair and gossiping together after a tough workout.

Only this place didn't have any blow-dryers. And Julie wasn't my friend.

She lunged for me, her leg flying upward in a perfect kung fu kick. Her flat heel smashed into my skull with tremendous force, spinning me ninety degrees before I started to crumple. My head cracked into the corner of the bench as I fell, then reverberated off the hard tile floor. I saw blood—mine—trickling across the floor and I wheezed in pain. But I didn't lose consciousness. I couldn't. Despite the black spots in front of my eyes, I saw my car keys inches away from me under the bench, where Julie had dumped them. But I couldn't risk crawling over to get them.

I tried to stand up, figuring I'd make a run for it. But as I got to my knees, Julie landed another kick, this one to the back of my neck. I fell down flat, unable to move. Had she severed my spine? I groaned and managed to turn onto my side in time to see Julie ripping one of the shower curtains from its hooks. Then she was back, rolling the fabric around and around my limp body. I tried to fight her off, but my hands just clawed at the air, and in a moment, my arms were bound at my sides. I was wrapped as tightly as King Tut. The slimy plastic covered my mouth and nose and I coughed, fighting for air and trying to breathe.

"No, you can't die yet," Julie said, pulling the material down. "I learned my lesson with Nora. Easy to mimic suicide. But you don't move the body afterwards. You'll die when I'm ready to kill you."

She wrapped duct tape around my bound form, then disappeared for a minute, coming back wheeling a bright orange hand truck, the kind used to lug boxes. Or to move mats and weights in the gym.

She rolled the metal platform under me, then tipped it back, pushing forward now easily. She might have been transporting a dumbbell. And I guess she was.

I couldn't see where we were going, but then she seemed to jam the hand truck against a wall.

"Scream and I'll tape your mouth shut," she said. I thought of

Gracie's directive to shout "Fire!" but I wasn't in much of a position to holler anything. Just to be sure, Julie pulled the plastic back over my face and left.

I'd almost passed out by the time she returned, but I made myself snap back in time to realize we were moving again. I heard the sound of a cheap metal door squeaking. And then we were outside, in what I guessed was an alley behind the gym. The night seemed damp and sticky—or maybe that was just how I felt inside my plastic tomb. Suddenly I was rising. On my way to heaven so soon? No, just a lift on the hand truck hauling me about three feet off the ground. Julie gave a mighty push, and I landed first on a soft cushion, then slammed down hard on a stiff, bumpy surface. I craned my neck until I was able to see out an inch and realized I was in the backseat of my own Lexus. Julie must have pulled it around. I'd bought the car for the extra cargo space. Who knew the cargo would be me?

Julie got in the driver's seat, and then threw something back to me. My Michael Kors bag.

"I sent the 'OK' message again. Wouldn't want anyone to worry. I'll keep sending it until you're dead," Julie said nastily.

"You don't have to kill me, Julie." My voice was so muffled that I wasn't sure she could hear. "I'll do anything you want."

"I'm not going to kill you, you're going to kill yourself," Julie said, turning on the motor and starting to drive. "It's all planned. Your suicide note is right here. It's very touching. You confess that you killed Nora because she knew too much. You can't bear the pain anymore of what your husband did. You ask that your friend Molly raise your children when he goes to jail."

Inside my sweaty, stale casing, I swallowed hard. Nobody was raising my family except Dan and me. Who else could talk to Grant about string theory, to Ashley about stringy hair, and to Jimmy about string cheese? And then there was Ashley's plan to redecorate her room. What if I wasn't around and instead of the Persian I'd picked, she bought one of those pink shag carpets from Pottery Barn Teen? I'd be spinning in my grave.

My situation was definitely grave—in every sense. But there had to be a way out. I closed my eyes and tried to concentrate. What would Sammie do in her screenplay?

Pleading was out. Telling Julie I'd do anything hadn't made any impression. Trying to connect on a human level? Hadn't done any good that day with Johnny Devito, and I wasn't sure Julie had a human side, anyway. I'd certainly never seen it. Maybe Molly would get nervous after all and call the police. But they'd know only to go to Sanford's gym. Jerry DeVito wasn't about to tell them where we'd gone. In fact, he probably didn't even know. Julie had turned crooked after the rest of the family went straight.

"So how do you want to kill yourself?" asked Julie conversationally. "I have some drugs if you'd like to OD. But you don't seem very cooperative. With Nora, I cuffed her hands and put a plastic bag over her head. But there can't be any doubts with you that it's suicide. I have a gun and I don't mind using it. Definitely the quickest. But I'm partial to carbon monoxide in the garage. Kind of a woman's way to kill herself, don't you think?"

If she was expecting an answer from me, I didn't have one, because I was busy trying to work my right arm out of the casing. I'd managed to find a little slack in the material, and my hand was inching upward. At about my shoulder, it got stuck again, and try as I might, I couldn't budge anymore. I almost screamed in frustration.

But I'd been in tight situations before—like the night I wore that size 6 Dolce & Gabbana gown to a charity ball with Dan. I'd gotten into it, but it wasn't clear how I'd get out of it. I'd managed, after ten minutes of patient squirming. Now I had to get out of this. I turned my shoulders slightly and got my elbow in front of my chest, then pushed my arm up with all the energy I could muster. My hand flew forward, suddenly released from the tight wrapping. I wasn't helpless after all.

My little victory got my blood pumping again—quite literally. My arm had fallen asleep, and now that I could move it, pins and needles prickled from my shoulder to wrist. I clenched and unclenched my fist, and as soon as I got some sensation back, I groped around the small area I could reach, feeling for something I could use to defend myself. Under the seat of the car, my fingers squished into a handful of discarded raisins and the Legos that Jimmy played with on long rides. Then I felt a football, an electronic toy, and a pile of action figures—all the comic book heroes Jimmy worshiped. Boy, I could use a real Superman now. I'd even settle for Halle Berry as Catwoman.

Should I hurl one of the toys through the window to attract attention? I wouldn't get much leverage from my position on the floor, and even the heaviest would probably just bounce off the safety glass and land on my back. Aim for Julie? I remembered all the times I'd warned Jimmy and his friends that distracting the driver was dangerous. Maybe it was, but the likelihood of a tossed football getting Julie into an accident was minimal.

I listened carefully to the sounds outside the car. Local roads, not a thruway. Some cars passing. Not a completely deserted neighborhood yet. I didn't know where Julie was taking me. But once we arrived at the destination, I'd be dead in minutes. Julie had her plan. She'd probably already scrawled my signature on the suicide note.

I pulled myself forward, painfully crawling along the car floor an inch at a time. My free hand finally felt the door, and I reached for the handle. Please God, don't let Julie know about backseat child locks. I had one chance. We weren't going fast, but I couldn't imagine flinging myself from a moving car. Wait until we stopped, though, and it might be too late.

Even in my facedown position, I could tell we weren't in total darkness. Still an area with streetlights, which probably meant people around. Now or never.

In the smoothest move I could manage, I clutched the door handle and yanked myself upward. I flung open the door and launched myself forward.

"*Help!*" I screamed as loudly as I could. "*Fire!*"

A screeching of brakes from somewhere. The crunching of two cars colliding. Me, pitching to the pavement.

"What the hell . . ." I heard someone say.

And then I blacked out.

Chapter Sixteen

I *insisted on leaving* the hospital for Dan's court hearing, even though my neck was in a brace, my arm was in a cast, and I was having trouble breathing thanks to my broken ribs. But who cared? I'd had a concussion but not gone into a coma. The doctor shook his head and said I was a lucky woman. Which, frankly, was exactly how I felt.

The kids had also insisted on coming, and given the circumstances, Chauncey said it would be fine. We all sat down in the second row, and despite the hard bench, even Jimmy sat up perfectly straight, without squirming. He stared straight ahead at the judge's table, which was flanked by the flags of the United States and California. The room felt official and even a little intimidating—but really, it could use some sprucing up. Waiting for the proceedings to start, I decided that instead of the grayish-white paint on the walls, I'd probably recommend wood paneling for a more dignified feel. The IN GOD WE TRUST lettered above the judge's bench was a sickly yellow that could be replaced with shiny bronze. And whose idea had it been to cordon off the jury box with a barrier so tall it looked like the jurors were jailed? I envisioned a low, S-shaped wall as a gracious way to separate without dividing.

Molly and Tim arrived as they'd promised they would, gave a little wave, and settled several rows behind us. Mandy had come with her mom to show her support for Ashley. To show her support for the American legal system, she'd worn a white eyelet blouse that didn't reveal any midriff. Grant's friend Jake was sitting in the back row looking vaguely terrified. Probably good. If one visit to a courtroom could convince him he didn't want another, maybe he'd halt all hacking. A few of Grant's other friends arrived, and with safety in numbers, Jake seemed to relax. At least nobody was going to throw him in jail today.

The bailiff came to the door and sonorously announced, "All rise," and once we'd scrambled to our feet, the judge came in, an attractive woman in her fifties with dark hair and glowing skin. In this town, even a judge was ready for her close-up. Luckily for her, she looked good in black.

I knew the judge had been well briefed on the case. In chambers, Chauncey had played her my recording, which the police had rescued from the backseat of my car. Forget Prada, I'd never again carry anything but Kors. Every woman needs a zippered compartment in her clutch.

The judge didn't waste a lot of time on setup, just efficiently called the district attorney to come forward and present his case. Mr. Allan Vikars unfolded his lean, lanky form from a padded chair at the prosecution table. A hard-cover binder about six inches thick—the case against Dan?—was sitting in front of him. He glanced briefly at Dan, and I saw he had intelligent eyes and a serious, no-nonsense expression. Watching him lead the opposition during a long trial would be unnerving.

DA Vikars turned to face the judge.

"Your Honor, new evidence has come to light in this case. Therefore, we wish to drop all charges against Dr. Daniel K. Fields in the murder of Theresa Bartowski, aka Tasha Barlow, of Twin Falls, Idaho, and Los Angeles, California."

He stopped. The judge looked at him, waiting for him to go on. Apparently, district attorneys usually had a lot more to say. But he was done.

"Mr. Vikars, have you consulted with the Los Angeles Police

Department, and do you speak on behalf of the district attorney's office?"

"Yes, Your Honor."

She waited again, but he simply walked back to his chair and stood behind it.

"Very well," said the judge. "All charges are hereby dropped. Dr. Fields, please rise."

At the defense table, where he was sitting next to Chauncey, Dan stood up unsteadily, shaken to the core at having been a defendant for even five minutes. Though he'd just been cleared, his face was pale and I noticed a slight tic at his eye. Seeing him like this for weeks on end would have been too torturous to bear. My broken ribs were a lot less painful.

The judge shuffled though some papers. "Dr. Fields, on behalf of the People of the State of California, I order all charges against you dropped. You are absolved of any wrongdoing in this matter."

Ashley yelped, "Yeah!" and Jimmy clapped his hands. The judge picked up her gavel to bang it, but then gave a little smile and put it back down.

"Dr. Fields, I also would like to offer this court's apologies for the false arrest. I hope your wife has a speedy recovery and I wish you all the best as you resume your normal medical practice and good works."

Now she did bang her gavel, saying, "Case dismissed," and the whole courtroom broke into cheers.

We all stood up as the bailiff held the door for the judge to return to her chambers. Then Dan and Chauncey shook hands, and Dan came over to give me a tender kiss.

"Thank you," he said.

I smiled. "That's now the four thousand eight hundred and ninety-third time you've thanked me. Though I'm not counting."

"Words aren't enough," said Dan, and he pulled a small box out of his pocket and handed it to me. "This is also inadequate. But it's a small way of telling you how much I love you."

The velvet box said Cartier on the outside, and when I opened it, a diamond and ruby bangle sparkled up at me.

I gasped. "Dan, this is gorgeous. But I don't need it. All I need is you."

"You have me," said Dan. "And now you have the bracelet, too."

Ashley peered over my shoulder and reached out to touch it. "Wow, Mom. If you really don't want it, I'll take it."

"Not a chance," I said with a laugh.

I held out my arm to Dan—the one without a cast—and he latched the bracelet around my wrist. For flinging myself from a moving car, I was remarkably free of cuts and contusions. The plastic shower curtain had shielded me well from the road.

"Family hug," Dan said. He put his arm around Grant on one side and Ashley on the other, and then Jimmy and I joined the huddle, too. Despite my injuries, we managed one of our old-fashioned, good-as-it-gets family hugs.

"Thank you all for standing by me," Dan said. "I love you all. Now we get to start again. Fresh and new."

"One thing I've learned is to listen to my family," I said with a smile. "You were right about the emails, Grant. I should have paid more attention to your clue that they were coming from Tasha."

"Right, listen to me," said Grant with a grin. "Maybe it can keep you out of trouble."

Chauncey came over then to say that Dan was needed in the back, and as soon as they went off, Ashley and Grant slipped away to talk to their friends. Molly and Tim quickly appeared at my side, each giving me a double kiss on the cheek.

"I should have known you'd be the hero," said Molly with a grin. "The well-dressed decorator solves the case."

"If I do a story about you on the network, can I get exclusive rights to the tape?" Tim asked with an impish grin.

"I'll have to see what other offers I get," I said airily.

"Watch it or I'll never lend you another tape recorder."

"I hope I'll never need one," I said fervently.

"I haven't heard," said Molly. "Is Julie in jail?"

"Yup," I said. "The judge keeps putting off the bail hearing. Which is fine with me."

"And her brother?"

"Working as a grip somewhere, I guess. Dan's not going to press blackmail charges. In fact, he wants to do reconstructive surgery on his face at no charge." I rolled my eyes. But I knew Dan. He'd do it no matter what. And he'd make Johnny look good enough again to be on camera, never mind behind one.

"The only question I have left is about Roy Evans," said Tim. "What was his connection, anyway?"

"Just what you already know," I said. "He was making S-and-M tapes with Tasha, and when he found out she had been strangled to death, he panicked. But he's too dumb to kill and frame as cleverly as Nora did. So if you don't mind L.A.-style drugs and sex, nothing really criminal on his roster."

Tim laughed. "Does that mean I have to rehire him?"

"Definitely not," Molly said firmly.

"Julie had her little fling with Roy," I explained, "but she didn't know he was also involved with Tasha until I showed up. That first time I was in Julie's office and mentioned Roy's connection to his makeup girl, Julie looked shocked. Now I know why. She knew about Tasha from her brother Johnny."

"So Julie finds out the same girl who was screwing over her brother was also screwing her lover. No wonder she was mad enough to murder," said Tim.

Molly nodded. "What still gets me is that Nora, the Idaho rube, turned out to be the conniving manipulator."

"Casting against type," said Tim and I, at exactly the same time. We all burst out laughing. But then Tim glanced worriedly at his watch and Molly announced that they'd better get back—Tim had a show to produce and she had at least twelve hours of work to catch up on. I felt incredibly grateful. They were two of the busiest people around, but they'd been there when I needed them. After another round of kisses, I watched them walking out of the courtroom with their arms around each other. A silver lining.

To celebrate the day, I figured we needed a family celebration, and I knew just the thing. A blowout lunch at Spago Beverly Hills. I'd call Wolfgang Puck right now and ask him to get a table ready with champagne and Ashley's favorite smoked salmon pizza. I motioned to the kids, and when they came over, I described my plan.

"Um, Mom, if you don't mind, I was going to head back to school with Jake," said Grant. "He's my lab partner in physics and we're doing a really cool experiment this afternoon. We're measuring the force of gravity with lasers."

How could I complain? "Go ahead," I said.

"Same with me, Mom," said Ashley hesitantly. "I mean, nothing about lasers. But Mandy told her boyfriend that he could bring his best friend from camp to Starbucks after school to meet me. Isn't that cool? And I'm ready." She cleared her throat. "I'm getting a grande soy cappuccino, half-and-half decaf and regular, whip but no sprinkles."

"Good choice for impressing him," I said.

"And I have Davey's party!" said Jimmy. "Don't you remember? Ice cream and cake and then that scary movie."

"I thought you weren't going because you were afraid you'd be—"

"Scared?" asked Jimmy. He puffed out his little chest and stood as tall as he could. "I don't get scared anymore."

Dan rejoined us and I took his hand. "How about going out for a romantic lunch?" I asked him hopefully. "Just the two of us at a back table at Spago."

"Love to, but can we save it? Brandon Jackson called me. The hospital board is meeting this afternoon. They want to officially welcome me back."

I felt tears spring to my eyes and went to wipe them away. Dan noticed and immediately looked worried.

"Oh, sweetie, if it means a lot to you, of course I'll come," said Dan.

"Me, too," said Grant.

"Me, too," echoed Ashley and Jimmy.

"No way." I sniffled and Dan handed me a clean handkerchief. "It's just that I suddenly realize how happy I am. You're all too busy for me."

"That makes you happy?" asked Ashley, baffled.

"You bet." I blew my nose and then grinned. "I got what I wanted. Everything's back to normal."

Acknowledgments

I'm grateful to Jane Gelfman for her warm support of this book, and to Trish Lande Grader for her wonderful talents as an editor. I'm very lucky to have both of them on my side. To my new colleagues at *Parade*—I'm thrilled to be with you. I extend my admiration and appreciation to Walter Anderson, Lee Kravitz, Randy Siegel, and Ira Yoffe. I'm always thankful for Anthea Disney's advice and encouragement. My friends at the television networks have given me an inside view of Los Angeles (including some very good restaurants), and I appreciate their help and good humor. Warm thanks to Susan Fine, Ronnie Siegel, Lynn Schnurnberger, Margot Stein, Leslie Mintz, Anna Ranieri, Marsha Edell, and many others for being great cheerleaders. I was guided on court proceedings and law by a state Supreme Court judge who generously opened his courtroom to me. He is too ethical to allow his name to be mentioned, but I am thankful for his help.

My dad, Stanley Kaplan, gave me my first Sherlock Holmes book when I was ten and never stopped sending me his favorite mysteries. I miss him every day. Love to my mom, Libby Kaplan, to Bob and Nancy and their terrific families, and to Lissy Dennett. Finally, I am blessed to have my smart and handsome husband, Ron Dennett, and my Yale men, Zachary and Matt. Their wisdom always finds its way to my pages. They are the best in the world.

About the Author

JANICE KAPLAN is Executive Editor of *Parade* magazine, the most widely read publication in America. She has been the executive producer of prime-time television specials for Fox, ABC, VH1, and other networks, and was deputy editor of *TV Guide*. A former contributing editor at *Vogue*, she began her career as a sports reporter for CBS Radio and was a producer at *Good Morning America*. Kaplan has written hundreds of articles for magazines and appeared on television shows including *Today*, the CBS Early Show, and *Entertainment Tonight*. She's the coauthor of *The Botox Diaries*, *The Men I Didn't Marry*, and the national bestseller *Mine are Spectacular!* A magna cum laude graduate of Yale, she lives in Larchmont, New York, with her husband and two sons.

A Job to Kill For

1-4165-3213-7

TOUCHSTONE
A Division of Simon & Schuster
A CBS COMPANY

If I'd known Cassie Crawford would die, I might not have joked about wanting to kill her.

I'd been at her brand-new three-million-dollar penthouse overlooking Los Angeles for almost an hour this morning, making sure all the details were perfect. Fresh calla lilies in the Steuben vase. Stainless steel Italian cappuccino machine properly filled with organic shade-grown Sumatran ground beans. Electronic shades opened at the right angle to let in the light but not the UV rays. At 12:17, Cassie strode in, wearing a sheer white blouse, white jeans, and strappy gold high-heel sandals, looking even blonder and slimmer than last time I'd seen her. Our appointment stood at noon, but given the commission she was paying, seventeen minutes counted as on-time performance.

"Is everything done?" Cassie asked anxiously. Apparently we wouldn't bother with Hello, How are you? or even Nice to see you again. Cassie took off her Chanel sunglasses but didn't even glance up at the handmade Swarovski crystal chandelier that sparkled overhead, sending gleams of sunlight flickering across the foyer.

"Done," I replied simply.

"Thank God," Cassie said. She made a quick movement of hand against chest, and I thought at first she was crossing herself. But instead she religiously adjusted the seven-carat diamond pendant hanging just above her cleavage. As she patted it into place, the necklace clinked against her wedding band, so heavy with sapphires and diamonds that Cassie risked carpal tunnel syndrome every time she lifted a well-manicured finger. Of course, now that she'd married Roger Crawford, she never needed to lift a finger again.

Without another word, Cassie pivoted on the four-inch heels of her Jimmy Choos and headed to the bedroom. I followed, traipsing comfortably if not quite as elegantly in my Lilly Pulitzer pink flats. If the ability to stride seamlessly on stilettos was required before you married a billionaire, I'd obviously never be so blessed.

Or maybe cursed. Despite the perfect outward appearance, Cassie seemed to be in a controlled panic as she checked out the penthouse for the first time. Her eyes were bloodshot, and she raced around the room snapping her head like a Perdue chicken. She opened and closed the storage drawers I'd cleverly tucked behind floor-to-ceiling lacquered doors, then quickly moved on.

"Do you think Roger will like the bed?" she asked, sitting tentatively on the edge of the fifteen-thousand-dollar Hypnos mattress I'd had flown in from London.

"It's the same one Queen Elizabeth sleeps on," I said, as if that settled it. Though who knew where Prince Philip slept.

"And the sheets?" Cassie asked, running her fingers over the linens that were so soft they made 600-count sateen seem like sandpaper. "Frette?"

"Definitely not," I said firmly. "Frette is so last year. They're now used in some"—I lowered my voice—"hotels."

Cassie looked briefly uncertain, but then nodded. At age twenty-eight (according to the gossip columns) she couldn't know everything. I couldn't either—but being a little older meant I knew how to sound like I did.

She sighed. "Well, I'm counting on you to get everything right.

Isn't it funny? Until I married Roger, I lived in a furnished sub-let in Studio City. This is the first place I've ever decorated my-self."

She'd decorated this place herself? "You did a nice job," I said encouragingly. I'd been in the business long enough to know that the person signing the check got to take credit for the success. Cassie had turned up as a new client not long ago, calling me out of the blue and asking if I could furnish the just-bought penthouse from top to bottom while she and Roger cavorted on a three-week trip to Hong Kong and Tokyo.

"It'll be tricky with such a quick turnaround," I'd said.

"Price isn't a problem," she'd insisted.

With any luck, the combination of Cassie's bank account and my eye for style would land both of us in *Architectural Digest*. How-ever difficult she turned out to be, I'd cope.

Cassie and I had met twice about the design, but when I tried to show her samples and discuss the virtues of Carrera counters versus granite, her eyes glazed over.

"Whatever you think Roger will like. That's the only thing that matters."

"You should like it too," I'd said.

"Roger has to be happy," Cassie said firmly. "Pleasing him is my only job at the moment." Apparently, the calendar had flicked back to 1950 when I wasn't looking.

I'd never met Roger Crawford and Cassie happened to be his new (or at least newest) wife. But when it came to decorating, I didn't really need her advice on how to keep him satisfied. I just turned the penthouse into a marble-and-brass version of jewel-strewn Cassie: something to help him feel sexy and young, and make it clear to anyone around just how successful he must be.

I knew Roger would admire the result. But now Cassie contin-ued dashing around with an anxious expression. She came to a dead halt in the dining room, glancing at the gleaming onyx table and the chairs covered with zebra skin.

"The fabric's fake," I assured her. "A combination of silk, cashmere, and linen. Probably more expensive than importing the real thing from Africa, but ecologically better. And everything else in the room is so minimalist, I thought we could have some fun."

"Fun," Cassie said direly.

She marched into the second bedroom suite and began opening and closing drawers. She peeked into every possible nook and cranny, as if she were hunting for lost keys.

"Are you looking for something in particular?" I asked as she walked out of the walk-in closet. I'd lined two of the walls with mirrors, and Cassie's image reflected over and over, repeated forever. Her eyes flitted worriedly, but not a single line popped out on her forehead. Either she was genetically incapable of furrowing her brow, or she'd already had her first Botox injections.

"I don't know, something just doesn't feel right."

"Doesn't feel right?" To my eye, the place looked darn near perfect. But my client had to be satisfied. If she wanted a Prince poster instead of the Picasso, I'd dash out to find it a fabulous frame. "Maybe you don't like the pale green color on the wall," I said, trying to be helpful. "To me, it feels peaceful, but if you want something brighter, we could repaint it in daffodil. Or magnolia."

"No, it's not that. I can't really explain it." She shook her head. "Something's got me spooked. Isn't it weird? I feel like a little kid at Halloween going into a haunted house."

"No ghosts here," I said.

Cassie gave a rueful laugh. "I'm Roger's third wife. Trust me, there are ghosts everywhere."

From what I'd read about him, Roger Crawford had variously owned a ranch in Montana, a waterfront casa in Costa Rica, a town house across from Buckingham Palace, and a sprawling estate in Beverly Hills. I didn't know which of those had gone to previous wives, and which were now "home" to Cassie.

"The penthouse is brand-new," I reminded her. "All yours and ghost free. You and Roger start fresh here."

Cassie gave a little frown, then darted off. I followed her into the kitchen, where she gazed blankly at the six-burner Viking stove. She opened the door of the oven warily, as if nervous that the Pillsbury Doughboy might pop out.

"Combination heat, with electric and convection currents," I explained. "The temperature stays even, so it's ideal for baking."

Cassie nodded, but from the empty expression on her face, I realized she didn't plan to be whipping up big batches of Bundt cakes. Probably the only baking she'd do was at the Sunless Tanning Salon in Beverly Hills.

She sauntered over to the kitchen pantry, where the smooth-glide shelves rolled out effortlessly. Since she'd asked me to take care of everything, I'd stocked the pantry with life's necessities—from Hawaiian macadamia nuts to Macallan single malt scotch.

"Champagne and chocolate truffles on the bottom shelf," I said. "From my experience, that's the solution for any marital spat."

Cassie looked stricken. She'd been married less than a year so perhaps she couldn't imagine a marital spat. Or maybe my friend Molly Archer was right when she told me Cassie's marriage had veered into trouble.

As the head of Molly Archer Casting and able to influence most of the media hotshots in Hollywood, my old college pal stayed tuned in to everyone. She'd called me to report that Cassie and Roger had been seen arguing at the chic Japanese restaurant Koi a few nights earlier. After Cassie stormed out, Roger went over to the celebrity-packed Skybar, where he drowned his troubles in a martini. And left, several sources reported, with "an amorous but unidentified redhead."

"You realize what that means," Molly had said ominously.

"He's lusting after the ghost of Lucille Ball?"

"I like to think Lucy's happily married in heaven."

"Isn't Roger?"

"Darling, this isn't about passion. It's about the prenup." Molly had paused meaningfully. "Young Cassie gets a million bucks if she and Roger split anytime in the first year. After that, the payoff jumps to ten million."

"He's a billionaire. That's not exactly a kick in the wallet."

"He's a businessman," Molly corrected me. "He calculates his investments carefully."

Now looking at Cassie, I wondered if her panic about the penthouse could be connected to the expiring prenup. Maybe she figured that if she decorated right, she could buy herself another year and a bigger payoff. No wonder she seemed nervous. Much harder to decide whether the antique rug should be Tabriz or Turkish with nine million bucks on the line.

Turning away from me, Cassie opened the Sub-Zero refrigerator and unexpectedly gave a broad smile.

"Kirin green tea!" she said. "I didn't see this before. How did you know?"

I peeked inside the refrigerator, where three green bottles with Japanese letters stood neatly lined up.

"It's always been my favorite," she said. "A little bitter, but much better than anything you can get in America." She grabbed one of the bottles, cracked open the cap, and took a long swig. She gave a little shake of her head, then drank some more.

"Did you have this imported from Tokyo?" she asked. "I can't believe it. You're really the best, Lacy."

When I didn't answer, Cassie gave a tentative smile.

"I've loved this stuff since I went to Kyoto during spring break in college. This trip, I drank it all the time in Tokyo." She took another long sip, then smiled at me, relief written all over her face. "Roger told you to get it, right?" Her smile got even wider. "He's such a sweetheart, after all. He wanted to surprise me!"

She finished drinking, then put the bottle carefully on the countertop. I had a lot of questions I wanted to ask—including why any college kid would take spring break in Kyoto instead of Cancun—but instead I stared at the tea. I believed in giving credit where credit was due. But in this case, I didn't know from where it was due.

I picked the bottle up, puzzled, then put it back down.

"Oh, I just remembered something," Cassie said. "The Rothko in the study."

She hurried down the hallway into the room that had rapidly become my favorite. I'd had the floor in Roger's study bleached and cured to a pale maple and had the angular bookshelves that lined three of the walls tinted exactly two shades darker. A stunning brass-and-glass desk stood in the middle of the huge expanse, and the floor beneath it was accented with a checked-tile inlay. I'd provided rolling ladders so Roger could climb up and reach a book at the top of the towering shelves. But instead of the standard wooden library ladders, these were made of sinewy steel. The room felt familiar—but still fresh and modern. I liked giving a new twist to an erstwhile style.

Cassie pointed to the simple two-toned painting that would probably bring in six million bucks at auction at Sotheby's. "I think there's something wrong with the frame," she said.

The Rothko had been in one of Roger's other houses and I'd had it brought in. I'd used the most reputable art-trucking firm I knew. They'd never damaged anything before. And come to think of it, I'd inspected the picture carefully when it arrived. But sure enough, the lower right-hand corner of the frame was freshly broken off.

"No damage to the picture," I said, studying the orange and red color fields.

"Can you get it fi-fi-fixed?" asked Cassie, suddenly panting slightly. I looked over. Her forehead was beaded with sweat, and she clutched her stomach. Something had struck her other than art-lovers' distress.

"Are you okay?" I asked her.

She was almost doubled over now, and when she opened her mouth to speak, she seemed to be gasping for words.

"I-I have to . . ." Her eyes rolled toward the top of her head, and she seemed to be choking. But she grabbed for the ladder by the bookshelf and put a foot on the first rung. Swaying heavily, she started to pull herself up.

"Be careful," I said from across the room.

"Up-up," she said, gasping. "Have to g-g-get it." Her voice was raspy, and her face was suddenly whiter than a geisha's. She kept climbing, and I saw a spittle of drool dripping down from the side of her mouth.

"Cassie," I said anxiously. "I think you're sick. You'd better come down."

"Delta," she said. She stumbled on one of the rungs and barely managed to catch herself. She kicked off her shoes and the Jimmy Choos flew down, landing with a thump on the ground.

"Come down, Cassie." Worried, I took a step forward. "If you need a book, I'll get it."

Cassie shook her head. "Not coming down." The penthouse ceilings soared twenty feet high, and Cassie had to be eight feet off the ground now. Suddenly she gave a shout of pain and clutched at her throat with both hands. Nothing connected her to the ladder except her pedicured toes. Her head bobbed and then she plunged forward, her arms spread wide, as if she planned to soar across the room like an angel.

But Cassie was no angel. She wasn't even the Flying Nun.

She landed with a sickening thud, headfirst on the polished floor.

"Cassie!" I screamed, rushing over.

I fell to my knees next to her. A huge gash had opened in the back of her head. Cassie gave a little moan and then turned silent.

I watched in horror as the wound began spurting, covering the floor in blood, the deep red color of a Rothko.